La Charlière

A Novel by

William Grovère

La Charlière (2nd Ed.)

A Novel

Copyright © 2025 William G. Coors

(William Grovère)

First published (1st Edition) 2021, ISBN: 9-798732-725575

All rights reserved. No part of this book may be used or reproduced by any means, graphic, electronic, or mechanical, including photocopying, recording, taping, or by any information storage retrieval system without the written permission of the author except in the case of brief quotations embedded in critical articles and reviews.

ISBN: 979-8-218-99700-7

ISBN 979-8-218-99700-7

9 798218 997007 >

To the children of the children

yet to be born to my five grandchildren:

Faith, Logan, Jack, Travis, Avery—

Cedric's contemporaries—

to whom the challenge of making sense of the world will fall in 2084. This is when my grandchildren will have reached my age and will enjoy the accomplishments of their own grandchildren the way I do mine today.

Acknowledgements

With grateful appreciation to Sandrine Ricote for meticulous text editing, my wife, Sylvia, for tireless editing and Tom Waller for valuable feedback.

Special thanks to Gigipaws for the cover painting of the La Charlière airship.

La Charlière

A novel by

William Grovère

Table of Contents

Book 1

Introduction

The year was 2084. Five years earlier, the dinner gathering with Sandi Brundt, Vincent Gilbert, Brigid Andersen and Stephan at the restaurant in the Akershus Fortress overlooking the Oslo Fjord had not concluded until two a.m., when the proprietor had finally asked them to leave. Other than the ordinary trials and tribulations of their daily routines, the past five years for all four of them had been relatively uneventful. That is, except for Sandi and Vincent, who had fallen madly in love, and gotten married shortly after that dinner in Oslo in the Spring of 2078. The arrival of their first child, Louisa, had, of course, been anything but routine.

The Syndicate had gone into retreat and life had become tranquil once again.

Cédric Rothschild's ground-breaking theories about dark matter and the variable speed of light continued to gain acceptance, but slowly. This was in spite of all the mounting evidence in support of his work and the fact that a whole new era of energy technologies had been commercialized based on the discovery of supermassive clusters. People tend to believe what they are taught in school, and the belief in constant light-speed was no exception. Just like clinging to the Aristotelian earth-centered universe in Galileo's day, the theory of fixed light speed took a long time to fall out of favor. After all, there were plenty of people in 1592 who still believed that Christopher Columbus had not sailed far enough to topple off the edge of the flat earth. The scientists who knew better, or at least who should have known better, were reluctant to embrace new theories that would, otherwise, have required them to make major revisions to their published textbooks. Scientific orthodoxy has always been a hard thing to dislodge. The years following Cédric's death in 2062 were tumultuous in scientific circles and many just wanted to suppress these disruptive ideas and the implications they brought to theoretical physics at every level.

In 2084, Vincent and Sandi Gilbert were living a comfortable and almost storybook existence in Bretagne, where Vincent was rapidly ascending the corporate ladder at Ashleigh Airships Corporation. Life in France for them was lovely. This peace was shattered on October 4, 2084.

Chapter 1: Treachery in the North Atlantic

The blare of the emergency klaxons penetrated with difficulty the deep subconscious of Stephan's brain as he emerged from a drug-induced fog. Every beat of his pounding heart coursed through his temples painfully. The last thing he remembered was the sadistic grin of the captain wishing him "sweet dreams" as he slipped into oblivion at the dinner table. Through his mental fog he became aware of the creaking and groaning of the airship breaking apart as it pitched wildly in free fall. He knew he had only seconds to escape the craft if he were to have any chance at survival. The lights were flickering on and off, providing barely enough illumination to find the locker where the emergency escape gear was stored. The pressure suits were all gone. The crew had already used them to get off the craft, disposing of the spares. Stephan stared in disbelief at the last remaining parachute on the shelf. He grabbed it and buckled the straps with difficulty. It was a vain gesture. He knew that after jumping out of the airship at an altitude of ten thousand meters without a pressure suit, he would be unconscious from lack of oxygen within a minute. He set the parachute to automatically deploy at one thousand meters. Finally, he clipped the carabiner of a life raft to his belt and pried open the escape hatch. The sudden blast of cold thin air overcame him as he took one last deep breath and plunged out into the blackness of space with the tethered life raft package trailing behind him. The last thing he remembered before passing out was the ship breaking in half and hundreds of giant spheres spewing out like droplets in an aerosol. Overcome by gravity, they would fall to the North Atlantic Ocean below, settling some thousands of meters to the seafloor, where they would remain for eternity.

***

"Fifteen more minutes," said the pilot over the intercom. "What makes you think he's still alive?" he asked Brigid.

"You obviously don't know Stephan," replied Brigid without looking up. A navy diver in the back was pulling on his wetsuit. A medic sat patiently next to a gurney. All were silent in the dim red light as they approached the search area.

The pilot said, "You realize that without a locator beacon, the search envelope will be some ten thousand square kilometers," The hovercraft skimmed over the water barely two meters above the wave crests, heading southwest from Norway. Powerful jet engines at each wing tip were swiveled to the horizontal position for level flight. They whined at full power, propelling the craft forward at six hundred and fifty kilometers per hour on that moonless night. Brigid did not look up from the high-resolution forward-looking infrared display in the console of the copilot's seat. She glanced over at the navigation screen showing their position relative to the last known coordinates of the airship before it went down.

Brigid was momentarily blinded when the infrared screen went totally white.

"Look!" said the pilot, pointing to a flare arcing skyward on the starboard horizon. He turned the craft in that direction and began reducing the throttle.

Brigid picked up the heat signature once they were three kilometers distance, and she called out directions to the pilot. "I told you we would find him," she said jubilantly. The pilot began pivoting the jet engines to the vertical position for hovering and set down the craft on the dual pontoons about one hundred meters from the life raft before idling back engine power. A ramp at the rear of the craft was lowered and the navy rescue swimmer, seated on a jet ski, slid down on rails and into the water, disappearing into the darkness with practiced precision. He returned only moments later with the life raft in tow.

Brigid and the medic stood at the edge of the ramp to grab the rope. The dayglow orange of the life raft shone brightly in the floodlights of the hover craft. Stephan offered a grimaced smile, slightly raising an arm just high enough to make a slight wave, when he recognized Brigid. His lips were blistered from frostbite. The medic hopped into the raft to check his condition before bringing the new passenger on board, returning with the news that Stephan was seriously hypothermic and seemed to have a fractured right femur, but was otherwise alert. The medic temporarily splinted the leg and, with the help of the rescue swimmer, transferred him to the gurney and pulled him into the hovercraft. Brigid held his freezing hands as the jet ski was stowed and the craft was prepared for departure.

"Did you scuttle the life raft?" she asked the rescue swimmer as the rear ramp door was closing. He nodded and signaled thumbs-up to the pilot that they were clear for departure.

The medic began assessing Stephan's condition more thoroughly in the bright lights of the cabin, noticing for the first time a bad gash along his right thigh. "We need to get him out of these wet clothes," he said, as he began carefully cutting along the right pantleg with the surgical shears. Without looking up, after examining the gash more carefully, he said, "He would have bled to death from this wound if he weren't half frozen. I can't tell if the femoral artery is severed, so we can't begin warming his core until I check it." He gave Stephan a shot of sedative and began probing the wound.

With Stephan asleep and stabilized for the moment, Brigid returned forward to her copilot's seat. "Remember, absolute radio silence until we are well away from the rendezvous," she said to the pilot. He nodded in agreement.

It was still dark when the hovercraft approached the southern coast of Île d'Ouessant. The pilot pivoted the engine pods to slow down and reduce the noise. They were too low in altitude to be detected by the radar at the airport on the north end of the tiny island off the west coast of France. In stealth mode, the craft was practically undetectable as it crept effortlessly over the surf zone and slid up the beach to the remote farmhouse just half a kilometer inland. The front gate was open in anticipation of the craft's arrival. A host of farm animals scattered in every direction as the hovercraft entered the compound. The rear ramp was quickly lowered, and the gurney was wheeled out to a group of awaiting people indistinguishable in the pitch dark, who took charge of the gurney and rushed back indoors.

The entire exchange took barely one minute. The rear ramp was retracted, and the craft headed south to the beach and resumed its original heading back to Oslo.

Chapter 2: It's a Small World After All

"Are we there yet, Papa?" Louisa had asked the question every five minutes for the past hour in the charming manner of a four-year-old. Vincent smiled at his wife and consulted his wristwatch. "Almost, Darling," he said.

Louisa was bouncing up and down on her seat humming the tune to Libérée, from La Reine des Neiges, in eager anticipation of meeting Anna at Disney World in Orlando. Her flowing dress and costume matched the cartoon character in almost every detail.

"I can't believe I kept that dress after all these years," remarked Sandi. "My mother bought it for me at Disneyland-Paris when I was just Louisa's age." She looked over at Louisa lovingly and stroked her braided blonde hair.

"Your childhood couldn't have been all that bad if your mom took you to Disneyland," said Vincent.

"I have a few happy memories," she replied. "That is certainly one of them. I am just glad that Louisa gets to make this big trip with her daddy." Sandi stood up and said, "I think we will go for an ice cream. Do you want to join us?"

"No thanks," replied Vincent. "Georgia is more picturesque than I was expecting," he said, looking out the window of the maglev train at the pine forests of southern Georgia streaming by. The six-hundred-and-fifty-kilometer journey from Atlanta to Orlando would take an hour and a half. "I think I will just sit here and admire the view." He leaned back in his seat. This was the first true vacation he had taken in ten years, and he was feeling the stress of the prior two years start to melt away as he contemplated his future. He listened in the silence to the faint high-pitched hum of the levitating magnets. He looked around the once-modern coach that was now in need of refurbishment. Maglev trains were still the fastest mode of transport in much of the world. Most of the intercity portals in the Virginia Commonwealth were never completed. The planned evacuated subterranean portal connecting Atlanta and Orlando would have shortened the trip to a mere twenty minutes, but when the United States broke apart, such capital projects were deemed too extravagant. Vincent also knew that travel in portals, just like in high-speed maglev trains, was about to be rendered obsolete by timecharging.

His father, Charles Gilbert, had invented the first timecharger rotor, the original term coming from the French, *chargeur des temps*, for the phenomenon of borrowing time from the future and bringing it into the present. The term had stuck for lack of a better one. He had discovered that the speed of light was slowed down in the vicinity of a supermassive object, with the consequence that time itself was retarded. In other words, all of the clocks ran more slowly with respect to the external reference frame. A related phenomenon was that mass, itself, could be modified.

After the incident in the Caribbean, where a Virginia Commonwealth destroyer sank three Syndicate submarines, there was a public outcry. The demonstration of the timecharger effect was compelling, not so much because it enabled a navy destroyer to hop out of the way of a torpedo–although that was a very cute trick. No, it was the sudden realization that warships outfitted with timechargers could sail long distances undetected, and without consuming much fuel. This opened the door to using the technology for offensive purposes. It was argued that timecharger technology signaled a new arms race, so the United Nations headquartered in Geneva immediately banned any further development. They had requested that the research and development labs around the world stop working on the technology. It wasn't so much that the public was outraged, but the Syndicate had infiltrated the United Nations sufficiently by 2070 that they were able to stir up the sentiments among member states that Virginia would gain an unfair military advantage over the rest of the world. In reality, the Syndicate had received a near fatal blow to their aspirations of controlling the seas with submarines, and they needed time to recover. In any event, the Virginia naval power, largely left over from the former United States, was already considered too powerful, and was being forced to downsize.

Vincent's research had always involved a robust collaboration between the NRL in Alexandria, Virginia and the CNRS in Toulon, France. Vincent had returned to work in

Alexandria as the liaison officer between the French research organization, CNRS, and the Naval Research Laboratory. He was permitted to carry out his neutron winding experiments, albeit under the strict constraints that any work would be completely transparent and discoveries would be disclosed to the public. After his marriage, he and Sandi settled down in Alexandria, Virginia to start a family. His father's original timecharger rotor sat idly in a back room at the lab collecting dust, waiting to be moved someday to the Smithsonian–if it were ever to reopen.

While working at the lab he had developed a technique for manufacturing continuous filaments of neutrons wound into a helix. He pursued this research until work on neutron winding had progressed to the point where scale-up was practical. Vincent had understood the significance of structured neutron clusters from the beginning. The machine his father had built in Marseille was able to wind neutrons into tubes consisting of a few billion neutrons per micron of length. Vincent had dreamed for a long time of drawing neutrons into long filaments with a smaller diameter, like a string of pearls in order to distribute the mass in one dimension along the length of the wire. To this end, he designed a neutron winder to assemble neutron strands into a triple helix. He had developed a way to co-extrude the neutron strand on the inside of an aluminum fiber, which could be drawn continuously and wound up onto a spool as a ten-micron diameter filament, barely visible to the naked eye. The filaments had a tensile strength ten times greater than that of a spider's web, which was due to the strong magnetic attraction of the neutrons. A spool of the filament one kilometer in length weighed one hundred kilograms. The density of the filament was about 320,000 grams per cubic centimeter–more than 10,000 times denser than any other known substance. But this could not be explained by the known properties of neutrons. Based on the flux from the neutron source and the speed at which the filament was drawn, there would be about 10^{15} neutrons per centimeter of filament. The rest mass of these neutrons should weigh only about a nanogram. There were aspects of structured neutron clusters that did not make sense. At some point, Vincent hoped to be able to carry out the necessary scientific investigations to explain the phenomenon, but for now, it seemed to work in the new timecharger rotor design.

It was widely recognized, based on the pioneering work of the French scientist, Cédric Rothschild, that the speed of light slows down in the vicinity of supermassive objects, such as neutron clusters. Clusters of several million neutrons could be fabricated routinely, and these were the basis of microfusion reactors, which provided most of the world's electrical energy. These clusters were unstructured, with a rest mass ten orders of magnitude greater than what would be expected by the weight of the individual neutrons. A single neutron weighs about 1.7×10^{-27} kilograms. A billion of such neutrons should weigh only about 10^{-18} kilograms–too little to detect. In a cluster, however, the rest mass would be a few micrograms. If the cluster were placed on a scale, that is what it would actually weigh. It was still a matter of fierce scientific debate as to the exact nature of the mass discrepancy–why clusters of neutrons stuck together by their magnetic fields caused the collective weight to be so much greater than when neutrons were weighed individually.

It was the unexpected discovery that the weight of the cluster depends on its velocity relative to the earth's gravity that became the basis of the timecharging device. The speed of light in free space is 3×10^8 meters per second. In the vicinity of the supermassive neutron cluster, however, it is some nine orders of magnitude slower, or just thirty centimeters per second. The weight of an object near the surface of the earth is a function of the gravitational attraction between the object and the earth. This force is communicated by gravitons, which travel at the speed of light. If the neutron cluster is at rest, it will have an apparent weight equal to its rest mass. That is, the rest mass of the neutrons joined together in the filament, not the rest mass of the individual neutrons. But if the cluster happens to be moving perpendicularly to the gravitational force–say, at one meter per second–then the cluster will have vanished from the place where the earth expected it to be during the time required for the graviton to exit the cluster, so the apparent weight will be less. The effective mass did not change, only its weight. This simple idea galvanized the research community world-wide, and a race was on at almost every laboratory to find potential applications.

The timecharger rotor built by his father was made possible by the discovery of how to wind a strand of neutrons into a continuous helical tube. The original idea was spawned when Vincent was a little boy playing with a collection of neodymium iron boride magnetic balls. His father had watched him wind a string of the balls into a tube and realized that the very same principle could be applied to a strand of neutrons if a rotating magnetic field could be used to direct the strand into a circle. The first ordered strands were produced this way by his father and Cédric in the NaPiles laboratory in the Western Alps of France, in a small town called Saint-Michel-de-Maurienne, where Vincent grew up. A more refined neutron winder was subsequently constructed at his father's factory in Aix-en-Provence some years later. In order to build the rotor, filament segments had to be painstakingly attached to the outside rim of a rotor that resembled a bicycle wheel on its side. This process took weeks because every strand segment had to be oriented to be parallel to the axis of rotation. Furthermore, each neutron "tube" behaves like a toroidal magnet with a north and south pole, so the direction of each segment had to be alternated in order for the magnetic fields to cancel around the rim, ensuring that the completed rotor did not have a permanent net magnetic moment, which would have otherwise introduced a torque on the rotor when spinning. Getting the segments placed and aligned became the principal challenge preventing commercialization of the technology.

Vincent's innovation involved drawing a continuous filament, which could be wrapped around an aluminum rod bent in the form of an arc. The arc segments could then be joined to make the hoop for the timecharger rotor. Because the filament was wound continuously around the rotor, the magnetic field was completely cancelled. This single innovation would transform timecharging from a laboratory curiosity into a technology that could be exploited commercially.

Vincent had anticipated that his laboratory at NRL would be closing. Furthermore, about that time Ashleigh had been growing impatient to commercialize the technology in their freight division. So, for the past three years, Vincent had been working for Ashleigh Airships, headquartered on the West coast of France, and he and Sandi had moved to France to oversee the technology transfer. The company had been commercializing this new concept for transporting cargo across the oceans employing the weightless characteristic of the timecharging rotor, using Vincent's innovations.

Sandi returned to the seat after a while with Louisa in tow, licking drips of French vanilla from her fingers. The little girl hopped eagerly into her daddy's lap and Sandi stood behind Vincent's seat and touched his cheek lovingly. "You know, Vincent, I can't recall the last time I saw you this relaxed."

"I will be a lot more relaxed after the ribbon-cutting ceremony," said Vincent. "At least I am not expected to give a speech." He took Sandi's hand and kissed it gently. "Thank you for coming on this trip. Travelling together as a family is a joy for me. I am really looking forward to spending time with you and Louisa at Disney World. I feel like I have done nothing else but work night and day on the airship for way too long. As soon as it docks tomorrow and Jean-Luc cuts the ribbon, the airship line will be officially opened for business, and I will be out of a job."

"Promotion to vice president of business development is hardly what I would call 'out of a job'," replied Sandi.

"It's a desk job. I'm not sure I am cut out for it. I like building things with my hands, not explaining to people how they work," Vincent sighed.

"Who else is better qualified than you to explain timecharging?" said Sandi. "The success of Ashleigh's airship business hinges on you convincing investors that these things are really reliable."

"But cargo? Really?" responded Vincent. "What a waste! The airships should be transporting passengers."

"Give it time," said Sandi caringly. "Sooner or later Ashleigh will come out with a passenger version. Anyway, the stock options alone stand to make you a wealthy man."

"We don't need the money. Jean Luc said there are no plans for a passenger version as long as the international Geneva treaty bans timecharging travel," replied Vincent.

"Oh, you mean putting people inside the spheres," said Sandi. "Now that is far-fetched."

"Actually," protested Vincent. "We have both experienced the effect. You know it works." After a long pause, Vincent inserted, "I have been considering starting up my own company." This was the first time he had mention this to her. "My father thinks I should do it."

This comment caught Sandi by surprise. She sat quietly contemplating the implications before she finally said, "Even if you can demonstrate that timecharging is safe, how do you propose explaining how going slower is actually faster to a skeptical public?"

Vincent replied, "They will get used to the idea sooner or later."

"Are you really serious about starting your own business?" asked Sandi. "That sounds pretty risky. Anyway, I am afraid I am also one of those sceptics. I know you have told me over and over, but will you please explain to me again how this *timecharging* thing works? I just can't seem to get my head around it."

"I wouldn't worry. It's very complex and it takes a computer to do the calculation, but when all is said and done," he replied, "I think solving the old problem of jet lag will be my greatest achievement. Just think of it," he said looking at his wristwatch. "We would depart from the Le Croisic Aerodrome on the west coast of France at, say, ten in the morning—exactly fifty-nine minutes ago—and we would arrive here at the Orlando Aerodrome in thirteen more minutes—that is, at twelve minutes past eleven in the morning. Seventy-two minutes after we departed France."

Sandi was shaking her head dubiously.

"No, really," said Vincent. "It's just like driving a car or taking a walk along the beach for seventy-two minutes. There's no jetlag involved."

"What about the extra three days?" Sandi protested.

"You will never miss them. When we dock in Orlando, you won't even have to reset your watch to the local time. All you need to do is reset your calendar ahead three days," Vincent replied with a grin.

"I don't know, Vincent. All this time travel stuff makes me uneasy. How am I supposed to explain to anyone in Orlando that I am suddenly three days younger?"

"You will be just the same age as everyone else on this airship, and no one in Orlando will be able to tell the difference," Vincent said jokingly.

"Okay, but just one more time; walk me through how this works," she insisted.

Vincent said, "Can you hand me my notepad in the vest pocket of my jacket hanging by the door?" He shifted Louisa to one knee when Sandi handed it to him, and he flipped it open to consult the page where he had done some calculations. "Okay," he began "The distance between Le Croisic and Orlando is 6,788 kilometers. In the old days, flying in a jet aircraft at just under the speed of sound, the trip would have taken a little more than seven hours, and there would have been a six-hour time change. Travelling that way was just brutal. Even taking portals, the trip takes about two hours, and still there would be a six-hour time difference—you would actually arrive four hours before you departed, which really messes up everyone's body clock—particularly when going from west to east. For the first time in history, timecharging makes it possible for a world traveler to choose the departure time, the arrival time in a different time zone and," Vincent looked up at Sandi and paused for effect, "the trip duration."

"So, what's so magical about seventy-two minutes?" Sandi asked.

"Nothing, whatsoever," Vincent replied. "I could have arranged for the trip to take four hours, in which case we would all be restless and stir-crazy, or I could have arranged for the trip to last ten minutes, in which case we would have barely had time to get settled in our seats. Seventy-two minutes is just a nice duration for a relaxing trip as a family."

"I still don't understand how we lose three days," said Sandi.

"It will only take seventy-two minutes on the inside of the capsule as far as you are concerned," Vincent explained. "It only takes more than three days on the outside, but we wouldn't be aware of it because we are timecharging inside this capsule. The top speed of the airship would be about one hundred kilometers per hour. Even at thirty thousand meters up, there is still enough air resistance to impede our passage. Speed requires energy. In fact, it would take more than four times as much energy to double our speed, and the solar panels on top of the airship can only supply enough energy to propel us safely at about one hundred kilometers per hour—that is, the speed of the airship with respect to the ground. We could go slower but not faster without exhausting our batteries."

"I still don't get how we are supposed to arrive in Orlando three days later than when we left," said Sandi.

"That wouldn't bother you in the least if we were on a cruise ship making the same voyage. Except in that case, we would need a stateroom for eight nights and twenty-four meals plus a lot of idle time to kill."

"Oh, let's not talk any more about cruise ships," Sandi said with a shudder.

"Here is the point, Sandi," continued Vincent. "By our own clocks, we would have travelled almost 7,000 kilometers in seventy-two minutes. That's an astounding 5,800 kilometers per hour in the earth frame—four point six times the speed of sound––simply by reducing the speed of light within the capsule by a factor of sixty!"

"Then why three days and not two days or one day?" asked Sandi.

Vincent checked the calculations in his notebook, and replied, "If I wanted to arrive in Orlando seventy-two minutes after departing from France and arrive on the same day, our airship would have to be travelling 5,800 kilometers per hour—much too fast. Plus, we would still need to recover from jetlag. To arrive at the same time on the next day, we would need to add twenty-four hours to the trip duration of 1.2 hours and the time difference of six hours, or 31.2 hours. That means we would have to travel at 220 kilometers per hour—still too fast. In the same way, two days would require 55.2 hours, and the airship speed would have to be 125 kilometers per hour. That would have been possible but would have taxed the safety margins of our battery backup capacity. Anyway, what's the rush? It still feels like the trip lasts only seventy-two minutes, regardless of the airship speed. It's a simple matter of adjusting the timecharger setting. With three days, or 79.2 hours of flight time in the earth frame, to be exact, we get to lumber along at a very safe 86.3 kilometers per hour."

The maglev pulled into the Orlando train station right on schedule. They took the monorail to their hotel next to the Epcot Center. After checking in, Vincent said, "Why don't you and Louisa go up to the room and get settled? I need to check out the docking facility for tomorrow's arrival of *La Charlière*. I should be back in thirty minutes and then we can all go to Disney World. Jean-Luc should be arriving in time for a late dinner."

This was the maiden transatlantic voyage for *La Charlière*, which was cruising from its construction site in Le Croisic, France to the Orlando Aerodrome, where a grand celebration was planned upon its arrival the following day.

The encounter with Anna, Elsa and Olaf turned out to be anticlimactic. The real people dressed up in costumes did not live up to the expectation Louisa had for the cherished cartoon characters. The waiting line for the "It's a Small World" ride was short, so they decided to take it before catching the monorail back to their hotel.

"You know, Vincent," said Sandi as they waited in line, "My great-grandfather Brundt took this ride at the New York World's Fair in 1964, before it moved to Disneyland in California. My grandfather and father both rode it as children. It's sort of family tradition in America to take your children to Disneyland. I am the first Brundt in four generations that has never been on this ride." She paused to reconsider, "except the one in Disneyland Paris, which is not really the same."

Vincent just nodded. On the ride, Louisa sat on Sandi's lap, mesmerized by all the animatronic children singing in the timeless sonorities of every language about peace and harmony in the world. Vincent was preoccupied with his thoughts. He had believed he was helping to make it 'a small world after all' but it was becoming clear that a desk job career at Ashleigh Airships was not something he had ever aspired to.

"Are you okay, Vincent?" asked Sandi after they got off the ride and were strolling along the main promenade lined with flowers and waving Disney characters. "You seem a bit withdrawn."

"Oh," replied Vincent, sadly. "I'm trying to decide whether or not I am actually depressed, but I am definitely overwhelmed. The last couple of years living in France have been wonderful, but I have a growing restlessness, and I'm just not sure I want to stay at Ashleigh. I feel like I am starting to get ground up in the gears of a big corporation."

There was a message on his portable phone that he had previously not seen. He had disabled the notification chime when they entered the park, and he had forgotten to turn it back on. The message was from Jean-Luc Gallatin. "Jean-Luc is trying to reach me," Vincent said, looking at his watch. "He's probably at the hotel now. He's early."

It was just before six o'clock and Louisa was showing signs of wearing out and starting to get cross. "I will take her up to the room," said Sandi. "I presume you will be having dinner with Jean-Luc, so Louisa and I will just order something light from room service. Anyway, she will probably be out cold in twenty minutes, and sleep through the night."

"Jean-Luc tried to call me a while ago, but he did not leave a message," said Vincent. "I think I will just wait for him in the hotel lounge."

Chapter 3: Airship Down

Upon entering the hotel, Vincent glanced one more time over at the aerodrome in the distance adjacent to the Park. It was brightly illuminated against the night sky, having the appearance of a giant sports arena. Workmen were putting the finishing touches on the grandstands that had been constructed on either side of the landing pad. These would be filled with excited spectators and dignitaries the following day for the event–the maiden voyage of the airship from the west coast of France to Orlando.

Vincent sat in the hotel lounge waiting for Jean-Luc to arrive. They had planned to have dinner together to discuss the details of the arrival of *La Charlière* and the ribbon-cutting ceremony the next day. As the hours progressed, Vincent's glass of wine had turned into two, then three, and two bowls of pretzels and nuts had spoiled his appetite. He searched his phone for messages to no avail, and tried to contact the headquarters in France, but got no answer. He couldn't understand the reason he had not received any messages from Jean-Luc, who was otherwise, always prompt. As he waited, he was going over in his mind some ideas for more advanced timecharger technology that he hoped he would have an opportunity to discuss with Jean-Luc. He didn't want a desk job. All he wanted was for Ashleigh Airships to turn him loose in the laboratory to develop the next generation of timecharging airships, and he had a pretty good idea how to do it.

The breakthrough for Vincent had come at NRL three years earlier, before his lab had been shut down and his team of scientists disbanded. He had begun embedding the neutron clusters into bushings that slid in and out on spokes like those on a bicycle wheel, pushing against springs. Thirty-six of these spokes radiated outwards from the central hub of the rotor to the outer rim. When the rotor was stationary, the bushings congregated near the central hub presenting their ordinary rest mass. But as the rotor spun faster and faster, the bushings moved outwards by centrifugal force, increasing their radial velocity. Ordinarily, this would also increase their angular momentum, but Vincent had realized in a flash of insight that, due to the super massive nature of the neutron clusters imbedded in each bushing, the mass of the sliding bushings would actually decrease as the rotor spun faster and faster, because the time-lag due to the earth's gravitational field would be increasingly retarded. The faster the rotor spun the lighter it became, becoming at some point lighter than air. Some people tried to characterize the effect as anti-gravity, but Vincent knew this was not actually the case. All that was taking place is that the normal mass of the rotor assembly was being reduced by the slowing down of the speed of light within the neutron clusters and the consequent reduction in effective mass. The fundamental problem was how to control the time and mass independently. With his father's timecharger rotor, it was not possible to levitate a heavy object without simultaneously causing anyone nearby to experience retarded time. Vincent's modification to the rotor decoupled the reduced mass from that retarded time so that people outside the rotor assembly did not experience the timecharging effect.

The idea to place the rotor inside a spherical dome came to Vincent one day when he was playing with his collection of neodymium iron boride magnetic balls. He started with a close-packed hexagonal plane, consisting of thirty-seven balls, and stacked them layer by layer, giving a shape resembling a six-sided dirigible. He reasoned that the spheres would be practically weightless when timecharger rotors were at full power. By varying the speed of the rotor, the effective mass of the spheres could be adjusted for ascending or descending. After finding a schedule of air densities versus altitude and doing a few simple engineering calculations, he determined that a ten-meter diameter hollow aluminum sphere would displace about 100 cubic meters of air. The effective buoyancy would be able to lift about 120 kilograms at sea level or 12 kilograms at an altitude of 20,000 meters. Such a simple invention was truly astounding. It solved the underlying problem with gas-filled dirigibles because it was not necessary to carry ballast to be discharged for ascending or venting gas for descending. The idea was certain to revolutionize the transportation business because the energy required to propel the craft forward was much less than that required for ordinary flight because no energy was required for moving against the earth's gravitational field. Vincent had made the critical discovery that rendered timecharger technology really feasible in airships.

Finally, he decided to go up to the room to wait. Sandi and Louisa were sound asleep, exhausted from the travel and the amusement park. Vincent sat on the sofa, growing increasingly anxious by the minute for any word from Jean-Luc. Ultimately, a message showed up on his phone, "La Charlière has gone down over the North Atlantic. Please return to Paris immediately. J-L"

Vincent was in shock. He sat for several minutes to process the implications, then went to the bedroom to wake up Sandi. She followed him out of the bedroom so as not to awaken Louisa. "La Charlière has crashed," said Vincent grimly.

"What?" exclaimed Sandi. "Crashed? What do you mean, crashed?

"That's all I know. I just received this message from Jean-Luc." He handed his phone to her so she could read the message for herself.

She read the text and looked up. "He wants you to return to Paris immediately?"

Vincent was still having difficulty processing the news. "I guess if I go now, I can catch the eastbound North Atlantic portal and be in Paris in five hours."

"You should go then," said Sandi. "Louisa and I will manage just fine. We'll take the train to Bethesda and stay with Granddad until we hear from you."

"Why don't you stop by to see your mom?"

Sandi just stared and made no response.

"No, really," Vincent said. "You will be passing right through Savannah on the way. She has never met Louisa."

"Vincent, that's asking a lot. It's been fifteen years," said Sandi somberly. "I just don't know. I don't think she would ever want to see my face again."

"Give it some thought. At some point, the two of you need to make up." Vincent said, going into the bedroom to retrieve his travel valise which had not yet been opened. He kissed Louisa on the forehead and kissed Sandi goodbye and headed for the door. "I will let you know the minute I know anything more."

"Hello?" said a weak voice on the other end of the line.

"Hello? Mama? It's Sandi"

There was a prolonged silence. "Mama, it's Sandi. I will be passing through Savannah today and was wondering if we could stop by to say hello. There's someone I want you to meet."

Chapter 4: La Défense

Jean-Luc Gallatin stood up from his desk when Vincent entered his spacious office at the headquarters of Ashleigh Industries in Paris. Jean-Luc's face was grim. He said nothing, signaling for Vincent to take a seat in one of the over-stuffed chairs adjacent to the picture window on the sixth floor that perfectly framed the Eiffel Tower in the distance. Jean-Luc sat down in the opposing chair and poured both a cup of coffee from the decanter on the table between them. Vincent finally broke the silence. "I heard that six of the seven crew have been rescued." Jean-Luc nodded. "The seventh has apparently not been recovered–one of the engineering technicians. I suppose he has been declared lost at sea." Jean-Luc sipped his coffee and still made no reply. Vincent continued, "This is a horrible disaster, and I don't see how Ashleigh will ever recover." Jean-Luc still made no reply.

"Monsieur Gallatin, sir," Vincent continued. "I am deeply honored by your offer to make me the Executive Vice President of Ashleigh Airships. It is a dream position for me by any standard of measure." He paused to sip his coffee and rehearse in his mind his next sentence. "Monsieur Gallatin, I have decided to refuse your offer. My wife and I have been discussing this for days. The loss of *La Charlière*, perhaps, makes the decision easier, but frankly, I am just not cut out for a desk job."

Jean-Luc stood up to close the door to his office, and sat back down, staring into space for what seemed like an eternity to Vincent. Then he said, "I am told that you are acquainted with the Head of the French Intelligence Ministry, a gentleman named Abraham."

"Yes, Sir," replied Vincent. "My wife also knows him well. We interacted with him when we were trying to move the Timecharger to America. That was before we got married and started a family."

Jean-Luc responded tersely, "Abraham has been arrested."

"What?"

"He has been charged with an assortment of crimes and complicity with the Syndicate."

"That's not possible," exploded Vincent. "Abraham would never be disloyal to France."

"I know," said Jean-Luc. "He is being framed. Most of the top echelon of the Ministry has been wiped out." Jean-Luc paused and sipped his coffee while Vincent processed the news.

"What I am about to tell you," he continued, "will put you in danger and alter the course of the rest of your life." Vincent's silence signaled for Jean-Luc to continue. "The seventh man on *La Charlière* is a senior officer at the Intelligence Ministry."

"Is? He's not missing?" responded Vincent.

"We had suspected that Ashleigh Airships was being infiltrated by Syndicate operatives and that there might be an attempt to sabotage the maiden flight of *La Charlière*. Abraham and I arranged for one of his agents to pose as an engineer on the flight—someone you know. An agent named Stephan."

"Stephan! Is he okay?"

"For now, as long as he is presumed dead and lost at sea," replied Jean-Luc.

He poured both of them a second cup of coffee and leaned back in his chair, crossing his legs. "I always knew Ashleigh was being controlled by the Syndicate from the top. I chose to ignore it. They needed a capable executive to run the company in order to provide respectability in the international business community. They paid me handsomely and never interfered. That is, as long as I didn't ask too many questions."

He stood up and retrieved a folio from a file cabinet below the credenza, handing it to Vincent. It was bound by a string with a knot that had obviously never been untied. "When I purchased NaPiles from your father, this collection of papers surfaced. It was in a box of personal effects that belonged to your father's laboratory assistant, a man named Cédric Rothschild."

"Yes, I knew him as a child. He was the inventor of microfusion," replied Vincent.

"I never looked inside that folio," continued Jean-Luc. "It is really part of the legacy of NaPile. I intended to give it to your father someday, but I think it is fitting for you to have it."

Vincent stared in wonder at the folio, anxious to see what was inside. "Vincent," began Jean-Luc without expression, "You don't need to decline the position I offered you. The offer has been rescinded. I thought I had more influence around here, but there have been some charges made that place the responsibility for the crash on you. I am being forced to ask you to tender your resignation."

"Resignation!" shot back Vincent. "You know I had nothing to do with the crash."

A long silence ensued. Vincent was speechless and Jean-Luc wanted to phrase his following sentence carefully. "I have a very important mission for you. I need you to rescue Stephan from his current hideout and deliver him to somewhere else that is safe. He was badly injured in the escape from *La Charlière*. He is being hunted down as an international fugitive, and I fear if he is caught, he will be executed." Jean-Luc buried his head in his hand, rubbing his forehead with thumb and index finger. Then looking up at Vincent, "My letter of resignation is on my desk. I don't know what that means for me and my family, but I suspect this won't end well for me. I am too much of a threat to the Syndicate for them to just let me go free."

Vincent was speechless. The two men stared at each other. From the expression on Jean-Luc's face Vincent knew that a new bond was forming that transcended the prior business relationship of superior to subordinate. Jean-Luc stood up, retrieved the letter on his desk and walked out of the office without saying anything.

Vincent waited several minutes for Jean-Luc to return before becoming impatient and wandering out to inquire of his whereabouts from his administrative assistant. “Did Mr. Gallatin say when he would be back?”

“I don’t know, but I think he left the building,” she replied.

“I am going down to my office, then. Please give me a call when he returns.”

“I really don’t expect him back,” she said. “He took his overcoat.”

Vincent went back into the office to fetch the Rothschild folio and started towards the elevator. The administrative assistant held up an envelope as he passed her desk. “Monsieur Gallatin asked me to give this to you.” Vincent took it and got into the elevator to go to his office on the third floor. The envelope was sealed and had no writing on the outside. He opened it to find a card inside with a hand-written note which said, “Arnaud: La Porte du Conquet, Tonight, 9pm.”

Vincent eyed the strange message several times upon entering his office. He tossed the Rothschild folio onto his desk and grabbed his coat, turning off the light and locking the door behind him. It was already 4 o’clock, and he would have to hurry. He would catch the TGV Maglev to Brest, which would take about an hour. This would give him enough time to go to his apartment, grab a bite to eat, and get his car out of the garage for the short drive to the town of Le Conquet on the Bretagne coast, which he knew well. It had a magnificent beach which was one of his favorite places to go with Sandi on weekends.

As soon as he was seated on the train, he checked his watch and removed his portable from his briefcase, pressing Sandi's number.

"Hello?"

"Sandi, it's Vincent. I hope it's not too early to call."

"No, I have been up for a while. Louisa is still asleep," she said. "How did it go with Jean-Luc?"

"That was the strangest meeting I have ever been to." Vincent paused, not knowing where to begin. "I did it! I turned down the job. But it turns out that there is no job to turn down. The offer was rescinded." Sandi was quiet on the other end. "Guess what else? I got fired and they think I may be responsible for the crash."

"Oh, Vincent! I am so sorry," was all Sandi could manage.

"I was planning to visit the aerodrome in St. Nazaire tomorrow to assess the impact of the crash. All the work on new dirigibles has been suspended, and I suspect that the future of Ashleigh Airship is now in question. I was not looking forward to facing all my coworkers at the plant, but I guess that won't be necessary now."

"Do you want me to come to France to be with you?" asked Sandi.

"Perhaps in a few days. Let's give the news a chance to settle in before we make any plans. How is it going with your mom?"

"It's really remarkable," Sandi responded. "She's a completely different woman than I remember. We have been taking long walks together and unpacking a lot of hard things from the past. She's also in love with Louisa. Louisa just sprinkles joy and happiness everywhere she goes. What are your plans for this evening?"

"I am heading back to the apartment on the TGV now. Jean-Luc gave me a very cryptic assignment. I'm supposed to meet up with someone in Le Conquet. I'll take the car and maybe grab dinner there at that restaurant we love overlooking the bay. I will call you from there."

"I miss you, Darling," she said.

"I was planning to join you in Savannah in a few days. If it's working out with your mom, there is no reason for you to be in a rush to come to France. We will have a lot of things to sort out. Maybe we should consider moving back to America."

"That would be nice," she said. Vincent could detect a break in her voice.

By the time Vincent reached his apartment, it was getting late, and the drive to Le Conquet took longer than normal in the rush-hour traffic. He pulled into a filling station not far from the port to top off his hydrogen tanks for the drive home. It was already 8:45, and he would have to go to dinner later.

« Excusez-moi, je cherche quelqu'un qui s'appelle Arnaud » Vincent asked the attendant. *«Au port»* he responded without

looking up, pointing in the direction down the hill. Vincent reflected that even though Le Conquet was not very large, there had to be at least a dozen Arnauds in town. He pulled into the visitor's lot at the marina and got out of the car to look for someone to assist him. He asked the parking attendant the same question, who pointed in the direction of a ship tied along-side the pier about one hundred meters down on the right.

Vincent approached the ship that was all lit up and appeared to be preparing to depart. He asked a man maneuvering a mooring line from a dock cleat, if he knew someone named Arnaud. The man smiled broadly and pointed to the stern of the ship: the nameplate read, "*L'Arnaud*". It was some kind of a supply vessel. It was about thirty meters in length with an impressive assortment of cranes and gear on deck. A man smoking a pipe was standing at the top of the gangway. "You must be Vincent," he said. "Hop aboard. We have been expecting you," and turning, he headed inside, giving Vincent no opportunity to reply.

No sooner had he reached the top of the gangway than it was retracted, the mooring lines pulled in and the ship was underway, heading out to sea. The deckhand chuckled at Vincent's stunned expression and said, "The Captain is waiting for you on the bridge. Just up those stairs on the left," he said pointing to the entryway.

Vincent climbed up the steep stairs, that were more like a ladder and entered the bridge. "Welcome aboard," said the

Captain, turning to hand him a life jacket. "You are going to want to wear this. We are heading out into some pretty heavy seas, if for no other reason than to cushion you from breaking some ribs when we get knocked around."

"Where are we going?" demanded Vincent.

"Not far," replied the captain. "To a small island just off the coast. If you know Bretagne, you have probably already been there. It's called Île d'Ouessant."

"Yes, I have been there. It's a wonderful place to ride bikes," replied Vincent.

"Not this time of year, I'm afraid," said the captain.

"Why are we going there?" Vincent asked as the boat passed the breakwater and headed out into a night so dark, nothing was visible for miles.

"*L'Arnaud* is going there to make some emergency repairs to the hydrogen refueling depot, but I don't know why you are going. Thc order came in from above that we would be ferrying a VIP to the island tonight."

Vincent pondered this odd comment. None of this made sense to him and being called a VIP didn't help. "How long will it take?" asked Vincent.

"Just under an hour," the captain answered. "There's a fresh pot of coffee and some sandwiches in the mess. Make yourself comfortable."

The captain wasn't kidding when he said the ocean would be rough. The bow was regularly plowing into waves that towered over the bridge, drenching the windscreen with white foam in the headlights. Vincent remained on the bridge. He was very glad he had not had time to eat dinner. He was suddenly stricken with panic when he realized that he had left his portable phone in his unlocked car at the marina. "We'll be returning to Le Conquet tonight, then?" he asked. He knew the answer was 'no', but hoped he was wrong.

"Not likely," said the captain over the roar of the angry seas. "*L'Arnaud* is the only ship that goes to the island this time of year and the airport is closed due to the storm. We won't be returning until the repairs are finished, which will take a couple of days, I imagine."

Vincent fell into one of the swivel chairs on the bridge and buckled the seat belt, looking out the side window in a state of utter hopelessness. The only thing visible was the occasional blinding flash of the spray in the floodlight. The ship made practically no noise of its own. Three 500 kW hydrogen fuel cells generated all the electric power for the DC motors that turned the ship's screws and powered the lights and control systems. At full throttle the ship was consuming 100 kilograms of hydrogen per hour from the high-pressure Steelhead storage tanks below deck.

After forty minutes or so, Vincent caught a glimpse of the intense searchlight from the Phare de la Jument lighthouse off in the distance. *L'Arnaud* ultimately passed the lighthouse on the south side of the island and curled around to the port on the north. Immediately upon entering the harbor past the breakwater, everything became eerily calm. The ship sounded its airhorn to announce its arrival and gently maneuvered to the pier where it would dock for the night.

There was a person waiting dockside for *L'Arnaud's* arrival. Bundled in a heavy coat, a face was barely visible peeking out through the fur lining of the hood. "This is where you get off, Vincent," announced the captain, "Someone is waiting to see you."

Vincent headed for the stairs. "You might want to leave the life jacket," said the captain. "I don't think you will need it anymore."

The person waiting at the bottom of the gangway when Vincent exited the ship, turned and motioned for him to follow to a car standing nearby. Once seated in the driver's seat with Vincent in the passenger seat, she released the knot on the hood and pulled it back. "Brigid? Brigid Andersen? Is that you?" said Vincent in total astonishment. "What is this all about?"

"If you can wait just ten more minutes, this will all make perfect sense," she responded. With a big smile she said, "I am so glad you came." She drove along the narrow back roads from the port to an enclave on the other side of the island.

"What is this?" asked Vincent.

"This is one of Queen Camilla's summer residences," Brigid said, pulling the car into a detached garage. "There is a warm coat in the back seat for you, and there is someone here that is anxious to see you."

The house was warm and bright. At the sight of Stephan in the entryway, the conversation with Jean-Luc earlier that day suddenly made sense. Stephan was sitting in a wheelchair with his right leg elevated and in a cast from hip to toe. "Is it possible that it's you? Jean-Luc told me you were on *La Charlière* and may have survived the crash." Vincent gave him an embrace.

"Come, let's get out of the cold," suggested Brigid.

"Were you badly injured?" asked Vincent looking at the cast.

"I wrecked the leg up pretty completely," responded Stephan. "I had to shoot the first doctor who took out a scalpel to cut it off."

"I see that your dark sense of humor is still intact," said Vincent as they entered the Great Hall where a wood fire roared in a massive fireplace. A nurse positioned Stephan near the fire and straightened out the throw covering his legs.

"You are probably hungry," suggested Brigid to Vincent. "An assortment of food has been spread out on the dining table."

"Yes, famished," said Vincent, heading to the table.

"May I pour you a glass of wine?" she asked.

"So, when is someone going to explain why you brought me here?" asked Vincent.

Brigid started in. "I think you know that Abraham was arrested. No one has heard from him, so we can only assume the worst. Basically, anyone that ever had a hand in thwarting the Syndicate is being purged, at least so far, only in France. Stephan, as Abraham's right-hand man, is number one on their hit list. He is being hunted down for elimination."

"But everyone that knows Stephan was the seventh person on *La Charlière* presumes that he perished in the crash," said Vincent.

"Until they come up with a body, they won't give up the search," said Stephan.

"He is safe here for the moment," said Brigid, "but it won't last. The Syndicate has too many eyes and ears. We need to get Stephan out of France and beyond the Syndicate's tentacles. The problem is that Stephan cannot exactly walk away. He needs surgery to reset his compound-fractured femur, and after that, he will need months of physical therapy if he is ever going to walk again at all."

"And I cannot remain here," added Stephan. "Queen Camilla has been deposed. Brigid and the staff are here to prepare for the Queen's arrival in two days where she and the royal family will be held in exile. This entire island will be locked down, and no one will be able to come or go without the knowledge of the French government officials."

After a long contemplative silence, Vincent took a sip of wine and said quietly, "Jean-Luc knew that I could help. That is why he sent me." Standing up, he said, "I may have an idea. Actually, Jean-Luc probably had the idea and knew I would figure it out on my own. But it is after midnight, and I am exhausted. I need to spend some time thinking about how to pull it off. We can discuss it in the morning. Surely there is a room in this huge château where I can get a good night's sleep."

Brigid said, "Vincent, can you keep a secret?" Without waiting for a response, she said, "Stephan is my husband. We were already married when we had dinner with you and Sandi in Oslo. For obvious reasons, we have not been able to tell anyone, even the Queen. With the monarchy under assault, this would be an added danger to her."

"Secret?" Vincent chuckled. "Do you really think the queen doesn't know? The way the two of you have always looked at each other makes it rather obvious."

Chapter 5: Stowaways

Vincent caught a couple of hours of restless sleep before getting up to pace the room. He needed to return to the marina on the other side of the island to determine if his plan was even feasible. By four in the morning, he was unable to wait any longer, and bundled up as best he could, and slipped out of the door alone under the cover of darkness. He walked across the courtyard to the carport hoping that Brigid had left the key fob in the car, when the thought occurred to him that the château was probably already under surveillance. Based on the drive the previous night, he concluded that the walk shouldn't take more than an hour, but without his phone, he would have to navigate purely on instinct. He could hear the surf in the distance, which he knew was to the south, so he slipped out the side door next to the main gate and headed north in the darkness. His heart was racing so fast he didn't notice the cold at all, but he did notice a van by the side of the road with its engine running.

The cold gray disc of a full moon was directly overhead, whose light appeared and disappeared as fast-moving clouds streamed eastward. The changing dull light animated the shadows making Vincent nearly undetectable as he made his journey north. The only sounds were the occasional barking dog and some unsecured objects flapping in the wind. The marina was actually closer to the château than he had recalled, and he saw the pulsating red light of the harbor entrance as he crested the hill in the center of the small island after only about thirty minutes. Glistening in the distance was his objective, an enormous white dirigible anchored at the bow to a mooring tower in the middle of a field adjacent to the harbor. Its 100-meter-long body lay in a cradle on the landing pad at the aerodrome.

Vincent's first challenge was to figure out how to sneak through the chain link security fence surrounding the giant craft, which was well-lit by flood lamps. An unoccupied guard shack stood next to the entry gate, which to Vincent's surprise, had been left open. He could see a team of workmen doing something to the mooring tower, and he recalled that the skipper of *L'Arnaud*, the boat he had arrived on the previous evening, mentioning something about the need for some emergency repairs to the docking mechanism. Vincent's destination was a hatch midship of the dirigible. The workmen were preoccupied with their task and did not notice him pop open the hatch and slip inside. It was just as he had remembered. The control space was about three meters deep, two meters high and one meter wide–barely big enough to accommodate him and Stephan. He pulled the door closed behind him and surveyed the control panel. The various lights displayed the status of the airship. Vincent needed to ensure that there would be room for the two men and a few supplies for what might turn out to be a journey taking up to five days depending on weather conditions and prevailing wind. He checked the water level in the ballast tank and the neutral buoyancy indicator. Stowing away on a dirigible designed to deliver hydrogen was probably the most reckless thing he had ever contemplated, but it was the only way he could think of to get Stephan off the island undetected. The hydrogen nacelles were nearly empty—the remaining pressure in the airship being just sufficient to keep the bags inflated at one atmosphere for its return voyage in order to refill. When fully loaded with hydrogen at six atmospheres, there would be no possibility to carry additional weight. Vincent checked the navigation computer to confirm the destination of the location that the autonomous craft would return to once launched. Satisfied that everything was in order, he climbed back down to the tarmac and slipped away undetected out into the darkness.

Vincent returned to the château compound at a quarter to five and proceeded back to the bedroom to catch some sleep in order to be rested for the journey the following night.

"Where have you been?" inquired a voice from someone in a high-backed chair facing the fire in the grand salon.

"What are you doing up at this hour?" asked Vincent.

"I am not able to sleep much," replied Stephan. "The pain in my leg keeps me awake."

Vincent sat down on the hearth facing Stephan, glad for the warmth which was welcome now that he had shed his overcoat. He said, "I went to check out the possibility of escaping on a hydrogen delivery dirigible anchored at the aerodrome."

"So, what did you find out?" asked Stephan.

"It's a crazy idea," replied Vincent, "but I think the plan just might work. By tomorrow night we should be ready. There is a crew working on the mooring system, but I have no way of knowing when the repairs will be completed. My biggest worry is that they will finish up before we get a chance to get on board, and the craft departs without us."

"Why wait until tomorrow night?" said Stephan. "Let's go now."

"It's five in the morning," protested Vincent. "We don't have time before daybreak. We need to prepare some provisions for the trip, which could last for several days."

Stephan grabbed his portable phone and sent a message to Brigid to come to the grand salon immediately. When she arrived five minutes later, he explained to her what Vincent had described and said, "We need to be at the aerodrome by no later than six, which means we have about thirty minutes to get me ready." Brigid made no objection and headed into the kitchen to gather up some supplies. Stephan reached over to pull his wheelchair closer to where he was sitting. He stood up and took a couple of hops on his one good leg to get into it. With a pained grimace and exhale, he pointed to the front hall closet. "Would you mind fetching my coat?"

Brigid returned from the kitchen with several bags of supplies. "If you eat like birds, this might keep you alive for five days. I don't know about water, though. I could only find this one jug."

"That will suffice," said Vincent. "We can drink from the water in the ballast tank. We will need lots of blankets. It will be cold in the control space." He stared intently a Stephan. "Are you sure about this?"

Brigid spoke up on his behalf. "Vincent, I trust you, and I know you would not do anything to place Stephan in unnecessary danger. He has to get off this island undetected before the queen arrives. This seems to be a pretty good plan under the circumstances."

"Okay, then," replied Vincent. "We need to walk to the aerodrome, though. We can't drive. There is a van parked down the street that is surveilling the château."

This news caused Brigid and Stephan to exchange a concerned look of heightened alarm. "Don't worry about me, Stephan," she said. "When the queen arrives, she will be bringing a security detail with her, and I will be fine. I will go fetch some blankets and be right back."

With everyone bundled and blankets piled on Stephan's lap, the three headed for the door. "Do you have your pain pills?" Brigid asked Stephan.

"They are next to where I was sitting in front of the fire, but I won't need them," said Stephan.

Vincent wheeled Stephan out the front door as Brigid went back into the grand salon to fetch the bottle of pills that she knew her husband would be glad to have. Once out in the courtyard, the three stared around in wonder. A heavy marine fog had descended upon the island, so thick that they could barely see the yard light above the carport.

"We don't need to walk to the aerodrome," exclaimed Brigid. "We can drive. No one will see us in this fog and the car is equipped with forward-looking infra-red so we will be able to see where we are going without headlights."

This was a very welcome change in plans. They loaded the supplies in the trunk and positioned Stephan in the back seat with the blankets piled on him. Brigid drove and Vincent sat in the passenger seat. Brigid activated the FLIR and pressed the button to open the gate. The electric vehicle slipped silently into the fog, undetected and unnoticed by anyone.

When they arrived at the aerodrome, Vincent got out of the car to check the status of the security gate. Unlike before, this time it was closed. The guard shack was dark and unoccupied. Vincent tested the handle on the door and found it had been left unlocked. Inside there was a bank of video monitors along the wall, one of which was streaming the view from the mooring tower. It appeared that the workmen had finished the repair and had departed. There was no activity on any of the other surveillance monitors. He simply pushed the button labeled "Open Gate" and just like that, the gate slid open, and Vincent hopped back into the car, hoping that the rest of the journey would turn out to proceed as smoothly as it had up to that point.

"Wait a minute," Vincent said, hoping back out of the car and reentering the guard shack to switch off the video recorders.

They drove right up to the hatch that Vincent had entered only two hours previously. By the time Vincent and Brigid had transferred the supplies and blankets into the control space, Stephan had gotten out of the car and hobbled to the opening in the dirigible unaided and pulled himself inside, demonstrating his remarkable upper body strength. He piled up some blankets and made himself comfortable. He was smiling broadly by the time Vincent joined him and eager to begin the voyage. Brigid peered in from the entrance and said nothing. Vincent detected tears in the eyes of this woman who had never shown any trace of emotion. He waved and pulled the hatch closed.

"Wow, we really cut this close," Vincent said as he surveyed the navigational computer. "We are apparently scheduled to depart at seven. That's just twenty minutes from now. We need to release water from the ballast tank that is equal to our weight and the weight of all the supplies we brought on board. Otherwise, the ship won't be buoyant enough to disembark." He pulled a lever to let water out and watched the gauge that indicated the relative weight of the dirigible in the surrounding atmosphere. The ship was designed to be neutrally buoyant at sea level, and the humid air due to the fog also needed to be compensated for. This function was carried out automatically by the ship's computers, which also dynamically adjusted the trim by managing the pressure in each of the ten hydrogen nacelles. At precisely seven, they could hear the ground tethers disengage and the propellers in the stern come to life. The mooring mast automatically extended allowing the dirigible to swivel into alignment with the wind. At last, the bow tether was released, and the dirigible was off.

“How do you know how to do all of this?” asked Stephan.

“That’s a long story,” replied Vincent. “I would rather hear your account of what happened aboard *La Charlière*.”

Stephan answered, “If we are going to be cooped up in this thing for five days, we will have plenty of time to recount stories. By the way, where are we going?”

“Bermuda,” Vincent peeked at the navigation computer. “5,240 kilometers as the crow flies. This craft has a top speed of about 100 kilometers per hour, so without headwinds, the trip would take fifty-two hours, but it was not designed for speed. The navigational computer chooses the course to follow the path of least wind resistance, so the trip could easily take twice that long. As of now, the trip computer is estimating sixty-eight hours. That’s not too bad. I hope this holds. This ship was never intended to carry passengers. There is an indelicate matter to consider as we get under way, though. You probably noticed by now that there is no bathroom.” Vincent reached into one of the sacks and retrieved some paper plates and a box of plastic bags, handing them to Stephan. “The widows slide down, and I will leave it to your imagination to figure out the rest.” Vincent could tell by the grin on Stephan’s face that he was accustomed to such inconveniences.

“You know,” Vincent said, “They are trying to lay the blame for the crash of *La Charlière* on me.”

Stephan said, “We both know that’s not the case. Tell me about this craft.”

Vincent said, "This ship is totally autonomous. It is like a homing pigeon designed to find its way when, and if, it can. There are a couple of thousand of these ships in service around the world transporting hydrogen. Ashleigh Airships originally planned to use them for passenger service, along the lines of the Graf Zeppelins of the 1930s. The idea was a commercial flop, not so much because of safety concerns–the things that led to the Hindenburg disaster had all been corrected–it was just that the romance was gone. People who want to take their time prefer cruise ships and those who want to go fast take hyperspeed portals. There's just not much interest in travelling by dirigible. After my laboratory at NRL was closed down, I was furloughed. That was about the time we got together in Oslo, as you recall. Sandi and I fell in love not long afterward, got married, and Ashleigh offered me a job in France in their airship division. It was a shame, because I had just made a breakthrough in my research at NRL that would have revolutionized the way timecharger rotors are fabricated."

"Whatever came of your laboratory?" asked Stephan.

"I don't know," replied Vincent. "I disassembled the equipment and put what I could into storage with the thought that someday I would be able to resume the work. As soon as I joined Ashleigh and moved to France, I got pulled into other pursuits. Up to that point, the facility in St. Nazaire was building hydrogen dirigibles for transoceanic passenger service. They hired me to work on the next generation of timecharging airships.

When the whole idea of passenger service fizzled, they switched their focus to transporting freight. *La Charlière* was the first in the new class that was supposed to revolutionize the transoceanic freight business."

Stephan sat quietly listening to the story. The memories of his narrow escape from the craft just three days earlier were fresh on his mind. Vincent looked at him to give him a chance to jump in. "No, please continue," said Stephan. "I want to hear your side of the story."

"I always thought it was a stupid idea to use timecharging merely as an alternative to hydrogen in lighter-than-air dirigibles–that the real benefits of timecharging were to be found in using the effect to alter the experience of time for travelling passengers. By putting people inside the capsule with the timecharger the problem of jetlag would be essentially solved. It would be possible to arrive at your destination a few minutes after departing, albeit some increment of twenty-four hours later. Ashleigh had promised me that they would let me work on this once the UN ceased its restrictions. It never happened. I was shuttled off into the hydrogen dirigible business to transform the ships that were originally intended for carrying passengers into a fleet intended for merely transporting hydrogen. Ashleigh never had any intention of being in the hydrogen business. They only wanted to get the airship business ready to be sold off. That turned out to be my responsibility. This ship we are in is designated D1097," he said, turning to point out the nameplate above the control panel. “It is one of the fleet of ships I helped repurpose. I got a lot of hands-on experience with these craft, and Jean-Luc knew this.”

“You know, Vincent, it was Jean-Luc that arranged to have me aboard *La Charlière*,” said Stephan. “Perhaps he felt some responsibility for the accident. He never fully appreciated the extent of the subversive activities of the Syndicate in his company.”

“I think he does now,” said Vincent.

“I hope you will forgive me if I nod off for a while,” said Stephan. “I just took one of my pills. They are quite powerful and make me drowsy. This is the first time in a couple of weeks that I don’t feel I have to be on the alert. I haven’t slept well for several days.” Stephan’s eyes became heavy and closed. Vincent consulted the trip computer and stared out the window at the fog. The dirigible was gliding along at one hundred and twenty meters above the surface of the North Atlantic heading south by southwest.

Chapter 6: Bermuda

A blinding flash of light followed almost immediately by a deafening thunderclap awoke Vincent from a deep sleep. The hydrogen dirigible was rocking gently in the turbulence. He glanced at the video screen that showed their position to be a couple of kilometers south of a band of thunderstorms. They were making good time and were already about one thousand kilometers north of the Azores.

"Are you sure this thing is safe?" asked Stephan from the darkness on the other side of the cabin.

"So, the thunderclap woke you up as well?" Vincent asked.

"No. I have been awake for several hours. What time is it?" asked Stephan.

Vincent consulted the chronometer. "It is four in the morning, Greenwich time. These dirigibles don't keep track of time zones, so I can only guess that the local time is probably, five or six. How's the leg?"

"Throbbing," replied Stephan. "Could you pass me something to snack on?"

Vincent switched on the cabin light and began digging through one of the bags that Brigid had prepared. He pulled out a block of cheddar cheese and an almost-fresh baguette. "*Voilà!*" He passed them over to Stephan along with a knife. "Until the food runs out, we will be feasting like kings. I turned up the heater on the water tank and removed the insulating cover to see if I couldn't get some heat into the cabin. The tank heater was only designed to keep the water from freezing, but the idea seems to be working." There was another flash of lightning and thunderclap.

"You never answered my question," said Stephan.

Vincent consulted the navigational monitor again to check the location of the storm. "The ride wouldn't be too pleasant if we actually passed beneath one of those storm cells. The downdraft would probably drive us onto the surface of the sea. This does happen every once in a while, but Ashleigh has only lost a half a dozen or so in several years."

The expression on Stephan's face suggested that this answer was not very comforting.

"It's hardly a concern at all for empty ships. When they are full, they are carrying about ten tons of hydrogen and lumber along without much maneuverability. Empty, though, we are much nimbler and will easily skirt any bad weather. The bigger challenge is maintaining neutral buoyancy. The fuel cells powering the ship generate eighteen kilos of water for every kilo of hydrogen consumed. That water gets condensed out and stored in the ballast tank that I am leaning against to get warm. Would you like some?" He passed a jug to Stephan. "It's a bit warm but perfectly safe to drink. I wish I had thought to bring tea bags or instant coffee."

"What did you mean by "the bigger challenge"? asked Stephan.

"Are you sure you want to know? In a nutshell, if we were ever to lose the water ballast, we would drift off into the stratosphere," replied Vincent glumly. "These ships are designed for delivering hydrogen. When the mylar nacelles are filled, the pressure is adjusted for neutral buoyancy at sea level. The density of air is about one and a quarter kilograms per cubic meter. The density of hydrogen at one atmosphere is only about eighty grams per cubic meter, so a one cubic meter bag of hydrogen would be able to lift about two thirds of a kilogram of added weight. The nacelles in this dirigible hold about two hundred thousand cubic meters, which would be sufficient to lift one hundred and forty tons or so when empty. That is, the nacelles must be maintained at slightly more than atmospheric pressure to keep them inflated. This is what I mean by "empty". When full of hydrogen, the pressure is adjusted for neutral buoyancy including the weight of the ship and everything on-board, without water ballast. The water generated by the fuel cells is simply jettisoned during the outbound trip. But on the return trips, the water must be retained as ballast. During the development phase, there actually was a dirigible that accidentally discharged the water from an empty ship, and it drifted up to about thirty thousand meters where it loitered around for months before the seals on the mylar nacelles began to fail."

"I now have first-hand knowledge of the terror of trying to breathe at ten-thousand meters above the earth," said Stephan. "I have no desire whatsoever to repeat the experience."

"Not to worry," replied Vincent. "Other than the slow speed and uncertainty of the length of the trip, there is probably no safer way to travel than in an empty hydrogen supply dirigible. The computer has us arriving in Bermuda in forty-five hours, give or take ten hours. You should consider popping another one of those pills. The last one had you out for twelve hours."

"I have been reflecting on the crash of *La Charlière*," said Stephan. "Jean-Luc went to extreme lengths to conceal my identity. No one at Ashleigh could possibly have known it, so that leaves the Intelligence Ministry. There must be a Syndicate mole somewhere high up in our organization. The thought of this sends chills down my spine."

"What actually happened aboard *La Charlière*?" asked Vincent.

Stephan sliced more cheese and took a drink of water without responding for a while. "After the gold smuggling incident in the Paris-Longyearbyen Portal, Jean-Luc did some serious housecleaning at Ashleigh. The Syndicate seemed to be in retreat and most people believed that the threat had passed. Most people, that is, except Abraham. Abraham always seemed to have a deep-rooted suspicion about human nature. He believed that people with evil intent could disguise themselves and pretend to be just ordinary people to blend in. He had a remarkable ability to see through the façade. About six months ago, he concluded that the Ashleigh Airship Division had been infiltrated at the top by Syndicate operatives. Jean-Luc told him that the idea was preposterous but agreed to have an undercover field agent on-board for the maiden Atlantic crossing. That, of course, was me. I was hired by Ashleigh as an electronics specialist and was assigned to the crew of *La Charlière* for the pre-certification shake-down cruises leading up to the maiden voyage. I am really good at what I do, so there would have been no reason to suspect that I wasn't the real deal."

"The night we departed from France for Florida, everything was normal and working perfectly. The captain and the rest of the crew were jubilant, anticipating the historic cruise. We were all in the captain's mess celebrating and drinking champagne. The next thing I remember is falling over in my chair and hitting the ground. When I woke up, *La Charlière* was breaking up and going down. I grabbed a parachute and life raft and bolted out the escape hatch."

"At ten thousand meters?" exclaimed Vincent.

"What else was I supposed to do?" replied Stephan.

"Why didn't you wait until you were at a lower altitude?"

"That question entered my mind just before I lost consciousness for lack of air," replied Stephan. "Actually, the ship was breaking apart, and I didn't think there would be anything left to jump out of if I waited."

"Why did the captain drug you?" asked Vincent.

Stephan replied, "My cover had obviously been blown. The captain apparently knew all along who I was. At first, I allowed myself to think they were just using the crash to get rid of me, but then I realized that, in that case, all they needed to do was toss me overboard. No, for some reason, they needed to destroy *La Charlière*."

"But why?" shot back Vincent. "*La Charlière* was going to usher in a new era of global trade. It's out of character for the Syndicate to destroy the very things that could bring them a whole new stream of wealth and power."

"That question, my friend," responded Stephan quietly, "has been practically all I have been thinking about for the past three days."

"So, I guess that means it would be a good idea to keep you alive and get that leg fixed up," replied Vincent. Stephan just smiled and nodded.

Sandi's mom, Héloïse, was playing with Louisa when Sandi entered the kitchen. "How did you sleep?" her mom asked.

"I can't believe you left my room completely unchanged," Sandi said.

"Oh, after Frank left me, I thought I would sell the house," replied Héloïse, beginning to cry. "I just never lost hope that someday you would come home."

At this, Sandi burst into tears and the two hugged for a long time without words, allowing all the cords of bitter estrangement to melt and drip to the floor with their tears. All was forgiven in that moment.

“And now you have come home with my granddaughter, who brings me inexpressible joy.”

Louisa said, “Mama, Grandmama is going to teach me how to make pancakes.”

Upon regaining her composure, Sandi said, “I got a message last night from the police in Le Conquet. They found Vincent’s car parked in a loading zone at the marina. They said it was unlocked and Vincent’s cell phone was on the driver’s seat. That’s just not like Vincent, and I am really worried.”

“What do you think you should do?” asked Héloïse.

“I don’t know,” replied Sandi.

“Perhaps you would consider leaving Louisa with me. That way you could take the portal and be in Paris tonight.”

At that moment, the doorbell rang. “Who in the world could that be?” Héloïse went to the door and opened it to see a man bundled in a trench-coat looking out towards the street. “Yes?” she inquired.

The man turned. The hat, scarf and dark glasses obscured most of his face. “May I talk to Sandi Gilbert?”

Héloïse said nothing. She was not about to let a strange man into her house.

Sensing her reluctance, he said, “Will you kindly tell her that Jean-Luc Gallatin is here to see her?”

By this time, Sandi and Louisa had come to the entryway. “Mr. Gallatin?” she said, not a little surprised.

He removed his dark glasses and scarf so that Sandi could confirm his identity. "May I come in?" he said.

Sandi exclaimed, "Mama, this is Jean-Luc Gallatin, Vincent's boss!"

Once inside, he said, "I have a rather urgent matter that I need you to attend to."

Sandi made no reply before he continued, "I need you to go with me to Bermuda."

"When?" she asked.

"Right now. There's no time to explain. My plane is waiting at the Savannah airport."

"Your plane?"

"It is critical that we leave immediately. This involves Vincent, but there is no time to explain," said Jean-Luc impatiently.

"What about my little girl?" exclaimed Sandi in total confusion.

"She can stay with me," said Héloïse.

Jean-Luc handed Sandi a package. "Here, put this on, and then we must go."

Sandi opened it to find a black uniform and hat. She read the name tag on the front, "Who is Francine Duboite?" she asked, incredulously.

"My pilot," replied Jean-Luc.

"What?" Sandi returned, "You want me to pretend to be your pilot? I don't know how to fly!"

“Oh, that doesn’t matter. The planes these days fly themselves,” replied Jean-Luc.

“Where’s your real pilot?” inquired Sandi.

Jean-Luc flashed a mischievous grin. “I ditched her in Bermuda. By now, I am sure she is hopping mad.”

Sandi just shook her head in disbelief. “Mr. Gallatin, sir” she said, “You are a very strange man.”

“Not so strange, I think,” he responded. “There just comes a time in one’s life when it is necessary to take risks. You can’t always play both sides against the middle. At some point everyone needs to choose a side. Hurry. We must go. I will fill you in once we are in the air.”

The Dassault Falcon Xii climbed out of the Savannah airport on autopilot. Sandi Brundt Gilbert was in the pilot’s seat and Jean-Luc Gallatin was in the copilot’s seat. The twin ramjet engines gulped liquid hydrogen on assent to their twenty-five-thousand-meter cruising altitude where the trip to Bermuda at twice the speed of sound would take barely an hour. Sandi, pretending to be Francine Duboite, had had no difficulty gaining access to the tarmac with the borrowed identity and the control tower positioned them on the runway without incident. Except that she did not have a license to fly the plane, everything was otherwise, routine.

“So, is this your private plane?” she asked, once airborne.

“No.” replied Jean-Luc. “It belongs to Ashleigh.”

Sandi gave him a puzzled look. "Vincent told me you resigned."

Jean-Luc said, "That was my plan when I left the office after meeting with him the day before yesterday. I had the letter of resignation in my hand, and I was planning to tender it that afternoon." He looked out the window at the almost total blackness of space at that altitude. "By the time I got to the main floor, I realized that I would not be able to do anything useful if I resigned. By staying on, I have resources at my disposal."

"Like this jet, I suppose," said Sandi. Jean-Luc made no comment.

They both sat quietly contemplating the ramifications of the circumstances. Finally, Jean-Luc spoke up. "It is best that I tell you as little as possible. You can't trust anyone, so the less you know, the better. You have a reservation at the Hamilton Grand Hotel under the name, Francine Duboite. No one will ever know that there are two of you on the island with the same name. As soon as we pull into the gate, I need you to change out of Francine's uniform and hang it back up in the closet. There is a pair of coveralls hanging up. Put those on and slip out as one of the ground crew. As we discussed, I expect Francine to be storming out to give me a tongue-lashing. Fortunately, this isn't the first time I have gone off in the plane without her, so there is some precedent."

"What am I supposed to do at the hotel?" inquired Sandi.

"It is a bit late in the season, but the weather should still be nice. Enjoy Bermuda. I left ten thousand euros at the front desk for "Francine". Just don't use your personal credit cards."

"That's it? Just sit around and drink rum punches?" asked Sandi sarcastically.

"Not exactly," replied Jean-Luc. "There will be a supply boat arriving at the Hamilton Docks each morning at about ten from a ship operating off the coast. I don't know exactly which day, but Vincent will be arriving on that boat within the next three days."

"What did you just say?" Sandi said, snapping her head around. "Vincent?"

"That is all I can say," responded Jean-Luc. "If I tell you anymore, I will be placing you and a lot of others in danger. Vincent will be able to explain everything." Jean-Luc looked down at the communications console to see that they were being hailed by the Bermuda air control tower. "Now, remember what I told you to say: identify yourself, give them our tail number, and request permission to land. They will ask for an authentication to transfer instrument control to them. Then you can sit back and relax. They will bring us in and land us automatically."

"What if something goes wrong?" Sandi asked, suddenly overcome with a sense of fear.

"Don't worry. Everything will be fine," he replied comfortingly. "And Sandi, remember; you are Francine Duboite and speak to the controller with as strong a French accent as you can possibly muster."

Chapter 7: Bougainville

Captain Shaw braced his elbows on the starboard railing just outside the bridge to steady his binoculars. The air was crisp and clear, and the sun was just about to break the horizon. He caught his first glimpse of D1097 to the north-east by the glint of sunlight off its reflective coating. A huge hydrogen supply dirigible was secured in the forward cradle on the flight deck, filled and preparing for departure. It contained ten tons of pressurized hydrogen for delivery to an island in the Bahamas. The aft cradle was not occupied. Even though the ship could accommodate two dirigibles simultaneously, it was not safe to have a full one departing at the same time an empty one was docking. The captain scanned the horizon in all directions. The only thing he could see was one of the autonomous collection barges returning home to the well deck inside the huge ship. He went back onto the bridge. "D1097 should be docking in about forty minutes," he said to the first officer. It was unusual for the captain to take interest in any particular supply dirigible. "You have the bridge. I will be down on the flight deck."

D1097 inched forward from the stern to a position above the aft docking cradle. Four deck hands grabbed the ropes dangling from the dirigible and completed the docking manually, securing it into the cradle and hooking up the connection hoses. Captain Shaw was looking on and waiting until it was safe to open the hatch to the control cabin. He nearly died of surprise when the hatch opened from the inside and a man popped out. He had been told there was important cargo on board, but he never dreamed it would be human cargo.

"Hello, Shaw," said a beaming Vincent, enjoying the surprise as if he had just popped out of a birthday cake. "Would you please have someone fetch a gurney? The guy I have with me is in pretty bad shape and we need to get him to the infirmary immediately. Here, give me a hand. He has a fractured femur and is running a high fever from the infection. He has been slipping in and out of consciousness for the last twenty-four hours."

"Did you just come here on that thing all the way from Île d'Ouessant?" was all Captain Shaw get out.

"Yes, and I don't recommend it as a means of travel," said Vincent. "Is there an EMT on board?"

"It might be a stretch to call him an EMT, but yes, more or less," replied Captain Shaw, climbing into the cabin behind Vincent. "Who do you have here?"

"His name is Stephan. He is the French intelligence officer on the Dauphine Rêve," replied Vincent with a grunt, trying to position him on top of a blanket so they could pull him out of the cabin.

"The guy who authorized the sinking of the Russian yacht off Guadeloupe?" said Shaw. "I never met him face to face, but I sure admired his brass for doing that."

The gurney arrived with the EMT and the four men arranged to lift Stephan out of the dirigible. They raced the length of the flight deck to the other end of the ship and took the elevator down one level to the infirmary in the bow. Stephan's pulse was weak. The EMT suspected that Stephan was badly dehydrated and hooked him up to an IV as soon as they were inside the infirmary. "This man really needs a doctor," he said, looking up at Vincent.

"Do the best you can to stabilize him, and I will go to Hamilton to find one," replied Vincent.

"Let me call in a medivac helicopter," said Captain Shaw.

Vincent paused momentarily. "You can't do that," he said. "No one can know Stephan is here." Observing the bewildered look on the captain's face, "It's complicated. I just need to get to the island to find a doctor willing to come back here with me."

"The daily supply tender to Hamilton is due to depart any minute," volunteered Captain Shaw.

"Good," said Vincent. "Tell them to wait for me."

Sandi was watching for the arrival of the supply tender from the Bougainville operating thirty kilometers offshore to the east of Bermuda as instructed by Jean-Luc. There had been no sign of Vincent on any prior day. This day she saw him standing on the prow of the hydrofoil as it entered the harbor. She called out to him with joy and waved to get his attention. He never anticipated that she would be waiting for him in Bermuda, but like so many things that had taken place in his life over the past week, he was not actually shocked to see her. Dockside, there was a very happy and unexpected reunion. After a long embrace, Sandi said, "Wow, Vincent! You really need to take a shower." They both burst out laughing.

Sandi said, "When the police sent me the message that they found your phone in your unlocked car at the marina in Le Conquet, I was really worried. It's just not like you to go anywhere without your phone."

Vincent thought about this for a moment. "You know, Sandi, you are right. That's not like me at all. Until you just mentioned it, I had completely forgotten about my phone." He thought about this some more and stopped. "If I had had my phone with me for the trip to Île d'Ouessant and to here, someone would have easily been able to track my location. It strikes me as just one more strange thing in a string of strange things that have been happening to me over the past few days as if everything I do is being influenced by an invisible hand." They both contemplated this for a moment, then Sandi reached into her bag, retrieved her phone, and switched it off.

"How much do you know?" Vincent asked as they continued walking the two blocks to Sandi's hotel.

"Practically nothing," she replied. "Jean-Luc brought me here in the Ashleigh corporate jet the day before yesterday and told me to watch for you arriving on the supply boat from a ship called the *Bougainville*."

"Corporate jet?" responded Vincent. "He told me he was going to resign."

"Well, it seems he had a change of heart," she said.

"So, you don't know about Stephan?" he asked.

"Stephan!" she exclaimed, "What about Stephan?"

"Oh la la, we have a lot of catching up to do," he said, looking up to the sky. "Stephan is out on the *Bougainville*. I urgently need to find a doctor."

"Are you sick?" she asked.

"Not for me! For Stephan. It's a long story. I am going to need some clothes."

Sandi gave Vincent the key and sent him up to the room to shower while she went into the men's clothing store in the lobby. The best she could come up with was a wardrobe that would make her husband look like a character in a Rudyard Kipling novel. Vincent was out of the shower and pacing the room in a towel when Sandi arrived.

"Do you have any idea how many doctors there are in Bermuda?" he asked, clearly agitated. "I stopped by the front desk and they looked at me as if I had lost my mind. They gave me this." He handed her a brochure with dozens of pages of doctors with every imaginable specialty. "I don't know where to start."

"Well, why don't you start by getting dressed? We will figure this out."

At that moment, there was a knock at the door. Sandi peeked through the peep-hole to see two gentlemen that looked like hotel staff. "Who's at the door?" asked Vincent.

“A couple of guys from hotel security, I suppose. They have probably come to check up on the smelly derelict that entered my room,” she said smiling, and opened the door a crack. “Hello, can I help you?” she asked.

“You probably don’t remember me,” said one of the men. “My name is Vasi Spinu. I am the valet to Her Majesty, Queen Camilla of Norway. You saved my life on the *Polaris Explorer*.”

“Yes, of course, of course. Please, come in. My husband will be out in just a minute. You are the Moldavian gentleman that translated what the hijackers were saying over the radio in the queen’s stateroom.”

“Yes, ma’am,” he said removing his hat. “This is my cousin, Anatoly. He is Queen Camilla’s personal physician. She dispatched us here to take care of Stephan.”

The supply tender was still tied up at the Hamilton dock when Sandi and Vincent arrived with Vasi and Anatoly Spinu. The return trip out to the *Bougainville* on the hydrofoil took just under an hour, which gave Vincent an opportunity to bring Sandi up to speed and explain Stephan’s predicament. Sandi and Vasi also had time to get caught up on the events aboard the *Polaris Explorer* after the hijacking. Vasi had heard bits and pieces from Brigid, but this was the first time he had heard the whole story.

“You can’t imagine my surprise when the chief engineer aboard *L’Astrolabe* told me that the Mr. Spinu working for Queen Camilla was his uncle,” said Sandi.

"I should probably let you in on a little secret," Vasi said. "I am not really the queen's valet. I head up her entire intelligence operations. Brigid works for me. The valet thing is simply my cover when we travel."

"Oh my! If I had known..." said Sandi apologetically.

"Not to worry," he said. "As long as people treat me like the queen's lowly valet, it means my cover must be working. You know, it was your tip from Alexandre that opened up the investigation of the submarine base in Chornomorsk. After his father was assassinated in the coup, we fled to Norway. Alexandre was just eight years old. When he became older, he immigrated to Canada and I had lost touch with him until Brigid mentioned your encounter with him aboard the French icebreaker."

"It appears there are Spinus showing up all over the place," commented Sandi.

"My family ran Moldavia pretty much as a close-knit dynasty," said Vasi. "Anatoly was the leading physician in the country and the Health Minister before the coup. You can imagine that we all hold a deep-seated grudge against the Syndicate after they commandeered our beloved country."

The hydrofoil tender reached the *Bougainville* just before sundown and entered its cavernous well deck from the stern. The space which was designed for deploying landing craft full of heavily armed marines for amphibious assault missions now served to dispatch and retrieve a fleet of autonomous salvage barges that skimmed the waters off Bermuda for the tons and tons of floating plastic trash that circulated in the ocean gyres. The North Atlantic and Caribbean gyres collided just east of Bermuda, resulting in a concentration of floating debris in these oceanic waste dumps.

Captain Shaw was dockside when they arrived. Vincent introduced Dr. Anatoly Spinu and the group rushed down to the infirmary. "I think we managed to stabilize Stephan, but he has a raging fever and is mostly incoherent," said Shaw. Dr. Spinu went right to work, checking Stephan's heart with his stethoscope and measuring his temperature and pulse, shaking his head from side to side. He pulled back the cover and removed the fetid bandage covering the wound on Stephan's right leg. "The entire leg is badly infected," he said. "You don't by any chance have an x-ray machine?"

"Yes," said Captain Shaw, "If you know how to operate it. This hospital was designed to take care of about thirty marines with combat injuries, so I suspect you will find almost anything you need somewhere in here."

Dr. Spinu looked up at the EMT who was standing by to offer any assistance and remarked, "You did well, young man. You probably saved this man's life. I will need an X-ray before I can amputate."

"Um, Dr. Spinu, sir," said Vincent, "Before Stephan passed out for the last time, he made me promise not to let anyone remove his leg. He said he would rather die than go on through life disabled."

Letting out a deep fatalistic exhale, Dr. Spinu shook his head and said, "He may get his wish, but let me see what I can do." He handed the EMT a vial of antibiotics, "Here, add this to the IV. Now I need the rest of you to leave for now so I can concentrate."

As they all got onto the elevator, Vincent looked back and said. "Remember, doctor, no amputation. Stephan is very experienced with firearms, and you really don't want him mad at you."

Once on the elevator, Vincent said to Captain Shaw, "So, Richard, I don't think you were ever formally introduced to my wife Sandi."

"Ah, the famous Commander D'Arc, Dragon-slayer. I know all about you but by reputation only. It is, indeed, an honor to finally meet you in person," he said. "Captain Richard Shaw at your service. I believe you have the singular distinction of having commanded three different ships with three different ranks and aliases in just two weeks. You are a genuine maritime folk hero."

Sandi glared at Vincent, "What stories have you been telling this poor captain about me?"

"Not stories, ma'am," responded the captain. "I have first-hand knowledge. I was the skipper on the Trump when you made that incredibly gutsy maneuver to turn into the torpedo and take the hit head-on in that old icebreaker."

Sandi blushed slightly. "Between trying to get seven thousand people off the sinking *Polaris Explorer*, timecharging across the North Atlantic on *L'Astrolabe*, and engaging two Syndicate subs and a Russian yacht firing torpedoes at us on the *Dauphine Réve* in the Caribbean, I had more than enough excitement in those two weeks to last me for a lifetime. I am rather more content now to be settled down and raising a family. Anyway, it was the Trump that sank those three subs. I was just a spectator."

"Spectator? That's a bit modest," said Capitan Shaw, turning as the elevator door opened onto the bridge. "I don't know what everyone's plans are, but I would be honored if you would at least stick around for dinner. We have a fabulous chef, and we don't get many visitors this time of year."

"We would love to accept your offer," replied Sandi, "but Vincent and I have a scheduled video chat with our daughter in America, and we need to get back to the hotel."

Vincent added, "Between Stephan's groaning and bouncing around in thunderstorms, I haven't slept much in several days. We have a very nice room at the Hamilton Grand, and I was hoping to sleep in a real bed tonight."

"Fair enough," replied Captain Shaw. "This is not exactly the Hamilton Grand Hotel. How about you, Mr. Spinu?"

"I would be honored to join you for dinner," Vasi responded, "and if possible, I would like to remain on board until Anatoly is finished. Perhaps he will join us and give us an update on Stephan's condition."

"No problem," said the captain. "Make yourself at home. There's bunk space on this ship to accommodate an expeditionary force of about a thousand marines, so take your pick." He chuckled, being the only one to appreciate his dry humor. "Alternatively, I suspect that you might be more comfortable in one of our visitor suites. The investment group that owns this ship likes to bring VIPs out for a stay during their junkets to Bermuda. There are six really nice suites you can choose from." Shaw looked at his wristwatch and turned to address Vincent. "The tender to Hamilton is due to depart soon. I will show Mr. Spinu to his stateroom and then escort you and Sandi to the well deck. If you come back tomorrow, I will give you a chef's tour of the ship."

Chapter 8: Hydrogen from Trash

Captain Shaw and Vasi Spinu were waiting at the landing dock in the well deck when the tender arrived the next morning. "Look who we brought with us," said Vincent as he, Sandi and Brigid stepped off the hydrofoil.

"Hello, Captain. I'm Brigid Andersen. I don't think we have ever met." They shook hands. "Queen Camilla sent me to Bermuda to relieve Mr. Spinu, who is desperately needed back in Île d'Ouessant now that the queen is in exile."

"She came on the queen's private jet this morning," volunteered Vincent. "It is waiting for Vasi at the airport."

Vasi gave Brigid a welcoming hug, and said, "Don't worry. Anatoly told me this morning that Stephan, although by no means out of danger, is alert and stable. He is eager to see you." Then Vasi stepped onto the hydrofoil and departed directly for Hamilton International Airport.

They all first visited the infirmary to check on Stephan. Dr. Spinu was sitting in a chair by the side of his bed where he had kept vigil for the entire night. He stood up to embrace Brigid. "I think he is going to recover. He is incredibly strong-willed," he said to her.

"How about the leg?" she asked gingerly.

"It's still attached," replied the doctor. "When he regained consciousness this morning, his first words were that I would be a dead man if the leg was gone."

"I didn't really say that," mumbled Stephan.

"I suspect he will have a long and painful recovery, and need a lot of physical therapy, but there's a good chance that he will walk again," said the doctor. He handed Brigid a cup of water and a pill. "Here, see if you can get him to take this."

Sandi and Vincent took the elevator with Captain Shaw up to the top level. The elevator opened up into the bridge from which there was a good view of the flight deck five stories below. "We are now atop what is called the "island". We can't go outside until after the launch, but we can watch it through the windows from here. Refilling of D1097 could not be carried out until the control cabin where Vincent and Stephan stowed away has been cleaned up and the ballast tank water heater, which they disassembled, put back together. It is always necessary to launch a loaded dirigible before the next empty one in the queue can dock. Any accident during launch of a one filled with hydrogen pressurized to six atmospheres that could result in a puncture of one of the nacelles would be catastrophic if the hydrogen were to ignite. During a launch, all personnel must be safely secured in an explosion-proof bunker. Because of the delay in the launch, the arriving empty dirigible next in line is loitering a few hundred meters off the starboard beam," he said, pointing out the window.

"As you can see, this is a big ship, 257 meters long and 32 meters wide, with a displacement of 45,000 tons–a midget compared to your *Polaris Explorer*, Sandi–nevertheless, big enough to handle two 32,000 cubic meter dirigibles at once. Each of those craft carries about 10 tons of hydrogen when filled to six atmospheres. The nacelles are actually rated to ten atmospheres, but this gives us a comfortable safety margin. The energy contained in 10 tons of hydrogen is about the same as one half a kiloton of high explosives. Hydrogen won't actually explode unless enclosed in a space with enough air, but it can catch fire. You have all probably seen the newsreels of the *Hindenburg Zeppelin* crash in New Jersey in 1937. When hydrogen burns, it has no visible flame, so most of what you see in the photos is the color of flames from the burning fabric, but this is not to diminish the safety concerns when handling hydrogen. There is always the possibility of a leak and an array of infrared sensors on the flight deck are constantly watching for hot spots." He stepped aside to give the tour group a chance to take in the sight.

"The story behind this ship is rather interesting. The keel was laid down in 2019 in Pascagoula, Mississippi. *Bougainville* was the third ship of the America-class of amphibious assault ships designated LHA-8 by the United States Navy. She went into service in 2024 and served in the Atlantic fleet for twenty-six years up until her scheduled service life extension. She went into drydock in Charleston for refurbishment and a complete weapons upgrade in late 2050. Then came the disastrous naval battle in the South China Sea. When China invaded Taiwan, the Naval Command dispatched the Pacific Fleet to the area with two aircraft carrier battle groups and a contingent of amphibious assault ships intending to make a land invasion to retake Taiwan."

Sandi interjected, "My father was killed in that battle. In a submarine trying to defend one of the carriers."

"Oh, I'm sorry. I did not know," responded Shaw remorsefully.

"His name was Brundt, Captain Paul Brundt," she said. "My mom was pregnant with me when it happened, so obviously I have no memory of him."

"That was a sad day for the United States," said Shaw. "I was just ten. Two of the sister ships of *Bougainville* and a number of other amphibious ships were sunk while *Bougainville* sat out the war in dry dock. Then the United States broke apart. The *Bougainville* was simply forgotten. After I retired from the Navy of the Virginia Prefecture a couple of years ago, I was contacted by a group of investors interested in cleaning up the trash in the oceans. There were so many plastic bottles and shopping bags collected into islands of trash that you could literally walk across them in places. They had some ideas and technology for converting the trash into hydrogen, and they needed to construct a special-purpose ship for the project. They contacted me because they thought I could help them procure the architectural drawing from the naval archives for a ship with a lot of the same features as an amphibious assault ship. I started looking around for big-deck ships that might have been mothballed. Most had already been cut up for scrap, but I did find one rusting away at anchor in an estuary of the Savannah River. It was a junk heap. It was clear that refurbishing it would cost more than building a new one.

"Then an old Navy buddy who grew up in Charleston told me he thought there might be a ship in dry dock that I should look into. It was astonishing to discover the *Bougainville* right where it had been sitting untouched for thirty years. It was in pristine condition. In preparation for the service life extension, the entire ship had been coated with rust inhibitor and a scaffolding constructed around it. It was probably the scaffolding that was the reason it didn't look like a ship at all. With the collapse of the US Navy and the ensuing bureaucratic confusion, it seems the ship simply slipped through the cracks and was completely forgotten. It was perfect. The investors immediately wanted to buy it, but nobody could figure out who actually owned it. All the weapons systems had been stripped off and apparently, the title had been transferred to the commercial shipyard responsible for the upgrade. But then the shipyard company went out of business and the trail of ownership was somehow lost. How in the world do you purchase a billion-dollar warship from defunct entities that don't claim ownership? The United Nations got into the act and made an international plea that the ship was essential for cleaning up the oceans. Finally, the Prime Minister of Virginia

Prefecture convinced everyone that there was no possible use any more for an amphibious assault ship, and the ship was donated to the cause. Do you believe it? Now that is what I call serendipity."

D1097 finally departed and drifted off towards the northeast. A second empty hydrogen supply dirigible had shown up in the meantime and both of the 100-meter-long craft were secured into the deck cradles nose to nose, with tails protruding beyond the flight deck over the bow and over the stern. The tops of the dirigibles extended all the way to the level of the bridge. It was an impressive sight to see Bougainville dwarfed by these enormous craft.

"Let's head down to the well deck to begin our tour," said Captain Shaw, leading the way back to the elevator.

The elevator door opened at the same place where they had arrived earlier on the hydrofoil. Several very strange-looking boats that appeared to be some sort of barges without any apparent superstructure were lined up in the well deck. One of them had pulled into a chute at the front of the well deck and was disgorging its load of trash onto a conveyor belt that transported it through an opening in the forward bulkhead. Another barge was in line for its turn at the chute, and another empty one was on its way out of the well deck.

"These are the autonomous collection barges," began Captain Shaw. "They are remotely piloted by people up in the control center, where we will stop in a few minutes. The make-up of the trash varies a great deal from place to place so the pilots monitor a bank of cameras to make adjustments to the retractable sweep booms you can see stowed on the sides. All in all, it's pretty routine, but every once in a while we encounter a large floating object that requires some care, wood pallets, for example, are a constant menace–boat hulls, break-away buoys, and things like that. We once got a dead whale stuck in the grinder. Cleaning up that mess was a very unpleasant task. For the most part, the trash consists of plastic bottles, shopping bags and pieces of Styrofoam insulation. These get ground up and compacted in the hoppers in much the same way as with a garbage truck. Each barge has a capacity of about 200 tons. Then the trash is unloaded onto that conveyor belt where it is fed into a collection bin on the other side of that bulkhead."

The captain opened a water-tight door in the forward bulkhead and led the way to continue the tour. They proceeded down a corridor that was enclosed by windows. The contents of the collection silo could be seen feeding to an auger in the bottom.

"The smell is horrific," commented Vincent.

"We process about 200 tons of trash per hour," Shaw continued. "Everything gets ground up and turned into a thick sludge that goes into the gasifier. Follow me. This is not a place I care to spend much time for obvious reasons."

The group proceeded through another water-tight door and up two flights of stairs. The roar made hearing difficult, and the heat emanating from the walls made it uncomfortable. "The gasifier is just on the other side of this wall," yelled the captain.

"The temperature runs about 700 to 900 degrees centigrade, which turns virtually anything organic into a mixture of carbon monoxide, carbon dioxide, methane, some low molecular weight gases and, of course, a lot of hydrogen." He led the group on through another water-tight door into a portion of the ship that was much quieter and cooler by virtue of more than adequate air conditioning. A technician in white coveralls stood in front of a large control panel monitoring the process.

Captain Shaw greeted the operator, who appeared to be unaccustomed to seeing tour groups. "This is the nerve center of the whole process," he said. "It operates twenty-four hours a day, seven days a week. The real challenge is to ensure that enough trash is coming into the collection silo to keep the gasifier fed." He walked over to a computer monitor and pointed to the screen. "You can see here the output from mass spectrometers that continuously monitor the composition of the gas stream. The make-up of material feeding the gasifier is constantly changing, so real-time adjustments to the gasifier settings are required. If anything gets out of whack, we need to shut the gasifier down, glean out the mess and restart it. I don't need to tell you that we don't like it when this happens."

Moving over to another monitor he said, "This is where we track the flue gases before and after clean-up. There is a lot of stuff in this trash besides just hydrocarbons. There is an assortment of metals from labels and bottle caps, an occasional lithium-ion battery, halogens–chlorine from saltwater mostly–

traces of heavy metals and…you get the picture. These things cannot be allowed to enter the membrane reactor. They get scrubbed out and collected along with all the stuff that doesn't gasify, like nails from pallets, nuts and bolts, battery casings and the like."

The captain led the way up one more flight of stairs into an enormous space that appeared to run the length of the flight deck overhead. A line of refrigerator-sized enclosures extended the length of the space in four rows. Large cylinders labeled "Caution: Hydrogen under pressure" lined both walls. "This used to be the aircraft hangar bay, where jets, helicopters and tiltrotors were readied for their missions. Now it is where we make hydrogen. The cleaned-up gas from the gasifier is fed into devices called double-cells. Inside these enclosures are tens of thousands of electrochemical cells made from special ceramic materials that complete the conversion of carbon monoxide and residual hydrocarbon gases into just carbon dioxide and hydrogen. The hydrogen is extracted from the mixed gas stream through a ceramic membrane that purifies and compresses the hydrogen to about ten atmospheres. The process is called H2H, short for "hydrogen from hydrocarbons"–ocean trash in our case. We extract about one hundred kilograms of hydrogen from each ton of trash. We also produce about three tons of carbon dioxide per ton of trash. The pressurized hydrogen goes into those tanks along the walls and the carbon dioxide is collected in those pipes you see going down through the floor. This is probably a lot more technical than any of you care to hear, but the hot CO_2 passes through recuperators down below, where the recovered heat is what provides the thermal energy for gasification. Then the cooled CO_2 gets compressed and liquified. There's not much to see down there except a jumble of pipes, so if we take the elevator up to the control room, it will be easier to explain what happens to the liquid CO_2 from there."

The elevator opened up into a room that was nearly dark except for an assortment of video monitors surrounding work-stations manned by personnel intently watching the screens and maneuvering joysticks. "This is the operation control center," said Shaw. "When this was a warship, this was the combat information center. It is where command and control of all the warfighting activities were coordinated. Perhaps it is a reach, but in a sense, these people are conducting a kind of warfare against the piles of ocean trash. But before I explain what they are doing, let me finish the story of what happens to the CO_2. Come over here to this screen. What you are looking at is a closed-circuit video of the discharge end of a tube that extends down three thousand meters below the ship. The ship is positioned over a very deep point of the Atlantic Ocean. Liquid carbon dioxide is pumped into the top of the tube and gravity causes it to go down the tube because liquid CO_2 is denser than seawater. The reason the tube is so long is that it takes about 300 atmospheres of pressure to keep it in the liquid state, so the discharge needs to be at a depth in the ocean that exceeds that pressure. If you watch the video screen, you can see the turbulence from the mixing of liquid CO_2 with the surrounding saltwater near the outlet in the floodlight, and the subsequent sinking of it as it settles to the sea floor where it forms a lake and cannot reenter the atmosphere. At greater depths, it can be further compressed into a solid. In any event, the CO_2 gets sequestered for hundreds of years while it gets converted to carbonate minerals and perhaps hydrocarbons by a process called abiotic methanogenesis."

"What happens to the tube when the ship moves?" asked Sandi.

"The ship does not move much," replied Shaw. "We use GPS tracking to keep the ship stationary most of the time, but when we do reposition the ship or anticipate severe weather, the tube is just retracted onto a spool in the bow below the waterline."

"Now for the fun part," he said, positioning himself behind one of the operators and placing his hands on her shoulders. "Tanya, here, is one of our best pilots. The left joystick is how she remotely operates the salvage barge, and the right joystick is controlling the surveillance drone. The lower screen shows the position of the barge relative to our position, about 12 kilometers to the east. The ocean trash is not uniform. It clumps together to form floating masses that need to be hunted. That is what the surveillance drone is doing. It is dark now, so the drone is sending back infrared and microwave images. The drone sweeps out a search pattern ahead of the barge that Tanya determines, and then she directs the barge to the location of the floating debris to scoop it up. This is an around-the-clock activity, especially when the sea is calm like tonight. There are typically four barges operating at any given time. It takes about 100 tons of debris to make 12 tons of hydrogen, so it keeps these operators very busy collecting enough trash. Our goal is 1,000 tons per day, which provides enough hydrogen to fill ten supply dirigibles. The debris fields east of Bermuda have been diminishing somewhat, so we are considering relocating the ship to a richer area. This position off the coast of Bermuda for the past year has been ideal because many of the crew have apartments there, and they can come and go with relative ease on the hydrofoil, but we are limited to a collection radius of about 50 kilometers. It seems that either the centers of the gyres have drifted off or we have simply depleted the supply of trash in this area, so we may have to reposition shortly."

"That's about it. Does anyone have any questions?"

"I saw on the news last night that there is a hurricane forming off the Azores," said Sandi. "Does this cause you any concern?"

"Yes," replied Shaw. "We are monitoring it closely, but the chances of it hitting Bermuda are only 10%. If it strengthens and comes our way, we will have a week to prepare. The salvage barges would all be recalled and secured in the well deck. We would need to reel in the CO_2 tube, shut down the gasifier and idle the H2H modules and batten down the hatches. With the hydraulic tailgate on the well deck closed, Bougainville is probably the safest place to be even in a category 3 hurricane. We are in the middle of hurricane season, so let's just hope one doesn't come our way."

Chapter 9: The Hamilton Grand

Sandi and Vincent exited the elevator of the Hamilton Grand Hotel on the ground floor. The lobby was resplendent with old-world charm. A huge crystal chandelier hung prominently from the high ceiling in the center. One wall was lined with bookshelves. Overstuffed chairs and reading tables were spread around, giving the room the sense of being a pleasant place to just hang out. They walked up to the front desk and Sandi said to the clerk on duty, "Good morning. I am Francine Duboite in room 302. Are there any messages for me?"

The desk clerk checked the box and handed her an envelope. "Here you go, Madame Duboite, I hope you and Mr. Duboite are enjoying your stay with us," she said cheerfully. The attractive and perky desk clerk handed Sandi the plain envelope simply marked, "Duboite, room 302" and she slipped it into her pocket.

"You know, Vincent; There will be hell to pay when your wife finds out that you were having an affair in Bermuda with Francine Duboite," she said playfully to her husband with a poke in his ribs. Suspecting that the desk clerk had overheard her she turned around with a mischievous grin and put her index finger up to her lips and said, "Shh. It's a secret."

They entered the breakfast area on the spacious terrasse just off the side of the lobby. It was paved with white limestone tiles and surrounded by white trellises covered with purple bougainvillea. The sky was pristine blue without a single cloud in sight, and the air temperature was warmer than normal for so late in the year. The round table where they had had breakfast served every morning for the past week was prepared and waiting for them. “This way Madame and Monsieur. Duboite,” said the handsomely dressed host at the door. They were the only ones on the breakfast terrace except the couple seated at their table and awaiting their arrival.

“Good morning, Stephan,” said Vincent “You seem to be looking more and more chipper each day.”

Stephan smiled and patted the cast on his right leg. “Except for this, I am almost as good as new. I am just happy to have Brigid here to push me around in the wheelchair, and I’m glad to finally be off the ship.”

Vincent and Sandi seated themselves. Brigid said, “Dr. Spinu checked in on him again this morning before heading back to Île d’Ouessant. He said the breaks were clean and he didn’t think Stephan would need surgery. The bone seems to be healing nicely, the infection from the gash is mostly gone and the wound will be a memory before long.”

“I have an appointment this afternoon with a physical therapist,” said Stephan.

“You know,” said Sandi. “These past few days have really been fabulous. The last time the four of us were together was in Oslo. What was it? Five or six years ago?”

“Being secluded here in Bermuda with Stephan has been wonderful,” said Brigid. “We never got to take a normal honeymoon. We were always looking over our shoulders. It feels like Bermuda is as far away from the Syndicate as one can possibly get on this planet, and I am really enjoying the break.”

“Oh, Brigid! Don’t use that word around me,” said Stephan. They all laughed.

Vincent contributed to the lightheartedness, “And, if the Syndicate wanted to eliminate most of their opposition all at once, they would just place a bomb under this table.” In jest, he pulled up the edge of the tablecloth and peeked. His head did not come back up right away.

“Vincent?” said Sandi.

When he came back up, he was motioning with his index finger that there was something unusual under the table. “I think it’s a bomb.” They all laughed heartily at the joke. “No,” he repeated. “I think there really is a bomb. Don’t anybody move a muscle.” Vincent bent his head down again to look more closely. He saw a green flashing light on the device and there was a thin wire leading to one of the legs of Sandi’s chair. “I think it was activated when Sandi sat down.” He looked for other wires, and seeing none, he stood up and pulled his chair away from the table, climbing under to get a better look. This action caught the attention of the host who came over to the table.

"Vincent thinks there may be a bomb under the table," Stephan said with a grin, playing along with what he presumed was Vincent's practical joke.

"I think there is a pressure switch rigged to Sandi's chair," came Vincent's muffled voice from under the table. "I think this thing is set to go off if she gets up."

By this time, the host had fled to the front desk to summon security. "Come on, Vincent. Now you are starting to scare us," said Stephan, still convinced that it was a practical joke gone too far.

Vincent was on his knees next to Sandi, looking intently into her eyes. "Do not move a muscle," he commanded sternly before turning over on his back to study if there was anything obvious, he could see to disarm it. The host rushed back in followed closely by a couple of men from hotel security. They took one look at the device and called the Bermuda bomb squad on the 2-way radio. It took fifteen minutes for them to arrive. For Sandi it seemed like two hours. They placed an explosion shield over her.

"Get those two out of here," Vincent commanded, pointing to Stephan and Brigid. A technician from the bomb squad joined Vincent under the table. The two were laying side by side on their backs to survey the situation.

"This is not a very big bomb," said the technician, "But it would have certainly killed anyone at the table. I know this kind of device. It has been modified from a claymore mine. A pressure switch activates it, and it is set to detonate when the pressure is released. He reached up and flicked a switch on the side of the casing. The flashing green light went to solid red. A deathly stillness filled the room for a few moments. "I think we are okay now." Vincent slipped out from under that table and took Sandi's hand. "Sir, you need to leave." instructed one of the men.

"I'm not leaving my wife," he said defiantly.

The bomb squad technician shook his head and snipped the wire leading to Sandi's chair, while watching the lights on the device for a change of state. After waiting for a dozen seconds, he yelled, "All clear." And climbed out from under the table dripping in perspiration.

The lobby was filled with firemen, local policemen and a contingent of national police when Sandi and Vincent finally emerged from the breakfast terrace. Sandi put her hand in her pocket to discover the note the desk clerk had given her that she had forgotten about. She opened it, read it and handed it to Vincent. It said, "Do not go out to the breakfast terrasse this morning!"

Brigid and Stephan disappeared from the lobby during all the confusion. Sandi told Vincent, "See if you can find them. I'm going up to the room to pack."

"Madame Duboite, the Chief of Police wants to talk to you," said the desk clerk as Sandi passed her on the way to the elevators.

“I will be right back down,” she said.

Vincent went out the front door to see if Brigid and Stephan might be in the crowd of hotel guests mingling outside when the hotel was evacuated. There was no sign of them. Then he caught a glimpse of Stephan heading down to the marina as fast as he could get his wheelchair to go. Vincent yelled, “Stephan, where are you going?” Stephan did not stop. Vincent ran to catch up with him. “Stephan, where are you going?” he said out of breath.

“To the marina,” Stephan replied without stopping. “No one can ever know I am in Bermuda. An encounter with the police is the last thing in the world any of us can afford.”

“Where is Brigid?” asked Vincent.

“She went to the room to pack. She will meet me at the marina. We need to catch the morning hydrofoil to the *Bougainville*. It will be departing in less than ten minutes,” said Stephan.

Vincent said, “Here, let me push you.”

They arrived at the marina expecting to see the *Bougainville's* tender, but it was not there. “Where's the hydrofoil?” Vincent said to a dockworker, pointing to the empty slip where the tender should have been.

“Not coming today,” said the man. “*Bougainville* sailed away this morning before dawn to stay ahead of the hurricane.”

“What? Sailed away? Hurricane?” exclaimed a frantic Vincent. He did a full three-hundred-and-sixty-degree sweep of the surrounding for a clue for what to do next. He spotted some boats tied up not too far away with the sign "Water Taxi". "Wait here," he said to Stephan. "I will be right back."

One of the boats at the taxi stand was an inflatable with twin 500 horsepower outboards that he estimated could probably reach forty miles per hour. "Is this boat for hire?" he asked the boat operator.

"Yes, where do you want to go?" he queried.

"We need to catch up with the *Bougainville*," said Vincent.

"Oh, I can't do that," the boat operator replied. "They already have a five-hour head start. Anyway, they are in international waters and this boat is not licensed for such a trip."

Vincent thought for a minute. "How about the airport, then?

"That I can do," replied the boat operator.

"Okay, stay here," said Vincent. "I will be right back."

Sandi and Brigid were standing on the dock next to Stephan when Vincent reappeared. "I ran into Brigid in the third-floor hallway coming out of her room with suitcases," said Sandi. "She explained to me that she needed to get Stephan away from Bermuda. I had realized about the same time that I didn't want to have to explain to the Chief of Police who Francine Duboite was. So, here we are."

"Okay," said Vincent. "I hired a water taxi to take us to the airport. I have no idea what we will do when we get there, but hopefully by then, we will have figured it out."

The four hurried down to the awaiting taxi and got on board. Off they went out of Hamilton harbor to the west, into the Great Sound and rounding the point in the shallows between Spanish Point and Cobbler Island. They passed quickly along the north coast of the island, entering Castle Harbour at the inlet south of Ferry Island Fort. The marina at the airport was located next to the freight terminal on the south side of the airport, giving them a long walk to the main passenger terminal.

"How much do we owe you?" Sandi asked the boat operator.

"Ninety dollars each. Three hundred and sixty dollars," he replied.

Sandi retrieved her Francine Duboite envelope of cash. "How much in euros?"

The man gave the matter some thought and replied, "That would be three-hundred and sixty euros."

"Three-hundred and sixty euros?" Sandi exclaimed. "The exchange rate is 1.5! It should be more like two-hundred and fifty euros."

The man just shrugged his shoulders as if the matter was out of his hands. Sandi shelled out the cash and gave him look that would shame most people. He untied the inflatable boat and sped off, leaving the four looking around for a shuttle bus or some hint for how they were supposed to make it to the main terminal. "I guess we walk," said Brigid.

Vincent did not hear her say this. He had become distracted in his mind with a wild idea. He pointed to a helicopter behind a chain-link fence adjacent to the freight terminal only a hundred meters away. "That's how we get to the *Bougainville*!" he exclaimed. They started running to find the entrance. Vincent was pushing Stephan's wheelchair as fast as he could. The sign over the door read, "Scenic Helicopter Tours: Explore beautiful Bermuda from the air". Vincent explained to the tour operator that they wanted to take a one-way trip out to a ship sailing north at a slow speed and land on the deck. The tour operator was familiar with the Bougainville and had flown out to her a few times. It was agreed, and Sandi shelled out the three thousand euros for the trip.

"Okay, then," he said. "Let me go hail the skipper on the radio to get the ship's position and advise them to expect us."

"Um, Sir," said Vincent sheepishly. "Would it be possible to wait until we get close to the ship before contacting them?"

The tour operator and their soon-to-be-pilot lowered his glasses on his nose and frowned at Vincent. "I see," he said. And after a long pause, "Okay, then. In that case I will need eight thousand euros." Sandi shelled out almost all of what remained of Francine Duboite's cash. "I will find out where the ship is presently located and her heading on the Marine Finder," said the operator. "One more day, and we would have been closed to wait out the hurricane."

It took one and a half hours to catch up with the Bougainville. "There she is," said the pilot, pointing forward through the windscreen to a dot on the horizon. He switched on the radio and selected the correct frequency. “This is Bob Macky speaking. Hello, Richard, are you there? Over.”

“Captain Shaw here,” came the response. “What’s up?”

“Yes, Richard, I am three kilometers astern requesting permission to land,” said Macky.

“Is it an emergency?” asked Captain Shaw.

“No. I have four fugitives aboard who claim they know you,” said Macky.

“I will be waiting on the flight deck,” said Shaw. “We are doing just ten knots and the wind is light from the south. You should have no trouble putting down.”

There were no tethered hydrogen dirigibles aboard, so the flight deck was mostly clear of obstacles except for the cradles. The helicopter landed on the flight deck near the stern and idled the rotor. The door popped open, and the four passengers emerged, Stephan’s arm was around Vincent’s shoulder as he hopped on his good leg. They opened the luggage compartment to retrieve their things and Stephan’s wheelchair.

Captain Shaw yelled to the pilot, “Hey Bob, why don’t you hang around. Bev has cooked up a wonderful dinner.”

“Thanks, Richard. Another time, perhaps. I know your wife is a terrific cook, but I need to get back so I can secure this bird in the hangar before the storm hits.” Pausing, he added, “I told the Bermuda tower we were going whale-watching. Do you think they believed me? It is a little late in the year." The helicopter lifted off and disappeared to the south.

Chapter 10: Into the Storm

"This space reminds me of Captain Nemo's living room on the Nautilus," remarked Vincent as they entered the main salon of Captain Shaw's living spaces adjacent to the bridge aboard the *Bougainville*.

"Well, I suppose we did get a bit carried away," replied Shaw. "It's just that the investors in this project had a lot of money burning a hole in their pocket that they ended up not spending to purchase the ship. They instructed me to make it opulent and spare no expense. The idea was to create a venue where they could entertain friends and VIPs. They wanted it to rival the most extravagant cruise ships. They instructed me to do whatever it took to eradicate any reminder that *Bougainville* had once been a warship. Please, everyone, make yourself comfortable," he said, motioning to the plush chairs and sofas. Vincent strolled along the bookcase observing an impressive collection of nautical volumes. He stopped at a complete set of the works of Jules Verne, like the set his father had kept when he was growing up.

A woman entered the salon with a tray of drinks. "This is my wife, Bev," said Captain Shaw. "She's the cook and the Director of Human Relations, which mostly means just keeping me in line."

"I am very pleased to meet you," Sandi said, standing up to take the tray from Beverly. "We feel bad just dropping in uninvited."

"Nonsense," replied the captain. "Your visit is rather fortuitous. We departed from Bermuda short-handed. Many of the crew chose to return to the island where they had families. They mostly worked in the salvage operations, so it didn't impact us much. While on station, we didn't need a lot of crew to operate the vessel, but now that we are underway, that has all changed. Having an experienced skipper join us is more than just serendipity. It is an answer to prayer," he said, looking at Sandi.

"You're not serious," she responded. "Are you thinking of putting me to work?"

The captain motioned to a man who appeared at that moment at the door of the salon. "Ah, Alex, welcome. Come in, I think all of you may remember Alex Spinu, the Chief Engineer on *L'Astrolabe*."

Sandi put the drink tray down and went over to give him a big embrace.

"How in the world did you ever end up on the *Bougainville*?" asked Stephan, seeming quite surprised by this new development. Brigid stepped forward to introduce herself. "I'm Brigid, Stephan's wife. I don't think we have ever actually met."

"Uncle Vasi has spoken highly of you many times," he said, taking her hand. "I got to know Stephan on the icebreaker, but this is the first time I knew that the two of you were married."

Brigid said, "We had been keeping it secret, but there is not much point any longer. I guess *katten er ute av sekken*," she said in Norwegian with a wink. "The cat is out of the bag."

"Alexandre," repeated Stephan. "What in the world are you doing here?"

"It's a bit complicated," replied Alex, taking a glass of iced tea from Sandi and seating himself. He said, "I have been working undercover for Uncle Vasi for the past two years—actually, after my encounter with Commander Brundt aboard *L'Astrolabe*, she passed my tip about the secret submarine base in Chornomorsk to Brigid, who passed it on to Uncle Vasi, who contacted me directly and asked me to return to Norway to join him at the agency."

"Please," Sandi interrupted. "Don't call me Commander Brundt, It's just Sandi now."

Alex continued, "After some very intensive training, he dispatched me to Moldavia under a false identity to see what I could find out about something rumored to be very big that the Syndicate was up to. I will come back to that in a bit." He took a sip of tea. "Let me first tell you how I ended up on this ship. Uncle Vasi wanted to dispatch me to Bermuda to give Stephan a first-hand account of what I had seen in Moldavia. While I was waiting in Oslo, I saw a job listing for an engineering officer on the

Bougainville. The ship was scheduled to re-deploy into the Indian Ocean after the first of the year, and apparently, the current engineering officer lived in Bermuda and was unwilling to stay on the crew. It was the perfect cover for me. We knew Stephan was on board. Some strings were pulled, and here I am. What I didn't expect was that by the time I showed up for duty, Stephan had decided to live the good life at the Hamilton Grand." Stephan chuckled at this remark.

Sandi asked, "Did you write the note warning us not to go to breakfast this morning?"

"Yes," replied Alex, "But it wasn't a warning. I gave the note to the desk clerk yesterday afternoon before I went to catch the evening tender back to *Bougainville.* I was planning to return this morning to fetch Stephan. I just wanted to catch him before he went in for breakfast so we would have time to get to the tender scheduled to depart at 9:30 this morning. Uncle Vasi had received a report that Stephan had been spotted and thought it would be a good idea for him to disappear for a while. I was planning to bring him back onto the ship—that is, until Captain Shaw decided to depart one day early to stay ahead of the hurricane."

"So, you didn't know about the bomb," queried Vincent.

Alex Spinu and Richard Shaw looked at each other in shock and said at the same time, "Bomb? What bomb?"

"The bomb beneath our breakfast table," said Vincent.

"I didn't know anything about a bomb!" exclaimed Alex. "When I found out that *Bougainville* was to depart a day early and the tender wasn't going to go to Hamilton, I was completely panicked. Then, this afternoon you showed up out of the blue in a helicopter, and with the complete entourage."

Stephan said darkly, "Well, I really am glad to be here, but none of us are safe as long as I am on board. Now that the Syndicate knows that I survived the crash of *La Charlière*, they will stop at nothing until they have a corpse."

"Say, you're not by chance that French crewmember presumed lost at sea, are you?" asked Captain Shaw.

Stephan flashed a broad grin, "*C'est moi.*" After a long silence, while everyone contemplated the implications that the Syndicate probably knew by now that Stephan was on the *Bougainville*, "I fear that I have put all of you and this ship in harm's way," he said. "We should anticipate a Syndicate submarine attack in a couple of days."

"That's unlikely," said Shaw. "In the first place, unless they have made a substantial improvement in their torpedo technology, the best they could do is maybe poke a few holes in us. They would have great difficulty sinking Bougainville. In the second place, they haven't been spotted in open seas in a couple of years and the moment one of them tries to exit the Mediterranean they would pick up a French submarine escort. No, if they want to attack this ship, they will need to do it by air, with a landing party using helicopters or tiltrotors. I don't think we have much to worry about, though, until we get closer to the coast of Morocco. Tomorrow, there is something very interesting I want to show you."

"Dinner is ready," said Beverly coming out into the salon, untying her apron. "Will you be joining us, Mr. Spinu?"

"No. Thanks anyway, Mrs. Shaw. Duty calls. I need to figure out how to operate a ten-megawatt hydrogen fuel cell system." Alex stood up to excuse himself.

"Mr. Spinu," said Stephan. "I am really eager to hear what you have to tell us about the Syndicate activities in Moldavia."

"Perhaps tomorrow," he replied, exiting the salon. "I don't want you to have nightmares—at least, not tonight anyway. Everyone be safe and sleep well."

The dinner party followed Captain Shaw into the dining room. "Oh my," exclaimed Sandi. "This is more elegant than Captain Charpentier's dining room aboard the Nautilus."

"Perhaps," responded Shaw, "but I will wager that Captain Charpentier didn't have to help with the dishes after dinner." This brought on a laugh and somewhat lightened the otherwise somber mood.

"Are you aware that Captain Charpentier is now an admiral?" asked Vincent. "He is over the entire French submarine fleet. Were it not for the chaos in the French Naval Directorate, he would probably be a Vice-Admiral by now. I had dinner with him a month ago in Toulon...and another of Sandi's favorite people, "The Grand Inquisitor" himself." Stephan broke into a genuine laugh.

"Vincent, you need to stop teasing me about that encounter," responded Sandi. "I was scared to death. I thought I was about to be arrested and spend the rest of my life in a French prison. How was I to know that Captain Rousseau was just trying to offer me a job,"

Thoroughly enjoying the reverie, Stephan added, "That's when she called me a 'spook'."

Vincent and Stephan enjoyed this moment of levity, but Sandi did not.

"Everything is set out on the buffet, so please take a plate and help yourselves," said Beverly. "There is a choice of red wine, white wine, and soda if you prefer. A pitcher of ice water is on the table."

"Captain Shaw," asked Sandi, stepping up to the buffet to serve herself and handing him a dinner plate. "Is there any more news about the hurricane?"

"I checked a couple of hours ago," he replied. "It strengthened to a category 4 after passing over the Florida panhandle, but it doesn't look like it will hit Bermuda. It is moving up the East Coast and the eye is now heading for landfall near Hilton Head."

"Hilton Head!" gasped Sandi. "Vincent! Mama and Louisa!" She reached into her handbag for her phone to retrieve any messages. "Oh, No! Vincent. I forgot to switch it back on!"

Captain Shaw picked up a remote control and turned on the television to the weather station. The newswoman was leaning hard into the gusting wind and driving rain. The scene behind her was total devastation. Her voice was impossible to hear over the roar, but the streaming sub-caption read, "It seems that the worst of this storm is now over for Savannah, Georgia, at least. But as you can see, there's not much left standing."

"Come on, phone! Download! Download! Where are my messages?" Sandi was frantic.

The first voice message finally showed up. "Sandi, dear. This is Mama. You have probably been watching the news. Don't worry. We had plenty of warning and everyone is safe. Louisa is fine. It is unlikely that my house survived, so we are heading to France. We will meet you in Saint-Marc. I remember the code to get into your apartment. I love you."

Sandi and Vincent stared at each other in disbelief.

Beverly spoke up over the noise of the TV, "Come, sit down. We will figure this out, but there is no point in letting your dinners get cold."

A young woman hurriedly entered the dining room. "Sorry I'm late." She kissed Captain Shaw on the cheek and gave Beverly a big hug. "We are going to encounter some rough seas up ahead later on tonight, so I wanted to check that the seals on the tailgate were secure and that the well deck is pumped out and dry."

"This is our daughter, Tanya," said the captain. "I think you all met her in the Control Room, piloting a salvage barge and surveillance drone on your tour last week. While underway, I pretend to be the captain, but she is the one who actually runs the ship."

"That's ridiculous," responded Tanya. "*Bougainville* is just a big, slow salvage barge. I simply engaged the autopilot. At ten knots, how much trouble can we possibly get into? The next obstacle is the Azores, still 3,000 kilometers up ahead. We won't be there for six more days. This ship is not rigged for speed."

Sandi looked across the dinner table to Vincent. The sudden realization that they would be sequestered on the ship for two more weeks struck them both at the same time.

Early the following morning, Stephan was outside his stateroom awaiting daybreak. "Hey, Brigid. Do you think the United States Navy would have approved of these lavish outside balconies?" Stephan asked her as she came out with his morning coffee. The deck faced north. The sunrise could not be viewed from the port side of the ship's island, but the faint glow of dawn was visible, nonetheless, up ahead on their northwesterly heading. The sea state was rougher than the glassy waters off Bermuda, but the voyage was still comfortable in spite of the absence of stabilizers. The steady roll and pitch of the ship were therapeutic for Stephan. He had managed to hop onto the balcony during the night and position himself on a deck chair, covering himself with a blanket against the chill.

"How long have you been up?" asked Brigid.

"I haven't been able to sleep much. My leg hurts and I can't stop thinking about all my friends and colleagues at the Intelligence Ministry either dead or in prison. My heart aches for Abraham. He doesn't stand a chance at his age." He took the mug of coffee from Brigid and relished in the steam permeating his sinuses. "I hate this cast! I hate being completely helpless!" he finally said.

After breakfast, the group convened in the salon with Alex Spinu for him to relate his adventures in Moldavia. "Are you all ready to hear some pretty scary stuff?" he asked. They all nodded. "Okay then. I spent the last six months undercover in Moldavia at Uncle Vasi's request. As you probably know, after the coup and my father's assassination, Uncle Vasi took me to Norway for my protection. Moldavia is an amalgamation of Moldova and the Crimea and the southern part of what used to be called the Ukraine along the Black Sea. The capital is Odessa and is the place where I was born. I went there as a simple tourist. It is an ancient city with a rich history, but sadly, the city is at the crossroads of cultures and has experienced wave after wave of violence for centuries. The coup of 2048 is no exception. I was only eight years old, but the memory is still fresh. It was very painful to return to the places where I grew up. What was most striking about the city, though, was the oppressive darkness. No one was smiling. The people in the restaurants along the nearly deserted boulevards spoke only in whispers. A couple of weeks in the city was all I could take, but it gave me an opportunity to refresh my mother tongue."

"My destination was a broad plane in the Danube delta called Pādurea Letea, in the far east of what was once part of Romania. It is an extremely remote area about 180 kilometers southwest of Odessa and 20 kilometers inland from the Black Sea. The beaches along the Black Sea in that region serve as a popular vacation spot for boaters. There are no roads, so it is only possible to get there by water. I purchased camping equipment and supplies and rented an inflatable power boat in Odessa with extra petrol tanks for the trip. The beaches were almost completely deserted. There were only a few other campsites so finding a spot out of sight of the next group of people was not a challenge. I set up camp in a beautiful inlet near the mouth of the Danube from which, I could explore the estuary. From my campsite, it was only about twenty-five kilometers upstream to Pādurea Letea, and I could reach it in under an hour. There were always patrol boats going up and down the river. They would stop me from time to time, wanting to know what I was up to. I would just show them my fake credentials as a professor of ornithology from the university studying bird migration. After a while, they got used to my presence and just waved as they passed. The mosquitoes and black flies were something else!"

Alex paused to drink his coffee, which was lukewarm by that time. "They had no reason to expect that I was actually on an espionage mission," he continued. "There was an unusual amount of barge traffic coming down the river which was offloading at a dock at a tiny village called Periprava, where I occasionally stopped to buy supplies. There was a restaurant there that I frequented. This gave me a chance to get to know the locals and secure my bird-watching alibi. A constant stream of lorries went through the town from the dock carrying materials inland and returning empty. One of them stopped at the restaurant and I jumped in the back when no one was looking. It was filled with curved metal segments that I imagined could be joined into spheres."

"Oh, no!" exclaimed Vincent.

"Oh, yes!" responded Alex. "I rode in the back of the lorry for about ten minutes before it stopped. It was dark by then but when I got out, I saw dozens of ten-meter diameter spheres glistening in the moonlight."

"If that's true," said Stephan, "then they would show up on satellite images."

"Ah," replied Alex, "but that's the strangest thing of all. As I was looking out on this sea of spheres, they...well, they all disappeared from sight right before my eyes."

Vincent leaned forward in his chair and stared at the floor. He had a pretty good idea what was going on. "Alex," he finally said. "I need to know exactly what you saw. You say they disappeared? Just all at once?"

"Well, not exactly," replied Alex. "It was nothing I had ever seen before, so it's hard to describe. One by one, they seemed to take on a fuzzy appearance, like they were out of focus, and then just sort of dissipated over the course of a few seconds. Within a matter of just a few minutes, they had all just disappeared. It was very dark. There were no lights whatsoever, only a little moonlight."

"Here's the really creepy part," Alex continued. "There were a lot of people walking around carrying stuff. They were dressed in black clothing and were wearing some sort of goggles that I decided must be night vision goggles. There were no buildings that I could see and no structures whatsoever—nothing that would give any hint to the presence of a construction site. Some of them were taking the curved metal pieces out of the lorries and others were carrying something that looked like cylinders about thirty centimeters in diameter and a meter tall. They would attach the cylinder onto a base plate and then begin assembling the metal segments around it to form the spherical dome with a hatch in the side. The last thing they did was to install six seats, like the jump-seats you would find on an aircraft. These were arranged into a circle around the cylinder facing outward. I watched while they completed one of the spheres, which took more than an hour. They only spoke in soft whispers. Then they walked away and started building another. Before long, the finished sphere would take on that fuzzy, out of focus appearance and then dissipate into thin air. I couldn't believe my eyes. I stayed almost until morning and saw them build six more of these things until the moon finally set and it was too dark to see anything. I walked back to the dock to get my boat—no, I ran. I was terrified. The trip back to my campsite was the scariest thing I have ever experienced."

"Timecharging capsules!" said Vincent as he stood up and walked out of the salon. "They are preparing an invasion force."

Chapter 11: Quantum Couple

Captain Shaw came into the salon with a large hard-shell carrying case which he placed on the coffee table. "Where did Vincent go?" he asked.

"I would guess he needed to go outside for some fresh air," said Sandi.

Shaw undid the clasps on the case. "This is what I wanted to show you." He looked around at everyone with a broad smile as he opened the case.

"Good grief!" exclaimed Brigid. "That's a Viper X. Where in the world did you get it?"

"So, you know what it is?" he asked.

"Yes, we used those in the Norwegian army," replied Brigid "but those things have been banned by international treaty for years. They were the favorite weapon of terrorists."

Captain Shaw said, "There is a weapons locker on deck 3 full of these things, along with assault rifles and an assortment of handguns that could supply a small army. It seems that when *Bougainville* went into dry dock, someone forgot to clean out that weapons locker."

"But a Viper X?" said Brigid. "Surely it's not operational after thirty years."

"Eight new AA batteries, and it's as good as new," said Shaw, removing the shoulder-fired anti-aircraft missile launcher from the case, and turning on the power switch and handing it to Brigid. "Do you care to give it a try?"

Brigid turned off the power switch and handed it back to Captain Shaw with a disapproving scowl.

Shaw said, "This thing has a five-mile range and 30,000-foot ceiling. It is really lethal against airborne threats. There's practically no aircraft in the world this thing can't bring down."

"That's precisely why they have been banned," shot back Brigid.

"Yes," rebutted Shaw, "but the Syndicate doesn't know we have any of these. When they try to attack this ship with whatever type of aircraft they bring, we will be ready to blow them out of the sky."

Vincent walked back into the salon at that moment. "Those things won't work against *timechargers*," he said, walking across the room and standing to look out the window at skies that were turning increasingly dark and foreboding. The room went completely silent at this remark. Finally, Vincent turned around and said, "They won't risk a conventional boarding attempt if they have *timechargers*. From what Alex described this morning; the Syndicate has achieved a high degree of operational readiness. I doubt that they are capable of launching an all-out invasion, but a simple search-and-destroy mission like attacking *Bougainville* is certainly a possibility." Vincent went over to the buffet and poured himself a cup of coffee from a drip percolator that had been left on all morning. The coffee was lukewarm and had the consistency of coal slurry.

"Here," said Sandi, standing up. "Let me start a fresh pot."

All eyes were on Vincent. "I know what Alex was describing," he began. "I recognize the ten-meter disappearing spheres as the very thing we were developing at Ashleigh Airships. The Syndicate has turned them into war machines. My father warned us of this possibility, but we didn't take him seriously enough. Until this morning, I would never have dreamed that timecharging technology could be commandeered for this kind of evil."

He paced slowly around the salon. "Airplanes can be detected by radar, noise, heat signature...this is the reason nations have largely abandoned aircraft as a means of force projection. It is weapons like the one on the coffee table and high-powered lasers and rail guns that rendered military use of air power ineffective. I credit this with bringing fifty years of peace and tranquility to the world. Have you considered that other than a few border skirmishes, there hasn't been a major war anywhere in the world since the Battle of the South China Sea in 2051?"

Vincent sat back down and rubbed his weary eyes. "Timecharging spheres are virtually undetectable. They can go anywhere, anytime, and for whatever purpose—good or evil—at the will of the operator."

"Surely that can't be true," said Captain Shaw.

"When timecharging, the entire sphere and everything inside enters into a different space-time reality that is invisible to those on the outside," Vincent shot back.

"Vincent," said Sandi, "You told me once that, yes, it's true that no one on the outside can see in, but didn't you also say that no one on the inside can see out either. If that's the case, how can they navigate to where they are going."

Vincent closed his eyes, putting both hands on his head and entering a posture of deep contemplation. After a while, he popped up. "That's it! Sandi, darling, you are absolutely brilliant. They can't operate autonomously. They need guidance from the outside." He paced some more around the salon. Turning to Stephan, he said "Stephan, was there anything unusual about the spheres making up *La Charlière*?"

"No," Stephan replied, trying to reconstruct the fateful flight before the crash. "No, all the spheres were ordinary as best as I can recall. Of course, they were invisible in the dirigible when operating, and I couldn't see inside any of them. I assume each one contained a timecharging rotor set for weightless operation. All of the flight controls and superstructure were on the outside."

"But you told me the last thing you remember after jumping out was seeing the spheres in the moonlight. How is that possible if the rotors were operating?"

"I guess someone must have killed the power to crash the ship," replied Stephan.

"That would require the ability to communicate with the rotor controls on the inside while they are running. Someone on the outside knew how to switch off the rotors. Once the rotors are activated, the spheres will continue to timecharge until the timer, which is located on the inside, switches it off. If any particular rotor were to fail or switch off accidentally, there is enough redundancy to keep the ship aloft. It is unthinkable that all the rotors would switch off at the same time. The rotors would have been activated at the factory to run for the life of the batteries, which would have been days. There's no way to turn them off from the outside."

Vincent stopped in his tracks. "Stephan! That's why they want you dead. You saw the spheres."

"I don't understand," said Stephan.

Vincent responded, "If the superstructure of *La Charlière* had broken apart like the crew reported, the invisible and weightless spheres would have drifted off into outer space. You wouldn't have been able to see them at all."

Beverly came out of the kitchen carrying a tray. "I do not want to interrupt you, but it's past one and I thought you might be getting hungry, so I made a few sandwiches."

"Thanks, Bev," said Captain Shaw. He closed the Viper X case and placed it out of the way to make room for the sandwich tray on the coffee table. "I'm afraid we lost track of time."

"Would it be possible to have Alex rejoin us?" asked Vincent.

Shaw punched the button on the intercom. “Bridge,” responded Tanya.

“Do you know where Alex is?” asked Shaw.

“He’s in the engine room,” said Tanya. “He’s trying to figure out why we are consuming hydrogen faster than we should be.”

“Don’t bother him, then. That’s obviously a higher priority. If he comes to the bridge, just send him to the salon when he has a moment.” Captain Shaw pushed the intercom button a second time to switch it off.

Vincent said, “Everything Alex described this morning from what he saw in Moldavia is consistent with the timecharging spheres being produced at the Ashleigh Airships factory at St. Nazaire. This tells me that, not only does the Syndicate have access to the Ashleigh technology, but it seems there has been some technology transfer and corporate cooperation.”

“I would rather call it collusion,” said Stephan. “I think this is what Jean-Luc was hoping I would figure out.”

“Okay. Collusion, then,” said Vincent. “That’s a pretty sinister view. I was thinking more along the lines of corporate espionage, but collusion would certainly explain why the spheres that Alex saw look a lot like the ones we were building at St. Nazaire.”

“What makes you so sure they are the same?” asked Sandi.

“For one thing, the description of the rotor canisters,” said Vincent. “Alex described them as cylindrical, one meter tall and thirty centimeters in diameter. That’s the size of the next generation model based on my sliding bobbin innovation. This type of rotor is just now going into pilot production. Even *La Charlière* didn't have those installed yet. The rotors on *La Charlière* used the older hoop rotor and are twice the size and weigh about a ton. Even four strong men would not be able to move them around. The canisters that Alex described were being moved from the back of a truck by just two men." Vincent picked up a turkey and cheese sandwich and a napkin. "We have a huge advantage, though. The Syndicate would have no way of knowing what Alex saw, so they would have no reason to suspect that anyone has pieced together what they are up to." He took a bite of his sandwich.

"Except the loose end presented by me surviving the crash," added Stephan.

Brigid said, "This still doesn't solve our predicament. If they mount an assault on *Bougainville* using those things, and we have no way of knowing when, or even if, they are coming, we are just sitting ducks out here."

"Perhaps," said Vincent, "but I have been giving a lot of thought to what Sandi said a while back. We can't see them, but they also can't see us. They can't attack us without assistance from the outside. What makes a stealth fighter jet invisible? It doesn't actually disappear. It simply redirects the radar waves, so they don't reflect back to the fire control antennae. In much the same way, a timecharging sphere does not actually disappear, it just shifts the frequency of reflected light. We can see things because light reflects off solid objects. It is this reflected light that we see with our eyes. When a timecharging rotor is engaged it decreases the local speed of light within the sphere, including everything inside the sphere and the shell of the sphere. If you are inside the sphere, nothing seems out of the ordinary; it takes the same amount of effort to raise your hand above your head. Sound waves travel at the same speed so you can talk normally. Your heart beats at the same rate. I know all of this sounds bizarre, but this is the basis Cédric Rothchild's breakthrough discovery. The speed of light is not constant. It is localized. Light can never be sped up, but it can be slowed down. If you measured the speed of light on the inside of a timecharging sphere, you would get exactly the same result you would get on the outside. The only difference is that relative to the outside, the speed of light is orders of magnitude slower inside the sphere. Here's something to try to get your head around. Let's say someone on the inside is hooked up to a heart rate monitor measuring seventy beats per minute. There's no way to actually check his heart rate from the outside because there is no way for someone on the outside to see or measure anything on the inside. But if it were possible, the heart rate of someone on the inside would appear to be about 200 times slower, or one beat every three minutes or so. The effect of timecharging is to introduce extreme slow-motion relative to the outside. Seventy beats of our Syndicate commando's heart took one minute on the inside but 200 minutes on the outside. If his sphere is moving along at sixty kilometers per hour, or one kilometer per minute, according to an outside observer, in the minute it took his heart to beat seventy times, the sphere will have travelled two-hundred kilometers. According to his clock, he is travelling 12,000 kilometers per hour, or ten times the speed of sound."

Vincent paused to let this sink in. He knew that Sandi and Stephan had both experienced this effect several times first-hand, but the reality was still hard for them to comprehend. Even Captain Shaw had experienced the effect when his Arleigh Burke destroyer had travelled from the mouth of the Chesapeake Bay to the Caribbean off the coast of Guadeloupe, a journey of 2,700 kilometers, in just minutes. "Are you ready for more?" Vincent asked.

"So, not only is everyone and everything on the inside of the sphere running in slow motion, visible light striking the outside of the sphere is also timeshifted, or what we have been calling timecharged. The result is that the incident light within the visible spectrum is reflected with a frequency and wavelength in the deep ultraviolet that is way beyond the range of human vision. The signature of this effect is just what Alex described. It takes some time for the timecharging rotor to spin up to speed when it is activated. What happens is that the light reflecting off the sphere is shifted to higher and higher frequencies until it is no longer visible. Alex observed the spheres becoming iridescent, or "out of focus" as he described it, before disappearing from sight."

Brigid asked, "Do you think we could modify the tracker of a Viper X to work in the deep UV?"

"Unfortunately," Vincent replied, "light at those frequencies can only penetrate a few centimeters in air. In the laboratory we did use ultraviolet cameras so we could observe the spheres while timecharging, but there would be no way to see one far enough away to lock on and engage it at a sufficient stand-off distance. I don't think it ever occurred to any of us working at Ashleigh Airships that dealing with invisible things could ever have a practical application. Using the effect for cloaking as an offensive weapon just never crossed my mind. We need to understand the reason Ashleigh wanted to deploy timecharging spheres in freight dirigibles like *La Charlière* in the first place. They never intended to put people inside. I tried hard to convince upper management that the real benefit of timecharging was for personal mobility, because it solved the problem of jet lag. I climbed inside one on a couple of occasions to demonstrate that being inside while timecharging is perfectly safe. This did not set at all well with upper management, but that's a discussion for another day. As a lifting device, this is how they work. The volume of a ten-meter diameter sphere is a bit more than 500 cubic meters. The density of air at sea level is about one and a quarter kilograms per cubic meter, so such a sphere would displace 625 kilograms of air if there was just vacuum on the inside. If it were an ordinary balloon filled with helium, or better yet, hydrogen at one atmosphere, the gas on the inside would weigh less than ten kilograms. So, depending on the weight of the balloon, it could lift a payload of about 500 kilograms. The initial plan for Ashleigh Airships was to use ten-meter diameter hydrogen-filled spheres. The original dirigible design was basically the same as *La Charlière* with a lifting capacity of about 300 tons. This project just went nowhere because of ballast control issues and safety concerns. That's when they contacted me to help convert the hydrogen-filled spheres over to timecharging spheres. It was recognized by then that such spheres were practically weightless, dramatically increasing the load capacity."

"They also knew that you were the world's leading expert in the technology," interjected Sandi proudly.

Vincent continued, "With full power applied to the rotor, one of these spheres would accelerate upwards rapidly and ultimately drift off into outer space, which is what the spheres on *La Charlière* should have done. When we were developing the spheres in my laboratory in Brest, we enclosed them inside a fishnet that was attached to a scale that could measure the upwards force. One time a technician forgot to secure the tether to the scale and the sphere shot up to the ceiling like a party balloon where it remained until the timer switched off the rotor. In the Ashleigh freight dirigibles, one thousand such spheres are secured into the airship frame. The superstructure, including the front cabin, the control room, solar panels and the propulsion system weigh about ten tons, so the ship can carry about 500 tons of freight at sea level. In the dense air at low altitude, a fully loaded dirigible can only go about as fast as a container ship, but the big advantage is that it requires hardly any fuel to do this. The electricity to power the propellers for forward motion comes from the top-mounted solar panels during the day and batteries at night. The whole system requires only about a hundred kilowatts of power compared to fifty megawatts for a container ship. The real advantage, however, is the ability to operate at higher altitude where the air is less dense, and the dirigible can travel much faster. Ashleigh's plan was to compete in the intermediate market space between air freight and conventional shipping. For the maiden flight of *La Charlière*, there was practically no freight on board because the company wanted to impress the investors with how fast the airship could go at high altitude."

"Actually, the Ashleigh Airship business was on shaky grounds from the start. One of the secrets not widely known is that, although the airships had no difficulty ascending, bringing them back down to earth was altogether another matter. The rotor settings cannot be altered from the outside once activated, so it is necessary to set the internal timers to turn the rotors off at predetermined intervals. Once a particular rotor came to a stop, it could be programmed to a new setting and then switched back on for a new length of time. The ship's buoyancy was controlled by this almost ridiculous means, but there was no other option. We tried for years to figure out how to control a rotor from the outside without success. There was a group in corporate research and development rumored to be working on what they called a "quantum couple". As I understood it, they were trying to make two identical semiconductor devices with all the spins of all the atoms lined up in exactly the same way. If one of the controllers were put into a particular quantum state, then the other controller would enter that same state. The intriguing thing about this was that the information about the quantum state of the controllers was not communicated at the speed of light. In fact, it didn't matter how far apart the controllers were from one another, they were always instantly in exactly the same state. The only thing that would break the pairing was if any attempt was made to discover the state of one of the two controllers. Apparently, any attempt to measure the state broke the quantum symmetry. It is one of the profound mysteries of quantum mechanics that has puzzled physicists for more than a century. I never found out if they succeeded in making it work, but the idea would have solved the dilemma of how to control a running rotor from the outside."

"You don't suppose the Syndicate figured out how to make it work, do you?" asked Stephan.

"The thought has crossed my mind," replied Vincent. "How else can you explain all the spheres that Alex saw without any apparent containment structure unless they somehow figured out how to control each of the rotors from the outside?"

"Even if you could control the buoyancy remotely," said Captain Shaw, "it doesn't explain how anyone could direct their movement. This would require some sort of autonomous piloting device like the surveillance drones we use. For that, you need information about the present location of the drone and some way of steering it to where you want it to go."

Sandi jumped in, "Okay, so the spheres are invisible, but this doesn't mean that a small box attached to the outside has to be invisible."

"Wow! But of course!" exclaimed Shaw, "We don't see our own drones when they are ten miles out. The only way we know where they are is that they tell us. They have on-board GPS transponders, so the drones know where they are. This information is transmitted back to the remote pilot in the control room."

Vincent added, "Assuming that the Syndicate has figured out how to communicate to the inside of a timecharging sphere, and if they attached a small device to the outside with characteristics similar to a drone for propelling the sphere and directing its course, then we probably wouldn't become aware of its presence until it had landed on our flight deck."

"But we would surely be able to intercept the transponder signals," suggested Shaw.

"Do you think the Syndicate would be so stupid as not to encrypt the signals?" asked Vincent.

"It wouldn't matter," said Shaw. "We wouldn't need to know what the communications were saying, only that they were taking place. This would be our early warning system. I need to get Tanya in here. She's the one who really knows about such things."

"When do you think we can start expecting the attack?" asked Sandi.

"We are still a long way from the West Coast of Africa," responded Vincent. "If they truly have this ability, it is likely that they have already deployed the spheres from a land base somewhere. I doubt that they can travel any faster than a hundred kilometers per hour. The journey for the men inside lasts for only a few minutes but the trip on the outside would take at least a couple of days before they could reach our position."

"That is, unless they have a way to deploy them from ships or submarines," said Stephan grimly.

"Or aircraft," added Vincent.

"In any event," said Captain Shaw, "we are about to encounter some pretty bad weather up ahead. If hydrogen delivery dirigibles are any indication, no one will want to be bouncing around in Mid-Atlantic turbulence in a lighter-than-air vessel."

"I don't think the people on the inside would feel a thing," said Vincent. "Any acceleration forces on the outside would be smoothed out on the inside."

Chapter 12: Ponta Delgada

Vincent lay propped up on the bed in his stateroom. The room was dark except for the bedside light illuminating the book on his lap. He was watching the sheets of rain through the sliding glass patio door illuminated by the ship's floodlights. An occasional flash of lightning and thunderclap took him back to the night in the storm aboard D1097. The rolling and pitching of the 45,000-ton *Bougainville* were intense, but nothing compared to what he and Stephan had experienced on the dirigible.

Sandi entered the room quietly to see if Vincent might be napping. "Do you mind if I switch on the light?" she asked.

"No. Go ahead," he said. "It sure starts getting dark early this time of year. I was just lying here thinking about the past few days."

"You look awfully relaxed for someone who is about to be dispatched by Syndicate hitmen," she said, only partially in jest.

"I spent some time this afternoon with Tanya and Captain Shaw," he responded. "They activated the navigational transponder system for controlling the drones and routed the signal scanner to the bridge. I am confident that they will pick up anything in our immediate vicinity broadcasting position coordinates. We should have plenty of warning."

"Then what?" Sandi inquired.

"I have some ideas. We can discuss them after dinner," he said reflectively.

"What are you reading?" she asked.

Vincent replied, "It's a book written by Jules Verne called, "Five Weeks in a Balloon". My father had a copy that I read as a boy. It was in French. I borrowed the captain's copy from the library in the salon. I have never read the English translation. It is quite remarkable considering it was written more than two hundred years ago. I'm only as far as chapter one, but Jules Verne wrote through the voice of his principal character, a Dr. Ferguson. Quoting him, 'I do not follow my route, it is the route that follows me.' I think this applies to me, as well," Vincent said.

"I am going to slip into the shower and get changed for dinner," Sandi said. "We should probably be ready to head upstairs in about thirty minutes."

Vincent was sleeping soundly when she came back out. She pulled a cover over him and switched off the reading light. She kissed him gently on the forehead and headed up to the salon for dinner.

Alex Spinu was sitting alone in the salon when Sandi entered. He stood up to greet her. "Queen Camila sends her regards. She wanted to be sure you knew how grateful she is for loaning your husband to the cause of rescuing Stephan."

"Please tell her, 'Thanks', but I think the rescue is very much on-going and far from complete " she replied. "Did you ever figure out why we are consuming hydrogen faster than we should be?"

"I am a bit embarrassed for needlessly causing alarm," he said. "The fuel cell system is new to me. It turns out that the system that feeds the hydrogen boiling off from the liquid hydrogen tanks operates at ten atmospheres. I had been assuming that the pressure was three atmospheres, since that is what goes into the fuel cells. I failed to take into account the volume expansion, that's all."

"So, we have enough fuel to reach Ponta Delgada?" she asked.

"Yes," Alex replied. "We are consuming a bit more than six-hundred kilograms an hour. We had 150 tons of liquid hydrogen when we left Bermuda, so by my calculation, we will use only about 108 tons. We should be okay. I am working on trying to squeeze out a few more knots of speed. What we could really use is that timecharger device on *L'Astrolabe*."

"And the *Trump*," said Captain Shaw, entering the salon with Tanya and having caught the tail-end of the conversation. "I have good news," he said. "The company has landed a contract for cleaning up a plastic waste concentration about 500 kilometers southwest of the Azores. There is a trench there deep enough to sequester the CO_2 and all the permits have been granted. It will also knock about twenty hours off our trip since we won't need to go all the way to Ponta Delgada."

"Isn't 500 kilometers a bit far for the tender to bring in crew and supplies?" asked Mr. Spinu.

"The company leased a tiltrotor that will make daily flights from Porto Delgada. We won't be using the hydrofoil this time. It's not as convenient as Bermuda, but it's much closer to the delivery terminals in Europe for the hydrogen supply dirigibles," explained Shaw as he bent down to retrieve a beer from the refrigerator. He handed one to Alex and offered one to Sandi and Tanya.

"No thanks," said Tanya. "I'm on duty. Excuse me. I need to visit the bridge before dinner."

"May I join you?" asked Sandi.

The two women went forward onto the bridge, which was dark except for the flashing status lights and video screens that confirmed that everything was nominal. The seas were heaving and occasionally the bow would pierce the leading edge of a wave, sending a shower of sea-spray over the flight deck. Sandi walked forward to take in the view, grasping the railing below the window for balance. For an instant, her fondness for being at sea washed over her and all else was forgotten.

Tanya said, "My dad told me you graduated from the Maritime Academy in Copenhagen."

Sandi nodded without saying anything.

"I have applied for admission for next Fall. I am told it is the best maritime school in the world, but it is almost impossible to get into. I don't really think they like Americans."

This comment caused Sandi to smile. "Perhaps I can help," she said.

“Is it true that everyone in your family for five generations graduated from the US Naval Academy?” asked Tanya.

“Yes. My father was in one of the last graduating classes before the school was privatized—while there still was a United States Navy. My grandfather is still alive and living in Bethesda. He is a retired Vice Admiral.” The thought of her grandfather made her long to see him as soon as possible.

“My dad graduated from the Virginia Naval Academy after it merged with the Coast Guard Academy,” said Tanya.

“Why aren’t you applying to go to school there, then?” inquired Sandi.

Tanya did not answer right away. “Probably for the same reason you didn’t go there,” she finally said, turning to exit the bridge and leaving Sandi alone to unpack the innuendos of this comment.

Beverly emerged from the kitchen carrying two large pizzas and set them down on the coffee table in the salon. “Eat them while they’re hot,” she commanded.

“Do you always do all of the cooking?” asked Sandi.

“Heavens no!” she replied, handing out paper plates and napkins. “When *Bougainville* is on station, sometimes we have as many as thirty crew on board and I have plenty of help then. When we have VIPs on board, I generally bring in a real chef. I can’t cook in these rough seas, so tonight you have my specialty, frozen pizza from the microwave oven. Anyway, there’s only the eight of us on board." She looked around the salon to count noses. "Where are Stephan and Brigid?" she asked, "and Vincent?"

Captain Shaw replied, "Brigid took the sandwiches left over from lunch and said she and Stephan wanted to remain in their stateroom tonight. I think it is frustrating for Stephan to get around in his wheelchair on the pitching decks."

"Vincent was out cold when I left him," said Sandi. "I wrote him a note to join us if he wakes up, but I have a suspicion he is out for the night."

They had passed through the storm by the end of following day and the seas gradually became calmer. The days were short, and the nights were long and dark in the first week of December. The voyage was painfully slow, and the tedium was wearing on everyone, coupled with gnawing anxiety about a possible Syndicate attack. Sandi placed her mug of coffee in the gimbaled holder and climbed into the captain's chair for her assigned duty watch, which Captain Shaw had succeeded in convincing her to assume. It was four in the morning on the sixth day since departing from Bermuda. She checked the navigation computer to see what kind of progress they were making. Alex Spinu had somehow managed to boost their speed to twelve knots, which knocked a full day off their trip to the port of Ponta Delgada in the Azores. Sandi was stir-crazy and was eager to get home to her daughter and mother in France. She checked the radar screen for other ships in the area. All the ships in the vicinity were communicating over the collision avoidance system, executing any necessary course corrections automatically. Tanya had rerouted the drone transponder monitor from the control room to the bridge. It was silent this night as it had been for the past five nights, except for an occasional crackle from lightning in the distance. The night was cloudless and inky black. The Milky Way was so bright that it seemed to bath everything in starlight. Except for the running lights and floodlights on the flight deck, everything else on the ship was dark. *Bougainville* was travelling too slowly to generate much of a wake, but the phosphorescent glow of algae gently agitated by the ship's slowly turning screws illuminated the trail in the water behind them. Sandi grabbed the wheel. It was only a symbolic act since the autopilot was activated, but it flooded her with memories of wanting to be a ship's captain from her youth.

"Does this remind you of the night on the *Polaris Explorer*?" came a voice from somewhere at the back of the bridge.

"Stephan, you startled me!" she said, swiveling around in the chair. "What are you doing here? Your watch doesn't start for another four hours."

"I couldn't sleep," he replied. "I find the bridge to be a good place to think."

"It does sort of remind me of that night, especially now that Francisco Fernandez has shown up unexpectedly."

Stephan chuckled. "I had completely forgotten about that name."

"You were prepared to go down in the ship with me, weren't you?" Sandi asked rhetorically, looking forward once again.

"I guess we will never know for sure, will we?" he responded.

"You know, Stephan. This is the first big ship I have been on since you and I were on the *Dauphine Rêve*," she said. There was a prolonged silence as the memories flooded both of them. "Commander Darc," she mused. "I can hardly relate to that person anymore. The captain thought I was flirting with him when I was only trying to get him drunk and out of our hair."

Stephan said, "You told us at dinner in Oslo that you had lost your passion for the sea, but I know that's not the case. I noticed the way you sat in that chair and grabbed the wheel."

"Oh, it's just a distant memory now," Sandi said. "Vincent and I have a wonderful life. I hope you will get a chance to meet our daughter, Louisa, sometime."

"What do you think Vincent will do now that he has been let go from Ashleigh?" asked Stephan.

"He mentioned that he might want to move back to Virginia, but we haven't really had time to reflect on what the future holds," she said.

"He told me on the hydrogen supply dirigible that he was thinking of starting up his own business," said Stephan, rolling forward in his wheelchair from the back corner of the bridge.

"That has come up a lot lately," she said. "He was increasingly unhappy at Ashleigh. They kept trying to push him into management, but he was always happiest just working in the laboratory and inventing things."

"This may all be fruitless speculation," said Stephan. "It seems that once again we are being overcome by events beyond our control."

The two sat in the stillness of the bridge. The only sound was the gentle whistle of the wind on the stays outside. "I don't think they are coming," said Sandi finally. "It's been five days. I don't think they will try to board *Bougainville* until we arrive in Ponta Delgada."

"Perhaps, you are right," he said. "We should be arriving late tomorrow."

At that moment, there was a chirp on the drone monitor that was barely audible. "Did you hear that?" asked Sandi. They both listened intently. "There it is again," she said. The chirp repeated every five seconds, and the signal seemed to be getting stronger and stronger. "I think I should alert Captain Shaw."

Within about a minute, the captain showed up on the bridge with Tanya not far behind. They listened to the chirps and confirmed they were positioning transponders. Tanya put on headphones to listen more carefully and began feeding some commands to the navigational computer. After a few moments, she turned around in her chair and removed one earpiece. "The signals are not scrambled," she said. "I am picking up four separate transponders out at forty-two kilometers and heading our way at sixty kilometers per hour."

Captain Shaw disengaged the autopilot. "Sandi, you have the bridge," he ordered and then went with Vincent and Brigid to retrieve the weapons stashed in the chart room. Brigid took a Viper X from the case and turned it on to be sure the power was working before handing it to Stephan. She grabbed a second one still in the case and two assault rifles. Likewise, Vincent grabbed two Vipers and Shaw took the assault rifles. Stephan and Brigid went out onto the forward observation platform to establish their position while Vincent and Captain Shaw went out on the rear platform. These actions had all been carefully rehearsed in advance. These four had a commanding view of the flight deck fore and aft. Everyone was intently panning the sky through binoculars for any sign of the incoming craft. Alex and Beverly joined Sandi on the bridge, and Tanya continued to call out the range to the approaching craft. "These are not aircraft," she yelled out. "They are definitely drones!"

Everyone was breathlessly silent for the next fifteen minutes until Tanya finally called out, "One more minute!" Stephan and Vincent had their Viper X's activated and ready to fire, watching in the viewfinder for the first indication of an engageable target. The backup missiles were turned on and at the ready. Brigid cocked her weapon and disengaged the safety. The faintest high-pitched whine of the drone propellers was finally distinguished above the sound of the wind. One of the craft set down on the forward area of the flight deck, and a moment later, a second one set down aft. Two others hovered about fifty meters to starboard.

The first sphere began to materialize from iridescence, becoming clearly visible in just a few seconds. The instant Stephan heard the acquisition tone on his Viper, he squeezed the trigger. There was a click but no ignition of the rocket engine. He and Brigid exchanged a terrified look. By the time Stephan could pick up the second Viper, men were already coming out of the sphere. Brigid fired three short bursts from her assault rifle. Two men crumpled to the flight deck. The remaining men picked them up and dragged them back into the sphere, engaging the timecharger rotor and swiftly lifting back off. Vincent had better luck with his Viper. When it locked on to the aft sphere, he fired with practically instantaneous and decisive effect. The craft was completely obliterated along with a portion of the flight deck. Vincent let out a victory whoop.

"I think they are going away," called out Tanya.

This entire exchange lasted barely five minutes. The smoke from Vincent's rocket was still pungent in the air before anyone realized the fight was over. Brigid had tears in her eyes. "What's the matter?" asked Stephan.

"I have never killed anyone before. That's the first time," she sighed sadly.

"Don't worry. They were wearing body armor. It's unlikely that you killed anyone. Besides, timecharging at Mach 10 they will have them back to the emergency room at their base hospital in just minutes, wherever that may be."

Book 2

Chapter 13: Sémaphore

Vincent returned from Toulon to his parents' villa at the tip of Cap Ferrat after dark. There was no one home, so he assumed they must have gone to the Grand Hotel du Cap down the street, where they often went for dinner. He went into the kitchen to scrounge a snack and sat at the breakfast table to phone Sandi.

"Hello, Vincent," she said. "When did you get back from Toulon?"

"Just this minute," he replied. "I think my parents must have gone out for dinner."

"How are they doing?" she asked.

"My mom is doing fine but dad is a bit grumpy. I still don't think he feels all that great after his surgery."

"There is someone here who really wants to say, 'Hi'," she said.

"Papa, I drew this picture for you," said Louisa, holding her masterpiece up to the camera. The stick figures of a little girl, with long blond hair, was standing in between two women on either side holding her hands. Another stick figure was off to one side with a frown on his face. "This is you, Papa," she said pointing to the figure.

"Why am I frowning?" he asked.

"Because you are not with us, of course," she replied, happily hopping down off the sofa.

Sandi said to Louisa, "Go to Grandmama, now. I need to talk to Daddy."

"I hope Louisa hasn't written me out of her life just yet," said Vincent.

"She's only four," responded Sandi. "She has been through a lot recently and doesn't understand why you aren't home with us. That's all. How did it go in Toulon?"

"Good, but I can't discuss it over the phone. Did you get my car back yet?" he asked.

"Oh, the car," she said with a sigh. "You can't imagine what I had to go through to try to get your car back. We went to the impound lot expecting to pay the 350 euros fee and come right home; but they sent us to the police station. I got grilled by the Chief of Police. He wanted to know where you were. I think they had decided that you became despondent over being fired by Ashleigh and had plunged off the end of the breakwater into the Atlantic. I assured him that you were still alive, but he wouldn't release the car to me unless you showed up in person."

"Okay, sorry. I will take care of it when I get back to Saint-Marc."

"Oh, no. I got the car," replied Sandi. "At that point Mama jumped up and got in the police chief's face. She rattled off French invectives fast and furiously like only a really irritated French woman knows how to do. She said, 'Listen, mister! My son-in-law just snuck off to Bermuda with another woman for a love tryst. I don't know where he is now, and I really don't care, but my daughter and my grandchild need that car. If it's not parked in front of this building by the time we leave, you will be sweeping up broken beer bottles for the rest of your public service career.' I tell you, Vincent, that's a side of my mom I never saw before. I was biting my lip so hard to keep from laughing that I nearly passed out."

"She actually said, that?" exclaimed Vincent.

Sandi said, "Yes. I'm sure the police chief had hair when we entered his office, but when Mama was done with him, the poor man removed his cap to wipe the perspiration off his forehead, and he was totally bald. He looked at me in terror and asked, 'Is this true, Madame Gilbert?' I said, 'Yes. Her name is Francine Duboite. If you call the Hamilton Grand Hotel in Bermuda, they should be able to confirm it.'"

Vincent burst out laughing. "Are you jealous?"

Sandi said, "Jean-Luc showed me a picture of her. I can assure you; I have nothing to worry about."

"So, did the police chief have your car brought around?" asked Vincent.

"Yes, and he handed me your phone, and he even waived the towing and impoundment charges," replied Sandi. "Oh, by the way, a box arrived for you from Ashleigh Headquarters this morning. I think it is all the stuff from cleaning out your office."

"What are your mom's plans now?" he asked.

"Apparently, her house was completely demolished by the hurricane. At the moment, she is practicing her 'irritated-French-woman' thing on the poor insurance adjusters," she said with a chuckle, adding, "How are Francisco and Consuela doing?"

"I am heading over to the guest cottage to check in on them as soon as I get off the phone with you," he replied. "The doctor wants to insert a titanium rod in his femur, but this would require cutting the bone and a few extra weeks to heal. Francisco will have nothing to do with that. He just had the doctor remove the cast and put on a brace so he can swim. He obviously can't walk yet, so he spends two or three hours a day working out in the pool. He is the most hard-core and determined person I have ever encountered. I will tell you everything when I get home in a couple of days. I miss you, Darling.

"I miss you too. Bisou-bisou," she said, switching off the phone.

Brigid and Stephan were sitting out on the patio of the guest cottage when Vincent arrived. Stephan had just climbed out of the pool from his *avant le diner* workout. The evening was brisk enough to inspire the need for turning on the gas heater behind their lounge chairs. Despite the lateness of the season, though, the faint fragrance of some hearty flowers coming from the exquisitely manicured gardens was in the air.

"Vincent! Welcome! You are just in time for dinner," said Brigid. "There is a bottle of rosé in the ice bucket. Help yourself and come join us."

"How did it go in Toulon?" asked Stephan.

"Captain Rousseau still doesn't know you are alive," said Vincent, while pouring himself a glass of wine. "You assured me that he is trustworthy, and my father confirmed it, but just like everyone else, he thinks you died in the crash of *La Charlière*."

"So, he knew I was on board?" asked Stephan. "Then that information must have come from the Intelligence Ministry."

"Yes, but he apparently has no idea that you survived, or at least he did not let on that he does, so, he can't be connected to the Syndicate because they do know you survived," said Vincent. "I didn't tell him you are still alive."

"That's just as well," said Stephan. "He will find out soon enough. Did he accept your invitation to come to visit your father here at the Villa Sémaphore?"

"Yes," replied Vincent. "He will be here tomorrow morning at ten."

Brigid said, "I still can't get over your parents' generosity to let us stay here in the guest cottage while Stephan recovers."

Vincent responded, "It did work out rather well that their life-long friends, Francisco and Consuela Fernandez, from Barcelona decided to visit."

Then Stephan said, "You know, it was your wife's idea to dig up that old alias I used on the *Polaris Explorer*, but Consuela?" he said, looking over at Brigid, "don't you think that's a bit much?" Everyone laughed.

"How did the two of you meet?" asked Vincent, climbing into a lounge chair and pulling a woolen throw up over his knees.

"You tell the story," Stephan said, looking over at Brigid.

Brigid began, "You recall Dr. Christophe Connally. You and he were both aboard the *Polaris Explorer* the night it sank...I mean the night we thought it sank, although I don't believe the two of you ever actually met." she said.

"My father had just gotten to know him that morning at breakfast," said Vincent. "It seems they shared a lifetime in just a few hours. My father still often talks about him. It was at Christophe's memorial at Château de Pomerance in Bordeaux where my mother met Sandi for the first time."

Brigid continued, "You already know that Stephan and I were both aboard the *Polaris Explorer* that night, but our story goes back about a year earlier. I was working undercover for my father in the Southern California Intelligence Prefecture, or SCIP as we called it. I was working with Christophe at the headquarters of Ashleigh Systems in Santa Monica, California before he retired, where I was posing as a dingbat receptionist. The Vice President of the American division was a guy named Fred Simms. Everyone supposed he was just a marginally qualified playboy executive who had been 'Peter-principled' into the job. Nothing could be further from the truth. He was actually a guy named Trent Lachman, a particularly sinister senior operative of the Syndicate. No one suspected how dangerous this man was until it was too late. Stephan had arranged to have Christophe, who still owned an apartment in Santa Monica, come to California to help my father and me bring down a gold counter-fitting and smuggling ring."

"That was big news," said Vincent. "I remember it well."

Stephan carried on with the story. "What we didn't know at the time was that Christophe's involvement in uncovering the smuggling operation became known to the Syndicate, and they issued a contract to have him disposed of. Had it not been for a very unlucky cat burglar, Christophe would have been killed by the bomb in his suitcase that was intended for him. I came to California as quickly as I could to give him some protection, but none of us dreamed the Syndicate could act so quickly or so ruthlessly."

"Anyway," Brigid continued. "Miraculously, although badly shaken up by the whole affair, Christophe survived. We placed him on a sugar beet farm in Northern France where he would be safe and out of the way. He spent several months there rebuilding his emotional state. In the meantime, it had become clear that serious deficiencies existed in the cooperation between the various intelligence agencies in France and America. There was generally a lot of mistrust between these disparate organizations. Stephan was assigned the task of improving the communications between the French Intelligence Ministry and SCIP. He spent several weeks in Santa Monica, and we worked closely together." She looked up and smiled at Stephan lovingly. "I guess the rest is history."

"When did you get married, then?" asked Vincent.

"About a month later," replied Stephan.

Brigid said, "My father, the Director of SCIP, was the only witness at our wedding. All of us being agents in various types of undercover work, we obviously had to keep everything under wraps."

"Does this mean you were already married when we had dinner together in Oslo?" asked Vincent.

"Yes," said Brigid. "We pretended pretty well, don't you think?"

"In hindsight, I guess I should have noticed by the way you looked at each other on occasions when you didn't think anyone was watching."

"We will have been married for seven years this coming February," said Brigid proudly.

"But when did you ever get a chance to see each other?" asked Vincent.

Stephan responded, "Oh, we got to see each other from time to time, but spies need to make sacrifices."

Brigid said, "You know, these past five weeks are the longest time we have ever been together."

"It's been nice," said Stephan, "but I am haunted by the knowledge that while I am here recuperating in comfort, all my friends at the Ministry are either dead or in prison, and I can't do a thing to help them."

"You will be as good as new in no time," said Brigid, stroking his shoulder as she got up to serve dinner.

Captain Rousseau was standing on the front steps looking out at the magnificent view of the Côte D'Azur when Gabrielle Gilbert answered the front door. "Madame Gilbert," he said turning. "It is good to see you again. I had no idea you were so close to the Sémaphore Tower. I go there all the time."

"Welcome. Come in. Charles is expecting you in the den," she said, turning to lead the way. Charles Gilbert was seated next to a crackling fire and Vincent was standing next to him.

"Will you forgive me if I don't stand up?" said Charles "I recently had some surgery, and it is still a bit difficult for me to get up and down."

"Of course," said Captain Rousseau, walking across the room and extending his hand in greeting. "Hello, Vincent," he said with a smile.

"I will be right back with coffee," said Gabrielle, disappearing into an adjoining room.

Captain Rousseau said, "I was just telling your wife that I come to the Sémaphore Tower quite often. It is where we test all the most advanced surveillance equipment. Napoleon built it in the nineteenth century as part of a network of signal towers prior to the invention of the telegraph. It is quite historic, you know."

"Yes," said Charles. "Once a year they open it up to the public. I keep meaning to visit it, but something always comes up, so I have yet to actually go inside."

"You don't need to wait for the public opening," said the captain. "I can arrange a private tour anytime you want. Just let me know."

Gabrielle emerged from the kitchen with a tray of coffees and placed it on the table in front of Charles, who leaning forward, added two spoonfuls of sugar and considerable cream. "I don't know why I drink coffee," he said. "I don't really like the taste. My doctor thinks I should drink more green tea."

Vincent said, "I have briefed my father on all the matters regarding what we know about the Syndicate timecharging spheres, as I discussed with you in Toulon. But we wanted you to come here for an entirely different reason." At this moment, Brigid pushed Stephan in his wheelchair into the sitting room to join them. Captain Rousseau looked at Stephan as if he were seeing a ghost.

"Yes, it's really me," said Stephan with a grin.

"It's not possible!" exclaimed the captain. "You died in the crash."

"Apparently not," said Stephan. "I needed to see your reaction in person. The syndicate knows I survived the crash, and unless you are a terrific actor, it is pretty clear that you did not know. That's a good thing."

"No! I had no idea. How did you possibly escape?" he asked.

Stephan patted his right thigh and said, "It wasn't without cost. Brigid and Vincent saved my life."

Brigid stepped forward and smiled, shaking the captain's hand, "I have heard a great deal about you, sir, but I don't believe I have had the pleasure of meeting you."

"I just can't believe my eyes," said Captain Rousseau. "I trust that you know that the Intelligence Ministry in Paris was taken over by a front organization for the Syndicate. And that Abraham and most of the others are in prison?"

"Yes," said Stephan gravely. "I was hoping you might know where they are being held."

"I may have some ideas," said Rousseau, placing his full mug on the coffee table and taking a seat. "Do you have any idea how much danger you are in if the Syndicate has figured out that you survived the crash?"

Vincent entered in. "One of the things I left out in our conversation yesterday in Toulon is that we were all recently on a ship in the middle of the Atlantic called the *Bougainville*."

"The former US Navy amphibious assault ship?" asked the captain.

"Well, not anymore," replied Vincent. "Now she's been repurposed for cleaning up some of the five-hundred million tons of plastic trash floating in the oceans. The ship was being repositioned for duty south of the Azores when we came under attack by Syndicate timechargers. They knew that Stephan was on board, and we believe they intended to land on the deck and finish the job left undone by the crash of *La Charlière*."

“This is remarkable,” said Captain Rousseau. “Are you telling me that the Syndicate has already mounted an attack against an unarmed ship using these timecharging spheres? The ones Vincent described being assembled in the Danube delta?”

“Well, we were not exactly unarmed,” said Stephan with a grin. “We think we know how to defeat them now. We completely obliterated one of them and sent another fleeing for its life.”

“This development changes everything,” said Rousseau. “The Sémaphore tower you can see from the front steps has the most advanced surveillance technology in the world. It is part of a network of early warning outposts along the entire coastline of France. We monitor ships, submarines, aircraft and watch for incoming missiles for any sign of a threat to the French mainland. We are ready to repel any attempted invasion, but now you are telling me that the Syndicate has a whole new type of offensive weapon that we will never even see coming. I fear that France has just built another Maginot Line. We are set up for another ambush!”

“It’s only an ambush if you don’t know when to expect it,” said Stephan.

Chapter 14: The Maginot Line

Vincent was kneeling between the seats of the cockpit. To his left, the pilot was looking out through the forward windscreen of the VTOL. Captain Rousseau was in the copilot's seat on the right-hand side. "There she is," said the navy pilot, pointing to a dot in the distance. It was a perfectly clear day with visibility all the way to the horizon. *Bougainville* stood motionless in the calm waters dead ahead. The 1,600 km trip from Lisbon, after a refueling stop, had taken less than two hours.

The pilot made a fast pass over the ship at cruising speed and executed a high-banking 180-degree turn to rapidly decrease airspeed before pivoting the jet pods at each wingtip and settling gently onto the flight deck. Captain Shaw and his daughter, Tanya, were waiting nearby behind a blast shield while the jet engines wound down, then approached the craft once the ladder was deployed.

"Hello, Captain. Hello, Tanya," greeted Vincent. "I would like to introduce Captain Rousseau from the French Naval Intelligence Ministry."

"Welcome aboard, Captain," said Shaw. "We have been expecting you. This is my daughter, Tanya Shaw."

Vincent added, "Tanya is the electronics whiz-kid that figured out how to detect the approaching Syndicate timecharging spheres."

Captain Rousseau motioned for the other two men exiting the aircraft at that moment to step forward. "These are our very best signal intelligence specialists," he said. "They are interested in learning as much as possible about the encounter."

Tanya said, "I have a demonstration prepared in the control room. We can go anytime you are ready."

"Why don't you take these guys up with you?" said Shaw to Tanya. "Vincent, Captain Rousseau and I will head up to the bridge and join you later."

They all entered the elevator of the island at the flight deck. Tanya and the two specialists got off at level four and the others proceeded to the top level, where they went into the salon.

"Coffee?" asked Shaw.

"I was expecting to see a dirigible tied up on deck getting filled with hydrogen," remarked Vincent.

"Oh," said Captain Shaw with a sigh, "This field has been a total bust. There is nowhere near enough trash in these waters for us to operate effectively. So far, we have only been averaging about 100 kilograms of trash per square kilometer. That doesn't even produce enough hydrogen to power the collection scows. Break-even is about 200 kilos per square kilometer, and we would need to be pulling in twice that much to make enough hydrogen to ship some out. I have sent most of the work-crew home, and we are getting ready to deploy into the Mediterranean, where we will at least be able to process municipal solid waste brought in by barge. There are only a few places that are deep enough to sequester the carbon dioxide, so we are planning to take up station in the deep water between the island of Corsica and Marseille. That is, as soon as the permits are granted, we will be moving on."

"So, you haven't been making any hydrogen?" asked Vincent.

"No. Barely enough to replenish our own liquid hydrogen tanks," replied Shaw. "The only dirigible we have dispatched since we got here is the one we sent back to Corsica empty, with Stephan and Brigid stowed away in the control cabin."

"That's a very cruel way to travel," remarked Vincent.

"I don't know," said Captain Shaw. "We fixed it up pretty nicely for those two, with cots and a portable toilet. We even installed a microwave oven, and Beverly prepared all their meals in advance for the journey."

"Okay, I guess that explains why they never complained about the trip," Vincent said.

Captain Rousseau cleared his throat to change the tone of the conversation. "You commanded an Arleigh Burke-class destroyer, is that correct?"

"Yes Sir," Shaw responded. "The *Trump* was my last command before I retired from the Virginia Prefecture Navy. That's how I met Vincent. He showed up one day at the Norfolk Navy base with an order to load a crate onto the ship and head out to sea. The authorization came all the way from the top."

"That was the timecharger, I presume?" asked Rousseau.

"Yessir. Vincent had it bolted to the superstructure midship while we were steaming out of the Chesapeake and the next thing I knew, we were just off the coast of Guadeloupe. We apparently made the 2,100-kilometer trip in about twenty minutes according to the ship's chronometer. I think that means we had been travelling at Mach 5."

"Yes, I have seen the reports," said Captain Rousseau. "I first became aware of timecharging technology from Vincent's father, who discovered the effect. He was always worried that such technology could be a formidable weapon if it were to fall into the wrong hands. Apparently, that's exactly what has happened."

"It is ironic," added Vincent, "that the United Nations thought they could prevent an international arms race by banning the technology altogether..."

"Only to ensure a monopoly in the hands of the Syndicate," said Rousseau, finishing Vincent's remark.

Captain Rousseau looked directly at Shaw. "I have a very delicate matter to discuss with you." He paused to drink some coffee and choose his words carefully. "Every indication is that the Syndicate is planning to invade France. A hundred and fifty years ago, Hitler's army crashed through our defenses and took over our country in a matter of only days. We had what we thought was an impenetrable defensive perimeter called the Maginot Line, designed to thwart an invasion by all of the logical routes. No one high up in the military command, save perhaps General Charles de Gaulle, recognized the threat posed by the Panzer tanks, that plowed through the heavy forests or the Ardennes like straw stubble and over-ran our country practically unopposed. Sadly, military strategists always think they will fight the next war with the weapons that worked in the last one."

"I fear that France has once again been lulled into a sense of complacency. Our borders are heavily defended against traditional threats from air, land and sea. I am confident that my guys downstairs, with Tanya's help, will be able to come up with a means to have some early warning against an invasion by those timecharging menaces being assembled in the Danube Delta, but I fear it's not enough just to have some early warning. Just like with the Maginot Line, the Germans exploited a weakness, and by the time the French forces could respond, they were cut off and defeated. This will happen again if we don't take decisive action."

"What did you have in mind?" asked Captain Shaw.

"We must destroy their base in Moldavia before they have a chance to deploy their invasion force," answered Captain Rousseau.

There was a long silence in the salon to let this final comment sink in. Rousseau continued, "I have been giving this matter a good deal of thought. The French military has assets that could perhaps carry out a pre-emptive strike like the one that would be necessary, but the will to do so is lacking. By the time the high echelons in the military command could agree that the threat was credible, I am afraid it would be too late." He said, looking at Captain Shaw and then at Vincent, "I have an idea. It is so preposterous that even the Syndicate would never see it coming. I propose using the *Bougainville* for an amphibious assault on their base—the original purpose for the ship. A couple hundred French Marines would be all it would take. We would be in and out so fast that there would not be time for an international protest. *Bougainville* is no longer a warship, so no one would ever suspect she was doing anything more than just collecting trash in the Black Sea."

Vincent and Captain Shaw both exhaled with a whistle at the same time.

Vincent emerged from his bedroom, dropping his backpack on the floor and heading to the pantry to find a quick bite to eat when his mother, Gabrielle, entered the kitchen.

"Your father and I are going to the Hotel du Cap for lunch. Why don't you join us?" she said.

"Thanks anyway," said Vincent, unwrapping a chocolate protein bar. "I need to get home this afternoon. I promised Sandi."

"Vincent, Dear, I am worried about you. You seem so stressed lately. I think you need to slow down a bit," she said.

Vincent smiled and gave his mother a big hug. "Don't worry," he said. "I'm fine. I just have some things to tend to in Saint-Marc. I haven't been home since I was fired by Ashleigh."

"It is pouring rain in Bretagne now," said Gabrielle. "Why don't you just have Sandi and the family come here and stay through Christmas? We have plenty of room."

"It's complicated," replied Vincent with a sigh.

"What's complicated?" said Charles upon entering the kitchen and catching the tail end of the conversation.

"You know, Dad, I developed the neutron strand winder and the bobbin technology. I turned everything over to Ashleigh and agreed to assign the patents for one euro. The thanks I get is termination. One day I was being offered an executive position at Ashleigh Airships and the next thing I knew I was kicked out on the streets. I feel like I have been sucked completely clean. I need to get back home to figure out what happened."

"You know," said Charles, "that's how Ashleigh treated me over microfusion."

"Villa Sémaphore is hardly being 'kicked out on the streets'," shot back Vincent, smiling.

"Everything has a way of working out, Dear," said Gabrielle. "Just be patient."

"I need to go brief Stephan and Brigid about my trip to *Bougainville* ," said Vincent, grabbing his backpack and heading out of the kitchen wearily. "And I need to catch the Paris Maglev at two. I will let you know our plans as soon as I know them myself."

Stephan was in the lap pool, as usual. It had four twenty-five-meter lanes affording him a chance to push himself to the limits several times each day. He had requested that the temperature of the water to be lowered to fifteen degrees Celsius, about the temperature of the Mediterranean at that time of year.

"I think you are turning into a fish," Vincent called out while walking past the end of the pool to visit Brigid out on the terrace.

Stephan hopped out, putting on his bathrobe and grabbing crutches. "So, what do you have to report?" he asked.

"It would be best if you hear things first-hand from Captain Rousseau. I believe he intends to come by this afternoon," Vincent said. "The *Bougainville* is heading to Toulon. Captain Shaw convinced his investors that he needs the ship to be able to go faster if they want to keep repositioning to new waste sites. Captain Rousseau has arranged to have two microfusion reactors installed at the Toulon Navy Base. I will let him tell you the rest of the story. *Bougainville* should be arriving in eight to ten days."

Vincent stood up to leave. "Now, I need to head to Nice to catch the TGV Maglev to Paris. I promised Sandi I would be home for dinner."

"We think we know where Abraham is being held," said Stephan as Vincent was walking away.

Vincent stopped and turned around in his tracks. "What! Is he still alive?"

Stephan replied, "We can't be sure, but we think so. He is being held at Château d'If."

"That old tourist trap off Marseille?" exclaimed Vincent.

"That place has been closed to the public for years," said Brigid. "It was the place where political prisoners were interred for centuries. Now, apparently, the prison has been reactivated."

"You are planning to break him out then?" queried Vincent.

"It's not that easy," said Stephan. "The only reason they have kept him alive is to cause him to suffer. What better place than the cell that held Abbé Faria? The second anyone guarding Isle d'If senses an attempt to break Abraham out of prison, they have orders to execute him on the spot."

"How do you know all this?" asked Vincent.

"Let's just say, the Syndicate has its spies, and we have ours," answered Stephan.

"And all the others from the Intelligence Ministry?" asked Vincent.

"We have reason to believe they may be holding as many as eight of the most senior people at the Château d'If prison," replied Stephan.

Vincent shook his head and walked over to his autopod standing by to take him to Gare de Nice. He was totally exhausted and wondered if he would ever be able to find time to rest.

Chapter 15: Château d'If

Vincent jumped out of the autopod and strode briskly through the rain across the plaza to the front door of his apartment building. He entered the security code and waited for the click signaling that he could enter the lobby. He took the elevator to his third-floor apartment and punched in the door code. The instant he opened the door, he was greeted by a fluffy white Pomeranian yapping wildly to announce the intrusion.

"Max. Hush! You are going to wake up Louisa," came the voice of a woman emerging from the hallway, tying a bow on the belt of her bathrobe. "You must be Vincent," she said, extending her hand.

"Héloïse?" he said, taking her hand. "I am so glad to finally get to meet you. Thank you for all you have done. I don't know how we would have managed without you."

Sandi emerged from the bedroom at that moment, quietly closing the door behind her, "I see you have met Mama," she said, welcoming Vincent home with a kiss.

"Where did the dog come from?" Vincent asked.

"You didn't think I would just leave Max behind in the hurricane, did you?" said Héloïse, picking up the dog and letting him lick her face.

Vincent dropped his things in the kitchen. Sandi took a plate covered in plastic wrap from the counter and placed it in the microwave. "I saved your dinner for you," she said.

“I am so sorry I’m late,” he said. “The TGV from Paris was cancelled. I guess a portion of the track lost power from all the rain. I ended up having to take an autopod, and without my phone I had no way to call you.”

Sandi surveyed her husband in the kitchen light. “Vincent, you look exhausted!” she said.

“I am just glad to finally be home,” he replied. “I’m not really hungry. If you don’t mind, I think I will just head straight to bed.”

Sandi switched off the microwave and covered Vincent’s dinner once again in plastic and placed it in the refrigerator. “I opened the box from Ashleigh like you asked,” she said. “There wasn’t much inside. Just a few things from your desk.”

“How about all my laboratory notebooks?” Vincent asked.

“Sorry,” said Sandi, “The only thing was the Rothschild folio you mentioned.”

“Six years of timecharger research and development down the drain,” Vincent said in disgust.

“There was an envelope, though,” Sandi said, picking it up from the kitchen counter and handing it to him. “I think you should take a look inside.”

On the outside of the envelope was that handwritten text, ‘severance’. Vincent opened it to find a check from Ashleigh signed by Jean-Luc Gallatin, himself. There was a sticky note attached that just said, ‘Thanks’. Vincent stared at the check for a long time before looking up at Sandi, who was smiling. She had already seen it. “One million euros?” he exclaimed.

It was the dead of night. There was no moon, and the sea was calm. Two navy divers were slowly swimming through the water at a depth of ten meters. The diffusers connected to their pressure regulators generated no bubbles on their exhale that might be detected at the surface. Their light-weight carbon fiber air tanks adjusted for neutral buoyancy automatically so that cumbersome weight belts were not needed. They carried nothing metallic that might make noise or be sensed by magnetometers embedded in the sea floor. Every bit of skin was covered by insulating black silicone wetsuits so that when their heads finally broke the plane of the water at the shoreline, nothing would be detected by the infrared sensors spaced at intervals around the perimeter of the island. They moved slowly over the rocks so as not to trigger the motion detector and acoustic sensor near the point where they exited the water. One of them pulled a device from his swim bag and quickly disconnected the cable leading to the motion detector and inserted it into the device, hoping that the brief signal interruption would not alert anyone of their presence. If it worked as planned, the device would mimic the signal coming from the motion detector and the acoustic sensor would only pick up the normal noise of the shore break. They pulled up the bag that contained their weapons and gear for scaling the west wall of the ancient rampart of the fortress of

Château d'If. They prepared their gear on a small grassy landing at the base of the wall and then one of them peeled back a flap on the sleeve of his wetsuit to expose a two-way transponder. He typed in a code to indicate that they were in position and awaiting instructions.

On the other side of the island, another party of four swimmers was doing likewise. Every action was carefully choreographed in advance. They had determined from previous surveillance missions that there were never more than six guards in the fortress at any given time, but each one carried a dead man's switch so that at the first indication of an attempt to break out the prisoners, a switch would activate the release valve of the cannisters of deadly cyanide gas in each of the prison cells. They would take no chances that the prisoners, even though very high value as long as they were kept alive, would ever get off the island. The rescue party did not know how many prisoners were being held. It was believed that the number was no more than eight, but they were carrying twelve gas masks, besides their own, just in case.

Stephan had told them that, assuming the prisoners had the good sense to hold their breath, once the cyanide was discharged, they would have no more than thirty seconds to disperse the anti-cyanide agent and get the masks on the prisoners. In any event, the mission was incredibly risky. If even one of them were spotted before they were in position, there would be no way to get to the prisoners in time.

Two of the men from the east landing party scaled the wall and secured a rope ladder for the fifteen-meter climb to the rampart. Stephan went up first. Most of his climb was accomplished using sheer upper-body strength. His good leg was of practically no use on the rope ladder and the fiberglass brace on his right leg kept getting caught in the rungs. Brigid followed carrying their weapons. Once Stephan and Brigid were in position behind one of the stone blocks that lined the rampart, Stephan whispered to the other two men, "Remember, do not engage any of the guards until the replacement crew gets out of the sphere and the old crew departs. The prior crew will be distracted with the changing of the guard, and this will give you a chance to scramble across the open and take up positions around the prison compound. It will take the new crew about a minute to get their bearings once the sphere departs. That is when we strike."

Meanwhile, the two men from the west landing party had scaled the wall and were waiting for the signal to move in on the prison compound. Everyone waited eagerly for the timecharging sphere to arrive. Stephan looked at Brigid and whispered, "Are you sure you are up for this?" he asked.

"I was the best marksman in all of Norway," she replied. "I could put a hole in a one-euro coin at two hundred meters. The episode on the *Bougainville* proved to me that I can pull the trigger. I am ready for this."

Stephan smiled. “Okay, then. Headshots only if possible. I will take out the two on the left and you take out the two on the right.”

“What if there are more than four?” she whispered.

“Then we will flip for him,” replied Stephan, looking through the telescopic sight mounted on his sniper rifle at the tiny red dot on the distant wall of the compound before switching off the laser.

It was about an hour before the sphere appeared in the courtyard. One instant there was nothing and then in the blink of an eye, the shiny ten-meter diameter craft was sitting on the grass like a giant soccer ball. The hatch opened and five people got out along with some trunks that probably contained supplies. The guards being replaced emerged from the prison compound and handed over their dead man’s switches to their counterparts in a routine that was repeated twice each day. The guards going off duty entered the sphere, and just like that, it flashed an iridescent glow for about a second and disappeared.

Stephan and Brigid looked at each other and Stephan nodded his head. Four muzzle flashes and four guards lay lifeless on the turf. “Where did the fifth one go?” demanded Stephan.

“I don’t know,” replied Brigid. “He must have slipped away!”

There were a few seconds of nauseating silence before they heard the muffled pops of the cyanide capsules going off in each prison cell. Then there was a short burst of automatic weapons fire, followed by more agonizing silence. Two giant quadracopters suddenly appeared out of the sky and set down in the courtyard. Rear ramps dropped down and several marines ran out of each to take up defensive positions while others wearing gas masks headed into the prison compound. After a few minutes, the first rescued prisoner was seen, arms draped around the shoulders of two marines, legs dragging behind, not able to keep up with the fast pace of the soldiers. Gurneys had been unfolded by the medics, and one by one the freed prisoners were strapped in and wheeled up the ramp into the belly of the quadracopter.

Stephan watched intently for any sign of Abraham. Finally, a marine emerged running from the prison compound carrying a bundle that looked like a sleeping bag. A head was slumped backwards over his forearm in a lifeless pose. Stephan recognized the long white hair of his friend flowing from behind the gas mask. His heart sank as he supposed that they had come too late to rescue Abraham.

Stephan and Brigid stood guard, waiting for Syndicate reinforcements to show up at any time. They would have only seconds to engage them once the spheres began appearing. The last marine came out of the compound carrying someone over his shoulder and ran up the ramp into the first quadracopter. The ramp was still in the process of ascending when the craft lifted off and disappeared into the night sky. The remaining marines got back into the second quadracopter, and it likewise departed the scene. The entire event had lasted barely ten minutes, and once again the courtyard was completely still. The two navy swimmers who had arrived on the west shore gathered up everything that would leave any trace of their presence, including the device that had been attached to the motion sensor. There could be no evidence left behind that would allow anyone to connect the operation to the French Navy. They put on their scuba tanks and slipped back into the inky black Mediterranean water.

The other two navy swimmers who had arrived on the east side with Stephan and Brigid likewise packed up their gear and prepared to depart the island. The rope ladder was no longer necessary, as there was a footpath down to the water. Brigid gathered up the shell casings. Stephan just stared through his telescopic sight, waiting for the arrival of Syndicate reinforcements. He was generally not prone to anger, but the sight of Abraham in the marine's arms was more than he could bear. All he wanted to do was to pick off Syndicate commandoes one by one as they popped out of the spheres. Finally, three spheres did appear. Stephan readied his sniper rifle. One of the navy swimmers tapped him on the shoulder. "Stephan, it's time to go." Stephan ejected the round from his gun and allowed the man to help him to his feet. One of them on either side helped him down the ramp and into his scuba gear. The four slipped away undetected for the long swim back to Marseille.

A marine corporal popped his head into Captain Rousseau's office. "Captain, we have completed the interrogation of the prison guard captured at Château d'If last night. He seems eager to spill his guts. Would you care to see him?"

"Yes, send him in," he said.

The corporal escorted the Syndicate prison guard in and had him sit on the chair facing Rousseau, who made an intimidating sight on the other side of the desk. The corporal remained standing by the door. Rousseau thumbed through the file folder in front of him, pretending to see it for the first time.

"What's your name, son?" he asked.

"Sylvanus, sir," the captured guard replied.

"How old are you?" he asked.

"I will be seventeen next month, sir," the prisoner responded.

"Why did you try to kill all of the prisoners?" Rousseau demanded with an air of impatience.

"Kill the prisoners? I didn't try to kill anyone," the young man squirmed in his chair.

"You pushed the dead man's switch setting off the cyanide canisters," said the captain.

"Dead man's switch? I don't know what you are talking about!" he said.

"The button on the lanyard you had around your neck!" Rousseau's voice was booming by that time.

The young man looked down in dismay. "Sir," he said, voice breaking. "This was only my first day on the job. I received the lanyard from one of the prison guards going off duty. He told me not to push the button unless I was in real trouble and needed help... but I never pushed it...I was about to, and then this guy jumped in front of me and fired a bunch of times into the air above my head and shouted for me to drop the lanyard and put my hands in the air."

"So, you never actually activated your dead man's switch?" repeated Rousseau.

"If you mean the panic button, no, sir," replied the young man.

"Okay, let's start from the beginning." said the captain. "How did you get to Isle d'If?"

"I don't know," he replied. "What is '*ill-deef?*"

"The place where you were last night," said Rousseau.

"Oh, they never told us where we were going," he said. "I was supposed to be in training. My trainer was one of the guys with me in the sphere. When we got out of the craft, we were all just standing around waiting for the other crew to depart. I wandered off to check the place out when I heard gun shots. I turned around to see the other members of my crew fall to the ground and I dove behind a wall. The next thing I knew, this guy was firing at me, telling me to put my hands in the air."

"Why don't you tell me the story from the beginning? How did you get into the sphere in the first place?" asked Rousseau.

"From the beginning?" asked the young man.

Captain Rousseau nodded his head.

"My parents have a small goat farm about fifty kilometers south of Bucharest," he began. "Times are hard, and like nearly everyone else in our community, my parents began borrowing money from the bank to survive. The banks were all too eager to loan money and tricked my father into putting up the farm as collateral. It should come as no surprise that my father could not possibly pay back the interest on the loan. We were barely operating at break-even as it was. Some guys from the bank showed up one morning with a foreclosure notice. They told my family we had one month to vacate the premises. Then one of them looked at me and told my father that they would extend the loan for another year if he would let me sign up for what they called a 'work project'. I agreed, and the next thing I knew, I was on a boat with about one hundred other boys my age going down the Danube. We all got off not far from the mouth of the river where it flows into the Black Sea, and they took us to a construction site where the spheres were being assembled. Each time a new sphere was completed, they strapped six of us inside, closed the hatch, and the next thing we knew, the hatch opened back up on some kind of loading dock in space."

"Space? Did you say, 'space'?" asked Rousseau, nearly coming out of his chair.

"Well, I think it was space, sir. We all floated around like the guys on the Space Station videos. But there weren't any windows, so it was not possible to know where we were for sure."

Captain Rousseau scribbled a note and handed it to the corporal. "Dr. Vincent Gilbert needs to hear this. Will you see if he is still staying at his parents' home on Cap Ferrat?" He made some more notes. "So, Silvanus, how did you get that cut below your collarbone? Those sutures look fresh."

"Oh," he replied. "That's not a cut. That's where they inserted the chip."

Captain Rousseau jumped up from his chair and barked a command to the corporal who was heading down the hallway. "Forget Vincent! We need to get this man to the infirmary immediately and get that chip removed, then we need to get him to a safe house. He is in grave danger here at the base."

"They told me they would hurt my family if I ever tried to have the chip removed," the young man protested.

"Come with me," Rousseau said. "We will figure this out, but you can't leave that thing inside you. The Syndicate knows you were captured. If they think you are still alive, it surely won't be for much longer."

In the infirmary, the doctor took a high-resolution chest X-ray to see what he was dealing with. "I have seen this type of implant before," he said to Captain Rousseau. "It's a micro ekg. They are typically used in older patients with heart conditions to notify the hospital in the event of a cardiac event. What is this young man doing with one? Do you want me to take it out?"

"How does it work?" asked the captain.

"It monitors the electrical impulses that trigger the heart muscle and broadcasts the patient's status to receivers on cellular towers," the doctor replied.

"So, if you remove it, there will be no more signal?" asked Rousseau.

"Of course not," replied the doctor.

"Is there any way to mimic the signal?" he asked.

"Other than attach it to a heart-lung machine, no," the doctor replied sarcastically.

"Do you have one?" Rousseau asked.

The doctor looked up at the captain to see if he was being serious. "Why in the world would you want to do that?"

"It's a bit complicated," said the captain, "but we need the people monitoring this young man's heart to believe he is still alive."

"This will take some time," said the doctor. "I thought you just wanted me to take it out and throw it in the trash."

"Do whatever you can to keep the signal going out, doctor," Captain Rousseau said, "and set everything up in the brig. That is where they will expect him to be." Then turning to the marine corporal, he said, "Double the security detail. I need to go to my office to contact someone."

"This is Brigid," said the voice on the other end of the line.

"Brigid. This is Captain Rousseau. I need to speak with Stephan right away."

"He is still in surgery, Captain," she replied. "He fractured his femur again during the rescue, and this time they are going to reset it properly with pins and a titanium rod. He will be out of action for at least a week. Is there anything I can do for you?"

Chapter 16: The Rothschild Folio

Vincent prepared a cup of coffee at 5:30 in the morning and headed into his study. He turned on the reading light and sat back in the luxurious desk chair that he loved. It had been a birthday gift from Sandi. He had been away for a month, but now the familiar surroundings and serenity of his study were beginning to melt away the stress of the prior weeks. All his astrophysics textbooks graced his bookshelves along with an assortment of technical references that had been his companions during the times when he was doing his most active research and development. Now they stood on the bookshelf, unopened for a couple of years. A prominent gap between the volumes was where all his laboratory notebooks had once resided. He regretted having taken them to his office in La Defense in order to have them copied for the permanent archive at Ashleigh. He knew he would never see them again. Those notebooks contained all of his ideas and theories about timecharging. He would have to reconstruct everything again from scratch as there would be no way to get them back. Cédric Rothschild's folio lay unopened on his desk in the bright light of the desk lamp. A string was wrapped around it in orthogonal directions tied with a bow in front that had not been touched in years. It was dark outside. The rain had let up, but the sound of large drops falling from trees and drain spouts served as a reminder of the storm of the preceding day—an all-too-common occurrence in Bretagne in December.

Vincent stroked the bow and then gently pulled the end of the string to untie the knot. Louisa showed up and stood quietly next his chair waiting for her father to notice her presence. "Good morning, Sweetheart," he said taking her hand. "What are you doing up so early?" He lifted her onto his lap and covered her with the blanket she had dragged along with her.

"*Qu'est-ce que-tu fais, Papa?*" she asked, apparently unphased by his long absence and simply glad to have him back.

"I was just about to read some papers that have been given to me. They are some things written by a man who used to work for Grandpapa when I was a little boy," Vincent said, pulling the contents from the folio and spreading the articles out on his desk.

"Where is he now?" she asked.

"He died when I was a little boy," he replied.

She sat quietly contemplating this while Vincent surveyed the assortment of journals and manuscripts—some typed and some hand-written. He picked up a manuscript that he hadn't seen before.

"What does it say?" she asked.

"It's in English, Sweetheart," he responded. "I don't think you would understand it."

"Mama is teaching me English. Will you read it to me?" she said.

"Okay, here's the title," he said lovingly. "*Gravitron Theory and the Dynamics of Gravitational Fields Induced by Supermassive Objects in Motion, by J. Cedric Rothschild and*

Sonja Dumitescu, May 4, 2062." He began reading the introduction, while Louisa sat quietly in his lap.

"Who are those people?" asked Louisa.

"Cedric Rothschild is the guy who used to work for Grandpapa, and I have no idea who Sonja Dumitescu is. This is the first time I have seen this name. Maybe Grandpapa knows," replied Vincent. He began scanning the lengthy document of about fifty pages to make an assessment of how much effort would be required to read and understand it. There were lengthy derivations that involved a level of mathematics that he did not have the background to tackle on his own. The level was well beyond anything that he had seen in Cedric's *Dark Matter and the Time-Dependent Speed of Light* manuscript from 2027, which he had studied extensively.

Vincent began to read the abstract out loud. "We propose a new fundamental particle called a *gravitron.* Similar to electronic charges, which produce an electric field at a distant point, gravitrons produce a gravitational field. For fields generated by electronic charges, Coulomb's Law states that the force exerted on other charges in this field is proportional to the product of the amount of charge divided by the square of the distance separating them, and the force is repulsive for like charges and attractive for unlike charges. It is said that an electron has a negative charge, Q, that is invariant. That is to say, the ratio of the charge to the mass of the electron does not change with the electron motion up to relativistic velocities. The nature of charge is mysterious, but its existence must be taken on faith and the interactions are measurable and predictable."

"Is he in Heaven?" Louisa asked.

"Is who in heaven?" Vincent replied, not really paying attention to the depth of her inquiry

"That man you knew as a little boy," she said.

"I'm pretty sure he is, Sweetheart," he responded casually.

Max came into the study at that moment and placed his paws on the arm of the chair, letting out a single 'woof'. "I think Max needs to go out," Louisa said.

"Will you go see if Grandmama is awake yet to take him out?" Vincent said, as he lowered her to the ground. He was totally engrossed by the unpublished manuscript in front of him that began introducing him to some concepts he had never considered.

He continued reading the abstract. "The classical picture of how gravity works is similar to Coulomb's Law. The force that one mass exerts on another is proportional to the product of the masses divided by the square of the distance separating them. However, for unknown reasons, unlike Coulomb's Law, the gravitational force is always observed to be attractive. The proportionality factor between the force and the masses is referred to as 'big *G*', which has been assumed to be a universal constant. Just as thirty years ago we demonstrated that the speed of light was not a universal constant, we will show in this manuscript that the gravitational constant is, also, neither constant nor universal."

Vincent sipped his coffee, which was by that time at room temperature. He decided to plunge into the introduction as far as he could go before becoming overwhelmed by the mathematics which he could see coming up just ahead. He continued reading, "The flux of an electric current flowing in a wire is determined as the amount of charge flowing per unit time parallel to the direction of flow. The velocity of the charges does not come into play. The current flux is the same whether in a laboratory on earth or on a satellite in orbit. At non-relativist velocities the behavior of electric charges is invariant to the absolute velocity of the reference frame. This is not the case with gravitrons. A gravitron is an entity for which the strength of the field generated depends explicitly on its absolute velocity. 'Big G' in the classic sense is a scalar constant, but in our new model, G is the result of the mass density flux times the velocity of gravitrons. Unlike an electronic current, a mass density flux does depend on velocity. The proportionality between force and mass density also depends on the dot product of the respective mass velocities. Two masses moving in the same direction exhibit an attractive force, while two masses moving in an opposite direction exhibit a repulsive force."

"These forces are very small and are typically only manifested when large masses moving at high velocities are involved. For example, the earth revolves around the sun at about thirty thousand meters per second. The velocity due to the rotation of the earth on its axis or even the velocity of the moon around the earth are small by comparison. The earth and everything on it or above it, are travelling through space at about the same high velocity. When I toss a ball into the air, the earth and the ball are both traveling at the same velocity, so the force of gravity is attractive, and the ball comes back down in the familiar way. Now imagine placing another earth-sized planet into the same orbit around the sun but going in the opposite direction at thirty-thousand meters per second. One would expect that sometime in the ensuing months, the two planets would collide with horrendous consequences. But in fact, because the force depends on the dot product of the respective velocities, the interaction between the two planets is repulsive. The two imaginary 'earths' would actually oscillate back and forth in semicircles every half year. This fanciful mind experiment is hard to imagine and impossible to prove, but it is a direct consequence of the field theory that is to follow. The earth is not very dense so a large planet traveling at high velocity is required to produce a flux of gravitrons sufficient for gravitational effects to be experienced at all. On the other hand, supermassive objects, such as neutron clusters, have mass densities many orders of magnitude greater than normal matter. Such bodies moving at modest velocities can measurably impact the gravitational attraction or repulsion when the local speed of light is taken into consideration. Equation 1 provides the generalized case for the force between two moving masses in vector form."

Vincent stared at the complex equation for a while trying to decipher its meaning before concluding that it would be fruitless for him to continue, and he would not be able to understand any of the one hundred equations that followed. He laid the manuscript aside and opened Cédric's daily journal written during his time spent in Grenoble. Most of it described the evolution of his thought processes. He thumbed through the pages of sketches and derivations trying to gain insight into what was going through Cédric's mind.

After a while, Louisa returned to the study. "Mama sent me to tell you breakfast is ready." Vincent glanced at his wristwatch to see that three hours had gone by practically unnoticed. He got up from his desk and walked into the kitchen.

"I peeked in on you a little while ago," said Sandi. "You seemed so completely engaged I didn't want to disturb you. By the way; Welcome home!"

Vincent smiled and walked over to give her a big hug and kiss. His mother-in-law was cooking pancakes for Louisa. "Good morning Héloïse," he said. Then turning back to address Sandi, "I can't believe what I am finding inside that Rothschild folio. I was familiar with his paper on dark matter because my father had it published after Cedric died. But I would never have dreamed that Cédric was such a prolific writer and inventor. The folio is a treasure trove of things he wrote that I doubt that anyone has ever seen before."

"Come sit down before your eggs get cold," Héloïse said, placing a pancake on Vincent's plate.

Vincent sat down across the breakfast table from Sandi. "I knew about his theories that the speed of light was not a universal constant, but I was just reading a paper where he showed that gravity—that is, the gravitational constant—is also not a universal constant. Do you remember the experiment I was performing a few years ago using a torsion balance based on Cavendish's apparatus for measuring the gravitational attraction between lead spheres, but substituting neutron clusters?"

"Vaguely," Sandi replied. "As I recall, you never got it to work."

Vincent said reflectively, "The gravitational attraction between supermassive clusters should have been orders of magnitude greater than I was able to measure. Now I think I may know why. Cédric Rothschild proposed a whole new kinetic theory based on mass density. Most of it is way over my head, but I think I may finally be able to understand the theoretical basis for how timecharging actually works. I even found some sketches in his journal for a device for transporting people into space."

Sandi said. "Why don't you contact some of your colleagues at the university? I think you would probably be able to carry on a more productive dialogue with them than with me."

"That's a terrific idea," he said. "Perhaps there will be someone in the office next week after Christmas."

Hearing the word, Christmas, Louisa asked, "What did you get me for Christmas, Papa?"

"It's a big surprise, Sweetheart," Vincent said, looking over at Sandi in a panic, having completely forgotten to pick something up. The smile on Sandi's face let him know that she had figured as much and had everything under control.

Captain Rousseau sped out of the parking lot at the Toulon navy base and headed to the remote town of Collobrières, nestled in a valley in the hills to the northeast. His destination was a private hospital adjacent to the ancient *ruines de l'Eglise Saint-Pons*. The curvy back roads were clogged with last-minute Christmas shoppers in no real hurry. When he finally arrived at the hospital, they had been expecting him at the front desk and a doctor came out to greet him in the lobby.

"He is still in a coma. He received a near-fatal dose of hydrogen cyanide, but I think his prognosis is encouraging," said the doctor.

"Did you take a chest X-ray by any chance?" asked Rousseau.

"Yes. It's routine," said the doctor.

"May I see it?" asked the captain.

The doctor hesitated. "Certainly, but we didn't see any lesions caused by the gas. We can pull it up on the screen in my office if you like," he said turning to lead the way.

"There, you can see for yourself," said the doctor. "Abraham is in remarkable health considering what he has been through."

"What is that oval shadow just below his collar bone?" asked the captain.

The doctor put on his reading glasses to make a closer investigation. "Ah, that looks like a micro ekg implant—very common in men his age. We are still waiting for his medical records to show up, but I was not aware he had a heart condition."

"That's not a micro ekg for a heart condition, doctor," exclaimed Captain Rousseau, "that's a tracking device! You need to remove it immediately."

"A tracking device? It's the day before Christmas," protested the doctor.

"If you don't do something about that implant right now, there is a pretty good chance you won't be alive tomorrow to celebrate Christmas," said Rousseau dryly.

"Do you think the Syndicate inserted it?" asked the doctor. "If so, I should probably check the others. When they arrived this morning, everyone was dehydrated, malnourished and suffering from hypothermia and various levels of cyanide poisoning. In triage, we were looking for blood, not old scars."

"Are all seven still here at this hospital?" asked the captain.

"Yes, plus the guy in the morgue. He's not one of ours. The marine medic who brought him in said the poor fellow apparently was sneaking a nap in one of the empty prison cells when the rescue started. It seems he is the one who tripped the dead man's switch. I am going to guess he had no idea what was going to happen. He never stood a chance. They didn't discover him until the final cleanup of the prison compound. He was just a boy—sixteen, tops."

The doctor called for a nurse and instructed him to check all the rescued hostages for recent incisions below the left collarbone.

The two men sat quietly for a moment, contemplating the implications. "You know, Captain, the Syndicate always seems to be able to think of the unthinkable. Like with these micro ekg implants. They have saved countless lives and yet, it seems that the Syndicate has figured out a way to subvert them for evil purposes."

The nurse returned after five minutes to report that everyone had the same scar. "Get the operating room ready," the doctor said, "and ask Pauline to scrub for surgery."

Rousseau instructed, "Once you remove the tracking devices, wrap them in aluminum foil so they can't broadcast, and don't forget to remove the one from the boy in the morgue. I need to call in a security detail for this hospital and start making arrangements for transporting the patients to another safe hospital. It is likely that the Syndicate knows by now where all their escaped prisoners are."

"What about Abraham?" asked the doctor. "He is in no condition to be moved."

"Let me think about that," said Captain Rousseau as he departed the doctor's office.

Brigid pushed Stephan's wheelchair into the hospital room and positioned it next to the bed. His brand-new cast was elevated and extended the length of his right leg. Two 9 mm Glocks were laying on his lap. He looked over at Abraham and stroked his forehead gently. Even now, with closed eyes and ventilator hose extending from the mask over his nose and mouth, his face still exuded the same characteristic resolute determination. Brigid placed her assault rifle on the table next to her chair and sat down.

Stephan said to him, "No one, my dear friend, will get to you without going through us first."

Abraham stirred in the middle of the night and seemed to be having difficulty breathing. Stephan pushed the call button for the night duty nurse. Brigid jumped up to find out what might be wrong. He was clawing at his respirator. She unclasped it for him and set it to the side. His eyes were wide open. He looked around the room. Catching Stephan's gaze, he began to cry. "Stephan?" he said weakly. "Is that you, my son? They told me you were dead."

"No, Abraham. I survived the crash," Stephan said, taking Abraham's hand and stroking it. "I am glad you are awake. How are you feeling?"

"That was quite an ordeal," said Abraham. "I never dreamed I would ever come out of that prison alive. I just know too much." Brigid gently inserted the straw from his water cup between his parched lips.

“We have figured out almost everything about the Syndicate intentions,” said Stephan. “We are preparing a pre-emptive strike against their base in Moldavia before they launch their invasion of France.”

Abraham tried to sit up in bed without success. “France!” he exclaimed. “They aren’t planning to invade France. They are going to invade the entire world.” He lay back in bed exhausted.

“And how are they going to do that?” replied Stephan, thinking that Abraham was not yet fully coherent.

“From space!” he exclaimed. “From space!” His eyes closed and he went back to sleep. The night nurse checked his vitals and replaced his respirator mask. “He is very tired,” she said. “You need to let him rest.”

Abraham never woke up.

Chapter 17: Antigravity

Vincent entered the kitchen after another restless night.

"*Joyeux Nöel,*" said Sandi cheerfully.

"Merry Christmas, Darling," he responded. "I just got off the phone with Captain Rousseau at the Naval Intelligence Ministry in Toulon. Abraham died last night."

"Oh, that's such sad news to hear on Christmas," she said. "Did he die in prison?"

"No," replied Vincent. "Apparently, the rescue attempt was a complete success. They freed all eight of the prisoners seized from the French Intelligence Ministry headquarters in Paris who were being held at the Château d'If prison. The captain said Abraham died of some complications resulting from his harsh treatment."

Sandi handed him a package wrapped in bright green and red paper. "This is for you to give to Louisa when she wakes up. It is a stuffed Olaf doll," she said.

"Captain Rousseau is coming to Brest this afternoon," Vincent said without emotion, "and I told him I would meet his maglev at the TGV station."

"Today?" Sandi exclaimed.

"Yes, this afternoon," Vincent replied.

"Vincent! It's Christmas day," she complained.

"I know," he said, "but he told me he has something urgent to discuss with me and was hoping I could drive him to the naval base here."

"Can't you just say no?" Sandi said. "Mama and I have prepared a fabulous dinner. Why don't you see if the captain could join us?"

Vincent sat down at the breakfast table. He sipped his coffee and stared out the window at the bleak scene of mostly shades of gray in Bretagne in winter. "Do you remember the passage I read to you from Jules Verne on the *Bougainville*?"

"I remember you reading it, but I don't remember the context," Sandi said.

Vincent said, "There was this explorer in the novel, *Five Weeks in a Balloon* named Doctor Ferguson, who said, 'I do not follow my route. It is my route that follows me.'" Vincent paused for a moment to reflect. "I think Jules Verne was actually writing about me in that passage," he said.

Sandi sat down at the table across from him and took his hands in hers. "Vincent. You know I love you dearly. You always seem to know the right thing to do, and I will support you in whatever path you choose, but if it were up to me, I would tune the world out and live a simple life here in Brest the way it used to be for us." They both sat quietly together holding hands for a while. Such times had become far too infrequent.

Finally, with tears welling up in her eyes, Sandi said, "I am so sad to hear the news about Abraham." The memories of him were flooding over them both powerfully. "When I stormed out of the briefing room after watching the *Vega Explorer* sink, Abraham came running down the corridor after me. He stopped me and placed his hands on my shoulders. I was weeping uncontrollably and would not look him in the eyes. In the gentlest voice I have ever heard he said, 'You just can't run away from this.' Then he began reminding me of the five generations of Brundts who performed heroic actions at times when they would have preferred to run away." Sandi and Vincent looked intently at one another. "Vincent, Darling," she said. "You are the most remarkable man I have ever known. You have a calling that you can't walk away from. You must do what you must do."

Vincent smiled at her lovingly, searching for words that would not come. Finally, he said, "Did you see the news this morning?"

"No," she replied.

"It has begun," Vincent said gravely. "A group of monarchists took over the Palace of Versailles this morning and installed Napoléon X as the Emperor of Europe."

Vincent was double-parked in front of the Gare de Brest. The station was packed with people coming and going to their Christmas venues. He spotted Captain Rousseau emerging from the station and hailed him. To his surprise, the captain was accompanied by Brigid Andersen and a young man he did not recognize. He kissed Brigid on both cheeks, "*Joyeux Nöel,*" he said. "It is so good to see you."

Captain Rousseau's countenance was far from festive. To Vincent's surprise, Brigid slid into the passenger seat, the young man got in behind her, and while he was opening the driver-side door to get in, he felt a tap on his shoulder. Turning around, he saw Captain Rousseau pointing to himself and making a steering motion with his hands. He opened the rear door and indicated for Vincent to get in. The captain got behind the wheel and turned up the audio player to high volume. He briefly checked the status of the hydrogen tank pressure, selected 'drive' and sped away. "Where are we going?" asked Vincent. Brigid looked back and placed her index finger in front of her lips. The captain was monitoring the rear-view mirror. In the outskirts of town, he pulled into a filling station to top off the hydrogen tanks. Brigid started the filling process while Captain Rousseau pulled out a hand-held wand and began scanning for bugs. He found one attached magnetically under the rear wheel well and tossed it off into the grass. Back in the car, the wand began to squeal in the vicinity of the visor. He zeroed in on the garage door opener clipped to it, confirmed that it was the source, and tossed it off into the grass, as well. He switched off the audio that was blaring Beethoven's 9th Symphony. "You can talk now," he said. "But quietly, please."

Vincent was looking off into the weeds trying to figure out how he was going to get into his garage without the opener. "Are we going to the navy base then?" he inquired.

"No, Le Conquet," the captain replied. "We can talk once we get there. We are being tailed." Then accelerating out of the gas station, he took a sharp right turn and flew down the narrow lane of the north-west Brest suburb.

"I didn't know my car could do that!" exclaimed an astonished Vincent looking out of the back window at the fast-moving cityscape.

They pulled up alongside a ship at the marina that Vincent instantly recognized as *L'Arnaud*, the very ship he had taken earlier to Île d'Ouessant, just off the coast. To his relief, the captain instructed him to get into the driver's seat, saying, "I will be right back." Brigid and the young man hopped out and ran up the gangway of the ship, quickly disappearing inside. Captain Rousseau returned after a few minutes and hopped into the passenger seat. "Well, Vincent. Why don't you drive us to a quiet place where we can talk? There is a lot to discuss."

Vincent thought for a moment and then remembered his wife's invitation for the captain to join them for Christmas dinner. "Why don't we just go to my place?" he suggested.

"That would be lovely," said Rousseau. "I haven't seen Sandi for years and I will be very happy to meet your daughter and mother-in-law."

"How did you know my mother-in-law was staying with us?" asked Vincent.

Captain Rousseau was still breathing heavily from dashing up and down the gangway. "After you left the house this afternoon the gas pilot on your stove went out. Sandi called a service technician. Do you have any idea how hard it is to get service at the last minute on Christmas Day? Actually, one of my guys just happened to be in the neighborhood...after turning off the gas supply to your apartment." Rousseau said with a chuckle. "You know, he found seven bugs in your house."

Rousseau observed Vincent constantly checking his rear-view mirror. "You don't have to worry about being tailed anymore," he said. "We just needed to shake them long enough to get Brigid and Sylvanus onto *L'Arnaud* undetected."

"Was the young man with you, Sylvanus?" asked Vincent.

"Yes," replied the captain. "What a story! He was one of the Syndicate guards at the Château d'If prison. We captured him during the rescue. It doesn't seem he has much loyalty to the Syndicate. He says he only joined them to keep a bank from foreclosing on his parents' farm in Romania. During the interrogation, we found a tracking device implanted below his collarbone. He said if he ever had it removed, they would hurt his family. We took it out and installed it into a heart-lung machine that is now merrily pumping away in the brig in Toulon. By the time the Syndicate figures it out, Sylvanus will be long gone."

"I am in shock about Abraham," said Vincent.

"You know, Stephan and Brigid were with him when he died." said Captain Rousseau.

"What about Stephan?" Vincent asked. "Is he okay?"

"You heard that he fractured his femur again during the rescue. The doctors had to reconnect it with a titanium rod and a lot of plates and screws. He will be completely out of action for at least six weeks. After Abraham died, Stephan got all the rescued prisoners into safe houses around France and returned to his cozy retreat at Villa Sémaphore."

"What about Brigid? Doesn't he need her?" Vincent asked.

"Your parents arranged for around-the-clock care. Anyway, I presume you saw the news this morning about our new Emperor Napoleon. He is just a Syndicate puppet, but people seem to be eager to bring back the monarchy. It seems that whenever there is the least bit of chaos and unrest, people are all too willing to relegate authority to some king or queen."

"What about Queen Camilla?" asked Vincent.

"No," Rousseau replied. "She is on our side. The Syndicate-controlled pro-monarchists mobs in France are the very same as the anti-monarchists and ultra-nationalists that forced Queen Camilla into exile. Every monarchy in the world now is being toppled as we speak. There is only room for one Emperor," he said darkly as they entered the driveway at Vincent's apartment building. "Queen Camilla has refused to abdicate, so now she must flee for her life. Brigid is trying to arrange safe passage for her to America."

Vincent stared at the closed door leading to the underground parking garage, trying to decide whether to phone Sandi to open it or go to the front door himself. Captain Rousseau reached in his pocket and retrieved a transmitter. Pointing it at the door, he pressed the button, making the door go up. Then he handed it to Vincent and said, "Merry Christmas."

Upon opening the front door, Vincent called out from the entryway, "Sandi, I brought Captain Rousseau back with me for dinner."

Sandi came out with Louisa to greet him. "I'm so glad you were able to stay over. This is our daughter, Louisa," she said. "Won't your family be missing you?"

The captain removed his navy cap. "Actually, I have no family. My parents both died in the pandemic of '47 when I was about Louisa's age. It seems that after years in foster homes, I ended up married the navy."

"Then, welcome," Sandi said to brighten the mood and motioned to the living room. "Come in, Captain. Let me take your coat. What can I get you to drink?"

"Why don't you call me Jacques?" the captain said. "Captain is way too formal for a Christmas gathering. My real name is Jacques-Yves Rousseau. I was named after Jacques-Yves Cousteau; my parents wanted me to grow up to love the sea—it worked."

Sandi said, "I think the last time I saw you was on the bridge of *L'Astrolabe* during the transfer of the icebreaker to the Canadians."

"Yes," said Jacques. "And did you know, that was also the first time I met Vincent? I knew his father well, but that was my initial encounter with Vincent. I will never forget the look you gave him when he turned around and you saw him for the very first time."

"Was it that obvious?" asked Sandi.

"Oh, my, yes," Jacques replied.

"Did you come to Brest just to see Vincent?" she asked.

"No. Actually, I had an urgent matter to tend to, and I needed Vincent's assistance." he said.

"All I did was hold on for dear life," Vincent said. "Captain Rousseau drove my car and made it do some things I did not know it was capable of."

Sandi's mother came into the living room with a tray of eggnog. "Would you care for some of my homemade eggnog. I must warn you, though, it's loaded with brandy.

"This is my mom, Hélöise," Sandi said.

"I am very pleased to meet you," said Jacques taking a glass of eggnog from the tray. "I am sorry to hear about your home in Savannah. You know, Madame Brundt, your husband, Paul Brundt, was one of the bravest men I have ever heard of. I have read the accounts of his heroism in the South China Sea many times. Sandi is following in his footsteps."

"Actually," said Sandi, jumping in. "My mom knows nothing about my very brief naval career."

"Ahh," said the captain, apologetically. "Perhaps stories for another time then."

Vincent said to the captain, grabbing him by the arm, "Come with me to my study. I have something I want to show you."

Vincent entered his study and switched on the light, directing Jacques to a recliner next to the window. "I have been thinking a lot about what you told me that Abraham said last night before he died. You thought he might have been delusional, but I'm not so sure. And you also told me that the captured Syndicate prison guard described going somewhere with a feeling of being weightless. I have always thought of timecharging as something that takes place near the surface of the earth or at least below some limiting altitude. I always believed that the effect of the timecharging rotors was to reduce the weight of the enclosing capsule, but never to the point of weightlessness. In my mind, I was confusing weightlessness with buoyancy. A timecharging sphere ascends as long as its total weight is less than that of the displaced atmosphere on the outside. At Ashleigh Airships, we considered what the ceiling might be at maximum rotor speed, but we never actually tested it. We believed there would be some altitude where the air was so thin that the sphere could not go any higher. It would be impossible to make the sphere weightless in the sense of having no mass. This would violate all the laws of physics because an object with zero mass would experience infinite acceleration from even the slightest force. I have always argued that timecharging was not the same as antigravity. That is, until this morning." Vincent sat down at his desk and removed a manuscript from the folio. "As far as I am aware, I am the first person to see this document in more than twenty years," he said, passing it over to Jacques.

"It was written by Cédric Rothschild, the inventor of microfusion and all the technology that led to timecharging. He worked for my father at NaPiles, and when the discovery of microfusion was demonstrated, everything at the laboratory was declared, top secret, and moved to Grenoble. All of Cédric's work was sealed. He died a couple of years later but before then, managed somehow to continue doing a lot writing on his own without the knowledge of the French government. Jean-Luc Gallatin gave me this folio and said it was found among Cédric's personal effects. Also, check out that the paper has a co-author."

Captain Rousseau turned the pages slowly without looking up. "The vector calculus is way beyond me, but I can follow the derivations somewhat. It looks a lot like some kind of gravitational equivalence to electrodynamics," he said.

"Did you study physics?" asked Vincent.

"No. Just electrical engineering, but I encountered a lot of this in my E&M classes," he said. "It looks like he has made a direct correlation between current flux density and mass flux density and derived an expression for the gravitational field analogous to the electromagnetic field. This is radical stuff, if you ask me," said Captain Rousseau looking up.

Vincent said, "I'm afraid this matter is way over my head, but I know a lot about celestial mechanics. If these ideas have any merit. Everything we know about gravity would be turned upside down. I was planning to see what my old colleagues at the university in Nantes might have to say."

"I would like you to hold off on that, if you don't mind," said Jacques. "Can you make a copy for me?"

"Certainly." Vincent took the manuscript and inserted it into his office scanner. "There's actually something else that I think you should see." He retrieved Cédric Rothschild's personal journal and opened it to the page with the words, 'Antigravity' written across the top with some hand-drawn sketches of a device that looked a lot like a timecharging sphere. Vincent pointed to the date on the page: June 3, 2062. "That was just a month before he died. You realize that Ashleigh Airships didn't even consider deploying such timecharging spheres for another fifteen years, and that would not have been possible without the neutron winding technology developed by Cédric. This means that someone high up in the French government knew about this a long time ago."

"Who else has seen this?" asked Rousseau.

Vincent replied, "This morning, when I untied the knot on the string binding the folio, it didn't appear that the folio had been opened for many years. This does not mean that someone close to

Cédric may not have seen these documents. Obviously, this person named Sonja Dumitescu saw it. I searched this morning for someone with that name. If she exists, she apparently has no other scientific publications to her credit."

Jacques said, "If this material fell into Syndicate hands some years ago, they may have had a significant head start. Tell me again how you came into possession of the folio."

"Jean-Luc Gallatin gave it to me in his office the day he informed me that I was being let go from Ashleigh," said Vincent. "It was also the same day he gave me the cryptic note to look for Arnaud in Le Conquet, which led to my trip to Île d'Ouessant and then to Bermuda with Stephan stowed away on a hydrogen supply dirigible." Vincent reflected on his strange journey while sipping his eggnog. "Something else; You will never guess what was in the same box with this folio and the other things from my office at Ashleigh. There was a severance check for one million euros signed by Jean-Luc, himself."

Jacques stroked his chin. "I think there are quite a few loose ends in all of this," he finally said.

Sandi came to the door of the study and announced that dinner was ready to be served.

Chapter 18: Le Phare du Petit Minou

Vincent pulled out of the parking garage of his apartment in Saint-Marc in the quiet eastern suburb of Brest just after nine. "I appreciate you taking me to the base," said Jacques. "I would have been glad to have someone come get me."

"It's no problem really," replied Vincent. "Are you sure you have a place to stay?"

"Yes, I go back and forth frequently between here and Toulon. I maintain a room at the Naval Intelligence Command. They are expecting me." Jacques looked out the window as they proceeded towards the boulevard that ran along the marina on the south side of town. All the bars and restaurants were brightly lit and filling up. The gas heaters outside were turned on and firepits were ablaze. "It seems everyone is getting ready for the big game," he said.

"I'm sorry," said Vincent. "What game is that? I have been out of touch for a while."

"The Stanley Cup semifinals are being broadcast tonight from Toronto," replied Jacques.

"On Christmas?" asked Vincent.

Jacques shrugged his shoulders. "France is facing Russia and they say the French hockey team has a good chance to win and advance to the finals. I don't think the game starts until midnight, France time, but it seems that everyone is getting here early to secure a spot in front of the television. By the way, I am really sorry I brought up Sandi's father. I didn't know it was sensitive."

"No problem," replied Vincent. "Until recently, Sandi and her mother had not spoken in years. When her father was killed in action during the defense of Taiwan, Héloïse was living in Hawaii and only nineteen at the time when Sandi was born. She barely spoke any English, so she moved back in with her parents in Caen. Sandi's childhood was pretty tumultuous, as you can imagine. Her mom began seeing an American businessman and ultimately left her with her grandparents in France while she followed that guy back to Savannah, Georgia. Sandi went to live with her paternal grandparents in Bethesda when she was a teenager. You know, her grandfather is still living. He is a retired vice admiral from the former United States Navy. He taught her how to sail, and ever since, all she ever wanted to do was be on the water. He is the one who encouraged her to attend the Maritime Academy in Copenhagen and paid her tuition. I think you know the rest of the story, but her mother never had any clue. Obviously, they have a lot of old baggage to unpack."

"Was it hard for her to walk away from her naval career?" asked Jacques.

"Yes, at first," replied Vincent, "But she got pregnant almost immediately after we got married, and all she wanted to do after Louisa was born is to be a mom."

The traffic was getting snarled along the main route, so Vincent headed back north to get around it. "This is pretty unusual for Christmas night, don't you think?" he said.

"I'm not surprised, really. France has always been proud of its sports teams," said Jacques. "This is the first time ever France has had an internationally competitive hockey team. No one will be sleeping tonight."

As they drove along on a quieter street, Vincent asked, "You never explained the reason for the bugs in my car and my apartment. Are Sandi and I targets?"

Jacques let out a troubled exhale. "I don't think you are in any imminent danger, although both of you have a bad reputation with the Syndicate. Our intelligence is very sketchy at best. The surveillance operation on Ashleigh Airships was being handled by Abraham's people at the Central Intelligence Ministry in Paris. As you know, Stephan was working undercover at Le Croisic Aerodrome west of Nantes. By the time Abraham grasped the full extent of the subversion of his agency, his entire team had been arrested and *La Charlière* had crashed. Unfortunately, my group got into this late. After the fiasco at the Admiralty, Abraham trusted no one in the Navy. And for good reasons. Sadly, we are continuously discovering new infiltrators. I only trust a handful of the people around me these days."

"The bugs?" repeated Vincent.

Jacques paused to carefully frame his words. "They were ours." He paused again to clarify himself. "At least I thought they were ours. I can't say for sure anymore whose bugs they actually were."

Vincent nearly swerved off the road, trying to discern something more concrete from the expression in Jacques's eyes as they pulled up to the security gate at the Naval Intelligence compound. The guard recognized Captain Rousseau and waved them through immediately.

"It's the first building on the right," Jacques said, pointing to the Officer's Club. "Just let me off at the front door there. I have the copy of the Rothschild paper you gave me, and I will await the copies of the other documents in the folio that you promised to send me. I need to head back south tomorrow morning. The *Bougainville* is expected to round Cap-Ferrat next week and I wanted to spend time with Stephan at Villa Sémaphore to catch up before watching the ship go by from the observation tower. Please tell Sandi how much I enjoyed spending Christmas dinner with your family." Just like that, he hopped out of the car, grabbed his valise from the back seat, and walked inside without saying another word.

Vincent headed slowly back to the front gate, trying to process the last exchange. He pulled up to the boulevard and turned on his left turn signal to head back toward Brest but decided at the last minute to turn right instead. He had driven by this gate every day for almost three years on his way to work at the Ashleigh Airships Research Center but had never noticed the non-descript facility he was now leaving. He wasn't ready to go home just yet. His family would have been asleep by then and he needed time to think. He briefly considered stopping by one of the bars to see what all the fuss over ice hockey was about. Rather, he headed west a few kilometers out of town to the point of Petit Minou where the ancient lighthouse stood sentry over the sea channel coming in from the Atlantic. He knew it well. He had often walked there from work at lunchtime to take the footpath down to the sea to sit on a weather-smoothed rock to think and reflect. The massive campus of the Ashleigh facility sat on the rise above, just up the road. It was eleven o'clock and a full moon was just breaking the horizon to the east when he pulled into the parking lot. It was chilly and strangely cloudless. A mild humid breeze wafted inland from the sea. All was quiet and Ashleigh was dark and lifeless...except for some unusual activity at the loading dock of the timecharger assembly facility about 300 meters away.

Vincent watched from the park bench in front of his car. "It's Christmas, for crying out loud!" he said under his breath. "What in the world is anyone doing working there tonight?" He could make out the shadows of half a dozen people walking back and forth to some awaiting flat-bed trucks in the parking lot. A forklift emerged from the open dock door with a machine on a pallet that Vincent recognized as one of the pieces of the neutron filament winder he had developed. He watched intently as several pieces of equipment he recognized were loaded onto the truck and secured. After about an hour, the side flaps of the trailer were dropped down and a convoy of three loaded trucks stood ready to depart. Vincent surmised that the equipment was being cleaned out from the now-defunct Ashleigh Airship facility and being moved to a warehouse for safe-keeping. This would likely mean that the convoy would be heading to the harbor to offload onto a barge for transport to St. Nazaire.

He watched as the dock doors were closed and the yard-lights were turned off at the facility. Several men climbed into two vans with flashing red lights to lead and follow the procession to the wharf in Brest. But the convoy turned right out of the parking lot and not to the left toward Brest, as Vincent had expected. This piqued his curiosity, so he decided to follow. It also suddenly struck him as odd that the equipment was being moved while all of France was distracted by the hockey game. The moon was bright enough that he did not need to switch on the headlamps of his car. The convoy wound along back roads through regions of Bretagne that he had never explored, and entered the autoroute well north of Brest, heading east. He decided that the convoy must be headed to the Port of Le Havre, but this didn't make a lot of sense unless the equipment was being shipped out of the country.

At three-thirty in the morning, he got a message from Sandi that said, "Are you ever coming home?" He had completely lost track of time and forgotten to let her know. He messaged her back, "Sorry, I got sidetracked. Don't worry. I will be home in a little while."

Thirty hours later, after half a dozen truck stops and countless cups of coffee, Vincent was in the outskirts of Bucharest. He was so weary he could barely keep his head up as he pulled to the side of the road. He watched the trucks of the convoy slip through a high security gate manned by numerous heavily armed soldiers and disappear into a large warehouse building. He took some pictures and sent his GPS coordinates to Captain Rousseau before heading into the city to try to find a hotel.

"Oh, Vincent! I am so relieved to hear from you. You had us very worried," said Sandi when she picked up her phone.

"I am so sorry," he replied. "I am in Bucharest now. I found a very nice room at the same hotel downtown I stayed in for my astrophysics conference a couple of years ago."

"Bucharest? How in the world did you get to Bucharest?" she demanded.

"I drove," he replied.

"What? For two solid days?"

"No, just thirty hours. I am pretty beat," he replied. Sensing his wife's astonishment, "I guess following the convoy from Brest was a bit impetuous."

"Impetuous? Vincent!" she exclaimed. "You had us all worried sick." Then she said after a long pause, "Okay, I'm sure you have your reasons. These are strange and perilous times. As

I told you, 'You have to do what you have to do'. You seem to have an unusual calling for this type of thing. Please stay safe. And come home as soon as you can."

"Sandi, I need a favor," he said. "The Rothschild folio is on the desk in my office. I sifted through the things quickly the other day, but I vaguely remember seeing a handwritten note with an address for a church here in Bucharest. If you can find it, would you please take a photo and send it to me? I need to try to get some sleep now and I will call you when I wake up."

Vincent slept soundly for ten hours. When he awoke, there were two messages on his phone. The first was from Captain Rousseau saying that Sandi had filled him in on the circumstances and that surveillance had been initiated based on the coordinates he had provided. The second was an attached photo of Cédric Rothchild's note that said, "Pastor Joel, Church of the Risen King, Strada Izvor and Calea 13 Septembrie, Bucharest." He checked the location on the map and discovered that it was practically across the street from his hotel. He planned to go there as soon as he purchased a change of clothes and some toiletries and had a bite to eat.

"I am looking for someone named Pastor Joel," said Vincent, poking his head into the front office of the small church a couple of hours later.

“I am Paster Joel, how can I help you?” the man said, getting up from behind the desk and coming around to greet Vincent with a warm handshake.

“My name is Vincent Gilbert. I happened to be in Bucharest on business and I was wondering if you might remember someone by the name of Cédric Rothschild?” he asked.

“Oh, Cédric,” Pastor Joel said, putting his head down. “That is such a sad story. Yes, I knew him well. Did you know him?”

“He used to work for my father in France, and I met him several times when I was a little boy,” said Vincent.

“Can I get you a cup of coffee?” said Joel, inviting Vincent to take a chair.

“Yes, please. That would be nice,” replied Vincent, taking a seat. “Recently, I came into possession of some of his personal papers, and there was a note that brought me to this address.”

Pastor Joel went to the counter to pour him a cup of coffee. “Cream or sugar?”

“No, black, please. So, how did you know Cédric?” Vincent asked.

Pastor Joel took his coffee and returned to his desk. “Cédric was a godsend to our relief activities. For years, there has been a constant flood of peasants being pushed off their farms in the region due to bank foreclosures. The banks in the region are not regulated and a lot of loans are being made at outrageous interest rates. Cédric brought a lot of desperately needed financial support to our efforts to relocate some of these refugees to the West."

"My father told me Cédric left his entire estate to the Church for this cause," said Vincent.

"I don't know about any estate," replied the pastor. "When Cédric died, all the financial support dried up."

"I don't understand. What happened to the sixty-five million euros he left behind when he died of pancreatic cancer?" asked Vincent.

"Pancreatic cancer!" exclaimed Pastor Joel. "Cédric didn't die from cancer. He was murdered!"

"What? Murdered?"

"Yes, his girlfriend poisoned him," Joel said.

"Girlfriend? What girlfriend?"

"Her name was Sonja," Pastor Joel said. "She was a fellow scientist. They were collaborating on some new theories. Perhaps 'girlfriend' is a bit too strong. They hung out together a lot, that's all. Cédric was a dedicated and faithful Christian man. I am sure she had designs on him, but he was honorable, and their relationship was completely platonic as far as I knew."

"You said she poisoned him?" Vincent repeated in shock.

"Yes, for the money," the pastor said.

Vincent stared at the reflection of his face in his coffee cup, trying to synthesize the shocking news he had just heard. "Where is this woman now?"

"I don't know. She vanished into thin air. I tried to involve the police, but they could find no trace of a Dr. Sonja Dumitescu. It seems it was all a lie. Poor Cédric was so trusting and innocent. He refused to believe that she was anything other than a fellow scientist enamored by his non-conventional theories," said Joel, bowing his head sadly.

"But they said he died of pancreatic cancer," objected Vincent.

"I know," said Joel shaking his head. "I know, but an autopsy was never performed. He signed everything over to her and she had him cremated immediately to cover it up. She was wicked to the core. I tried to warn Cédric, but he was blinded by her intellect."

"So, you met her?" asked Vincent.

"No, not exactly," replied Pastor Joel. "She was living in Grenoble. Cédric showed me some letters she wrote him, but I never actually met her in person."

Both men sat quietly in reverie. After a long silence, Vincent asked, "Do you have any knowledge of a group called 'the Syndicate'?"

"Do I ever!" exclaimed Pastor Joel, shooting up out of his chair and slamming his fist down on the desk. "They control the banks and are responsible for this whole refugee crisis in the first place!"

Vincent thought about this some more and then asked, “Is there any chance that this Sonja Dumitescu was a Syndicate operative?”

“Perhaps, but why do you ask?” asked Joel.

Vincent closed his eyes for a moment to think. Then looking up at Pastor Joel he said, “You seem like a trustworthy fellow. I will confide in you some things you should know, but everything I am about to tell you is strictly confidential and must not be disclosed to anyone. Have you ever had this office swept for bugs?”

“No,” Pastor Joel replied, “but I can imagine why you want to know. Perhaps we should go somewhere to talk without worrying about being overheard.”

Chapter 19: Cap-Ferrat

"This is preposterous!" said Stephan as he looked over the copies of the sketches in Cédric Rothschild's journal that Sandi had provided to Captain Rousseau. "Antigravity? You can't be serious."

"You have to admit," said Jacques, "It does raise some interesting possibilities."

"Just because it is an interesting idea doesn't make it non-fiction," replied Stephan, handing the pages back.

Captain Rousseau rebutted, "We can't discount the possibility that timecharging spheres are being used for travel into outer space. We have the eye-witness accounts of Sylvanus and Abraham's final words."

Stephan replied, "If these Rothschild theories have any merit, where would we find someone qualified to evaluate them? The derivations use mathematics unlike anything I have ever seen," he said, leaning back in his lounge chair to relieve the pressure on his leg.

"We just can't go public with this," said Jacques. "If these antigravity theories are credible, and the Syndicate has figured them out, then we are facing a whole new level of threat. I was able to follow enough of it to comprehend the fundamental premise. You, yourself, experienced making a trip of almost two thousand kilometers in just over an hour—in a cruise ship. Why is it unthinkable to reach the earth's escape velocity of 40,000 kilometers per hour in a timecharging capsule?"

"Are you suggesting that the Syndicate wants to launch cruise ships into space?" asked Stepan sarcastically.

"No, really," replied Jacques. "Vincent explained to me that the apparent velocity and the time constriction in a timecharger has to do with the rotor speed. He thinks 40,000 kilometers per hour may, in fact, be feasible if the rotor were to be made to turn fast enough—more than 20,000 revolutions per minute. They never tried this at Ashleigh because of the risk of having the whole assembly fly apart, but Vincent thinks the idea may be feasible."

Stephan sat quietly for a long time contemplating the ramifications. Finally, he said, "I have been running the film-clip of the last few minutes of the disaster aboard *La Charlière* over and over in my mind. I was barely awake from the drugging, but there are just some images that I can't get out of my memory. When I went to the locker to get a pressure suit, there weren't any. I remember thinking at the time that they must have thrown the extras overboard to keep me from escaping alive. But what I now remember is that when I performed the security check prior to departure from France, I couldn't find the pressure suits in the locker where they should have been. I had made a mental note to mention this to the captain. I always assumed that they must have been stowed somewhere else in order for the rest of the crew to have abandoned ship. Now, I'm not sure there ever were any pressure suits." Stephan leaned forward to pour himself a glass of ice water from the carafe on the cart next to his lounge chair. "There is something else I can't get out of my mind. I just assumed it was a hallucination up until now. I remember seeing members of the crew climbing inside one of the spheres. As crazy as it sounds, I think that is how the others escaped the crash."

At that moment, the Gilbert's housekeeper came out to the terrace to address Stephan, "Mr. and Mme. Gilbert have gone to lunch at the hotel. Lunch is ready for you and the captain whenever you want. There is a man at the door who says he would like to see you," she said, handing him a card.

Upon seeing the name, Stephan sat up with a huge grin. "Send him back here, *s'il vous plait.*" Stephan hobbled into his wheelchair.

The housekeeper returned to the patio door with the gentleman and pointed in the direction of the guest cottage, where Stepan and Jacques were sitting. "Tor! What a surprise!" said Stephan, exclaiming to Jacques "This is my father-in-law, Tor Anderson. Tor, I want to introduce you to Captain Jacques Rousseau of the French Naval Intelligence Directorate." The two shook hands.

"I know you by reputation," said Tor, "and it is an honor to meet you now in person."

"What brings you to the South of France?" asked Stephan, pouring a cup of coffee and handing it to him.

"Brigid sent me," he said, looking around at the exquisite grounds of Villa Sémaphore. "But I am having difficulty feeling very sorry for you."

Stephan pushed the button on the intercom to the kitchen. "We are ready any time for lunch, and we will be adding an additional person, please," he said.

"You seem quite settled and comfortable," remarked Tor.

"Jacques and I have been solving all of the world's problems," Stephan replied with a laugh. "But surely this is more than just a social call."

"I can't stay for lunch," said Tor, "Actually, I really came to see Captain Rousseau. I need a favor. As you both know, the *Bougainville* will be passing Cap-Ferrat in about two hours. I have an inflatable waiting down at the port. I need you to get a covert message to Captain Shaw to slow down when they pass by and lower the tailgate for the well deck so we can enter the ship undetected."

Captain Rousseau's eyes enlarged. "Even if I could signal the *Bougainville*, the people in the observation tower would see the inflatable. This is just the type of activity they are trained to keep an eye out for," said Jacques.

Tor smiled and looked reassuringly at the captain. "Captain Rousseau, I know you are a man of considerable resources, and I have been told by reliable parties that I could count on you to pull this off."

"What is this all about?" asked Stephan.

Tor replied, "The prison guard that Captain Rousseau interrogated and helped escape with Brigid, the young man named Sylvanus, is waiting for me at the port. He and I need to get on board the *Bougainville* undetected in order to brief the chief engineering officer, Mr. Spinu, before they reach Marseille."

"You mean Toulon," corrected Jacque.

"There has been a change in plans," Tor said. "You are probably wondering why you are hearing about this from me for the first time," he added.

"Yes, that question did cross my mind," said Captain Rousseau.

"You are, of course, aware of the Network in France," said Tor. The captain nodded affirmatively. "What you may not know is that the Network extends well beyond just France. It is a global network of men and women committed to bringing down the Syndicate. Just like in France, no one knows the identity of the other members. On rare occasions, one of us is asked to deliver a message in person. Some things are just too sensitive to trust to ordinary lines of communication—even secure ones. This is one of those times. You are aware of the plan to use the *Bougainville* to launch a preemptive strike on the Syndicate base in Moldavia."

"Of course," said Captain Rousseau. "I'm the one who initiated the idea."

Tor said, "Then, you must know that you cannot do any such thing while wearing the uniform of the French Navy. This includes allowing the ship to dock in Toulon. You now serve at the pleasure of the Emperor Napoleon X. For you to participate in any type of covert activity such as an invasion on the soil of a foreign sovereignty would be considered sedition and treason. You would go to prison."

"I have been very discreet with whom I talk to about this matter," said Jacques, defensively.

"Indeed," replied Tor, "but the Syndicate is aware of your role in orchestrating the prison break on Château d'If. I did not learn of this from my daughter, Brigid. I received a tip from the Network through someone working undercover deeply embedded in the Syndicate hierarchy."

At this remark, the color drained from Jacque's face. "Do I need to resign my commission?" asked Captain Rousseau.

"Absolutely not!" replied Tor. "The raid on Château d'If caught the Syndicate off guard. They will be monitoring you closely from now on, but it is unlikely that they will try to interfere with your routine activities. In the very same way, people loyal to the Syndicate have infiltrated nearly every aspect of civil government, the Network relies on key persons of influence like yourself. You just need to be aware that, as part of the Network, you answer to a higher authority than the chain of command in the French Navy. The Syndicate is powerful, but they are not omniscient. They survive by preying on the left-over provincialism of the Old-World Order. They derive their power by allowing the various branches of governments to retain the illusion that they are in control. There is no better example than the French Navy, which you know has been infiltrated for a long time. France can't defeat the Syndicate. No single nation or coalition of nations can. The Syndicate is an extranational entity that is everywhere and nowhere at the same time. They will only be defeated by a similar extranational entity. This is what the Network is."

"I didn't even know that I was part of this network of which you speak," said Jacques.

"Oh, but you are," said Tor. "You just didn't know it. This is the prime reason I was sent to you to deliver this request in person. Now I must go, but I will return in a couple of days. I will know that you succeeded in your mission when I see the tailgate of the *Bougainville* drop down."

The personnel on the observation deck of the Sémaphore tower complex stood to attention when Captain Rousseau reached the top of the spiral staircase.

"At ease," he said. "What is the status of the *Bougainville*?" he asked.

"She departed Genoa this morning and is just coming into view," said the officer of the deck.

Captain Rousseau went outside on the promenade without saying a word and removed the cover from the signal lamp. It had not been used for years, so he turned it on to be sure the bulb was working. He had briefly refreshed his knowledge of Morse code from the reference card in his front pocket. He began flashing the message over and over.

Tanya was on the bridge of the *Bougainville* keeping an eye out for small craft through binoculars. She saw the flashing light emanating from the Sémaphore tower and called her father over to take a look. "I think that might be Morse code," he said, looking through his binoculars. "I'm a bit rusty, but I will give it a try, 's-l-o-w-t-o-3-k-n-o-t-s-a-n-d-l-o-w-e-r-t-a-i-l-g-a-t-e-t-o-r-e-c-e-i-v-e-i-m-p-o-r-t-a-n-t-c-a-r-g-o'. Slow to three knots and lower the tailgate to receive important cargo," he repeated for Tanya. He went outside and plugged in his own signal lamp, flashing back, 'w-h-o-i-s-a-s-k-i-n-g-?'"

The response came back, 'r-o-u-s-s-e-a-u'

Captain Shaw then responded, 'r-o-g-e-r' and said to Tanya, "You have the bridge. I need to go down to the well deck. Slow to three knots on my command."

Being satisfied that his message was received, Captain Rousseau re-entered the observation deck. "*Bougainville* seems to be slowing down, sir," said the junior officer. "Also, there is an inflatable heading out to her at high speed. Do you want me to hail her to see if there is a problem?"

"No, just keep an eye on her for now," said Rousseau. He then went down the spiral staircase and tripped the circuit breaker at the bottom of the stairs, killing the power for the entire building. He knew the electronic equipment would be off for about five minutes before the backup generator came to life. He then went back up the staircase to the panicked operators running around in the dark and did as much as he could to promote the ensuing pandemonium.

Chapter 20: Bucharest

Vincent paced back and forth anxiously in the arrivals hall of Bucharest Central Station, waiting for the announcement of the maglev from Venice to show up on the screen overhead. Most of the trains were either cancelled or delayed. No trains were leaving the station, and only a few were making it in as a result of the freak winter storm bearing down from the Transylvanian Alps to the north that had already dumped twenty-five centimeters of snow and was expected to drop another twenty-five by morning. The train from Venice was already one hour late, and Vincent could not determine if it was going to arrive at all. Finally, the screen showed the train arriving on track 4, and the arrivals hall erupted in cheers.

Sylvanus and Alexandre Spinu exited the train, looking around for any sign of Vincent in the rush of passengers scurrying to depart the packed platform. Vincent spotted them immediately and hailed them from behind the security fence. “You need to go through the checkpoint,” he yelled. The passengers were doing their best to be civil as they cued up to pass through a narrow gate manned by a single policeman who seemed in no rush at all to let them into the country. Alex and Sylvanus were both travelling under fake credentials, Sylvanus as a college student returning from holiday and Alex as a professor of ornithology visiting from Austria.

Vincent met them on the other side of the checkpoint and led the way to his car parked out front. "This storm has caught the city completely unprepared," he said. "The traffic is backed up all over, so I have no assurance that we can even get out of the train station." The blizzard was ferocious, and Alex and Sylvanus were nearly frozen by the time they reached the car. Vincent popped open the tailgate for their bags and they gladly slid into the seats of the car that was still somewhat warm.

"So, Sylvanus," said Vincent, turning around in the driver's seat to greet him. "We finally get to meet formally. I will need your help to navigate to your farm. The main highway south is blocked, and I'm sure you know some back roads."

"This is a really nice car!" Sylvanus exclaimed, admiring the leather interior.

"I would never have bought a car like this on my own," replied Vincent, running the windshield wipers to clear the windscreen and checking the rear-view mirrors before pulling out of his parking space. "This car was all my wife's idea. She insisted on all-wheel drive. This Range Rover even has a snow gear. I never dreamed I would actually ever need one."

Mr. Spinu was sitting in the passenger seat. "We picked up the two microfusion reactors in Genoa," he said casually, "and managed to get the *Bougainville* into dry dock in Marseille without incident."

"How long will it take to install them?" Vincent asked.

“About a month,” Alex replied, “as long as they don’t encounter any difficulties. They will need to cut a hole in the side of the ship. They are too big to fit through the machinery hatches. I expect the reactors to give the ship a top speed of about twenty-five knots. That trip from the Azores was really painful. I could have done it in a canoe in half the time.”

It was not possible to turn right out of the train station. The traffic was completely snarled. “If you turn left,” said Sylvanus, “I can show you how to get around this.” This maneuver required Vincent to aggressively inch his way across three lanes of stopped traffic, prompting a lot of blaring horns and expletives yelled by irate drivers. Finally, they made it through, and the traffic on the other side was much lighter.

“I guess your parents will be glad to see you,” said Vincent.

“They don’t even know I am still alive,” responded Sylvanus, looking intently out the windows for landmarks in the near white-out conditions.

It took more than two hours to make the thirty-kilometer journey. When they finally turned into the goat farm that had been in Sylvanus’ family for four generations, Vincent observed tears welling up in his eyes in the rearview mirror. Sylvanus’ father was on the tractor, trying to keep the courtyard clear of snow. The heads of several curious Nubian goats could be seen peeking around the door of the milking barn where they were sheltered from the storm. The car had not come to a complete stop before Sylvanus popped out and darted for the front door. His mother came outside wailing as the two embraced. Several younger siblings gathered in. "Thank you, Jesus! Thank you, Jesus!" she kept repeating.

Vincent retrieved Sylvanus' bag from the back and laid it by the door before getting into the car and starting to drive away, when Sylvanus' father wrapped on the window. "Where are you going?" he asked.

"Back to Bucharest," Vincent replied.

"No, no, no, you must stay for dinner," he said. "You will never make it back to the city in these conditions. Just pull your car in there," he said, pointing to the open barn door where the tractor was usually parked. Vincent obliged and he and Mr. Spinu got out of the car and went inside.

"Mama, this is Dr. Gilbert," said Sylvanus. "He is French. And this is Mr. Spinu. He is Moldavian." His mother was still completely overcome with joy. His father shook hands with both guests and directed everyone into the sitting room, where a wood fire was roaring in the fireplace.

"My name is Gustav," he said, "Gustav Dutschescu. Thank you for bringing our son back home. We never thought we would see him alive again after the Syndicate took him."

Alex said, "The story of his rescue will take him hours to recount. He has become an invaluable asset in our crusade against the Syndicate."

Gustav, overcome with emotion, said, "In the midst of this darkest hour of winter and the threat of losing our farm, miracle upon miracle has been happening. Yesterday a man came by and gave me two hundred and fifty thousand euros in cash with instructions to buy our farm back from the bank, and today our son is restored to us. How can we possibly contain our joy?"

Sylvanus' sister emerged from the kitchen with a carafe and tray of glasses. Gustav began pouring. "Hot cider, anyone?"

Sylvanus looked at Vincent and said, "He calls it cider, but watch out; it has a kick that will make you forget where you are." Everyone laughed.

"So, what brings you to Bucharest, Dr. Gilbert?" Gustav asked, handing him a glass of his hard cider.

"Just call me Vincent," he said, taking his first test sample of the elixir. "It's a long story," he replied. "I have been tracking down some equipment that was stolen from the company in France I used to work for. It seems that the perpetrators have set up a factory just outside Bucharest to make a counterfeit device that was never authorized by that company."

Sylvanus jumped in, "Father, they are making the engines for the spheres that took me into outer space."

"Slow down," said Alex. "There is a lot to unpack here. Your parents may not be ready to hear it all at once."

"Well, yes," said Vincent. "I think they are fabricating the 'engines', as Sylvanus calls them, in the factory southwest of Bucharest and shipping them by truck to the port of Giurgiu on the Danube, where they put them on barges and send them down to the assembly facility on the Black Sea."

"That's the place they sent me and launched me into outer space," added Sylvanus.

"I have been tracking the daily truck convoys to the port," said Vincent.

"Can you describe what these convoys look like?" asked Gustav.

"Well, there are usually three trucks, black as night, that look a lot like a military convoy," answered Vincent.

Gustav left the room and returned momentarily with a pair of binoculars. Opening the front door and pointing to the expressway barely visible in the snowfall beyond the service road, he handed the binoculars to Vincent and said, "Do the trucks look like those? They haven't moved a centimeter for the past three hours. The expressway is totally blocked to the south because of a pile-up."

Vincent stared through the binoculars in total astonishment as he recognized the three black trucks that he had been tracking all week. "Oh, what I would give to be able to take a peek in the back of one of those," he said, handing the binoculars back to Gustav. "Perhaps, after dark, if they are still there, I might be able to sneak into one."

"I have been monitoring the traffic," said Gustav, "and it looks like the wreck is about to be moved out of the way, so the traffic should start moving again before too long."

"I have an idea," said Sylvanus. "I still have my uniform and Alexandre doctored my ID badge. Why don't we just drive up next to them on the service road and pretend to be sent from the factory to check the status of the batteries? By the time they discover that my badge number is not in their database, we will be long gone."

"How do you know about the batteries?" asked Vincent.

"They always told us to keep a close eye on the charge level of the batteries. They said if the indicator ever dropped into the red, our sphere would drop out of the sky," said Sylvanus.

"That's exactly right", said Vincent. "The batteries keep the rotors spinning. If the batteries were to die in this cold weather, the timechargers would weigh a couple of tons each. Then the trucks would have a bigger problem than the snow. Do you think we could pull this off?" he asked.

"It's worth a try," replied Sylvanus. "Let me go put on my uniform and I suggest that you borrow some work clothes from my father."

Vincent activated the hydraulic lifts on the Range Rover to give it an additional ten centimeters of clearance and he and Sylvanus departed from the barn with a supply of tools. They took side roads to the north so that it would look like they had been traveling south on the service road and pulled to the side of the road abreast of the lead truck. Sylvanus got out and grabbed his coat and woolen cap from the back seat. Vincent stayed in the car while Sylvanus trudged through the snow, climbed over the guard rail and stepped up on the running board of the lead truck, tapping on the window. The startled driver lowered the window.

"I was sent from the factory with a mechanic to check on the status of the batteries on the engines," he said, pointing to Vincent in the car. "Here is my ID." Sylvanus passed him the badge and stepped down, turning to look at Vincent for reassurance and blowing on his frozen fingers with a cloud of condensed steam from his breath.

The driver studied the badge and passed it to the man in the seat next to him, who shrugged and handed it back to the driver, who passed it through the window back to Sylvanus. "Okay," said the driver, motioning with his thumb towards the back of the truck, rolling the window back up and making no indication that either of them had any interest in getting out of the truck into the cold to offer assistance. Sylvanus signaled to Vincent, who opened up the back of the Range Rover, removing a step ladder and strapping on a tool belt that he had borrowed from Gustav. Sylvanus began loosening the strap on the side flap, making an opening big enough for Vincent to enter. Vincent secured the step ladder and removed a utility light from his tool belt, which he switched on and climbed into the back of the truck. Sylvanus stood guard, completely forgetting about the cold for about ten excruciatingly long minutes while he waited. Finally, Vincent's head emerged from the opening, and he handed Sylvanus a round canister about the size of a block of cheese and climbed down without saying a word. He collapsed the step ladder and took the canister back from Sylvanus and headed to the car in the ensuing twilight. The blizzard had intensified so that the visibility was no more than ten meters and Vincent disappeared from sight almost immediately. His tracks in the snow had already been obliterated. Sylvanus reattached the strap from the flap and proceeded forward to notify the guys in the cab that everything was okay. The driver did not lower his window, but just turned his head with a scowl and nodded. Sylvanus waved to him with a smile. He could see break-lights up ahead that told him the traffic was starting to move again.

Goats scattered in all directions as they drove into the barn, many of them scrambling up to the tops of stacked bales of hay. Vincent switched off the engine and stared ahead. They both sat quietly in the car, decompressing from all the excitement. Finally, Vincent exclaimed, "Did we just do that?"

"That was the most intense thing I have ever done," said Sylvanus, "except maybe doing back flips in zero gravity in outer space."

"What makes you so certain you actually were in outer space?" asked Vincent.

"I don't know," he replied. "That's what they told us. The feeling was a lot like I imagine the astronauts in the movies experience, but I was only there for a few minutes before they shipped us off to the moon."

"What did you just say?" Vincent burst out.

"You mean about the moon?" Sylvanus said, "They took us to a huge base on the surface of the moon for training. We couldn't see the earth, so I assumed we were on the back side somewhere."

Vincent turned his head and opened his eyes wide, staring at Sylvanus. "Surely you are kidding," he said.

"That's what everybody says," replied Sylvanus defensively, "but I'm not making it up."

"How did Alex react when you told him this?" asked Vincent.

"Just like you and everyone else. He suggested they may have been giving me hallucinogenic drugs," he said.

Vincent slowly opened the car door and got out. He retrieved the canister from the back seat and headed indoors in a daze with Sylvanus trailing behind.

"How did it go?" asked Alex.

Vincent held up the canister, "I have no idea what this is, but every timecharging rotor in the back of the truck had one. I would guess this one will be missed before too long." He then looked intently at Mr. Spinu and asked, "How long have you known about the Syndicate base located on the back side of the moon?"

This question caught Mr. Spinu completely off guard. "You don't think that's possible, do you?" he responded.

Mrs. Dutschescu came out of the kitchen just then. "Good. You're back," she said. "Dinner is ready."

The family gathered around a large oval table with extra chairs to accommodate the two guests. Once seated, everyone held hands and Gustav blessed the meal. "Dear Lord, your mercies to us are beyond comprehension and we thank you. You restored our son whom we never expected to see again. You provided money to pay off our loan. On top of this, you shower us daily with good things to eat and good health. Bless us, dear Lord, and may we be mindful of all those needy ones around us to share your blessings with others as you have blessed us. We pray this in the name of your beloved son, Jesus. Amen."

"So, Vincent," said Gustav as he began piling some goulash onto his plate, "what do you think is inside that canister?"

Bowls of food were circulating clockwise around the table. "Help yourself," said Mrs. Dutschescu. "Here, have some potatoes. They are from our own root cellar."

"Thank you, Mrs. Dutschescu," Vincent said. "This is a lovely warm dinner on such a cold stormy night." Then addressing Gustav, he replied, "I don't know. I recognized the timecharging rotors. They look just like the ones I designed. I couldn't inspect the neutron windings without dissembling one of the rotors and that would have taken too long. Anyway, the windings are sealed in a vacuum enclosure with air bearings, so if I did try to take one apart, I would have ruined it and it would have been obvious that someone had tampered with it. The canisters are odd, though. These are something I have never seen before. There was an electrical cable running from the speed controller on the rotor into them. I unplugged one and unscrewed it from the base of the rotor."

Mr. Spinu asked, "Do you think this might be the type of device you described on the *Bougainville*?"

"You mean a quantum couple? The thought has crossed my mind," responded Vincent. "I have no way to peek inside, and even if I did, I wouldn't know what I was looking at. If it is a quantum couple or any kind of device for controlling the rotor speed remotely, I need to get it to Captain Rousseau's lab for analysis as soon as possible."

"It could hold the key to how we might interrupt the action of the spheres," Mr. Spinu suggested.

Vincent said, "I was hoping to go to the Syndicate base near the mouth of the Danube with you and Sylvanus, but now I think it is more important for me to head back to Toulon. I don't dare try to ship the canister. I need to deliver it in person."

"Not before you try my fresh-baked rhubarb pie," said Mrs. Dutschescu.

"I really should be heading back to my hotel in the city," said Vincent.

"That would not be wise tonight in this blizzard," said Gustav. "I think you should plan on spending the night here." Vincent knew it was an offer he couldn't refuse. He settled back in his chair to relish the fresh coffee and watched the fire while Mrs. Dutschescu walked around the table, serving everyone a slice of the pie fresh out of the oven.

Chapter 21: Little Green Men

Vincent tapped at the door of his father's study at Villa Sémaphore. "Come in," said Charles. "So, I see you made it back from Bucharest. That's a long drive. You must be exhausted."

"Not as long as going for thirty hours straight through from Brest to Bucharest," replied Vincent. "At least this time, I stopped along the way to catch some sleep. Do you by any chance still have that little 'pea' that Cédric Rothschild gave you?"

"Yes. I keep it on the bookshelf." Charles got up from his recliner and took the little box down from the shelf. "I also have the magic sphere. Would you like to see it as well?" Charles asked.

"No, just the little pea will do," he said. "The aluminum globule with the embedded neutron nanocluster from when Cédric blew up the reactor. I just want to do a little experiment." Vincent took the little pea and dropped it from above his head. As was done many times before, it drifted slowly to the floor, landing at his feet. Then he picked it up and threw it as hard as he could against the heavy draperies on the other side of the study. After a few seconds, they both heard the sound of it hitting the wall. Vincent went to look for it and discovered it embedded in the plaster. "Oh, I am so sorry, Father. I think I put a hole in your wall. I was aiming for the draperies," he said, prying the pea out of the indentation.

"What in the world are you doing?" asked Charles.

“Where did the idea of mounting neutron clusters in the rim of a rotor come from?” Vincent asked.

“From Cédric, probably,” replied Charles, “I don’t really remember, but it was a pretty obvious way to keep the clusters in motion. After he was shipped off to the national laboratory in Grenoble, we did not communicate any longer. It actually was my original neutron winder that made the idea feasible.”

“Did you know that he did not die from cancer?” said Vincent. “He was murdered.”

“What? How is that possible?” replied Charles. “Murdered?”

“Yes,” said Vincent. “Poisoned by a female scientific colleague who made off with all of his money.”

“Everyone told me that he died from pancreatic cancer and left his entire sixty-five-million-euro estate to his church.”

“Apparently, that never happened,” responded Vincent. “The church in Bucharest he was working with on relief for Eastern European refugees never saw a cent. It seems she was a Syndicate conspirator and swindled him out of everything and then murdered him. The Syndicate had every reason to conceal the truth.”

“That’s really shocking,” said Charles. “I don’t know what to say.”

“How did Ashleigh get hold of the neutron winding technology? Did you sell it to them?” asked Vincent.

"Absolutely not!" shot back Charles. "I always assumed they got it from the NRL. When Jean-Luc Gallatin bought my company, Ashleigh was only interested in microfusion. The scope of the patent and royalties never included timecharging. I always considered that technology far too disruptive and kept it secret. Remember, that's precisely why we smuggled the rotor out of my factory in Aix-en-Provence to America."

Vincent said, "There is quite a bit of stuff going on that doesn't make a lot of sense. When I was at the NRL, all our research on timecharging was considered top secret. We were on the verge of making some really astounding discoveries when my laboratory was shut down and everything was transferred to Ashleigh Airships. Frankly, at that time, I agreed with the decision. No one in Virginia wanted to fund the work and I just figured that transferring it to Ashleigh was better than nothing. But a few things are starting to come into focus now. I'm really sorry," said Vincent apologetically, looking at the damaged plaster of the wall. "You are probably wondering why I threw Cédric's 'pea' at the drapes."

"Yes," responded Charles. "That really was rather unexpected."

"Well," said Vincent, "At the NRL, we were doing some groundbreaking research on the timecharging effect by embedding neutron nanoclusters into artillery rounds and firing them at the Dahlgren naval gunnery range. The idea was to make it impossible to tell that a shell was incoming or even the direction it was coming from. The problem was that they could never get the rounds to hit the target, often missing by a lot. No one ever figured out why and the project was finally abandoned. We observed the same effect in our indoor range using small caliber rifle rounds. We would sight in the target with regular rounds, but the rounds containing neutron nanoclusters always veered to the right or left for no apparent reason. That's why I threw Cedric's 'pea' at the drapes. I simply didn't expect it to go so far off-course. It is a good thing I didn't break your window." They both laughed.

"How well do you know Jean-Luc Gallatin?" asked Vincent.

"Not really well at all," replied Charles. "After we closed on the sale of NaPiles and settled the patent royalty issues, that was the last I saw of him. You always told me you liked working for him."

"After the crash of *La Charlière,* he fired me, you know." said Vincent, "and then he sent me on a very strange mission." He paused and then asked his father, "Have you by any chance ever heard of something called the Network?"

Charles did not answer but sat back down in his recliner. "Okay, then," said Vincent. "A couple of weeks ago, Ashleigh sent me a box containing the personal effects from cleaning out my office in La Defense that included a folio that Jean-Luc gave me of personal papers from Cédric Rothschild as well as his journals. The box also contained a check, signed by Jean-Luc, himself, for one million euros." Vincent stared at his father who showed no reaction. "But why is it that I get the impression you already know all of this?"

"Go on," said Charles.

"There was an unpublished manuscript co-authored with this woman, Sonja Dumitescu, who ended up murdering him. Judging by some notes in the margin, they apparently did not see eye-to-eye on a few points, so the paper never got submitted for publication. The paper is quite advanced and difficult to read dealing with some pretty far-out gravitational field theories."

Charles stood up and walked over to his desk. "Is this the paper?" he asked, handing it to Vincent. "Jacques Rousseau came by this morning and gave me a copy. He is out on the terrace right now with Stephan and Stephan's Father-in-Law, Tor Andersen."

"This manuscript is way over my head," said Vincent, "but some of the most interesting things are not actually in the manuscript but in his hand-written journal. He theorized that a moving body generates a gravitational field that is proportional to its mass times velocity. Some of it is all covered in this manuscript," he said, passing it back to his father. "What is not in the manuscript are some derivations in his journal that show that the gravitational field generated by a moving body is perpendicular to the velocity vector, so the effect is not observed when a supermassive body like your magic sphere is simply dropped. But when a body moves parallel to the surface of the earth, like when I threw Cédric's pea at the drapes, if it is massive enough and travelling fast enough, there is a sideways torque, which explains the hole I just punched in your plaster. The gravitational field of the earth is radial, but the field lines are distorted by the gravitational field of the moon, so the torque is influenced by the relative position of the moon with respect to the earth. I think this explains why the trajectory of the bullets and artillery shells was unpredictable." Vincent could tell that he had lost his father in this last bit of detail.

"Don't worry if you don't understand," Vincent said, "The important thing is that the Syndicate has known about this all along and Sonja Dumitescu was undoubtedly how they obtained this knowledge and why Cedric's discoveries were never made public."

Charles smiled broadly and said, "Everyone out on the terrace is eager to see you. Katherine has prepared a nice buffet lunch for us, and your mother and I are planning to join you. I am confident that you will soon figure out how to thwart this new Syndicate menace. Don't forget your package," Charles said as Vincent was leaving the study.

"Oh thanks. I almost forgot it," said Vincent. "I need to deliver this canister to Captain Rousseau. It's the whole reason I drove here all the way from Bucharest."

"Hey, Vincent. When can we expect to start seeing the invasion of the little green men from outer space?" said Stephan with a chuckle.

"Nice to see you too, Stephan," said Vincent, handing the package to Jacques Rousseau and walking over to greet Tor, whom he had not previously met.

Vincent poured himself a cup of coffee and sat down on one of the lounge chairs. "I think the good life is starting to make you soft," he said to Stephan jokingly. "I wish we were dealing with aliens from another galaxy. At least that way, the entire world could band together to defeat them like in that old movie, 'Independence Day'. What we are dealing with are not aliens at all–just some of the darkest elements of the human race. The saddest thing is that most of their minions who do their bidding are just ordinary farm kids like Sylvanus who have been pressed into service as a consequence of the corrupt systems operating right under our noses. If it weren't so credible, I would think it was fiction. I spent a lot of time this past week with a pastor in Bucharest who explained the whole wicked racket to me. First, the Syndicate takes over the central banks, which is ponderously easy in unstable countries. Next, they finance political candidates to gain control of the governments. Of course, this is all accomplished under the guise of freedom and democracy. These same elected officials grow the size of government, which means they need more and more money to perform the duties they claim are needed by the people they serve. It all looks very legitimate, and no one complains because these elected officials stay in office by doling out favors to all the people who keep them in office. Then they slowly rachet up taxes, such as property taxes on subsistence farmers like Sylvanus' parents. These farmers don't have any cash, per se, and the governments won't take payment in goat cheese, so the farmers are forced to sell stuff to raise cash. There is never enough, so they have to borrow from the banks–the very banks responsible for bankrolling the politicians in the first place. Of course, the loans are secured by the value of the farms, and when the farmers can't keep up with the usury interest rates, the bankers show up one day with foreclosure documents and threaten to kick the farmers off the land that, in many cases, was in their family for generations. If the farmer happens to have a healthy teenage son or daughter, they offer to defer the loan payments in exchange for what they call 'community service', which means being pressed into the service of the Syndicate." By this time, Vincent was pacing back and forth, venting in a near frenzy.

"This all makes me so angry," he said. "The same scheme has been going on for decades and probably all over the world. I wish we could just start blasting these spheres out of the sky and take the fight to the Syndicate but all we would be doing is killing countless people with no real comprehension of what they are doing. Just like Sylvanus, they have no idea that they are involved in an evil pursuit." He sat back down and sipped his coffee. Stephan and Jacques remained silent.

Vincent continued his tirade, "This is what Cédric Rothschild was doing with every spare minute. He saw what was going on. He was in the process of setting up a cooperative with his own money to offer low-interest loans to strapped farmers and small business owners. That's why the Syndicate…" Vincent looked around at his friends and said, "Wow, I guess I got a little worked up just now."

Stephan said, "You might want to consider cutting back on the coffee intake, Vincent."

Tor spoke up. "What you did for Sylvanus' family was incredibly generous."

"What do you mean?" asked Vincent.

"The two hundred and fifty thousand euros you gave his father to redeem the farm from the bank," said Stephan.

"How did you find out about that?" asked Vincent.

"Sandi told me," said Stephan. "She didn't know how to get the cash you requested to Pastor Joel, so she asked me if I had any ideas. I asked Tor to see if he could arrange the delivery."

Vincent folded his hands in his lap and nodded appreciatively. Charles and Gabrielle were strolling down the walkway towards them from the main house followed by Kathrine, pushing a cart with hot lunch for six.

Chapter 22: The Canister

"I am very pleased that you volunteered to drive me back to Brest," said Vincent. "I was planning to spend a few days at Villa Sémaphore to recuperate, but it will be nice to get home to Sandi. I am just glad you are doing the driving."

"I really like driving this car," said Jacques. "This trip is working out nicely. There is no one in Toulon qualified to evaluate what is inside that canister. My best electronics technicians are all in Brest. You said there was one of these devices attached to each of the timecharger rotors?"

"Yes," said Vincent, "Mounted on the top, with a wire leading down into the speed control panel. All I can imagine is that it is some sort of autopilot device. There would be no way to communicate with it from outside the sphere while timecharging, so one thought I have had is that it is one of the quantum couples I heard rumored about at Ashleigh."

"If that's the case, there is probably no one in my shop in Brest that will understand it either," said Jacques; "They are really good at all kinds of signal intelligence. They can do almost anything involving the electromagnetic spectrum, including optics, but I'm sure quantum coupling is beyond their reach."

Vincent said, "You know, controlling rotor speed is one of the grand challenges of timecharging. If you are on the inside, you have control, but you can't see out to tell where you are or where you are going, and if you are on the outside you can't communicate with anything or anyone on the inside to command the timecharger where to go. It is a quirk of the discontinuity in the speed of light between the inside to the outside. The Syndicate spheres that attacked the *Bougainville* used an antenna hanging down with a frequency converter on the inside. It was a bit of a kluge, I think. Nothing that depends on the speed of light for communication works very well."

When the car exited the long tunnel under the French Maritime Alps connecting Gap and Valence, it was already dark. The traffic on the main autoroute heading north along the Rhône was light. The Gap tunnel shortened the drive from Nice to Lyon by more than an hour, but it would still take six hours before they reached Brest.

"I think I will doze off for a while, if you don't mind," said Vincent. "Wake me if you need me to take the wheel." Vincent was exhausted and it felt good for him to close his eyes. He reclined the passenger seat and wrapped up in his coat.

"Except gravity!" Vincent exclaimed, tilting his seat forward again. "Gravity doesn't travel at the speed of light. Forget quantum couples. I think I know what the purpose of the canisters is."

"Well, are you going to tell me?" asked Jacques.

"Sylvanus told me something that didn't click until just now," said Vincent. "He told me that he had departed in one of the spheres from the base on the Black Sea and then spent a few minutes in weightlessness before going on to the moon. I assumed that he continued on in one of the spheres, but he never actually said that. There would be no reason to use the spheres for space travel. The only purpose of the spheres is to get into orbit around the earth. The timecharging spheres we were developing at Ashleigh were designed to be lighter-than-air as an alternative to helium or hydrogen-filled balloons. They were nearly weightless, but not exactly weightless. The point is that their buoyancy is determined by the weight of displaced air on the outside. At sea level, that is about one and a quarter kilograms per cubic meter. The whole reason the spheres are so large is to displace a lot of air to give more lifting capacity. But the atmosphere gets thinner and thinner as the sphere rises so there is always a ceiling above which the craft will not go, no matter how light, because the buoyancy force becomes less and less at higher altitudes with the decreasing air density. Even if the spheres were totally weightless, they would bounce around at the top of the stratosphere and eventually drift off into space propelled by the solar winds—not a particularly useful application for the craft. The rotor speed of the spheres on *La Charlière*, for example, were set to a maximum speed for a given payload so this couldn't happen by mistake."

"What Sylvanus described as feeling weightless suggests that he was in orbit around the earth. It is not possible to go into orbit even in a totally weightless craft. It would take a boost to propel the sphere far enough away from the earth that it could go into orbit. This wouldn't require much force, just enough to nudge it to a higher altitude. Timecharging alone could never get you there, even into low earth orbit. I like the idea of antigravity. It has a lovely science fiction ring to it. Based on Cédric Rothschild's predictions it might be possible, but the strain on the rotor at the necessary rotational speed is not something I think is feasible with the current design. And I don't think antigravity is even necessary. All it would take is a tiny booster rocket. Maybe not even a rocket. A blast of compressed air would suffice. Okay, now, let's assume this would get the sphere far enough away from the earth, but it still doesn't get you into orbit. In order to be in orbit around the earth the craft would need to have mass. Otherwise, it would drift off into space. How do you give a timecharging sphere some mass? You turn down the rotor speed. And how do you know when to do this? Ahh, that's the challenge. The mass must be precisely tuned for the particular orbit and must be turned off at just the right rate at the right altitude for the craft to enter a circular orbit. Once you are in orbit, getting to the moon is a piece of cake."

"Then, are you going to tell me how they do that?" asked Jacques.

"Gravity," responded Vincent. "It's so simple and so elegant. Gravity."

"What do you mean, gravity?" demanded Jacques.

"The gravitational field is invariant to timecharging. It is the same inside and outside. The strength of the gravitational field drops off as the inverse square of the distance from the center of the earth. The effect is measurable, especially for large distances. All you need is a precision scale. The square root of the change in weight of an object on the scale is proportional to the distance above the earth. That's what I bet you are going to find in the canister, a simple electronic scale. Do you think we could stop for dinner? I'm suddenly famished."

Over dinner at a roadside restaurant where they stopped near Lyon, Vincent asked, "Do you trust your guys in Brest?"

"Mostly," replied Jacques. "A couple of them I would trust with my life."

"But not all of them?" asked Vincent.

"The Navy has been infiltrated just like everything else in France," replied Jacques.

"Then I suggest we open the canister at my apartment," said Vincent. "We can swing by the base when we get to Brest to pick up your most trusted electronics technician and then head to my apartment."

"It will be three in the morning by the time we get there," said Jacques.

"Who can sleep at a time like this?" responded Vincent, looking off into space.

It was four in the morning by the time Vincent had dropped Jacques off at the officer's quarters and gotten back to his apartment. His curiosity got the best of him and he could not wait until the next day to pop the cover off the canister. It was just as he had suspected. There were three gimbaled load cells for redundancy, a microcomputer and a keypad for entering the desired altitude. What did catch him by surprise was that the altitude was set for 35,786 kilometers, the radius of geosynchronous orbit. This was much farther out than he expected, and would complicate the trajectory to the moon, but he was too tired to figure out the rationale.

The following morning, Captain Rousseau and one of his technicians called from the lobby at ten. Sandi let them in and waited at the door for the elevator to open.

"*Bonjour*, Sandi," said Jacques.

"Good morning, Captain," she replied. "Vincent is still sleeping, and I hate to wake him."

"That's not a problem," said Jacques. "He sent me a message last night that the device was on the dining room table."

"Come in, then," she said. Looking at the technician, she commented, "Aren't you the guy who fixed my gas range on Christmas?" He just smiled and followed Jacques into the apartment without saying anything and went right to work on the canister sitting open on the table.

"Let me pour you a cup of coffee. My mama bought fresh pain-au-chocolates this morning at the boulangerie," she said, heading into the kitchen to check on Louisa, who was sitting at the breakfast table coloring.

Jacques followed her and said to his technician that he would be in the kitchen and to let him know if he needed anything. Sandi handed him a cup of coffee and laid out the pastries, indicating for him to have a seat and make himself comfortable. Then she sat down next to Louisa.

"I am very worried about Vincent," she said. "He is so stressed lately, and I don't think he has been sleeping very well."

"Vincent has a very strong character," said Jacques. "I know there are limits of human endurance, but he is doing things that only he can do. I wouldn't worry too much. He is home now and there is not much more he can do than what he has already done over the past two weeks. He has figured out almost everything about the Syndicate's operations in Eastern Europe." They sat quietly for a while savoring their morning coffees.

"Tell me something, Sandi," Jacque said. "Why did you walk away from your career in the French Navy?"

"I wasn't aware that I had one to walk away from," she replied.

"A lot of brass in Paris took careful notice of your performance on the *Polaris Explorer* and then *L'Astrolabe,* not to mention the *Dauphine Rêve*. No woman ever received the kinds of commendations you received for uncommon valor in action."

"Mama, where is the red crayon?" asked Louisa.

"I think it must have rolled onto the floor," said Sandi. "You know, Jacques" she said with a sigh. "When *L'Astrolabe* made it to Washington with the timecharger, I was feeling pretty good about myself, but I think the stress had taken a bigger toll than I realized. Vincent and I had our first date the following day. Well, it wasn't really a date, we just met at Washington Park to hang out. We were out on the observation deck of the President's Tower when he placed his hand on mine. I had never been in love before then, but when he did that, I tumbled head over heels in love with him. All I wanted from then on was to be with him. We had lunch at a posh bistro on Pennsylvania Avenue and I remember thinking life couldn't possibly get any better. That afternoon I watched Syndicate hijackers murder hundreds of civilians aboard the *Vega Explorer*, and I guess I just snapped. It was Abraham who brought me back to my senses, but I knew I would never be the same. In the course of just four hours, I had gone from a place of untold happiness, being with Vincent in Washington Park to the most hideous experience of my life, watching all of those people plummet from the deck of the *Vega* as it broke apart. I think I stopped caring about the world's problems at that moment."

Héloïse came in the door with groceries just in time to keep Sandi from breaking down in tears. "Mass was lovely," she said. "I wish you would come with me sometime." She kissed Louisa on the top of her head when she noticed Jacques. "Hello, Captain. What brings you here?"

"We were just reminiscing," he replied.

"She told me about her encounter with you in Toulon," said Héloïse. "She said you scared the dickens out of her."

"It was just a little misunderstanding," he said. "Anyway, Vincent's father was on hand to straighten things out."

This caused Sandi to let out a loud laugh. “Some help!” she said.

“What’s all the ruckus?” Vincent said as he entered the kitchen.

“Good morning, darling,” Sandi said. “I expected you to sleep all day.”

“I figured it all out,” Vincent said. “They are operating a space station in geosynchronous orbit directly above the launch site on the Black Sea. They are using the timecharging spheres to shuttle people and supplies into orbit and using the space station as a launching platform for going back and forth to the moon. No one has ever seen it because it is too far away.”

Book 3

Chapter 23: Napoleon

Vincent showed up in the kitchen rested and cheerful for the first time in weeks. "The sun is trying to peak out," he said. "It might be a good day for a trip to Aquariopolis. The public is being allowed to view the new polar bear twins for the first time. I think we should go."

"That's a wonderful idea," said Sandi. "Mama, will you come with us?" she added.

"Certainly," said Héloïse. "Let me call them to be sure we can reserve some tickets. We haven't seen the sun for weeks so everyone in Brest is probably having the same idea today."

The four piled into Vincent's Range Rover. Sandi put Louisa's stroller in the back and off they went for the short trip to the park near the waterfront. The place was packed as Héloïse had suspected, but she had been able to reserve the tickets, nonetheless.

"I will let you out at the front gate and go try to find a place to park," said Vincent. "Have them hold my ticket at the ticket counter and I will meet you at the Arctic Wildlife exhibit in a few minutes."

Vincent finally found a space big enough for his car that was barely closer to Aquariopolis than their apartment in Saint-Marc. He locked the car and as he was heading towards the Park, a black van pulled up in front of him and four men got out. They shoved him into the back and jumped in next to him without saying a word as they sped away. One of them held up a sack and told Vincent to empty his pockets. He could tell by the fierce look in their eyes that if he failed to comply, they were prepared to strip him naked. "And the watch," the man said, pointing to Vincent's wrist.

"What is this all about?" Vincent protested. "Where are you taking me?" They made no reply. The van entered a security gate at the Aéroport Brest Bretagne and drove out onto the tarmac to an awaiting VTOL. The men pulled Vincent out of the van and shuffled him up the rear ramp of the plane. The ramp closed and off they went to the east.

"Where are we going?" he demanded again. He got no response. The men sat quietly for the thirty-five-minute flight. Vincent recognized the grounds of Château Versailles as the VTOL transitioned to vertical flight and dropped down onto the landing pad next to the palace. The realization that he was in big trouble struck him suddenly.

Two of the men held him by each arm and the other two followed closely in front and back as they ushered him into the palace and into a large room. The walls were ornate and covered with old paintings of French monarchs, but the only pieces of furniture were two chairs and a huge Louis XVth desk. They plopped him down into one of the chairs in front of the desk and waited at attention.

The wait wasn't long before the sound of the latch on the side door signaled the arrival of the dignitary. Two of the men grabbed Vincent by the arms and forced him to stand at attention. The dignitary sat down behind the desk and dismissed all the other men, who left and pulled the double doors of the main entrance closed behind them. The man scowled at Vincent for a long time before finally indicating for him to be seated. "Well, Dr. Gilbert," he began. "Do you happen to know who or what is behind the restoration of the French monarchy?"

Vincent made no reply. The silence was deadly before the man slammed his fist on the desk and bellowed, "Failure to answer my questions is not an option!"

"I don't know, sir," Vincent said.

"Sir?" he repeated in disgust. "Do you know who I am? It's 'Your Majesty' when you address me!"

"I don't know, Your Majesty," said Vincent.

"Not knowing the answer to one of my questions is not an option," he bellowed. "Tell me Dr. Gilbert, who do you think is behind reinstating me to the rightful throne of Napoleon Bonaparte? I know you know the answer."

"The Syndicate, Your Majesty," Vincent answered weakly.

"Now we are getting somewhere," Napoleon said. "Tell me about the Syndicate base on the moon."

Vincent's life raced before his eyes. He knew he was being set up to confess to things that would bring him a life sentence. "It's only hearsay," he said. "It's just the speculation of a pretty unreliable witness."

"Quit lying to me, Dr. Gilbert," said the emperor. "Why would the Syndicate want to have a secret base on the moon?"

"To launch an invasion," Vincent said. He regretted saying it the minute the words left his mouth.

"An invasion?" the emperor repeated slowly. "Of the earth, I presume. And why would the Syndicate want to invade the earth?" the emperor demanded.

"I don't know," Vincent responded.

Napoleon slammed his fist on the desk again. "I told you not to lie to me. Of course, you know why."

Vincent was trapped. "In order to rule the world," he said.

"That's right," said Napoleon. "Today I am Emperor of France and by the end of the month, I will be Emperor of all of Europe." He got up from his chair and walked over to the window that had a commanding view of the palace grounds. "Tell me, Vincent—is it okay if I call you Vincent? Tell me how these invaders are coming and going from outer space?"

Vincent hesitated, prompting a glare from the emperor. "They are using timecharging spheres—the ones I designed for Ashleigh Systems, Your Majesty."

"Go on," said the monarch.

"They are coming and going from a launching facility on the Black Sea to at least one space station in geosynchronous orbit."

"And you know this how?" he asked, turning to look directly at Vincent.

“From the altitude setting on the rotor speed controller that I borrowed,” said Vincent.

“Borrowed?” repeated Napoleon. “That is a very interesting choice of words,” he said. “You should know, this device you ‘borrowed’ last week has some people very stirred up.”

Vincent was speechless. He felt like he had just confessed to a capital crime. The emperor returned to his seat. “That will be all,” he said. “You are free to go.” As Vincent was heading towards the door, Napoleon stopped him. He turned and made eye contact with the man who suddenly had a different countenance. “Vincent,” he instructed in a lower voice. “Do not let your fear of what the future holds distract you from doing the right things in the present. Do not be like the servant who hid is master’s money in the ground. The Syndicate is powerful, but they are not omniscient.”

The double doors opened at that instant and the four men from before took Vincent through the palace to the entrance closest to the TGV station. One of them handed him the bag containing his belongings and pointed to the train station, saying, “The next maglev to Nantes departs in ten minutes. He turned and closed the gate, leaving Vincent on the outside, completely baffled by what had taken place over the prior hour.

“Where are you, Vincent? We are worried sick.” This voice message was repeated four times on his phone. Vincent called Sandi from the train.

"Vincent! Where the heck are you?" said Sandi when she answered.

"It's a long story, but nothing I can talk about over the phone," he replied. "Are you still at Aquariopolis?"

"Where else would we be?" she said, expressing her irritation. "You have the key fob for the car, and you are the only one who knows where it is parked."

"I am really sorry," he said. "I will explain everything when I get home. Can you call for an autopod?"

"I already tried. There is a one-hour wait," she said. "Anyway, we are having a wonderful time, and Louisa is showing no signs of wearing out. When do you think you will be here?"

"About two hours. I just departed the Versailles station," he said.

"Versailles!" she exclaimed. "What in the world are you doing in Versailles?"

"I told you it is a long story. I must change trains in Nantes. I will call you from there," he said.

"Oh, Vincent," she sighed. "You have to quit doing this kind of thing."

"This time it wasn't my choice," he replied after a brief pause deciding it would be unwise to say anything more over the phone. "I will explain everything when I get back."

The train from Nantes was an hour late, and by the time Vincent finally got home, it was after ten. Sandi met him at the door and gave him a big hug. “Louisa is sound asleep. We really wore her out.”

Vincent said, “I am so sorry. I thought I could make it to the park in time to bring you home.”

“That’s okay,” she said. “Once the sun went down, it got cold, and people started leaving. We stuck around for dinner and by the time we were finished, there were plenty of autopods standing by.” They strolled together into the living room where Héloïse was sitting reading. “So, Vincent,” Sandi said, “when are you going to tell me why you were in Versailles?”

“Emperor Napoleon sent for me,” he said. “He sent one of his private planes to pick me up.”

“I beg your pardon,” said Sandi.

“Actually, he grilled me rather intensely. About half-way through the inquisition, I was sure I was about to be marched off to the guillotine,” he said, poring himself a glass of red wine from the decanter. “At the end, he said some very curious things. He told me not to let my fear of what may take place in the future distract me from my present mission. Then he spoke in riddles. He said something about not becoming the servant that buried his master’s talent in the ground.”

At this, Héloïse spoke up. “That’s from the Bible. It is from one of the parables Jesus preached!” She grabbed her bible from the table next to her chair and began thumbing through it to find the passage.

"And then," Vincent added, "he said the most remarkable thing to me just as I was leaving. He said, 'The Syndicate is powerful, but they are not omniscient.'" Vincent sipped his wine reflectively. "Sandy, I have heard this expression before. I think it is some sort of code. Do you think it is possible that Emperor Napoleon X is actually part of the Network?"

The effect of the traumatic encounter with the emperor finally struck Vincent at three in the morning and he was unable to go back to sleep. He went to the kitchen to make tea and find a snack. Héloïse's Bible lay open on the counter to the passage of the Parable of the Talents in the Gospel of Matthew. He read it while the water was heating on the stove. He had practically no knowledge of these scriptures, which he had always considered to be ancient and irrelevant. This parable, however, captured his imagination and he spent several minutes trying to understand the significance of this third servant who buried his master's money. On the surface, it seemed like a perfectly logical thing to do if the servant had doubted his own ability to invest the money wisely. Apparently, the other servants in the parable had no such self-doubts. Where did they get the confidence required to press on in the face of all the implied risks and having to answer to a demanding master?

He took his tea into his study and sat at his desk to read Cédric Rothschild's personal journal. He had only thumbed through it casually before when he came upon the drawings of the antigravity device. However, this night he began reading it more carefully to gain some insight into this strange scientist that had worked so faithfully for his father for years—the man that taught him how to play two-handed bridge when he was a child. The journal was punctuated by random thoughts, mathematical derivations, sketches, and writing, which he called *Reflections*. One of these called "Credit and Glory" caught his attention and he read it to himself out loud.

Cédric had written,

For more than twenty years, I have been working on a coherent theory of the variable speed of light. There have been times when I had flashes of insight, and elements of the mathematical model would seem to be credible but other parts would break down, requiring revision after revision. Some of the ideas were basically right, but things never worked out on the whole. Recently, I picked up the pursuit again, taking the different approach of looking at just the birth of galaxies from Black Holes rather that the whole Universe all at once, and everything suddenly fell nicely into place.

Needless to say, this Sunday morning, as I went to church, I was feeling pretty good about myself. I could now begin to make a compelling case for variable light speed. As I sat in my pew meditating on the passion of Jesus and reflecting on the Crucifix above the altar, it dawned on me that the One who spoke the galaxies into existence was hanging on the cross in my place. He was condemned to die unjustly in my place for supposed blasphemy and heresy. I was overwhelmed with the unfairness. It was me that belonged on that cross, not Him." I said, "Lord! It's You who created the Heavens. Why are you revealing Your secrets to me? I will be receiving the credit and glory that belongs to You." He said to me, "You may actually receive some of the credit, but you will never get the glory. The glory is

Mine alone." It came with a gentle reminder that if I were ever to seek glory for myself, He would find someone else to get the credit."

The entry in Cedric's journal preceding this, showed the first successful derivation of how time-dependent mass and the speed of light are linked together in a common, local time frame. This led to his comprehensive theory of the nature of dark matter, as an artifact of increasing light speed when galaxies form, and was the foundation for his seminal treatise, "Dark Matter and Time-Dependent Speed of Light", dated July 28, 2029. The treatise was not actually published until Vincent's father had it posted on a public domain website after Cédric's death. It was never peer reviewed and it never appeared in any astrophysics journal, but it transformed forever scientific theory and led to the discovery of the timecharging effect. The thought occurred to Vincent that perhaps Cédric was one of those servants mentioned in the parable that doubled his master's money.

As Vincent was slowly reading through the pages of the journal and savoring the deeply personal glimpses into Cedric's soul, he noticed for the first time that the leather binding of the journal was merely a cover for an ordinary cardboard journal. He carefully studied the flyleaf, and when he pulled the leather cover off, he noticed an envelope taped to the front that had been hidden for years. Inside the envelope, he found five transparencies that appeared to be some sort of microfiche. He held one of them up to the light, but all he could make out were some unintelligible lines and squiggles that looked like hieroglyphics. There was an address on the envelope that read, “12 Place Antoine, Saint-Martin-d’Hères, France”, followed by a name that nearly stopped his heart; “Sonja Dumitescu”.

Chapter 24: Sonja

Vincent's autopod crept through ten centimeters of snow up the long tree-lined driveway to 12 Place Antoine in the eastern suburbs of Grenoble. A large white villa stood at the end with red roof tiles protruding through the snow in places. A broad staircase led up to the front door. It was bitter cold and the fresh snow from the night before had not been shoveled from the stairs. Vincent had the autopod wait for five minutes while he went to see if he was at the right address. He pressed the button on the box mounted next to the doorway.

"*Allô*," came a female voice over the speaker.

"Yes. My name is Dr. Vincent Gilbert," he said. "I am looking for Sonja Dumitescu."

"There is no one here by that name," the voice replied. "Go away!"

Vincent noticed the surveillance camera above the door and suspected that he was being watched. He reached in his pocket and withdrew the envelope holding it up to the camera. After a long silence, he heard the door lock click.

"Come in," she said.

The entryway was completely dark once he closed the door behind him. "Hello?" he said as a question.

"Where did you get that envelope?" said a voice from the far end of the hallway.

"It was hidden in the cover of Cédric Rothschild's journal," Vincent said. "Are you Sonja Dumitescu?" he asked.

She switched on the light. "Heavens no. My name is Magdalena. Sonja doesn't exist. She never existed. Cédric and I created her." She maneuvered her electric wheelchair forward and made a right-hand turn into the kitchen, flipping on the light. "Coffee?" she asked. "I will need your help to make it. My daytime caregiver called in late because of the snow. It's strange that your autopod didn't seem to have any trouble getting up the driveway this morning. The machine is there on the counter. Just select your type of bean—I prefer the Java—and push start. Oh, and the mugs are in the cupboard above." The espresso machine started grinding the beans and going through a sequence of automated procedures. "So, you are looking for Sonja," she said, moving to the other side of the kitchen.

"You must admit," Vincent responded. "What you just said is a bit curious. If Sonja doesn't exist, then who poisoned Cédric?"

"Grab your coffee," she said. "Let's go into the living room by the fire to get out of the chill. This will take a while to explain. I hope you aren't in a hurry."

"Would you like me to make you a cup?" Vincent inquired.

"Yes, please. That would be nice. I will be next to the fire. I'm freezing," she said, exiting the kitchen. "There is cream in the refrigerator. Put a dash in my coffee if you don't mind."

Vincent brought the coffees and sat down on the sofa across from her.

She began telling her story. "Cédric and I met at the nuclear research laboratory in Grenoble. When your father's company was confiscated, Cédric and I worked together on microfusion, but his heart wasn't in it. I could tell he was working on something else in his mind. He didn't talk much. I had such a crush on him, but he wouldn't give me the time of day until he encountered a math problem he couldn't solve. He knew I was a mathematician, so he asked for my help. That is when it all began. We started seeing each other more and more. He said it was to work on math problems, but I knew better. I started going to church with him. He was such a gentleman. He treated our relationship as purely platonic. I don't think he was aware that I had fallen madly in love with him."

"One spring day after church, he invited me to go horseback riding with him. He was an accomplished horseman, and he was eager to teach me to ride. It was the first time I had ever been on a horse. It bucked me off, and just like that, I broke my back. And here I am, a paraplegic. You can imagine how badly he felt. He covered all my medical bills and spent hours with me in the hospital, hoping I would recover."

She stopped to take a sip of coffee. Vincent saw a tear form in her eye and drop into her mug.

"He asked me to marry him," she continued. "I said no. I thought he was asking me just because he felt sorry for me. Now I know that I declined because I was actually feeling sorry for myself." She paused again. "I wish I had said yes, but this was all before we found out about his pancreatic cancer. It was very sudden. He passed away within six months of the initial diagnosis. And no, I didn't poison him. That was all part of the ruse. It started out innocently enough. Cedric had been working on his gravitational field theories and wanted to write a paper to submit to a journal for publication. As you know, he had had a bad experience with journals in the past, so he thought if he had a co-author, it might help make the manuscript more palpable to the reviewers. He created Sonja, this off-the-charts brilliant Romanian woman scientist. He created her curriculum vitae. He made it up! Did you know that hardly anyone ever checks the authenticity of a CV? I am convinced that Sonja could have been awarded a Nobel Prize before anyone would have known that she didn't even exist. As you can imagine, Cédric and I had a lot of fun with this." She put her empty mug down on the table. "I need another coffee. Would you mind?"

Vincent got up and went into the kitchen to make two more coffees. "Did I add the right amount of cream last time?" he asked from the kitchen.

"Perfect," she said.

Vincent said upon returning to the living room, "I get the sense that you are just getting started telling this story. You just met me. How do you know you can trust me?"

"Cédric trusted everyone," she said. "He knew the value of his discovery to mankind, and he wanted to share it with the world. His instructions to me were to have the manuscript published after he was gone, but I could never bring myself to do it. I don't think he ever fully comprehended the implications of what he had discovered. After he died, I gathered up all of his papers and journal and hid them because I knew the consequences if they were to ever fall into the wrong hands. I held on to them for more than twenty years, until a couple of months ago, I decided it was time to pass them on to someone who could be trusted. I removed what I knew were the critical five pages from the manuscript and encrypted them so that if anyone did get hold of it unintentionally, they would not be able to use it. I figured that sooner or later someone would find the envelope in the cover of the journal and come looking for Sonja. Then I sent the folio to Jean-Luc."

"Jean-Luc? Jean-Luc Gallatin?" exclaimed Vincent.

"Yes," she replied, guiding her wheelchair over to the other side of the room.

"How in the world do you know Jean-Luc Gallatin?" he said.

"Don't you remember?" she replied, "He is the one who ended up purchasing the rights to the microfusion technology from our laboratory. He also had a pretty good idea what Cédric was up to. I sent him the folio with instructions to pass it on to your father, but now I see that he wisely gave it to you instead. That turns out to be a good decision, I think." She pulled out a key attached to a lanyard around her neck and unlocked the captain's desk, lowering the top. Then she pulled out one of the drawers completely. Taped to the underside was an envelope, which she removed with care. “Do you know what is inside your envelope?” she asked.

“Only what appears to be some sort of microfiche films with strange hieroglyphics,” he replied.

She went back over toward him. “Here, hand me your envelope.” She removed the films from it and held them up to the light one by one until she found the right one. She took the films from her own envelope and did the same. Then she superimposed two films and held them up to the light to confirm the match before handing them to Vincent. “What do you see?” she asked.

Vincent looked carefully and readjusted the alignment. “I think I see characters–some text and maybe some equations. It’s pretty small to make out without a microscope,” he replied.

“Those are the five missing pages from his manuscript,” she said proudly.

“What manuscript? What missing pages?” Vincent asked.

“The May 4, 2062 manuscript, *Gravitron Theory and the Dynamics of Gravitational Fields Induced by Supermassive Objects in Motion, by J. Cedric Rothschild and Sonja Dumitescu,*” she replied. “You didn’t notice that pages were missing?”

“To be honest, I barely got past the introduction,” he said.

“Oh,” she replied, “then perhaps I should explain a few things. Cédric discovered antigravity.”

“I got that much from the introduction,” Vincent said.

"But you don't know how it works. You need these missing five pages for that," she said, handing both envelopes to Vincent. "Take good care of these."

"Does Jean-Luc know about Sonja?" he paused, "and could you also explain why Pastor Joel in Bucharest thinks you, that is Sonja, poisoned Cédric?"

"That's rather more complicated, so stick with me," she said. "Pastor Joel was Cédric's friend. As you probably know, they were working together to create a foundation to help address the root cause of the refugee problem from Eastern Europe. I will come back to that in a minute, but first, let me tell you why Pastor Joel was led to believe that Sonja murdered Cédric. Pastor Joel never met me. Everything he knew about Sonja was from letters I wrote. I was sorry about deceiving him, but I needed him to believe that this wicked Sonja woman was actually a Syndicate spy who got her hands on Cédric's invention and absconded with all his money, because ultimately, I needed the Syndicate to believe it. They're not just a big club. They generally don't even know who the other members are. They're not all that smart. The Syndicate is powerful, but they aren't omniscient."

Vincent looked up at this remark and detected the flash of a smile on Magdalena's face.

"You know, Vincent," she continued. "Cédric never lived in this house. He was always a perfect gentleman. He lived in the studio apartment above his workshop in the back. Before he died, he transferred ownership of this property to me and established a generous trust for my care. He set up his relief foundation with Sonja as executive director. The plan was to transfer in all of the money from his inheritance, which was being held by an investment firm in Paris. He told me it was worth almost sixty-five million euros, and he asked me to assign the royalties from any antigravity licenses to the Foundation. Then he died suddenly before the transaction was completed. At first, there were the anticipated testate issues that dragged on for a couple of years. I waited and waited until one day a certified letter arrived in Sonja Dumitescu's post office box in Grenoble where all the correspondence for the Foundation was received. It was from the investment firm managing Cédric's account. It said, "We are sorry to inform you that your account is overdrawn. Please remit €965.23 at your earliest convenience."

"You're not serious," exclaimed Vincent. "How is that even possible? What did you do?"

Magdalena sighed. "I couldn't exactly hop on a train to Paris and pretend to be Sonja Dumitescu. Needless to say, they never received their nine hundred and sixty-five euros, but I did investigate the matter. It seems that the people managing Cédric's account were some old cronies of his father. They were churning his investment portfolio, making increasingly risky investments until there was nothing left. I found stacks of unopened statements from the firm in Cédric's apartment. As I told you, he trusted everybody."

"And Jean-Luc knew about this?" Vincent inquired.

"Heavens no," she replied. "Jean-Luc only came back into the picture recently. I think he was trying to tidy up some loose ends regarding Ashleigh Airships. That's when he tracked me down."

The daytime caregiver finally arrived at that point. They could hear her stomping her feet by the back door. "Sorry I'm late, Miss Magdalena," she yelled. "The streets are a mess. I brought you some fresh pastries from the boulangerie," she said, walking into the living room. "Oh my," she exclaimed upon seeing Vincent. "I'm so sorry. I didn't know you had company."

"Not to worry," said Magdalena. "This is Dr. Vincent Gilbert. Cédric worked for his father when he was a boy. Just leave the pastries on the table."

Magdalena took a croissant and passed the tray to Vincent, then continued. "You can imagine that this put me in a bit of a bind. I wasn't sure how I was going to explain to Pastor Joel that there was no money, and the Foundation was bankrupt. I'm sure he would have understood, but there was another problem: how in the world was I ever going to explain about Sonja. You can't imagine the sleepless nights until I had the idea to have Sonja turn out to be a sinister Syndicate spy dispatched to steal Cédric's secrets, then murder him and make off with all his money. At first, I was just having fun with the idea in my mind, but after a while, I came to the realization that there was no better way to safeguard Cédric's secrets. As long as everyone believed that Sonja made off with everything, they wouldn't come looking for his papers. It's not in my nature to deceive people, but the ruse held up for twenty years. Other than Jean-Luc, no one ever came looking for Sonja until you showed up this morning." Magdalena drank down the rest of her coffee and said, "Come with me, there is something I want to show you."

They went out the back door. The groundskeeper was just finishing up shoveling the sidewalk that led to several outbuildings. Magdalena wheeled herself up to the door of one of them and punched in the security code to disarm the burglar alarm. "This is Cédric's workshop. Nothing has changed. I left it exactly the way it was when he died." She flipped a large circuit breaker near the door and bright overhead lights illuminated everything.

Vincent stood motionless in astonishment. Spread out before him was an assortment of sophisticated equipment. Some items he recognized, but mostly they were things he had never seen before and could only guess at their function. Magdalena went over to a cabinet against the far wall and took out a box about ten centimeters square and placed it on one of the workbenches. She looked up at Vincent beaming, and opened it. Inside was a shiny metallic sphere about the size of an orange. She took it out and gave it a spin on the workbench. The sphere drifted up off the table and headed towards the ceiling. "I'll bet your father's magic sphere could never do that," she exclaimed with glee.

Chapter 25: Top Secrets

Vincent came in through the back door of Villa Sémaphore and had meant to pass through the kitchen on his way to the guest bedroom in the back where he stayed while visiting his parents. His mother, Gabrielle, and Kathrine were preparing lunch. It was pouring rain for the first time in weeks and Vincent was drenched from the sprint from the autopod that dropped him off out front.

"Hello, Vincent. My, you are soaked!" said Gabrielle. "Are you trying to grow a beard?" she asked, looking at him more closely. "Sandi has been going crazy trying to get hold of you. Why aren't you answering your phone?"

"I left it in the apartment in Saint-Marc," replied Vincent. "I didn't want anyone to know where I had been."

Gabrielle said, "Sandi's granddad had a heart attack—not too serious apparently, but he needed a couple of stents. Sandi and her mom are headed to Bethesda with Louisa to visit him in the hospital. They are probably there by now. You need to give her a call to at least let her know you are still alive. She is frantic."

"Mom," he replied. "No one can know where I am. Will you please send her a message that I am fine, and I will join her in America in a couple of days?"

"Are you in some kind of trouble?" she asked.

"No," he replied. "I am just laying low. I think I will slip into the back and tidy up a bit. A shower and a shave and I will be good as new. Is Stephan still here?"

"Apparently," she said, looking out the window. "I don't know anyone else crazy enough to be swimming in this thunderstorm. Is he expecting you?"

"No. Is Dad around?" Vincent asked.

"Yes." she replied. "He is in the den. We will be having lunch in about an hour. I hope you will join us. Maybe Stephan would also like to join us."

Twenty minutes later, Vincent emerged from the back room. "Much better," said Gabrielle, looking him over. "Stephan and your father are in the living room. Here, will you take this plate of *hors-d'œuvres* with you? Lunch should be ready soon.

"Hello, Stephan," Vincent said upon entering the living room. "Hello, Father." Then, seeing crutches next to Stephan's chair, "Aren't you rushing things a bit?"

"It's been ten weeks," Stephan smiled. "The doctor has me in a brace. He thinks the swimming is why my leg is healing so well. Anyway, it's time to get back to work, don't you think?"

Vincent just shook his head.

He passed the plate of *hors-d'œuvres* and took a seat. A clap of nearby thunder reminded them all of the raging storm outside.

"That sounded like it hit the Sémaphore," Charles remarked, waiting for the alarm that would signal that their power had gone off in the observation tower next door.

"So, Vincent, your mother told me you are hiding out," said Charles.

"I just returned from Romania, and I didn't want anyone to know where I had been. That's all. The reason why I stopped by was to get some fatherly advice."

"What interesting things did you learn in Romania?" asked Stephan.

Vincent replied, "As you know, the timecharging spheres become invisible in the optical spectrum, but they plainly show up in the angstrom wavelengths where X-rays and gamma rays occur. Jacques was able to demonstrate the ability to observe them using an imaging system developed for detecting radioactive materials being smuggled in shipping containers. He and Alex Spinu installed the imaging device on a tower he had built for his wildlife conservation 'bird watching' project in the Danube Delta that has a view of the Syndicate base. They set up a surveillance post on a goat farm south of Bucharest in order to keep track of what the Syndicate is up to. What they have discovered is that the base is only used to launch spheres at night. They are averaging about twenty-five launches each night, and they assemble the spheres on site in the dark, which explains why no one has ever seen what is going on. We have yet to observe any spheres come back and land, however. Apparently, they return to earth by some other route. We have located the space station. It is in geosynchronous orbit directly above the Black Sea base. We conjecture that the spheres are going straight up and entering orbit in the vicinity of the space station and then get picked up and drawn in somehow. The spheres that are being launched are mostly carrying supplies and a few people. With a payload capacity of about 500 kilograms, they can put up more than ten tons of payload each night, so it is clear that there is a sizeable activity going on up there in space. Everything is now in place to take out the base on the Black Sea and destroy the spheres and all the infrastructure supporting them."

"That's wonderful news," exclaimed Charles. "Why do you need my advice for that? Destroy them while you can."

"Here's my dilemma," Vincent said. "We don't know how many people are on the moon base, but perhaps hundreds by our estimate. A lot of them are just farm kids and homeless kids that have no idea that what they are involved in is evil. Without the supply lines provided by timecharging spheres they would be marooned on the moon and left to die of starvation. This is really unsettling to me."

"Innocent people always perish in war, Vincent," said Charles. "The Syndicate must be stopped at all costs."

"There's more. It seems that I may have gotten myself into something a bit over my head," Vincent said. "I wanted to seek your counsel about how to deal with the knowledge of disruptive technology that could be used for good or evil purposes. When you started fabricating neutron clusters at NaPiles, at what point did you begin to worry that the technology might be used with bad intentions if it were ever to fall into the wrong hands?"

Charles replied, "I think I have always worried about the impact technology might have on society. But I would have to say, when Cédric blew up the reactor and explained that it was the result of microfusion—that is probably when it dawned on me that I needed to bring the French government in. As you recall, I went to the nuclear research laboratory in Grenoble to tell them about our discovery. It took a while to convince them, but once they realized what we had done, they immediately recognized the national security implications and commandeered everything going on in my lab and classified it top secret. That's, of course, how Cédric ended up in Grenoble."

"Yes," said Vincent. "But microfusion never led to an arms race. The technology was available to anyone who wanted it from the beginning."

"Anyone willing to pay license royalties to Ashleigh, that is," said Charles.

"True," said Vincent, "but nobody ever used microfusion to gain a military advantage. I am actually thinking more along the lines of timecharging. There had to have been a point at which you decided that your rotor was not safe in France and that's why you thought it was imperative to move it to America."

Charles contemplated this for a moment while he spread some camembert on a cracker, and finally said, "Timecharging was different. From the beginning, Cédric had a sense that he had made a more fundamental discovery than just a new way to make energy. You know, when he gave me that blob of molten aluminum with the neutron cluster inside—the one you threw at my wall last week—he had a curious grin on his face. He told me to hold on to it. I didn't think anything of it at the time. I just placed it on my bookshelf with the rest of my interesting artifacts. It wasn't until much later, when I was cleaning out my office and it rolled off the shelf and drifted to the ground that I had a glimpse of what subsequently became known as timecharging. I have often wondered if Cédric hadn't also observed the same phenomenon but wanted me to discover it for myself. We never discussed it, but I was aware that he was working on some new gravitational theories."

"He pretty much worked out a theory of antigravity," said Vincent. "You have a copy of his manuscript that Captain Rousseau gave you."

Stephan jumped into the conversation at that point and said, "Jacques told me there are some pages missing. His best scientists couldn't make any sense of it. They concluded that Cédric was probably delusional as a result of the poison toward the end of his life and that his theories are nonsense."

"Well," said Vincent, "I went looking for his co-author, Sonja Dumitescu. It turns out, she doesn't exist. Cédric invented her. His estate doesn't exist either. He was wiped out by a bunch of unscrupulous money managers who squandered everything."

Stephan said, “It’s sad to say but it seems that poor Cédric had become a paranoid schizophrenic before he died.”

Vincent kept silent and made no comment. Then, looking back at his father, he said, “Back to the timecharger, there had to have been a point where you considered burying the technology altogether.”

“Yes,” replied Charles, “I did consider this—even seriously at one point. I had plenty of money from microfusion royalties, and there was no pressing reason to build a neutron winder and the rotor in my laboratory in Aix.” He took a deep reflective breath and said, “At the time, I had been reading the accounts of Albert Einstein and the other scientists that recognized the implications of nuclear fission for building a bomb of unprecedented destructive power. They went to the United States to convince President Roosevelt that if Germany were ever to be the first to build such a weapon, the Third Reich would have ruled the world. I naively thought that if France were to be the first to introduce timecharging technology, they would use it for good purposes. That is how I got to know Jacques Rousseau in the first place.”

“That is also the point where Abraham became aware that there was a Syndicate spy working for you,” added Stephan.

“To be honest,” said Charles. “I probably should have destroyed the timecharger, but I considered it a bit of a kluge without much potential as a weapon. Moving it to the Naval Research Laboratory in Virginia seemed like a safe place and a good idea at the time. I guess I never dreamed that you would come along and develop a neutron filament winder that would make the technology commercially viable."

"And I never dreamed that the NRL would transfer such classified top-secret research to Ashleigh Airships," added Vincent.

"Yes," added Stephan, "and the United Nations played right along by implementing an international ban on timecharger development for fear that it would trigger a new arms race. Ashleigh got around the ban by claiming that their spheres could only be used for lifting freight, and people would not be allowed to timecharge inside them. Now, the Syndicate has uncontested exclusivity to use the technology for world domination. I can hardly imagine a more devious or well-executed plan."

"So, Vincent," asked Charles, "you said you needed some fatherly advice?"

Vincent paused for a moment before responding. "Here's the thing. The Syndicate has deployed time charging spheres for a totally unexpected purpose, to get their minions into geosynchronous orbit. That is a monumental achievement that they must have been working on for many years. I suspect they have been building the moon base for at least ten years. I am pretty sure that they scuttled *La Charlière* because they needed the Ashleigh Airships business to fail in order to cover up their true intentions to relocate the rotor manufacturing operation to Bucharest. If Abraham hadn't put it all together, I suspect that the Syndicate would have continued to grow in strength and become totally unstoppable at some point. The interesting thing about the ten-meter diameter spheres is that they are ponderously slow in the real-time frame. They are much lighter than air, but not absolutely weightless. They have to push a lot of air out of the way in order to ascend. This is particularly the case when they launch from sea level. Once they are above the earth's atmosphere, they can travel pretty fast, but they are simply sitting ducks when close to the ground. We will have no difficulty destroying them. But I just can't get all those farm kids on the backside of the moon off my mind."

"They are all serving the Syndicate, whether they know it or not," said Charles.

"You know they are merely pawns in the Syndicate strategy," replied Vincent. "The Syndicate's power base isn't on the back side of the moon. Their top people are all living the good life on earth. For sure, we could take out their means of getting to the moon with a preemptive strike on the Black Sea base. That would set them back, but it would hardly stop them. They would simply build another base and more space stations somewhere else. As long as they have a monopoly on timecharger technology, we will just be playing catch-up." Vincent stood to pour himself another cup of coffee. Then turning, he said, "What if I thought I knew how to shut down the moon base and rescue them at the same time?"

"What? You think you know how to go to the moon?" said Stephan sarcastically.

"Perhaps," replied Vincent, "but I will need some months and a lot of money to pull it off."

"That's just crazy," said Stephan. "We don't have months to sit around while the Syndicate grows in strength."

"I need to construct another neutron filament winder like the one I had at Ashleigh," replied Vincent. "It took me a year and cost ten million dollars to build it at the NRL."

"Well then," replied Stephan, "if all you need is a neutron winder, let's simply steal yours back."

"Now who's the crazy one?" replied Vincent. "I saw first-hand the level of security at the compound where they took the winder in Bucharest. Anyway, at the first sign of an attempted assault on that facility, they would surely destroy the winder."

"Vincent," said Stephan. "That's not how we operate. We never go in through the front door with guns blazing. If all you want is your winder back, you shall have it."

"Where would you put it?" asked Vincent.

"Just leave that up to me," said Stephan.

Charles added, "Once they know they are being surveilled, they will be in a total panic. Everything they do requires complete secrecy. It would be wise not to do anything to spook them. If you really think you can get the winder back, it must be done in such a way as to catch them by total surprise."

Kathrine stood at the door and announced that lunch was ready in the dining room.

"I need to go the America," said Vincent. "Sandi has been incredibly patient with me up to this point, but I think this is one of those instances where I need to act more like a husband and father. If you can work out a plan to retake the neutron winder, we should discuss it when I get back in a few days."

"I will do better than that, Vincent," said Stephan. "Your winder will be waiting for you when you return."

Chapter 26: Connecting the Dots

Vincent fumbled in the dark for the light switch. The Saint-Marc apartment in Bretagne was dark and lonely the last week of January. Sandi had turned off everything and had lowered the thermostat before leaving, so the apartment was cold. Absent was the delighted squeal from Louisa that, 'Papa was home' or the yapping of Héloïse's dog to announce his arrival. The first order of business was to call his wife in America.

"Ahh, Vincent," Sandi said, recognizing him by his caller ID. "I'm so glad you called. I was wondering when I would ever hear from you again."

"I'm really sorry I didn't get back to you sooner," he replied. "My mother said you were frantic."

"She was just over-reacting," said Sandi. "You know I never get frantic. I just needed to be sure you are okay and to let you know that we had to go to Bethesda in a hurry."

"How is your Grandad?" asked Vincent.

"He is doing pretty well for an eighty-four-year-old," said Sandi. "The doctors think he will be able to come home tomorrow. Louisa and I are staying at his townhouse. Mama has gone down to Savannah to haggle with the insurance adjusters. There's someone here who wants to say hello."

"Hi, Papa," said Louisa. "When are you coming to see me? I really miss you."

"The day after tomorrow, Sweetheart," said Vincent. "Are you and Mama taking good care of Great-Grandad?"

There was no answer, as Louisa had passed the phone back to her mother. "I see you called us from the computer in your office," said Sandi. "Is your phone not working?"

"I think the internet is more secure than cellular," replied Vincent. "I worry that it is just too easy to eavesdrop on my mobile phone."

"Are you still hiding out?" she asked.

"No," he replied. "I have pretty much finished everything I needed to get done. Now I am looking forward to joining you in America. After my run-in with the emperor, I don't feel safe in France. There is too much strange stuff going on and I can't wait to get away from it."

"What are your plans, then?" she asked.

"Right now, I am exhausted from all the travel, so I am looking forward to spending a night in my own bed," he replied. "I booked a seat on the Paris-Longyearbyen portal for tomorrow at five, but there is no point in arriving in America late in the day, so I made a reservation for tomorrow night at the Northern Lights Resort and Spa. This will give me a chance to unwind. I should arrive in New York in the morning, the day after tomorrow and be in Bethesda by noon. If that's okay with you"

"That will be fine," replied Sandi. "It will be good to see you. Do you have anything going on in America?"

"Actually, no, if you can believe it," he replied. "I was thinking of stopping by the NRL to say hi to some old friends, but besides that, I am just looking forward to hanging out with you and Louisa. If the weather is decent, maybe we could all go to Washington Park."

"I would like that very much," said Sandi. "Maybe we can find that lovely bistro on Pennsylvania Avenue where we first fell in love."

"You mean, where you first fell in love with me," replied Vincent. "I didn't fall in love with you until Oslo."

Sandi laughed. "I love you, Vincent. Please be careful."

Vincent terminated the video call and went over to the bookcase, feeling for the recessed latch at the bottom which released a catch. It swung outward, revealing a hidden compartment where he kept his important papers and other valuables. He retrieved the Rothschild folio and laid it on his desk before going into the kitchen to pour himself a glass of rosé from a box in the refrigerator.

He sat at his desk for a while, staring at the mysterious folio that had caused him so much inner turmoil. Finally, he pulled out the journal and slid the leather cover off the flyleaf. He reached into his inside coat pocket and took out the envelope containing the five microfiche transparencies which he had taken with him to Grenoble plus the five new ones Magdalena had given him. The burden imposed on him by the knowledge contained in that envelope overwhelmed him. Any decision about what to do about it would now have to wait. He carefully taped the envelope back in place and slid the flyleaf into the leather cover. He thought he would just close the folio and place everything back into his secret compartment and go to bed. But instead, he started turning the pages of the journal slowly. His eyes fell on one of Cédric's reflections near the beginning of the journal. It was dated May 12, 2060. That was Vincent's birthday and the day he had turned ten. The title of the reflection was "Connecting the Dots". Vincent thought back to the times he had stopped by NaPiles after school. Cédric had always been able to find time to drop everything and sit down to chat or play cards. As he read the words, he distinctly remembered the sound of Cedric's voice.

"Ancient mariners gazing into the night sky imagined patterns in the constellations resembling various forms. It's hard for me to see rams and crabs in the stars. It's just as easy for me to connect the stars in the pattern of a quadracopter or a Teddy bear, but this underscores the natural tendency for man to want to connect the dots. Images of clusters of galaxies from space telescopes have shown us that the universe is every bit as strange and foreboding today as it was to the unaided eye of ancient mariners. Nevertheless, man draws comfort from seeing patterns and relationships between objects in an attempt to reduce complexity to something intelligible. It doesn't matter whether stars are superimposed on the form of a crab or a unifying theory of gravity is sought; complexity is troubling to the human intellect, and mankind is compelled to make logical sense of things he does not comprehend. Compounded with apparent chaos, the world we inhabit seems unpredictable and uncontrollable. By connecting the dots, we think we are bringing order to the universe, and we gain a sense of security. (This is true whether man attributes a predictable influence on the zodiac on human behavior or presumes to unravel the mystery of the 'Big Bang').

The term 'connecting the dots' originates from the puzzles familiar to us from childhood, where an apparently random pattern of numbered dots appears on the page. Solving the puzzle consists of drawing straight lines between dots in numerical order to reveal an underlying image. The term 'connecting the dots' is a metaphor illustrating an ability (or inability) to associate one idea with another, to find the big picture, or salient feature, in a mass of data. We learn from an early age that the ability to connect the dots in clever and innovative ways is a good indication of professional acumen. Highly effective people are skilled at it. It demonstrates the ability to make good plans and then execute them. These are prerequisite skills for successful living, we are told. In my career, I was pretty good at networking: identifying critical elements that, once they could be connected together in just the right fashion, would certainly lead to some disruptive transformation. I could think outside the box and envision novel ways to connect the elements together. Just like all the famous inventors, I envisioned myself as being able to fit the pieces together and could articulate the vision for executing the plan. The ability to connect the dots is viewed as a gift that those who possess it can use for strategic advantage. They think it gives them a glimpse into the future. I desired to use my insight into how events might unfold to help move things along. I simply wanted to forecast the future."

Mankind hates uncertainty and the inability to predict the future. We hunger not only to know the weather forecast for next week but when to expect our sun to burn out. Why is this? Even if we were to know the future with certainty, what value would this have? Perhaps one could make a killing in the stock market or in gambling casinos, but if everyone else could see into the future, there would be no such thing as gambling. There would merely be a waiting for such a predetermined future to come to pass — a very dull existence if you ask me. So, what's the point?"

In the 18th Century, scientists had concluded that the universe was inherently deterministic. That is, once all the differential equations that determine behavior were known, they would be able to predict the future with certainty. This notion was very appealing to secular humanists because it provided the very framework for viewing the world as a giant clockwork that did not require any attention from the outside. One hundred and fifty years ago, this whole notion of causality went out the window with the advent of quantum mechanics. Not only was the universe not predictable, but it was also no longer even knowable. Mankind has been struggling with the implications ever since. How can we possibly inhabit a huge sphere careening through space at high speed if the universe is as chaotic and unpredictable as quantum mechanics now claims? How can we possibly discover the meaning of life if we have no hope of influencing our own destiny?

This question more or less stalked me most of my adult life. After a long career of struggle and unfulfilled dreams, I was faced with bad health, and was forced to abandon any hope that my accomplishments would have any lasting significance. That is when God led me to the realization that my attempts at 'connecting the dots' were nothing more than witchcraft and idolatry. This may seem a bit harsh, but here's what I mean. Just like with ancient mariners, I had been connecting the dots according to familiar earthly things, like crabs and rams, rather than heavenly things which I had never actually seen and that possibly did not yet exist. God showed me that, as with bright stars in a distant constellation, there was nothing wrong with the stars which I had identified as significant. The problem was with my insistence on connecting them together with imaginary lines to make figures that looked like things I knew, that were familiar to me. This is why astrology is witchcraft—it assigns the power to human forms that really belong to God alone. Like children connecting the dots of the puzzle, we draw straight lines between the dots. In fact, if the lines aren't straight and in the right sequence, there is a pretty good chance the underlying image won't be recognizable. This is because the creator of the puzzle started with a familiar object that served as the template on which the dots are placed. Then the original image was erased to make the puzzle. But this is precisely how we view the future—as a puzzle to be solved by craft and cunning to reveal the underlying image that we hope to ultimately recognize.

So, where does this leave us? Is every human endeavor simply hubris? Is there no point in pursuing dreams and visions? The first hint at the answer came to me from the book of Exodus in the Bible. The Israelites were wandering around in the desert without food or water. The first order of business was survival. In this context it is indeed curious that God chose to provide their daily sustenance in the form of a mysterious bread-like substance called manna. It was some sort of food that no one had ever seen before (or since). But even more curious was the admonition to only collect as much each day as they could consume on that day, except the day before the Sabbath, when they could collect a double portion. Why didn't God just airlift in piles of barley? Why give some strange substance that became foul in twenty-four hours? Wouldn't it have been better to just get them to the Promise Land where they could fend for themselves? Better yet, if He could kill off the firstborns, why didn't He just annihilate the Egyptians and let Israel assume control of the fertile Nile Delta? The answer is that God needed to teach them, first and foremost, to live by faith. I can tell you from first-hand experience that living by faith is terrifying for someone like me, who always wants to be in control.

So why is it so wrong for His creatures to want to be in control? After all, that is what we desire for our children, that they learn self-reliance and leave home at some point. Doesn't God want the same for us? This leads right back to the issue of idolatry and witchcraft. Inevitably, people choose self-reliance in the form of some golden calf to lead the way. We want to get our clues regarding what the future holds from the zodiac and fortune-tellers rather than from the very God who created our future. Thinking we are in control is the ultimate trap because the future is not determined by crabs and rams, but by an eternal loving God. We would engineer our future based on things we have seen—things from the past. The future that God offers consists of things yet to be seen. The book of Hebrews in the Bible says, 'Now faith is the assurance of things hoped for, the conviction of things not seen.' What possible benefit can there be in a future based on past things rather than a future based on new things that don't exist yet?

At this point, it is necessary to make a critical distinction between dreams and visions, and the act of 'connecting the dots.' Man on his own tries to discern patterns according to his own wisdom and understanding in order to predict the future. This is idolatry. God occasionally gives visions and dreams about what the future holds to prepare us for the totally unexpected. Orion's Belt consists of three bright stars roughly in a straight line. God posed the question to Job, 'Can you lose Orion's Belt?' Why, that's ridiculous. Of course not. This would require moving around a few stars. That would mean violating the laws of physics. This absurd rhetorical question affirms that such an act is well within God's abilities if He chooses, but totally unnecessary. More importantly, when people see three dots in a row, they naturally connect them with a straight line. This is how our brains are wired. It is the logical step in Euclidean geometry. Of course, there are an infinite number of paths that can be drawn through those three dots if not restricted to straight lines. But contemplating this introduces a degree of complexity that our human brain has difficulty dealing with. Just like with the Heisenberg Uncertainty Principle, once we embark on this path, by permitting the dots to be connected by curves, we give up all hope of solving the puzzle on our own. Orion's Belt is not a belt at all, just three points in an infinity of shapes. God does not need to move the stars around to reveal new forms. He merely needs to adjust the curve that connects them. Occasionally, He even gives mortal man a peek at the true shape, but since it doesn't exist yet, we generally have trouble recognizing it. The future is never familiar. Some things are predictable and reliable, like the sunrise and appearance of manna each morning. Everything else relies on faith that the future will unfold according to His perfect plan.

I must admit that what follows is a bit radical. The idea flows logically from Chapter 4 in the book of Hebrews, 'For we who have believed enter that rest, just as He has said, 'As I swore in My wrath, they shall not enter My rest', although His works were finished from the foundation of the world.' Apparently, those who fail to enter His rest are those lacking the faith to do so. But what does this mean, 'His works were finished from the foundation of the world'? When it says, 'He rested on the seventh day.' This does not mean He was just taking a break. The work was finished. There was nothing more to do. We enter His rest by entering His works that have already been completed. We are not tasked with completing His unfinished business. God did not pause to catch His breath and then carry on with creation on the eighth day. There was nothing more to create. It was completely finished on the sixth day! The implications are profound. Not only was the design for the DNA that determines why my eyes are blue completed, but also things like how to string neutrons together were figured out. I merely get to experience the exhilaration of solving His puzzle.

This raises the troubling issues of 'predestination' and 'foreknowledge'. Don't such things rule out free will and rob us of the ability to create new things on our own? After all, what good is the Mona Lisa if it pre-existed De Vinci's canvas? The answer lies in whether De Vinci was fulfilling God's plan and purpose or his own. The same test applies to neutron coils and microfusion reactors.

Returning again to the puzzle analogy: I dare say, people like me derive pleasure from solving them. The sense of accomplishment would be less if we solved a puzzle that we already had the answer to. Jigsaw puzzles are perhaps a better example. People spend countless hours on them to complete and reveal the underlying image. When they complete one, they simply start another. The image of God's finished creation is no different, except besides being ponderously huge and complex—allowing us to work on only a small section at a time—this puzzle has the added difficulty that Satan has mixed in a bunch of pieces from another puzzle that don't fit into this one. Where we really become frustrated is when we waste time trying to figure out where these wrong pieces go. They don't. At the end of the age, when all the true pieces of the puzzle are in place, all of these extra pieces will go into the fire. Only the works that are consistent with God's perfect creation will remain. I hope this includes the Mona Lisa and antigravity, but only time will tell. In the meantime, I shall continue to experience the joy of working on His puzzle and stop trying to convince Him that his Work needs a little improvement.

The important thing is that we can't connect the dots because the things in God's creation that they point to don't exist yet. By faith, Noah built an ark (Heb. 11:7). An ark? No one had ever seen a boat, let alone an ocean-going vessel 450 feet in length. Noah could never have connected the dots to do this based on anything familiar to him. No amount of connecting the dots could have produced such a vessel. But in fact, the dots had already been connected. All Noah had to do was follow instructions by faith. Could Noah have possibly envisioned a future postdiluvian world with clouds and rainbows and rain and snow?

Recently, some projects I have been working on for years—'my' dots—started falling into place. I was so excited that when I showed the puzzle that was beginning to take shape to God for approval, it was as if He said, "That's nice, but it looks a lot like a crab to me. Why don't you be patient for a while longer. Your dots won't connect to form anything you have ever seen. — J. Cédric Rothschild, May 12, 2060."

Vincent carefully closed the journal and placed it back inside the folio with the rest of Cédric's papers. He had a strange sense that the reflection he had just read had been written as a letter specifically to him. Cédric had anticipated a day when someone else would have to 'connect the dots' of antigravity.

Chapter 27: The Network

"Do you have a reservation for Vincent Gilbert?" Vincent asked stepping up to the reception desk.

"Good evening, Dr. Gilbert. We have been expecting you," the receptionist said, handing him the reservation card. "Is this your first time at Northern Lights Resort and Spa?"

"Yes," replied Vincent. "I have always wanted to stop over on one of my transatlantic trips and never made the time."

"Well, you are in for a real treat," said the receptionist. "The Northern Lights are in their full glory tonight and the sky is practically cloudless. The blizzard we were expecting never materialized. The best viewing is from our spa, which is encapsulated by a glass hemisphere. You are in room 302. The elevator is on the right and everything you will need for the spa is in your room. Enjoy your stay."

The resort was a popular stopping-off place for portal travelers coming and going to North America or Asia, affording an opportunity to recover from *décalage horaire*, or jet lag, caused by hyperspeed travel that typically traversed seven time zones in about an hour. In Vincent's case, he was still on Paris time, so there were no effects of high-speed travel—at least, not yet. His room had a picture window overlooking the glacier flowing into the bay on Svalbard Island. It was bathed in green and blue iridescent light from the Aurora Borealis that shimmered mysteriously overhead. He made a dinner reservation for eight o'clock and then selected a swimsuit from the assortment in the wardrobe. Putting on the bathrobe and slippers provided by the hotel, he headed to the world-famous spa.

It was not as crowded as he had expected. The hotel was enormous and was designed with ample room to give every guest plenty of space. Vincent headed straight for the grottos, which were a series of hot pools created among natural boulders. The temperature of each pool decreased as the water flowed down from the steaming hot inlet at the top. He found a pool with a temperature to his liking and slipped in up to his neck. The steam rising from the hot water of his pool encompassed him like a blanket. The only light was coming from the Aurora, which cast faint shadows through the glass dome overhead. Every worry on his mind began to melt away. He closed his eyes to relish the experience.

"Hello, Vincent," came a vaguely familiar voice from the other side of the pool out of the fog.

"Who's there?" Vincent asked.

"Tor Andersen," he said. "Do you mind if I join you?"

"Tor! What a happy coincidence!" Vincent said. "Please, come join me. Isn't this magnificent?"

"Meeting up with you is not exactly a coincidence," Tor said, coming over to Vincent's side of the pool. "There are some things we need to discuss."

Vincent stared at Tor Andersen in disbelief. "Really? Is no place safe? I can't even get away from all this in the grottos in Longyearbyen?" exclaimed Vincent.

Tor smiled at him and said, "This may be the safest place on the planet right now. I need to explain a few things to you. You can't do all this by yourself. The burden is too heavy. You need to learn to trust the Network."

"What is this 'Network'?" Vincent asked. "I heard you mention it to Jacques."

"That's precisely why I am here, to explain it to you," replied Tor. "Have you heard the term, 'supranational entity'?"

"You mean like the United Nations?" asked Vincent.

"No," said Tor. "The United Nations is not a supranational entity; they are an international entity. There is a big difference. The UN is a collective of member states that considers matters of global, as well as regional, concerns. They must agree by democratic consensus. In principle, no nation, large or small, has primacy over the others. This is not the case with a supranational entity, which operates globally beyond the reach of individual sovereign states. Of course, you recognize the Syndicate as being such an entity. Individual states and even collectives like the United Nations are defenseless against them. The Syndicate does, or at least tries to do, whatever it pleases, anywhere it chooses and at any time of its choosing, without any oversight. Who makes up their top echelons, we can only guess, but they have infiltrated nearly every instrument of government and civilian society in key positions where they can exert the maximum influence. They are heads of state, government officials, business owners, military officials, you name it. We generally don't know who they are because they operate covertly among us. But we see their influence everywhere we look. You have seen how this works first-hand in Romania, where an already weakened government was infiltrated by elected officials that colluded with bankers and big business to squeeze out private ownership, not only of family farms but to drive thousands of small enterprises out of business. Individual freedom is the enemy of the Syndicate. They increase their power by subverting freedom and enslaving people to do their will."

"Yes," said Vincent. "I have been battling them my entire adult life. But how do we stop them? Destroying their base in the Black Sea and blowing up a few timecharging spheres is certainly not going to do it."

This made Tor smile, and he said, "You are absolutely right, Vincent. There is another way. The Syndicate is not the only supranational entity that exists. There is another one."

"The Network?" Vincent asked. "Is that what my father is involved in?"

Tor lowered his voice and said, "One thing about the Network that I must make clear from the start; we never disclose anyone's name or relationship in conversations." He paused, adding, "and we never use the word 'Network' except in direct conversation like we are having now. Never use the word on the phone or in written communications or in emails. Is that clear?"

Vincent nodded.

"The Syndicate is powerful, but they are not omniscient," said Tor.

"I keep hearing that expression," said Vincent, "and..."

Tor raised his index finger to stop him. "You have probably figured out by now that this is code. You only use those words when you have absolute trust in the person you are telling it to and you must never, I mean never, disclose to any third party who you heard say those words."

Vincent leaned back on the bench in the grotto, eyes wide with surprise.

Tor looked intently into them until he was certain that the admonition had sunk in. "Okay then," he continued. "The Network is a supranational entity, just like the Syndicate, with a very significant difference. Whereas the Syndicate exercises control by subversion, the Network does not seek to control anyone or anything. Its objective is to set people free. It is a lot easier to enslave people than it is to set them free, so those committed to Network principles not only have a greater challenge, but they also have a higher calling."

"Sandi used to say, 'she was tired of slaying dragons'," said Vincent. "I think I have reached the same point. I'm not sure I can do this anymore."

"That's because 'slaying dragons' is an individual pursuit. No one is equipped to keep that up for long," said Tor. "Are you ready for your new assignment that doesn't involve slaying dragons?"

"I don't know what that means," Vincent replied.

"Vincent," said Tor with emphasis. "You have been entrusted with an important talent."

"What talent is that?" replied Vincent. "I'm not sure what more I am capable of doing."

"This talent is not the kind of talent you have in mind," said Tor. "You have knowledge of something that will impact the future of mankind for all time."

"I still don't know what you mean," said Vincent.

"Antigravity," said Tor.

"Antigravity?" responded Vincent, "How do you know about that?"

The mention of antigravity took Vincent completely by surprise. "If there were such a thing as antigravity," he said finally, "if it were ever to fall into Syndicate hands, the world as we know it would be finished."

Tor smiled and said nothing.

"I'm serious," said Vincent. "The Syndicate monopolized timecharging technology and we are facing the greatest threat in history. They stole my neutron filament winder and everything I developed at Ashleigh Airships. Can you imagine what would happen if they ever got their hands on an antigravity device?"

Tor leaned back and sat quietly, gazing up at the magnificent light show overhead. Then he looked back at Vincent and said, "So you have a dilemma. You can bury your talent in the ground because you fear the consequences of failure, or you can put it to work for the good of mankind."

The reference once again to the parable in Matthew's Gospel was clear to Vincent. He sat quietly, going over the cryptic admonition he had received at the end of his strange encounter with Emperor Napoleon at the Château de Versailles. "I can't make this decision on my own," he finally admitted.

"I was hoping you would reach that conclusion," said Tor, stepping out of the grotto and grabbing his towel.

"I have an eight o'clock dinner reservation," Vincent said. "Will you join me?"

"I'm sorry," Tor replied. "I need to catch the portal back to Paris. My work here is done. I will be in touch. Give my regards to your lovely wife." Then, he walked out of the spa.

Hydrogen supply dirigible number 0864 lumbered silently to the south over Bucharest. The sight of these huge vessels was not in the least bit uncommon, but on this particular dark and moonless night, the airship was barely visible. No one would have considered it unusual to see the craft flying at low altitude above the ground.

It loitered imperceptibly above the compound in the southern suburb of the city and settled down on the roof of one of the buildings. Four marine commandoes jumped out and carefully removed a few roofing tiles after cutting through the plastic liner. The factory was dark except for one security floodlight. Two of the marines dropped down on ropes to the floor below. One of them plugged a closed-circuit video image into the security camera while the other disconnected the power lines and attached slings to the underside of the machine. Two cables were lowered by the marines on the roof, attached to the slings and brought taught. The gate valve on the ballast tank was opened to release water weighing the same as the machine, and in barely an instant, Vincent's neutron filament winder was hoisted into the cargo bay of the dirigible. The ropes were retracted, pulling up the marines from below. The roofing tiles were replaced, and everything was secured back into the airship, which silently ascended once again to one thousand meters before heading south.

Stephan was waiting anxiously on the bridge of the *Bougainville* which was stationary in international waters in the Black Sea, carrying out a routine cleanup of the accumulated floating plastic trash.

"Dirigible 0864 inbound," announced Tanya over the intercom. "ETA is 0610 hundred hours."

Stephan glanced at the chronometer on the wall, noting that the dirigible would not be arriving for another hour. His gaze was fixed on the video monitor hooked up to the gamma ray imaging system that had been installed on the superstructure overhead along with the radars. It could see over the horizon, so he would know immediately if any unusual hostile Syndicate activity was detected. He checked the firing status of the Viper X antiaircraft missile on his lap. Tanya had modified the sensor to track incoming enemy craft in the ultra-short wavelength regime that would make the timecharging spheres visible. In the event that the Syndicate might have detected that the neutron filament winder had been stolen from their compound in Bucharest, he was ready to blow them out of the sky.

Captain Shaw emerged from his quarters after catching a little nap. "Don't you ever sleep, Stephan?" he asked.

Stephan simply shook his head without taking his eyes off the gamma imaging screen.

"Your idea to modify one of the dirigibles with a cargo bay was very clever," Shaw remarked.

Again, Stephan simply nodded to acknowledge that he had appreciated the captain's comment without losing his focus. Captain Shaw brought him a cup of coffee, for which he was very grateful. The first streaks of daybreak could now be seen, and the captain picked up a pair of binoculars to scan the horizon. He caught a glint of sunlight coming from 0864.

"There she is!" Shaw exclaimed, pointing to the horizon. Stephan did not take his eyes off the gamma screen. The fact that the dirigible was visible was of no consequence. It was the timecharging spheres he was worried about. The movement of the dirigible was agonizingly slow. She finally approached the

Bougainville from the stern and gently dropping down into the aft docking cradle, where the deck hands secured it with cables.

"I'm heading down to the flight deck," said Captain Shaw. "Are you coming?"

"No," replied Stephan. "I need to remain here to keep an eye out for any incoming Syndicate spheres. I won't breathe easily until the device is safely stowed below deck."

A forklift was on hand on the flight deck to greet the arrival of 0864. The cargo bay doors opened, and the marine commandoes disembarked first, more than just a little relieved to be on board the ship. The neutron filament winder was lowered onto the forklift and moved to the elevator platform, which descended to the deck below and into the room next to the ship's machine shop that had been prepared for it.

Stephan arrived at that moment to survey the scene and check out Vincent's machine.

"No signs of Syndicate spheres, then?" Shaw asked him.

"Apparently not. It seems my guys pulled the mission off without being detected," Stephan said, proudly. "It's true that the Syndicate is powerful, but they are not omniscient," he said to Captain Shaw under his breath. Then he went over to his men, who were standing at attention and went down the line giving each of them a grateful handshake and a kiss on both cheeks.

Vincent's autopod dropped him off at Vice-Admiral Brundt's front door in Bethesda. Sandi and Louisa ran out to greet him. He embraced Sandi and picked up Louisa, who wrapped her arms around his neck and laid her head on his shoulder.

"Did Grandad make it home from the hospital?" he asked.

"Yes," replied Sandi. "He is resting. Come inside. Have you had lunch?"

They walked arm in arm into the house. "I'm dying to hear what you have been up to," Sandi said.

"I have so much to tell you," said Vincent. "I don't know where to start. I think I know how to build an antigravity engine. Cédric worked it all out. But I learned a lot more from his journal than just the pure science."

They sat together in the breakfast nook holding hands across the table. Vincent glanced up at the crucifix that Sandi had left with her grandmother when she went away to college that was hanging on the wall above her head.

Vincent said, "Cédric's writings have altered my perspective on life. The responsibility of having the knowledge of how to build an antigravity engine and the implications for the future of humanity have been weighing heavily on me, as I think it did on Cédric. It turns out that Cédric struggled with many of the same issues that I am struggling with. The difference is that he didn't go down that scientific path by himself. He walked a spiritual path at the same time and sought guidance from God. The anxiety of carrying this burden by myself has simply been wearing me out. I thought it would be up to me to figure out every detail of the Syndicate's strategy so that I could lead the crusade to defeat them. It turns out that we were never meant to go slay dragons by ourselves. I have discovered that there is a whole constellation of stars involved in this pursuit with a complex network of interactions that are hidden from view."

Sandi said, "I think what you are describing is the reason I couldn't bring myself to pursue a naval career after the *Dauphine Rêve* incident. What does this mean for you?" she asked.

"That guy I met in Bucharest, the one on that note in Cédric's folio?"

"Pastor Joel?" asked Sandi.

"Yes," replied Vincent. "I think he had a lot to do with Cédric spiritual walk. Perhaps when things blow over, you and I could make a trip together to Bucharest. He is someone I would like you to meet."

Vincent and Sandi sat quietly together, reflecting on all that had taken place in the prior months that neither of them seemed to have any control over. Finally, Vincent said, "One thing is certain. I am done trying to fight this battle on my own. Do you remember the dinner we had at the Officer's Club with your grandfather and that other guy named Jonathan?" Vincent asked.

"Vaguely," replied Sandi.

"He was the guy that arranged to have the Timecharger installed aboard Captain Shaw's Arleigh Burke destroyer," said Vincent. "I need to talk with him. He may have some answers."

Sandi said, "When Grandad wakes up, maybe he will know how to contact him."

Vincent looked intently into her eyes and said, "Sandi, Darling. I think the time has come for us to give up the crusade for slaying dragons, at least for a few days." They both laughed.

Chapter 28: The Talent

Vincent woke up late the following morning and wandered into the kitchen at about nine.

"You look rested," commented Sandi. "Did you sleep well?"

"Yes," he replied, "except for the weird dreams. I can't remember the last time I had such vivid dreams. I thought I would remember them when I woke up, but now they are gone. Where's Louisa?"

"She went with Mama to the store," said Sandi. "They should be back any minute,"

"I thought your mom was in Savannah," said Vincent.

"She came back this morning with a big check from the insurance adjusters," replied Sandi. "She says she is done with Georgia's cold winters and hot summers. She is thinking of moving back to France."

"I'm not sure Bretagne winters are much of an improvement," commented Vincent.

"No," she replied. "She is thinking more along the lines of the Côte D'Azur. Saint-Tropez, maybe."

"It must have been a very big check, then," said Vincent, poking his head into the refrigerator for something to snack on.

"There's not much in there, I'm afraid," commented Sandi. "Mama said she planned to pick up some croissants for breakfast. Granddad is awake and asked to see you when you get up."

"Let's go say 'hi' to him, then," said Vincent.

"No, he only wants to talk to you," she replied. "He said he has something to tell you in private."

Vincent knocked quietly at the Admiral's bedroom door, which was ajar. "Is it all right if I come in?" he asked.

"Vincent! Yes, come in, come in. It's so good to see you again. It's been more than a year," said the Admiral, sitting up in bed and stuffing some pillows behind his back. "When I had the heart attack, I thought maybe it would be the end of me, but here I am, with two brand new stents, and now I am better than ever. There is something important I need to tell you." He picked up the empty glass on the bedside table and handed it to the attending nurse. "Betsy, would you be a dear and fetch me another glass of orange juice?" he said, "and pull the door closed when you leave?" His smile was broad and welcoming as he surveyed Vincent up and down. "It looks like you have lost weight, my son. Please, have a seat," he said, pointing to the chair next to his bed. "Would you like me to have Betsy bring you some coffee?"

"No, thank you, I'm fine," replied Vincent. He desperately wanted to ask the Admiral for advice about what he should do with the antigravity discovery, but he was beaten to the punch.

"Vincent," the Admiral began. "Do you remember the dinner at the Officer's Club when we first met?"

"Vividly, sir," Vincent answered.

"You probably assumed I was assessing you to determine if you might be someone suitable to have my granddaughter keep company with," he said. "Actually, I already knew the answer was affirmative. You passed the test."

"Thank you, sir," Vincent replied.

The Admiral continued, "but that's not why I invited you to have dinner that night. What I was really more interested in was hearing from you about timecharging." He paused to enjoy the suspense. "Do you recall the other person who was at the table with us, a man named Jonathan?"

Vincent nodded to the affirmative. "Actually, sir," he said. "I was hoping you might be able to tell me how to contact him."

The Admiral responded, "You may remember my comment concerning Jonathan that, 'In Virginia, there is the Admiralty, and then there is—well let's just say I am part of another group.'"

"I remember it well, sir," said Vincent.

"Do you have any thoughts on who that other group might be?" asked the Admiral.

"I have an inkling," replied Vincent. "I seem to keep bumping into people who share my passion for bringing down the Syndicate."

"Then you must be aware, Vincent, that the Syndicate is powerful, but they are not omniscient," said the Admiral with careful deliberation. "That man, Jonathan, shares your passion for bringing down the Syndicate. The things you came to discuss with me are best left to discuss with him. He is waiting for you in California."

California was the last place on earth Vincent expected to go next, but he nodded to acknowledge that he had understood the order and would follow it.

"There is a jet waiting for you at Andrews," said the Admiral. "They will be taking you and your entire family to Southern California. I can assure you that you won't regret it."

"I will arrange for Héloïse and Louisa to stay at a hotel, then, while Sandi and I are gone," replied Vincent, not knowing what else to say.

"No, no, you didn't hear me," said the Admiral. "the whole family, including Héloïse and Louisa." He paused and chuckled, "and Max, of course."

Vincent could not imagine the wisdom of taking his mother-in-law, her dog and his four-year-old daughter on one of his dangerous missions, but he dared not challenge the command. "Yes, sir," he said, standing to leave.

"Vincent," said the Admiral, whose smile had never left his face. "You have no idea how proud I am of you."

A van was waiting out front of Vice-Admiral Brundt's townhome in the naval retirement community of Bethesda. Sandi and Louisa got in the back after handing their bags to the driver. Héloïse was carrying Max, who was smartly dressed in a knit sweater. The confused dog yapped at the driver, who paid no attention.

“He doesn’t like strangers,” she said, and hopped in the back of the van.

Vincent got into the passenger seat. “Do you know where we are going?” he asked.

“Yes, sir,” said the driver. “It will take us about forty-five minutes on the Beltway barring unexpected traffic.”

Vincent sat quietly, looking out the window at the woods covered with two-week-old snow. The trees stood lifeless, waiting patiently for the return of spring. The sky was opaque gray with low-hanging clouds threatening more snow flurries. California? He asked himself. Why in the world would the Admiral be sending him to California? Hardly anything made sense anymore. The people around him seemed to know a great deal about a lot of things, but then again, not one of them seemed to know everything. What was going on around him was a matrix of random encounters that seemed to follow some sort of logical pattern that he could not discern. He had lost any hope of connecting the dots. Now he was just along for the ride. Just like Doctor Ferguson in *Five Weeks in a Balloon*, ‘I do not follow my route, it follows me’.”

When the van arrived at the airfield, it was waved through the security gate by the military guards on duty. It pulled up to the rear entrance of a large hangar and someone came out immediately with a luggage dolly, and a dog kennel for Max. The driver began retrieving their things from the back.

“Hello, Dr. Gilbert. Welcome,” said a woman who introduced herself to everyone as their aide-de-camp for the trip. The oak leaves on her lapel were those of a colonel. “Come this way,” she said. “The jet is waiting.”

The plane taxied out of the hangar and, only moments later, was screaming down the adjacent runway with more acceleration than Vincent had ever experienced. Louisa was understandably anxious and sat in his lap clutched in her father’s reassuring embrace. The jet headed skyward at a more rapid rate than Vincent would have thought possible, and in about ten minutes, the noise of the engines ceased, and the passengers began having a sense of weightlessness. Vincent peered out the window at the totally black sky above and the brightly illuminated earth far below.

“Are we in orbit?” he asked the colonel.

“Yes, low earth orbit,” she replied with a smile. “We are now 120 kilometers above the earth traveling 3,600 kilometers per hour. We should be arriving over California in about seventy minutes.”

“What kind of a jet is this?” asked a very shocked Vincent. By this time, Louisa had begun to enjoy the sensation of weightlessness and was flying back and forth across the aisle to her mother.

“This is called a hypersonic transport,” replied the colonel.

“Why have I never heard of it?” Vincent asked.

The colonel smiled and said, “Because it doesn’t exist.”

"What do you mean, it doesn't exist?" said Vincent. "I'm riding in it."

"The plane is real enough," she said, "but it was constructed under a top-secret program. The general public has no knowledge of this craft. It is hardly taken out of the hangar anymore because it is too costly to operate. It is only used to transport VIPs."

Vincent looked around for other passengers. "Is there a VIP on board?" he asked.

"Just you, Dr. Gilbert," she said with a chuckle. "Would you care to know more about the plane?"

"Definitely!" Vincent replied.

"As I said, the plane is called a hypersonic transport. It was designed to go anywhere in the world very fast. It has a top speed of Mach 7.5, which is faster than we are going now, but our speed is determined by the distance to San Clemente Island."

"San Clemente Island?" queried Vincent.

"Yes," replied the colonel. "That is our destination. Let me tell you more about the plane. It has twin SCRAM-jet engines that operate on liquid hydrogen fuel. While in earth atmosphere, it uses oxygen from the air, but at the cruising altitude we have now reached, oxygen is provided from onboard liquid oxygen tanks. I don't need to tell you that this plane is a technological marvel. The problem is that it consumes a lot of fuel just to reach altitude. We consumed about one hundred tons of liquid hydrogen just to get into orbit, and we will only burn about a ton more before we reach San Clemente Island. So, as I said, this is a very costly plane to operate. It requires authorization from the very highest level to take it up."

Vincent was completely amazed. He looked across the aisle at Sandi, who had been listening in on the briefing and seemed equally astonished.

"You can imagine, Dr. Gilbert," continued the colonel, looking directly at Vincent, "what it would mean for hypersonic travel in low earth orbit if we didn't need to burn so much fuel just to escape the earth's gravity."

Vincent and Sandi locked eyes. Both knew instantly what the trip was all about.

A light turned on overhead followed by a chime. "I see we are about to start our descent," said the colonel. "It is generally quite bumpy on the way down, so I suggest that everyone fasten their seatbelts, and I will see you again when we land."

Vincent recognized Jonathan standing on the tarmac next to the single runway on San Clemente Island. After the plane came to a stop and the stairs were deployed, a van pulled up to the bottom of the staircase to retrieve the passengers and the luggage, and a liquid hydrogen tanker truck approached the plane to begin refueling it for the return trip to the East Coast. The colonel remained at the top of the stairs and waved goodbye. A hot Santa Ana wind swept the desert island located one hundred kilometers off the coastline of Southern California that once served as a bombing range for the US Navy. Everyone was introduced and piled into the van, which took them to a small dock on the leeward side of the island, where a bright orange lifeboat tender was tied up.

"Where are we going?" asked Vincent.

Jonathan pointed to a ship a few hundred meters away.

"That's a cargo ship," exclaimed Vincent.

"No ordinary cargo ship, I can assure you," replied Jonathan. "Just wait until you see what is in store for you."

They took the short ride out to the ship. Lines were lowered which the deck hands secured to the tender, and they were hoisted up onto the deck of the ship which was stacked with standard forty-foot shipping containers of every color. The captain came to greet them as they climbed out of the tender. "Welcome aboard *Fast Transit One*," he said. "I am Captain Tom Waller, and this is Commander Ferguson. He will be your escort while on board." Then, looking at Héloïse, he said, "It would be a good idea to keep your dog on a leash. Otherwise, he might get lost among the shipping containers. Let's head to the bridge now. I have prepared some snacks if anyone is hungry. The voyage should only take about two hours."

"Where are we going?" asked Héloïse.

"Hawaii, Ma'am," replied the captain.

"Hawaii?" she exclaimed. "That's three thousand miles away."

"Two thousand five hundred and twenty-five, to be exact, Ma'am," said the captain, heading up the stairs as the ship was getting under way.

Once everyone was on the bridge, Sandi and Vincent stepped outside onto the catwalk to take in the view. Inside the bridge, Héloïse asked again, "Captain, did you really mean two hours?" He looked at Jonathan and they both grinned. Outside, Sandi lingered at the railing, gazing at the waves and taking in the ocean breeze. "Oh, Vincent," she said. "I never thought I would be glad to be back at sea." Vincent put his arm around her lovingly.

The captain informed everyone, "We will be sailing west for another few minutes in order to be well over the horizon. The Long Beach Harbor Master gets very agitated when ships suddenly disappear from his radar screen." He turned to the officer on deck and said, "Tell me when you are ready."

"We can deploy the decoy in five minutes," he replied. The captain lifted Louisa up onto the captain's chair and let her sound the foghorn. This startled Max and caused him to whimper.

Sandi and Vincent came back inside after several minutes. Héloïse said to them, "The captain was just joking that we are going to Hawaii." The captain and Johnathan exchanged amused looks once again.

"It's time," said the captain to the pilot, who pushed a red button on the console. The ship began to vibrate and the scene outside switched to an iridescent glow. Vincent and Sandi shared a moment of surprise upon recognizing the familiar effect of timecharging.

Vincent's eyes were wide as he looked over at Jonathan for confirmation, who was smiling broadly. Jonathan said, "How else did you think we would make it to Hawaii in two hours?"

"Where did you get the timecharger?" asked Vincent.

"From the Trump," replied Jonathan.

"That's not possible," said Vincent. "That was my father's timecharger. It is sitting in the warehouse at the NRL, just outside my former office."

Jonathan took a sip of coffee and asked, "Did you ever try to switch that one on?"

"Of course not," Vincent replied. "It was under the ban."

The glow outside became dim, indicating the start of the first night.

"So then, how can you be sure that it was actually your father's timecharger?" asked Jonathan, deriving immense pleasure from watching the expression of total surprise on Vincent's face. "It's a dummy, you know. What? Did you really think we were going to turn the real timecharger over to the NRL to let it rust in a corner after what you did with it off Guadeloupe?" He said, "Come over here. There is something I want to show you. We learned this trick from you on *L'Astrolabe*, when you figured out how the Syndicate submarine was able to track you." He pointed out the window at a cylinder extending twenty meters into the air. That pipe is heated to four hundred degrees to give it just the right heat signature in order for the drone that is following us to track us. The drone is just an inflatable with a navigational transponder on board so that people outside will think they know where we are, even though we are invisible."

"But timecharging has been banned by the United Nations by international treaty," protested Vincent.

"I suppose you mean the same treaty that the Syndicate is abiding by?" shot back Jonathan, heading to refill his coffee mug. "There are sandwiches in the mess. Would you like one?"

Vincent followed him off the bridge. "But Jonathan," he said. "How in the world have you been able to keep this secret?"

"That's a very interesting question," Jonathan replied, stirring some cream into his coffee and selecting a finger sandwich. "These are very good. Would you like one?"

Vincent stood motionless and just shook his head in disbelief.

"Let me explain something," said Jonathan. "I was planning to go into detail once we reached Pearl Harbor, but now is as good a time as any. Something very significant happened when the United States broke apart. The Pacific Fleet had been decimated in the Battle of the South China Sea. Pearl Harbor had become irrelevant as a strategic base in the Pacific. There were fewer and fewer commercial airlines serving the islands because of the high cost of jet fuel. Cruise ships quit coming, and the islands were too remote to ever consider constructing a submarine portal. Hawaii no longer retained its recognized status as an American possession, and it was never claimed by any of the resulting prefectures because it would be too difficult to administer from the Mainland. Hawaii was simply forgotten amidst all the chaos. For a while, it reverted back to its primitive state where those hardy inhabitants who stayed behind just lived off the land in total isolation, much the way Captain James Cook discovered it in 1778. This all changed with timecharging. A voyage of two hours in a container ship meant that supplies of all kinds could be brought to the islands and people could come and go once again. The interesting thing is that, due to the obvious need for secrecy, only a handful of people actually know this. More importantly, that handful of people turned out to be people universally devoted to bringing down the Syndicate. As far as we can tell, the Syndicate hasn't figured out what we are up to in Hawaii. They are powerful but they are not omniscient. There is no safer place on the planet for launching a counteroffensive against the Syndicate than where we are heading. There are two supranational entities about to square off with most of the world oblivious to what is actually going on."

"Does Admiral Brundt know about this?" asked Vincent.

Jonathan looked at him disapprovingly. "Vincent," he said, "weren't you instructed to never use proper names?"

"Yes," replied Vincent with growing anxiety. "I appreciate all of this," he said, "but why are you taking me and my entire family to Hawaii?"

Jonathan cast a puzzled look at Vincent. "Why? To develop the technology of antigravity, of course," he replied.

"Antigravity? How do you know about antigravity?" asked Vincent.

Jonathan, just smiled and said, "Don't you know? With the technology of antigravity, we would be able to defeat the Syndicate once and for all."

"What makes you so sure there even is such a thing as antigravity?" shot back Vincent.

Jonathan peeked at his wristwatch. "We should be emerging from timecharging in about ten more minutes," he said. Then he looked at Vincent with a very serious expression and said, "There are plenty of people who are convinced that antigravity is simply a myth. I just don't happen to be one of them. Why that is, I am not at liberty to say. But I do know that the Syndicate is gaining strength and right now we have no ability to respond."

Jonathan went over to the table and selected another finger sandwich. "Are you sure you don't want one of these?" He went on, "The United Nations banned timecharging because they feared the technology would trigger an arms race. The entire world has been looking backwards to the times when nations invaded other nations by land, sea and air. They viewed timecharging as opening up the possibility for armed aggression and throwing the world back into the war-ravaged epoch of previous centuries, and they thought they could keep this from happening. Their intentions were noble but completely misguided. They never contemplated that timecharging would be deployed in spheres dropping out of space. They never looked up. They couldn't imagine the world being invaded by a force coming from secret bases on the back side of the moon and dropping down in invisible craft everywhere, all at once. Abraham at the French Intelligence Ministry was the first to figure this out. He attempted to sound the alarm in Geneva at the United Nations Security Council, but they found such notions to be preposterous. Trying to find someone who would listen to him ultimately cost him his life, but once some of us began looking up instead of out, his warnings started becoming credible."

Jonathan walked over to Vincent and placed a hand on each of his shoulders. "Vincent, it is far too late for us to develop any kind of defense against this threat using any known technology. At best, we may have a year to prepare. The Network built up its defensive capabilities over the past few years, deploying timecharging technology in warships because we always expected the invasion to come from land, sea and air. In the end, the United Nations ended up triggering the very arms race they feared, but they gave the early head-start to the Syndicate, who was shrewder in how to gain the superior advantage. I have a pretty good idea you know how to tip the balance back to our side."

Vincent responded, "Do you have any clue how much good could be accomplished for humanity with antigravity technology? And now you want me to help you turn it into a weapon?"

Jonathan bowed his head and closed his eyes, taking in a deep breath and exhaling slowly. Then he said, "I can see why you might want to bury your talent in the ground to keep it from falling into the wrong hands. But perhaps you need to be willing to take the risk that your talent will multiply for good in the right hands."

Fast Transit One emerged from timecharging right on schedule. Diamond Head was just coming into view.

Chapter 29: Pearl

Fast Transit One inched into the entrance of Pearl Harbor, meeting up with the tugboats that would escort the ship to its berth at the Southeast Loch. The gantry cranes were in position to unload the arriving containers and replace them with empty ones for the return trip to Long Beach. Vincent and Sandi stood on the catwalk with Louisa, taking in the sight. It was 74 degrees and balmy. The warm fragrant air was a welcome respite from the cold dampness of the west coast of France. Héloïse remained inside, sitting quietly with Max on her lap. She was suddenly overwhelmed by the memory of waiting in the common area with all the other Pearl Harbor spouses for any news from the South China Sea engagement. The growing apprehension arising from the delay of any positive reports had been crushing. Finally, the news came that the Pacific Fleet had been decimated. Then, the reports of ships lost or damaged began to trickle in agonizingly. At last, the report had arrived that SSN-824, her husband's submarine, had been sunk with all hands lost. Héloïse had collapsed and gone into premature labor at that moment. Now, she sat quietly in the corner of the bridge, stroking Max and brushing away tears that hadn't flowed for thirty years.

Sandi came back inside with the others to prepare to disembark. Seeing her mother crying, she said, "Are you okay, Mama?"

"Oh, I will be fine," she said. "The sight of Pearl Harbor brought back some hard memories."

"You've been here before?" Sandi asked.

"Your father and I were stationed here for two years," Héloïse said, beginning to sob once again. "You were born right here at the base hospital."

"Mama!" exclaimed Sandi. "You never told me any of this."

"I know, I know," replied Héloïse, her voice trailing off.

"You always told me I was born in Caen," Sandi said.

"I know. It's complicated," Héloïse said, standing up to attach Max's leash. She turned to follow Vincent down the stairs. Sandi was still in a daze by the time she reached the end of the gangway. She walked up beside her mother and took her arm reassuringly. Héloïse laid her head on Sandi's shoulder, acknowledging the gesture.

Everyone was milling around on the dock while the luggage was loaded into the awaiting van. "Hello, Sandi," came a voice from someone standing with the greeting party.

"Madeline!" exclaimed Sandi, giving her a hug. "What are you doing here?"

Jonathan asked Sandi, "Do you know Ensign Calvi?"

"Yes," Sandi replied enthusiastically, "She accompanied me from Toulon to Bordeaux when I took command of *L'Astrolabe*."

"Wonderful," said Jonathan. "She will also be your liaison officer here at Pearl. She will be showing you to your quarters."

"Quarters?" asked Vincent.

"Yes," replied Jonathan. "If you don't mind, Madeline will show everyone to their housing arrangements, and Vincent, I would like you to go with me for a short tour of the facility." The others climbed into the van, and Vincent and Jonathan departed from the dock in a golf cart.

The cart pulled up in front of a dilapidated building. The sign out front said "acific leet eadquarters". Apparently, the capital letters had fallen off a long time ago. Jonathan told the driver not to wait around because they would not be coming back this way. The glass in the front door was held in place with duct tape. Jonathan pulled the door open with some effort and indicated for Vincent to go in. The foyer was dark except for the light coming in from the entrance. Jonathan inserted a card into the reader next to an elevator and the door opened immediately. He signaled for Vincent to enter and came in behind him without saying a word. The elevator descended some distance before opening up into a brightly illuminated concourse with people scurrying around like in the shopping mall at Christmas.

"Welcome to the Network," Jonathan said.

"These are all civilians," Vincent commented, noting the casual attire of the people.

"Oh, don't be fooled," Jonathan said with a grin. "If you are disrespectful to one of those guys in a Hawaiian shirt and shorts, there's a pretty good chance he or she may be an admiral."

"Without uniforms," asked Vincent, "How does anyone know who's who?"

"You would be surprised how quickly people figure out the pecking order," Jonathan said, leading the way to a two-story window looking in on a wall of video consoles and control panels. Turning around, he said, "What you see is the largest neural network computer in the world. Actually, the computer itself is buried deep inside the mountain to our north, where the US Navy once stored its strategic petroleum reserve in huge steel tanks. These tanks make wonderful Faraday cages, and the computer is virtually impregnable. The rest of Hawaii could disappear, but I dare say, the neural network computer would go on operating for centuries."

"What is the computer used for?" asked Vincent.

"Monitoring the activities of the Syndicate, mostly," replied Jonathan. "We call it MAX, not after Héloïse's dog, although that is ironic," he said after pausing to enjoy his own humor. "MAX monitors every piece of information on the planet. It tracks everything. If Jimmy falls off his bicycle in Hoboken, MAX knows it. That's not important news to you or me, but it is to Jimmy and his frantic mother. The Syndicate gained power in the world beginning by controlling the dialogue. They were able to put just the right spin on the narrative to control public opinion. Some called it "fake news", but it was far more sinister than that. If the Syndicate wanted Jimmy's bicycle crash to become an international news story, they had the ability to do it and reap millions of dollars from a fraudulent insurance claim. This is a silly example but imagine carrying out such subterfuge thousands of times every day. Elections were rigged, careers were made and ruined. The Syndicate had learned how to manipulate masses of people into believing they were thinking independently when, in fact, they were being led slowly into serfdom. How do you counter that?" asked Jonathan rhetorically. "With truth," he shot back, answering his own question. "What MAX does is analyze the trillions of bits of information generated every second and assigns a credibility score to each one of them, then reassembles the composite narrative. Did Jimmy really fall off his bike and was his mother really frantic? A million people working around the clock could not carry out such a task, but MAX is perfect for the job. The United States Navy started building this computer twenty-five years ago in order to avoid another fiasco like what happened in the South China Sea, which was the direct result of bad information, misinformation and poor judgement." He turned and walked briskly down a corridor. "Come," he said, "We have a plane to catch."

"A plane?" Vincent said, trying to keep up. "Where are we going?"

"Not far," replied Jonathan. "Just a couple of islands over."

They got into an elevator that took them back up topside where a quadracopter was waiting. "Have you ever ridden in one of these?" asked Jonathan, opening the starboard side door for Vincent and running around to the other side to get in. He assisted Vincent with the harness straps. "Pull them snug," he said. "Sometimes this thing flips over inadvertently." This caused the pilot to glare back with a scowl. "Just kidding," said Jonathan. "He only does that trick when I beg."

The four rotor pods of the quadracopter spun to life and it leaped into the air, heading southeast. The craft completed the two-hundred-kilometer trip in just twenty minutes and settled down on a concrete pad outside the Haleakala Observatory atop Mauna Kea. A man came out to meet them and led them inside the domed building where the biggest telescope was housed.

"Everything is set," the man said to Jonathan. "The viewing conditions are almost perfect." They went into a darkened room with a large video screen mounted on the wall. Vincent could make out a cylindrical object bouncing around on the screen. Their escort said, "The volcano is really active today and causing the telescope to move around." He pushed the intercom button and said, "Can we have a little more image stabilization, please?"

"What are we looking at?" asked Vincent.

"That is the Syndicate space station in geosynchronous orbit directly over the Yucatan Peninsula. It is almost one hundred thousand kilometers away, but you can count the rivets with this powerful telescope. There is another one of these which we can easily see that is over Kamchatka, but it is in the dark now. We generally can observe two of them and sometimes three. We think there are at least six and we just found out about the one over the Black Sea, which is not visible from our position."

Vincent and Jonathan made eye contact with the mention of the space station over the Syndicate base on the Black Sea.

"Can you switch on the gamma lens now?" requested Jonathan.

Their escort spoke into the intercom again to relay the request. A constellation of bright blue spheres suddenly appeared on the screen in the vicinity of the space station. Vincent glanced at Jonathan in astonishment. "How long have you known about this?" he asked.

The escort said, "We started seeing these space stations appear about four years ago. We suspected that they had something to do with the Syndicate but had no idea what they were up to. A couple of months ago, it was suggested that we should switch on the gamma detector. I think that idea originated with you, Dr. Gilbert. It seemed preposterous to us at the time, but now we are watching these strange spheres coming and going all the time."

Jonathan said, "I was eager to have you see them for yourself. We have been watching them come and go, and we have a pretty good idea now what they are planning, but we don't have a clue how to stop them." Jonathan stood up and headed for the door. Vincent continued to watch the video screen in wonder. It had the appearance of a swarm of jellyfish coming in and out of the mouth of a giant whale. "Come along Vincent, we need to get back to Pearl before dark."

Once they were airborne again, Jonathan looked over at Vincent, who was deep in thought. The last rays of amber sunlight were radiating off his face as the sun completed its plunge into the western horizon up ahead of them.

Jonathan said, “I don’t know which time zone your body is locked into right now, but I suspect your brain thinks it’s the middle of the night. Let’s call it a day. Tomorrow, I will show you your new office and introduce you to your team.”

“My team?” asked Vincent.

“Yes. Thirty of the very best engineers on the planet,” Jonathan said proudly.

The quadracopter settled down on a grassy area below a row of homes. Sandy, Louisa Héloïse and Max were on hand to meet their arrival.

Sandi said excitedly, “Vincent, you’re not going to believe what Jonathan called our ‘quarters’. We are in a ten-bedroom mansion…with a maid…overlooking Mamala Bay!”

Jonathan said apologetically, “It actually belongs to some uber-rich movie actress from Hollywood. She hasn’t been here in ten years, and we really don’t expect her back anytime soon.”

Vincent looked at Louisa. “What are those things on your arms?” he asked.

“They are called water wings,” Sandi replied. “Louisa and Mama have been in the pool all afternoon. And guess who lives next door?”

"Snow White and the Seven Dwarfs?" volunteered Vincent, showing his fatigue.

"No!" replied Sandi. "Queen Camilla and her entire entourage."

The following morning, Jonathan rang the doorbell at Vincent's residence as pre-arranged. The maid answered, "Please come in. Everyone is in the kitchen having breakfast. Can I get you something to eat?"

"No, thank you," replied Jonathan.

"How was your first night in Hawaii?" he said upon entering the kitchen. "It looks to me like you are all getting pretty well settled. There is a car in the garage, so I hope you will spend some time exploring the island."

"Thank you so much," said Sandi. "All of this is just incredible. I ran into Brigid Andersen, who is staying next door with the queen and we are planning to get together for lunch at their pool."

"I need to borrow Vincent for a few hours if you don't mind," said Jonathan, "but he should be back later this afternoon."

Vincent got up from the breakfast table and said, "I am ready to go."

Jonathan and Vincent hopped into the back seat of a golf cart and Jonathan told the driver, "Building 1, topside."

Then he said to Vincent, "This morning I want to introduce you to your team. They are all anxious to meet you."

Vincent sat quietly, trying to process the events of the prior twenty-four hours. As the cart entered a tunnel, Jonathan commented, “The entrances to the facility are concealed from satellite view. We don’t want to attract the attention of anyone who might be watching us from space. The US Navy left behind an ingenious system that sweeps the sky continuously using infrared lasers that perturb the atmosphere overhead just enough to blur the view from above, but not so much as to raise suspicion. We still must be careful. More than ten thousand people work here. Hours are staggered, and a lot of people work remotely as much as possible. You probably noticed the absence of parking lots. There is underground parking, but we do everything possible to disguise the magnitude of this operation.”

They took the elevator down to the same concourse as the day before. Jonathan led the way into a large bullpen area filled with desks and open cubicles. “Here it is,” said Jonathan, “your new office.” Vincent surveyed the room carefully to find an enclosed office with a door in the customary sense. He did not notice one. “Where are all the engineers you mentioned?” he asked.

Pushing the crash bar on a double door at the side of the room, Jonathan said, “They are waiting for you.” They stepped into a brightly lit lecture hall with seats in curved rows sloping upwards towards the back. Everyone stopped talking the instant the door opened and became attentive. All one hundred seats in the hall were occupied. Jonathan signaled for Vincent to take his place behind the laboratory-style bench at the front and he took a seat reserved for himself in the front row.

Vincent stood before the whiteboard that spanned the width of the room and peered out at the crowd. He scanned the faces that were totally focused on him and then looked at Jonathan for directions, who simply nodded his head up and down several times to indicate that it was time to begin. A minute passed in total silence while Vincent tried to figure out what he was supposed to say. An avalanche of thoughts swirled around in his brain. He was unprepared to talk. Finally, he said, "I suspect you have all come to hear me talk about antigravity." He cleared his voice and said more distinctly so people in the back could hear. "What if I told you that antigravity is a hoax? That it's impossible and it doesn't exist?"

No one stirred. No one looked around the room to exchange expressions of disappointment. They all sat quietly with pens and notebooks at the ready. Vincent looked at Jonathan for some more clues and got nothing at all except the same reassuring smile. He leaned forward against the laboratory bench with his hands spread out. Looking down at the assortment of colored markers. He took a deep breath and exhaled. He realized the time had come for him to share the 'talent' entrusted to him. Looking back up at the crowd of people that had yet to move a muscle or shift in their seats, he said, "It seems that none of you believed me when I said antigravity was just a myth. Okay, then..." Vincent grabbed a black marker and turned to face the whiteboard, paused, and wrote in large letters near the top, 'GRAVITRONS'. "Gravitrons," he said, turning back to face crowd with a stern expression. "I will tell you about gravitrons, but I must first warn you: From this day hence, the world as we know it will never be the same. The matter I am about to disclose to you has the potential for tremendous good as well as tremendous evil if it were to fall into the wrong hands. I am trusting each and every one of you that you will make a solemn commitment to not permit that to happen. The temptation will be to turn what I am about to describe into a weapon. Perhaps I can't keep that from happening. The strategic advantage afforded by antigravity is unimaginable. My sincere hope is that you will catch a vision for antigravity beyond its use merely as a weapon."

Chapter 30: Gravitrons

Vincent turned back to the whiteboard and wrote the equation, $F = -GM_1M_2/r^2$. He turned back around and said, "You are all familiar with this expression that originated with Sir Isaac Newton. It merely states that the gravitational force of attraction between two bodies is proportional to the product of their masses divided by the square of the distance between their centers. This is the force you must overcome to get your airplanes to stay in the air. In this case M_1 is the mass of your plane and M_2 is the mass of the earth. Pretty simple. So, what is mass, really?" he held up his marker. "Suppose I were to place this marker on a pan balance, and it weighed ten grams. What that means is that the balance has been calibrated to read ten grams on the surface of the earth. If I were to measure the number of carbon, oxygen and hydrogen atoms in the plastic of the marker and multiply these amounts by their respective atomic weights, I would get ten grams. Ten grams is the weight of the marker which just happens to also be its mass because the balance was calibrated to make them equivalent. On the moon, the balance would have to be calibrated differently in order for the mass and weight to be equivalent. Back on earth, if I placed ten identical markers on the scale, it would read one hundred grams, because everyone knows that mass is an extensive scalar quantity. Pretty simple, right? Newton's law of gravity also tells us that the force between the bodies is always attractive by virtue of the minus sign. The distance between objects is always positive and the masses are positive, so the force must be attractive. For a few centuries, science fiction writers got around this problem by inventing negative mass, or antimatter. Besides being patently ridiculous, the notion of negative mass would violate every known law of physics. There is no such thing as negative matter. If you are looking for it somewhere, let me save you the trouble." Glancing over at Jonathan, Vincent said, "Could someone please bring me a bottle of water?"

Vincent continued, "A scientist named J. Cédric Rothschild, who I am sure you all know about, was the first one to put variable light-speed theory on a firm foundation. This same Cédric Rothschild wrote a monograph a few years later entitled, '*Gravitron Theory and the Dynamics of Gravitational Fields Induced by Supermassive Objects in Motion*'. Is there anyone here who has ever heard of this work?"

Every hand in the lecture hall shot up. Vincent looked over at Jonathan in surprise. Turning back to the audience, he said, "So, I just wasted the last ten minutes of everyone's time. All right, then. If you have seen a copy of the manuscript, then you are all aware that there are five missing pages?" Every head nodded. "Good," said Vincent, "Then I will be able to tell you something you don't already know. The five missing pages reveal the nature of 'gravitrons'. Gravitron is short for gravitational polatron. Unless you happen to know what is in those five missing pages, you would have no idea what a polatron is. So, I am going to tell you now." He turned to the whiteboard and wrote '*mv*'. Turning back to face the audience, he said, "That's a polatron." He savored the puzzled looks on the faces of his audience for a moment. "You probably recognize this as mass times velocity, or momentum, '*p*'. We say a body of mass, *m*, moving with a velocity, *v*, has momentum *p*. This idea holds up just fine as long as the mass is invariant. A neutron has a mass of 1.67 x 10^{-31} kilograms. A mole of neutrons has a mass of 100 nanograms based on the neutron rest mass. That is how much a mole of neutrons would weigh on our earth-calibrated balance. But we all know that by bringing together a mole of neutrons into a supermassive cluster, the speed of light is slowed down some nine orders of magnitude inside the cluster. This, of course, is the basis of microfusion. If we put this supermassive cluster into motion relative to an external gravitation field, we get the timecharging effect. What Cédric realized is that the masses in the Newtonian gravitation law I just wrote on the board refer to the effective mass, not the rest mass. In the case of ordinary matter, there's not much difference between the two, but if we give a supermassive cluster of neutrons a velocity perpendicular to the earth's gravitational field, the effective mass decreases as a function of the velocity because of the time lag resulting from the movement of the position vector, the *r* in the denominator. The fact that the denominator is squared masks the fact that it is actually the magnitude of the vector product of the distance from the center of the earth to the moving cluster at two different times. Again, for ordinary matter, the displacement of the radius vector with time is of no consequence, but when the speed of light is retarded by nine orders of magnitude, the effect is profound."

Vincent turned back to the whiteboard and erased the M_1 term and replaced it with m_{eff}. "M_2 is still the mass of the earth," he continued. "But now we have a dilemma. How do we handle the effective mass when it depends on the velocity of that body?" He paused to watch the faces of some of his audience brighten at the moment they realized the answer. "The only explanation, as I think some of you have just figured out, is that 'Big G" in Newton's formula is not actually a constant at all. It depends on the speed of light inside the neutron cluster. Albert Einstein spent the last years of his life in a futile attempt to come up with a unified field theory that incorporates gravity based on the presumption that *G* was a universal constant. His instincts that gravity and electromagnetism had to be somehow linked were correct, and I suspect he would have discovered that *G* was not a constant had he not held so tenaciously to his bias that the speed of light was constant. I need to make another modification to the gravity equation." Vincent turned back to the board and erased *'-G* and replaced it with *'G(c(t))'*. "I left out the negative sign on purpose since there is now no reason to assume that the force is always attractive. *G* is now an explicit function of the speed of light, *c*, which is a function of time. The velocity term has been incorporated into this new function, and now we can gain some insight into what a polatron is. It is a body moving with velocity,

v, that has a variable effective mass. A polatron is described by a vector, just like with ordinary momentum, but the bookkeeping of the effective mass is taken care of by the time-dependent function, 'G'.

I suspect that you all know how timecharging works. What is interesting about timecharging rotors is that a ring of some billions of neutrons is rotated around a central axis which reduces the effective mass of everything coupled electromagnetically to the rotor. The faster the rotor turns, the more pronounced the effect becomes. But the rotor can never become weightless. The effective mass approaches zero only in the limit of infinite rotational velocity. You can see in the modified gravitation equation that in this limit, the effective mass, m_1, goes to zero, so, the force also goes to zero. The Syndicate is using timecharging spheres merely as a lighter-than-air device. As clever as this is, it is rather limited. For one thing, there is an altitude ceiling above which the spheres can't go without a boosting force. The other thing is that, just like with hot air balloons, they have no lateral control. They can ascend and descend vertically, but cannot, otherwise, navigate without being pushed around by conventional means.

Let's go back to Newton's gravitational equation. I just demonstrated how gravity works for a supermassive object in the earth's gravitational field, but how does a supermassive body behave in the presence of another supermassive body close by?" Vincent turned back to the board and substituted 'p_2' for 'M_2'. He continued, "'*p*' is a vector quantity, as I just said. The masses can't be negative, but the velocities certainly can be. There is something else revealed in the five missing pages of Rothschild's manuscript. The gravitational force is not just the vector product of the momenta, but the cross product of the velocities, v_1 cross v_2." This last statement produced a rustling among the audience as they started writing furiously in their notebooks all at once. "This discovery by Cédric is so simple and so elegant that it takes my breath away. For one thing, it means that the gravitational force is a vector quantity that is orthogonal to the respective velocities of the supermassive bodies. For another thing, which I gather from your commotion, that you have figured out already, it means that the gravity vector has a direction. It points up or down depending on the relative motion of the bodies. When it points down, the effect is attractive, but when it points up the gravitational force is repulsive. This is antigravity." Vincent smiled for the first time in days as he took a big drink of water to allow the implications of this last statement to sink in. There was a general uproar among the audience as people began conversing with one another.

Vincent waited until the room quieted down again and then continued. "It's no wonder that this effect has never been observed." He held up two markers. "If I place two markers next to each other, there is certainly a gravitational attraction between them, but it is minuscule. In his famous experiments, Cavendish actually succeeded in measuring the attraction between heavy metal spheres in a torsion balance, but of course, the force is always attractive, just like the force that holds planets in orbit around the sun. No one ever thought to measure the force between massive objects moving past each other at a high rate of speed. Even if you could carry out such an experiment in a laboratory on earth, the effect would be undetectable because the relative velocities of the two bodies would be eclipsed by the much greater velocity of the earth in orbit around the sun. Cédric recognized that in order to observe any such effect, much greater masses would be required. He began experimenting with neutron clusters in his workshop in Grenoble, where he began conducting tests with counter-rotating rotors. He started constructing rotors inside of the rotors. I recently observed one of his prototype devices float effortlessly to the ceiling of his lab. If the outer rotor was spinning counterclockwise while the inner rotor was spinning clockwise, the device floated upwards. If the direction of the rotors was reversed, the opposite would happen, and the device got heavier. He recognized this as a manifestation of the right-hand-rule, and the cross-product of the respective velocity vectors. He deduced something else. He realized that the direction of the gravitational field vector could not only be switched from up to down, but also it could be moved with respect to the vertical, by quickly changing the speed of the inner rotor relative to the outer one. This produces a lateral torque that makes the device steerable like a helicopter."

Vincent paused to give the people in the audience, who were busily taking notes, a chance to catch up. Then he said, "And that's when Cédric died unexpectedly. We will never know if he fully grasped the implications of his discovery, but his colleague and co-author, Sonya Dumitescu, certainly did. She is the one who removed the five pages from his manuscript and encoded them after he died. So now you know how to construct a steerable antigravity engine, at least in theory. It doesn't require much imagination to think up things to do with such a device. What you will need in practice, though, is a strong neutron source and a filament winder like the one I designed at the Naval Research Laboratory in Washington."

Vincent stuck around for an hour of questions and answers. He was astounded at the depth of insight and inventiveness of the engineers in the audience. There was no longer any doubt in his mind that he had made the right decision to release the secret of antigravity. A follow-up lecture was scheduled for the next day, but Vincent wasn't sure he had all that much more to talk about. After the last questioner departed, the lecture hall was quiet again. Vincent collapsed into the chair next to Jonathan. "The cat is out of the bag now," he said. He heard the characteristic sound of someone coming down from the top of the stairs behind him on crutches. "Stephan," he exclaimed. "How long have you been up there?"

"The whole time," Stephan replied. "It seems you created quite a stir."

“Have you ever met Stephan?” Vincent asked Jonathan.

“Not in person,” Jonathan said, “but I know him by reputation.” He shook Stephan’s hand. “You’re the guy who sank that Russian yacht off Guadeloupe without proper authorization.” They both laughed.

“But Stephan,” said Vincent. “How in the world did you get here? I just saw you last week at Villa Sémaphore.”

“It’s interesting,” replied Stephan. “They got a bit carried away with the microfusion reactors they installed on the *Bougainville* and now she has a top speed of forty knots. Captain Shaw is elated. He commands the fastest amphibious assault ship ever built. We made a short excursion into the Black Sea and then slipped through the Suez Canal and came straight to the Pacific plastic waste dump two hundred kilometers northwest of here. I just arrived this morning. Sandi and Brigid are hanging out together at the pool. I fear the two of them may be enjoying the good life a bit too much.”

Vincent proposed, “Then we should go join them for dinner.”

“I brought you a present, Vincent,” said Stephan. “Your filament winder.”

“My what?” exclaimed Vincent.

“I told you last week in France that if all you wanted was your neutron winder, you would have it. It is waiting for you on the *Bougainville*. I have another surprise,” Stephan said, “The two microfusion reactors generate so much surplus power that you will be able to make as many neutrons as you could ever want."

The three filed out of the lecture hall to take the elevator topside. "I don't think I can handle any more surprises," said Vincent.

Chapter 31: Quads

As was customary, Vincent was up at the crack of dawn sipping his coffee on the patio and waiting for the first rays of morning to bathed the volcanic cliffs on the far side of Pearl Harbor as the sun peeked over the top of the mountains behind him. The southern tip of the island of Molokai was just barely visible from the mansion perched on the side of the mountain where he had been staying with his family for the past three months. He watched a supply dirigible from *Bougainville* descend to the depot on Ford Island in order to deliver its load of hydrogen as an empty one drifted upwards.

Sandi came out with her coffee to join him. "Good morning, Darling," she said. "Isn't this view just stunning?"

"Happy Birthday," he said.

"Oh, my birthday," she groaned. "I had completely forgotten. Do you have any idea what it's like to discover that you are actually three months older than you thought you were your entire life?"

They both laughed. "I think April 20th is a wonderful day to celebrate your birthday. And springtime in Hawaii! It doesn't get any better," said Vincent.

"So, today I am 34 and a quarter," Sandi said, with a giggle.

"I think it was an honorable thing your mom did so you wouldn't have to celebrate your birthday on the same date your father was killed in action," said Vincent.

"Yes, but she forged my birth certificate," replied Sandi.

"All she did was turn the '1' into a '4'," replied Vincent.

"Yes, but I was born on January 20th and not April 20th," she replied.

Vincent said, "I have always liked celebrating your birthday in April. By the way, I have a very special birthday present for you. I need to head out to the *Bougainville* this morning to check up on the progress with the antigravity engine production, and I will be back this afternoon with your present."

Héloïse and Louisa emerged from the house together at that time. Héloïse handed Vincent a fresh cup of coffee and a plate of pastries and said, "Happy Birthday, Sandi." Sandi gave her a big smile that showed that she was over the shock of discovering that April 20th was not actually her birthday.

"What do you and Brigid have planned for today?" Vincent asked Sandi.

"Brigid is not here," she replied. "She and Stephan went off on some sort of 'secret' mission yesterday. Now that he is fully recovered, I suspect that maybe they went for a hike and overnight camping trip."

"Say," said Vincent, "in that case, why don't you come with me out to the ship, and I will give you your present onboard *Bougainville*. It's been a while since you last saw the Shaws."

Sandi could not think of a good reason to decline and glanced over at her mom.

"You go, Sandi," said Héloïse. "I will look after Louisa."

Thirty minutes later, Sandi and Vincent were in the rear seats of a four-seater quadracopter, or 'quad' as it was called, heading northeast over the featureless Pacific. Only a few puffy clouds dotted the horizon. The pilot and one of Vincent's engineers sat up front. As the *Bougainville* came into view, the pilot pointed to the ship and began feathering the craft for descent. Four circular cowlings enclosed the turboprops extended from the fuselage in the form of an 'X'. The high-pitched whine of the turbine engines decreased in intensity as the craft settled effortlessly on the landing spot that was only accessible when there was no dirigible tethered to the aft mooring station. The three passengers hopped out and three new people boarded the quad for the scheduled twice-daily round-trip to Pearl for exchanging personnel. Vincent and Sandi headed to the bridge to greet Captain Shaw.

"Look who I brought with me today?" Vincent said to Shaw as they entered the bridge.

"Welcome aboard, Sandi," Captain Shaw said. Mrs. Shaw came out of the salon, and everyone exchanged hugs.

"Today is Sandi's birthday," said Vincent. "I thought I would give her the surprise aboard *Bougainville*." Captain Shaw smiled knowingly. "Happy Birthday, Sandi," he said. "Vincent's secret is safe with me."

"How is the salvage operation going, Richard?" Vincent asked.

"Unbelievably well," replied Shaw. "We are at full capacity. I can hardly believe how much plastic trash there is out here and more and more seems to drift our way every day. As we head into Spring, the currents are shifting to the north, so the trash is just coming to us. We haven't had to reposition the ship in a month."

Vincent said, "I would like to go down and see how things are progressing with the antigravity engines. Is it okay if Sandi remains with you?"

"Of course," said Mrs. Shaw, taking Sandi by the arm and leading her back into the salon. "We have a lot of catching up to do."

Vincent took the elevator down to the aircraft maintenance hangar, one deck below the flight deck. The space was originally configured for servicing and arming jet aircraft after returning from combat missions. It had never been utilized for hydrogen generation and had previously sat vacant other than the well-equipped machine shop that occasionally was used to repair broken equipment. Today, a dozen quads lay spread out on the floor, their turboprop engines removed, leaving only the circular cowlings. Workmen were busy extracting the fuel tanks from under the seats and replacing them with hydrogen storage tanks and fuel cell modules. The quads were all in various stages of refurbishment. Vincent approached the foreman, who was overseeing the removal of the outer enclosure of a cylindrical canister in the back of one of them, and said, "How's it going?"

The foreman beamed. One of Vincent's engineers stepped forward and said, "We just took her out for a spin. I wanted to inspect the rotors again before I turn her over to you."

Vincent peeked into the craft to see for himself. With the cover removed, he could view the two toroidal windings of the counter-rotating rotors of the antigravity engine, nested one inside the other.

The engineer said, "Right now, we are just waiting for delivery of the motor control modules that are being assembled at Pearl. Everything else is on hand to finish the other quads, but this one is ready to go. As soon as I get the covers back on, I will take her up to the flight deck so you can go for a ride."

Vincent said, "I will go notify the pilot and meet you on deck in thirty minutes."

He went up to the drone flight control center and tapped Tanya on the shoulder. "Can you get away?" he asked.

"Sure," she said, signaling for one of her co-workers to take over her console and assume operation of her drone.

Vincent said, "The quad should be delivered to the flight deck shortly, and I will head to the bridge to fetch Sandi."

As planned, the quad was sitting on the flight deck when Vincent and Sandi arrived. Tanya Shaw was seated in the right front seat and Vincent helped Sandi get into the left front seat and secure her harness before hopping in the back.

“Hello, Tanya,” she said, “It’s so good to see you again. Vincent mentioned that he had a very special trip planned for my birthday. Where are you taking us?”

Tanya grinned. “I’m not taking us anywhere. You are the one in the pilot’s seat.”

Sandi looked back at Vincent in a panic. “What do you mean?”

“This is your birthday present,” said Tanya. “Your first flying lesson. There’s nothing to it. It’s just like flying a drone. You have two joysticks in front of you. The one on the left controls lateral movement and the one on the right controls vertical movement.”

“Like this?” asked Sandi, pushing on the right joystick. The quad shot up into the air fifty meters before Tanya regained control of the craft.

“Gently!” she commanded.

Sandi took her hands off the sticks and placed them over her ears. “What did I just do? The engine wasn’t even turned on yet.”

Vincent and Tanya broke out laughing. Vincent said, “Sandi, this quad doesn’t have turboprops. It is an antigravity quad.”

Tanya coached Sandi to take hold of the left joystick and gently push it forward. The craft eased forward. “Give it a little more,” said Tanya, “so we can be well clear of the *Bougainville*. Now you’re getting the hang of it.”

"My heart is really pounding," Sandi said.

"Okay, now release the stick," instructed Tanya. The craft began to hover in place. "Now I want to teach you how to execute the first important maneuver."

"I'm scared," said Sandi.

Tanya smiled at her reassuringly and said, "Just grab the left slick and twist it clockwise slowly without tilting it." The craft rotated clockwise. "Now twist it counterclockwise." The craft responded accordingly and started rotating back counterclockwise.

A faint smile began to form on Sandi's face. "I think I may be getting the hang of it," she said with growing excitement.

"The right stick is a bit trickier," said Tanya, "as you already discovered. It takes us up and down. We need a bit more altitude, so gently push it forward. Watch your altimeter," she said, pointing to the numerical dial ahead in the cockpit. "You can see it reads fifty meters now. Take us up until it reads four hundred meters."

Sandi executed the command and looked over at Tanya with a satisfied expression.

"See, I told you there was nothing to it," said Tanya.

"Where is the fuel gage?" asked Sandi, looking at the instrument panel.

"This craft doesn't use fuel," Tanya replied. "It uses your husband's antigravity engine. Let's go flying."

"So, you will take control, then?" suggested Sandi.

"No, no," replied Tanya. "You will fly the craft. Just like before, rotate the quad until our heading is two hundred and sixty degrees on that compass there," she said, pointing to the screen on the console. Sandi executed the turn as instructed. "Now, gently push the left joystick forward." The craft tilted forward and started moving. "Give it a little more," said Tanya, "or we won't make it back to Pearl before dark. The number on the left is your groundspeed indicator. Take us up to two hundred kilometers per hour. That's good." She said, looking around for obstacles and checking radar and the collision avoidance system. "Are you ready to execute a turn?"

"I think so," said Sandi. "Vincent, this is a blast!"

"Okay, tilt the left stick to the left, and keep an eye on your heading until you reach one hundred and eighty degrees," Tanya instructed. "Very good. Now tilt it to the right until you return back to two hundred and sixty degrees and let go. The craft will return automatically to level flight and take us to Pearl. There's a lot more to learn, of course, but congratulations. You are well on your way to being an antigravity quad pilot."

Sandi whooped with joy. "Vincent, I've got to have one of these."

"Let's head for home so Tanya can get back to work," said Vincent. "Your next flying lesson is scheduled for later this week."

"Oh, Vincent," Sandi exclaimed. "This is the best birthday present I have ever had."

Tanya dialed in the coordinates of their home overlooking Pearl Harbor and showed Sandi how to follow the navigation indicator. When the craft was directly above the driveway, Sandi went into hover mode as Tanya looked around for trees and other obstacles. "Okay, Sandi," she said, "gently, and I mean very gently, pull the right joystick towards you." The antigravity quad slowly descended to the pavement and came to a stop. Tanya switched off the power to the rotors and said, "Nicely done, Sandi. I will teach you to do flips and corkscrews in the next lesson."

Sandi was beaming as she jumped out of the craft onto the ground and did a victory lap around it, hands in the air, unaware of the applause of the crowd which had gathered, that included Queen Camilla. She ran up to Vincent and gave him a big hug, tears streaming down her face, and said, "All my life I thought I was destined to pilot ships. It never occurred to me that I was destined to fly aircraft."

Some days later, Vincent noticed a quad in the driveway as he was getting ready to leave for the Network. Sandi and Tanya were chatting enthusiastically out on the patio. A strong bond of friendship had formed between them. "Good morning, Vincent," said Sandi. "Tanya just got here to give me another flying lesson. She thinks I am ready to solo."

The doorbell rang and Héloïse let in Jonathan. "Everyone is out on the veranda," she said, turning to lead the way.

Jonathan's face was grave. "I just received a call from the Haleakala Observatory. They have been keeping an eye on one of the Syndicate space stations that is being repositioned directly above *Bougainville*. I can only conclude that they are planning an attack on the ship. Stephan went out to the ship this morning to oversee the defenses. I have called for a quad from Pearl to take me out."

"Why don't we take mine? It's sitting in the driveway," said Tanya.

"I would like to go along," said Vincent.

"Me too," said Sandi. "I have first-hand experience dealing with these Syndicate thugs."

Forty-five minutes later, the antigravity quad settled onto the deck of the *Bougainville*. They were met by a flight crew who propped the craft up onto a dolly and quickly headed for the flight deck aircraft elevator. Tanya went up to the drone control center while Vincent, Sandi and Jonathan stayed with the quad to descend to the maintenance hangar, where they were met by Stephan out on the shop floor. There were two dozen antigravity quads standing ready for service.

"All the modifications are nearly complete," said Stephan.

Vincent walked slowly between the rows of quads, inspecting the work with a scowl. "Are those Vipers being mounted to the nacelles?" he asked.

"Yes," replied Stephan, proudly.

“Take them off,” said Vincent, “take them off right now. I didn’t reveal antigravity to you so you could build fighter aircraft!” Vincent’s anger was barely controlled. He stormed out of the maintenance hangar to take the elevator up to the bridge. Sandi ran after him while Stephan and Jonathan stared at each other in disbelief, trying to make sense of Vincent’s outburst. They followed after a while to give Vincent time to calm down.

Vincent was sitting in the Shaw’s salon with Sandi next to him when they arrived.

“What in the world was that all about?” asked Stephan.

Vincent was breathing heavily, and his agitated state was apparent, but he made no response.

“*Bougainville* is about to come under attack, Vincent,” said Stephan emphatically. “We must be prepared. What better way than engaging the spheres with Viper X’s fired from quads?”

Vincent stood up and locked eyes with Stephan, finally saying, “I am no pacifist, Stephan. You know this. There wasn’t a more relieved person on the planet than me when the Trump fired the ASROC missile to sink that Syndicate submarine.” Vincent paused for several seconds to compose himself. Then he continued, “There were more than sixty souls aboard that submarine. Do you think they were all evil Syndicate thugs? Isn’t it more than likely that only a handful of bad people controlled the destiny of the others? Those others were farm kids like Sylvanus, maybe runaways, maybe kids just looking for some excitement. Not everyone aboard that submarine was evil, but they all died, nevertheless."

Vincent began to pace back and forth in deep thought. "We will know when the spheres start dropping from the space station. We will be able to see them as they approach the *Bougainville*. There is no doubt that this would constitute naked aggression, and we would have every right to respond accordingly. Have your men stand guard with Vipers. Fire if you must. The Syndicate controllers will figure out in a big hurry how vulnerable they are, and they will retreat just like they did when they attacked us off the Azores. But by mounting these anti-aircraft missiles on antigravity quads, you have just opened up a whole new arms race. It won't be long before the Syndicate figures out antigravity. Then they will start constructing more and more lethal weapons. We will have to respond with even more lethal weapons. The cycle will repeat over and over until the earth is in flaming ruins. After all, that's ultimately what the Syndicate wants in the end. I did not teach you about antigravity to start an arms race. No!" he said, turning to look at Stephan. "The arms race stops here! We must find another way."

Chapter 32: Liver Transplant

"Vincent, Darling," you really need to get some sleep," said Sandi, glancing at the bedside clock that read 3:23 AM.

"I just can't get the image of all those quads with Viper X's strapped to the nacelles out of my mind. Timecharging spheres are no match for antigravity quads equipped with anti-aircraft missiles now that we know how to see them and home in on them. I know how this ends, Sandi. We have five thousand years of human history to instruct us. Once we deploy a superior weapon, we will force the Syndicate to step up their efforts to field an even more deadly weapon and the race goes on and on. Yes, the Syndicate is evil but that doesn't mean everyone working on their behalf is necessarily evil. Sylvanus proved that."

The doorbell rang. "Who in the world could that be at this hour?" said Sandi.

Héloïse answered the door before Sandi got there. Brigid was standing in the entryway.

"What's the matter?" asked Sandi.

"I am so sorry to bother you in the middle of the night," said Brigid. "I just got a message from Stephan that the *Bougainville* came under attack. Apparently, they thwarted the assault, and everyone is safe, but they took some prisoners. He said several of them are Norwegian and a few don't seem to speak much English. He needs me to fly out to the ship to interpret for them. He is expecting another wave of assault and is hoping to get some intelligence about their intentions."

"Do you need me to arrange for a quad to come pick you up?" Sandi asked, heading to the kitchen to retrieve her phone.

"Actually," said Brigid, "I was hoping you would fly me out."

"Oh, I can't do that," responded Sandi as she entered the Network emergency number. "I just did my first solo flight, and I am not certified to take passengers. Anyway, I'm not allowed to fly at night."

"Nonsense," said Brigid as she turned to head toward the quad that was sitting in the driveway.

Sandi peeked out to notice another person already seated in the back. "Who is that sitting in the quad?" she asked.

"Queen Camilla," replied Brigid as she climbed into the vacant seat next to the queen.

Vincent hurriedly got dressed and came into the entryway. "What's going on?" he asked.

"Brigid and Queen Camilla want me to fly them out to the *Bougainville*."

"In the middle of the night?" exclaimed Vincent.

She rolled her eyes and turned her palms upward.

"Then I am coming with you," said Vincent, heading out to the craft and getting into the front passenger seat. "Good evening, Your Majesty," he said with a smile.

As the three waited for Sandi to get dressed, Brigid began briefing Vincent on everything she knew about the attack.

Sandi opened the pilot's door on the left-hand side of the quad and stuck her head in, staring intently at the three awaiting passengers who showed no sign of abandoning their intentions. Then she said, "You people have all lost your minds!" before hopping into the seat and strapping on her harness. They all sat in silent anticipation as Sandi switched on the antigravity rotors and activated the screens on the flight console. The faint whine of the rotors coming up to speed was barely audible above the noise of the crickets. She entered the last-known coordinates of the *Bougainville* into the navigational computer and searched unsuccessfully for some way to turn on the running lights. She finally shook her head and said to Vincent, "I don't think this craft is equipped with lights. Would you kindly mention to your engineers to take care of that oversight at some point." She took a deep breath and pushed forward on the right joystick, ascended to one thousand meters to hover before taking another deep breath and pushing the left joystick forward, heading out over the cliffs of the Oahu volcano that had been inactive for millennia.

The sparkle of light from a full moon danced on the water as the *Bougainville* came into view. The unmistakable shape of a hydrogen supply dirigible moored in the forward cradle glowed in the moonlight. The ship was otherwise completely dark.

"Don't you think we should let them know we are coming?" suggested Vincent.

"That would be a good idea if I knew how to operate the radio," Sandi replied.

"What if one of Stephan's marines thinks we are hostile and shoots a Viper at us?" Sandi looked sideways at him at the mention of this shocking possibility. He removed the microphone from the cradle and pushed the button to talk. "*Bougainville, Bougainville*. This is Vincent Gilbert. Come in, *Bougainville*."

"Yes, Vincent. This is Tanya speaking. We see you on radar and we are expecting you."

Vincent looked over at Sandi with a grin, saying, "See? There's nothing to it."

"Come to a heading of sixteen degrees and approach the ship from the stern," said Tanya. "There is a flight crew waiting for you. They will guide you into position." Then she said, "Hey, Sandi, I am really proud of you."

Stephan was standing on the flight deck when they touched down. "Good evening, your Majesty," he said, helping the queen get out of the craft. "We turned one of the barracks into a makeshift brig. We never anticipated prisoners." Stephan led the way to the elevator. Sandi stayed topside with her quad to be sure it was safely stowed.

Stephan continued talking as they walked along, "Four spheres landed on the flight deck last night. I don't think they had any idea we could see them coming. There were others hovering in the air, I presume, waiting for space on the deck to clear up. Our marines stood outside the spheres as they landed. When the hatches opened, the unsuspecting Syndicate commandos emerged and my marines simply took them prisoner, and that was that. The other spheres went away and never came back. We didn't have to fire a single Viper."

Stephan led everyone into a lunchroom where a terrified young woman was sitting alone. She was swimming in her camouflage uniform that was at least three sizes too large for her. She was holding a slip of paper, reading it over and over. Stephan said, "One of the spheres contained a contingent of Norwegian combatants. The two commanders were surly and so far, have been totally uncooperative, but the other four seemed to be all too glad to be captured and none of them put up the slightest struggle. I think this one is Norwegian like the others, although she is so traumatized that she will not say anything."

Brigid slid into the bench next to her and stroked her hair. "What is your name?" she asked in Norwegian.

"Christiana," came the weak and timid voice.

"Will you show me the slip of paper you have been holding on to?" Brigid asked. The girl handed it to her. Brigid recognized the handwritten text to be Norwegian. She read it and passed it to the queen with a look that her heart was about to break.

"What does it say?" asked Vincent. The queen translated, "It is a verse from Psalm 140 in the Bible. It says:

'Deliver me, O Lord, from evil men; preserve me from violent men, who plan evil things in their heart and stir up wars continually.'"

The girl nodded and began to sob.

"Do you speak English?" Brigid asked in Norwegian. The girl nodded again. Brigid looked around at the others not knowing what to say.

Stepan asked gruffly, "Why did you attack our ship?"

The girl sobbed uncontrollably and said, "They made me."

"Who made you?" asked Brigid more gently.

The girl regained her composure somewhat and began relating her sad story. "My husband is in a hospital in Oslo. He needs a liver transplant, or he will die. He is only twenty-six years old. We have two small children..." She began sobbing uncontrollably once again. Brigid continued to stroke her hair reassuringly. After a while, she continued, "We had no more money. The bank foreclosed on our home. Josh couldn't work and we were totally desperate. His doctor told me that the only way he would authorize the transplant procedure was if I would enlist in the army."

"The Norwegian Army?" Brigid responded with alarm.

"No," said the girl. "They just called us 'Freedom Fighters'. I joined. The next thing I knew, I was on the moon getting trained in hand-to-hand combat and receiving daily indoctrination about setting the world free from what they called the 'Old Empires'. They are ruining our country. Norway is in shambles. They forced the queen out. They took over the government and put all their cronies in charge..." she buried her face in her hands and began to sob again.

Queen Camilla sat down on the bench on the other side of her and took her hand. She gently asked in Norwegian, "Do you know who I am?"

The girl looked up at her and stopped breathing momentarily when she recognized Queen Camilla. She put her other hand over her mouth and gasped, "Your Majesty!"

Camilla looked up at Stephan and said, "Get me in touch with Dr. Spinu. Hopefully, he is still in Oslo."

"But your Majesty," said Stephan. "He doesn't run the health care system anymore. What can he do?"

"Dr. Spinu is a man of untold resources," she said. "He will know how to find a loophole." Then she looked a Brigid and said, "I'm taking Christiana back to Pearl with me. See if you can find her something more appropriate to wear."

"She probably has a chip, your Majesty," said Stephan. "We can't take her to Pearl. The Syndicate will track her there."

"Then I guess you will need to remove it," said the queen. "Surely there is an infirmary on this ship." She stood up and patted the young woman's hand and said, "Everything will be all right, my dear." Then, looking at Vincent, she said, "Now I would like to meet this Captain Shaw and his wife that I keep hearing about."

Stephan escorted Christiana to the ship's hospital and waited for the medic to arrive. Stephan recognized him immediately and said, "Do you remember me? You saved my life off the coast of Bermuda."

He smiled, studying Stephan carefully. "It looks like you made a complete recovery. To be honest, I never thought you were going to have the full use of that leg again. What can I do for you?"

"This woman has a locator chip implanted just below her right clavicle," Stephan said.

"Let's have a look," said the medic.

Christiana slipped her fatigues down over her shoulder.

"Here's the thing," said Stephan. "The Syndicate knows she has been captured. If you damage the chip while removing it, that would be a problem. Also, we need them to think she is still here on the ship when she isn't. The chip is a micro-ekg, and it monitors her heartbeat and body temperature."

The medic began giving the matter some consideration. "You are in luck," he said at last. "There is a blood transfusion machine in here somewhere that might work." The medic got up and rummaged around in some closets before wheeling out the cart. "I will need to take an X-ray," he said, guiding Christiana over to a hospital gurney. He checked on the progress of the transfusion machine as it heated up and installed a bag of plasma that he had removed from the hospital refrigerator. He poked the intravenous needle into the top of the bag so that the plasma would recirculate continuously. He then switched on the infirmary ekg machine to generate a calibration signal and attached the leads to the outside of the pump. Finally, he inserted a small vial in-line with the high-pressure side and looked at Stephan for approval. "Do you by any chance know your blood pressure, my dear?" he asked.

"120 over 70," she said. "At least that is what it was when I was donating blood for my husband, Josh. It is probably a good deal higher right now, I suspect."

"That's not a problem," the medic said, adjusting the pressure gage on the machine. "Do you have any allergies to local anesthetic?" he asked.

She shook her head and did not flinch when he inserted the needle. "Once you are numb, this will take no time at all."

As he began the procedure, Stephan said, "You are doing that as if you have the hands of a trained surgeon. You are not an ordinary medic, are you?"

The medic did not look up. He removed the chip and gently placed it in the vial inline with the warm blood plasma and then sewed the incision back together with masterful care. He said, "Now the Syndicate won't be able to track her. They are powerful but they are not omniscient."

Tanya came into the infirmary with a stack of clothes and placed them on the table. "You and I are about the same size," she said to Christiana. "You should be able to find something here that fits you."

"What in the world are we supposed to do with all of those prisoners in the brig?" asked Captain Shaw, pacing the bridge.

“We can’t do anything with them until the locator chips are removed,” said Stephan.

“How much do we know about these captives?” asked Vincent.

“None of my men are trained interrogators,” replied Stephan, “but it is clear that a few of them are hard-core evil. They would bite your head off given the chance. A few seem to be loyal to the Syndicate, perhaps with backgrounds in violent gangs. The majority seem to be just disenfranchised youths without anything better to do. The Syndicate gave them a sense of belonging, I guess. Then there are the ones like Christiana who have been conscripted under compulsion for fear of the consequences if they don’t obey orders. It would take an army of social workers to untangle the mess.”

“They can’t remain on board *Bougainville*,” said Captain Shaw.

“Let’s at least start removing the chips,” said Stephan. “We know what to do with the chips from the bad guys. A simple tap with a ball-peen hammer and they will cease to exist, and we can cart them off to prison somewhere.”

“You know,” said Vincent, “Molokai was once a penal colony for pirates. Perhaps we could drop off some empty shipping containers for shelter and airdrop some food from time to time.”

“Fine,” said Queen Camilla, “but what about the ones like Christiana who are serving against their will? If you destroy their locator chips, they have good reason to fear that their loved ones back home will be harmed."

Stephan replied, "The medic has come up with a pretty clever way to keep the chips active after removal, but this doesn't solve the problem of what to do with those prisoners."

"Well, I am taking Christiana back to Pearl with me," said the queen, "and I will figure out some way to get her home to Norway. I don't know about the others, but we need to learn to help them one by one."

At that moment, Stephan received a call from one of his men on the flight deck. "Stephan, what do you want us to do with these captured timecharging spheres? Should we just push them overboard?"

"No," replied Stephan. "They could be a valuable source of intelligence."

"We need the space, Sir, and they are two big to fit below decks unless we disassemble them."

Vincent's and Stephan's eyes met, and both had the same idea at exactly the same moment. "*La Charlière*" they shouted. "How much do you think they weigh?" Stephan asked his man.

"Not more than two hundred and fifty kilograms, Sir. Four men can move them around with ease."

Vincent had gone outside onto the catwalk to look at the flight deck below. Coming back onto the bridge, he asked. "Captain, is that dirigible in the forward cradle full or empty?"

"Empty," replied Shaw. "It arrived last night before the attack, and about the same time we suspended all operations."

"With your permission," said Vincent. "I would like to open the tail section and deflate a couple of the hydrogen nacelles to make room for the four spheres."

"Why?" asked Captain Shaw.

Vincent replied, "If you deliver them to Ford Island as a routine shipment, I will pick them up and take them to my laboratory at Network to study them."

"My men will help," said Stephan.

Brigid walked in at that moment and said, "Your Majesty, it's time to go. I am worried about your safety. Sandi has the quad ready to return to Pearl."

The queen looked at Vincent and said, "Do you mind staying behind? The quad only has four seats."

"By all means," he said. "I have work to do here. Perhaps I will ride back to Pearl inside the dirigible for old time's sake." He looked over at Stephan. "Maybe Stephan will join me," he said with a laugh.

Chapter 33: More Subs

Upon entering the Network engineering offices where Vincent was deep in thought, Jonathan asked him if he had received the message that two Syndicate submarines had just passed through the straits off Tierra del Fuego and were heading their way.

"Yes," he replied. "Stepan told me this morning."

"At 30 knots it will still take them seven or eight days to get here," said Jonathan.

"They are a long way from home," commented Vincent. "I am surprised that they would venture so far. They must consider the *Bougainville* a more strategic target than I would have imagined."

"Captain Shaw is in the process of suspending operations, and he will be bringing the ship to Pearl in a couple of days," said Jonathan.

"You realize, don't you?" said Vincent, sitting straight up in his chair, "that bringing the *Bougainville* here will paint a target on Pearl Harbor. As far as we know, the Syndicate has no knowledge of what goes on here. Are you sure you want to tip them off that this is where the Network is headquartered?"

"How would they ever find out?" replied Jonathan. "They will think it is just a routine port call."

"That just happens to coincide with the arrival of their submarines?" queried Vincent. "And then, won't they just lurk off the coast and wait for *Bougainville* to come back out? And what happens when they discover that Pearl Harbor is heavily fortified?" Vincent put his face in his hands and rubbed his weary eyes.

Jonathan stood silently without answers.

"Jonathan," said Vincent getting, up from his chair, "if we let them bring the fight to us here at Pearl, the Network will be on the defensive for the foreseeable future. I have a meeting with a couple of my engineers down at the boatyard. They said they have something interesting to show me. Would you care to come along?"

Vincent and Jonathan entered a warehouse in an area of the old Pearl Harbor Navy Base that had not been used in many years. The warehouse was dark and musty. The engineers who had been waiting for Vincent had opened the sliding doors wide to let in as much light as possible.

"I know there must be a light switch in here somewhere," said one of them, "but I will be darned if we can find it." He turned to walk to the far end of the warehouse, where two large, folded canvass rolls at least twenty meters long and ten meters in diameter stood.

"Dr. Gilbert," said one of the engineers, "in your lecture on antigravity, you gave us all a very stern admonition not to use antigravity for offensive warfare. We all took this very seriously. We have been doing a lot of soul-searching ever since. Frankly, when you delivered your admonishment, many of us thought you were just a disillusioned dreamer. I hope you will forgive me for saying that. The obvious thing to do with new technology as disruptive as antigravity is to deploy it in more capable and lethal weapons. After all, this is exactly what the Americans did with the discovery of fissile chain reactions, which brought a swift end to the Second World War. But as we all know, it only took fifty years before twenty-five countries had nuclear weapons and ten of those had the ability to launch thermonuclear hydrogen warheads from submarines. So, we understand your sentiments, Dr. Gilbert."

Another of the engineers stepped forward. "None of us could dismiss what you said, and it has haunted us for weeks. We brought you here because we think we know how to defeat the Syndicate submarine threat using antigravity without turning it into a weapon." He motioned for Vincent to follow and stopped in front of the towering canvas rolls, "These are portable inflatable drydocks."

Vincent squinted in the dark to look at the huge rolls and try to comprehend their significance.

"Dr. Gilbert, sir," he said. "We think we know how to build a lifting platform using a hydrogen supply dirigible with antigravity assist. We propose transporting the inflatable dry dock out to a location where it can be positioned beneath the enemy submarine. Once the drydock is inflated, the submarine will float to the surface, where it can do no more harm and where it can be towed as far away from the scene of the engagement as you care to tow it. Then you can do whatever you want with it and its crew."

Sandi positioned her quad two meters over the calm water with uncommon skill as the sonar technician in the seat next to her lowered a hydrophone to a depth sufficient to be away from any surface noise. He was listening carefully on his headphones for the sound of the screws of the Syndicate submarine. The *Bougainville* was in sight about five kilometers up ahead. After a few moments, he turned to Sandi and gave a 'thumbs up'. He adjusted his equipment to get a precise location and depth.

"The sub has come to a stop and is starting to come up," he said.

Sandi watched as the sub's video camera pierced the surface of the water. The ominous dark shadow of the submarine had become clearly visible from above in the crystal-clear Pacific. A second quad moved in to slip a shroud over the protruding camera. "That should keep them busy while they try to figure out what just happened to their periscope. They won't fire without visual confirmation," Sandi remarked.

A dirigible that had been modified with antigravity engines to serve as a heavy lift freighter came up behind them. Its giant cargo bay doors opened, and a massive canvas roll was lowered to the surface of the sea and unfurled flat to make a rectangle one hundred meters long and twenty meters wide. Eight more quads moved in to attach control lines, four quads on each side, as the inflatable drydock began to sink under its own weight. After the depth and position were confirmed by the sonar operator, the quads slowly moved it forward beneath the unsuspecting submarine that was now stationary in the water at a depth of ten meters. The entire procedure had been carefully choreographed and practiced several times in advance. The quad pilots could clearly see the submarine silhouetted against the white shape of the drydock below it as they inched it into position. When all was set in place, the signal was sent to open the valves of the network of compressed air tanks embedded in the device. The sidewalls began to inflate in only a matter of seconds, forming a rectangle whose perimeter completely enclosed the sub. The eight quads released their lines and headed back to the *Bougainville* while the Syndicate Shark Class submarine was slowly raised to the surface.

A hydrofoil pulled up alongside with a contingent of marines that jumped off to fan out across the top deck of the captured sub to prevent any of the crew from opening the hatches and escaping. They wrapped a sturdy cable around the screw, that was now partially out of the water, to prevent it from turning. An awaiting tugboat came forward next, attaching a cable to the back of the sub so it could be towed to Molokai. Once the prisoners were offloaded onto the island, the submarine would be towed out to sea to be scuttled.

The sonar operator reeled back in the hydrophone so Sandi could go in search of the second Syndicate submarine. This turned out to be unnecessary, as the second sub had watched the entire event unfold through its periscope. It subsequently dove to maximum depth and headed east as fast as it could go to get away. A French Nautilus-Class submarine trailed it for three hours before returning to its duty station in the vicinity of the *Bougainville*.

Jonathan was sitting in front of the video screen at the Haleakala Observatory, watching the live images of the Syndicate space station directly overhead. A giant cylindrical object came into view, which completely engulfed the entire space station.

"That's just incredible," he said.

The man sitting with him was very high up in the echelons of the Network Space Command. He said, "We won't know for a while how many people were on that station, but as soon as it is evacuated, we will jettison it back to earth to burn up on reentry. For years, we have been trying to come up with a feasible way to collect space junk and service broken satellites stuck in earth orbit without having to use rockets. We just demonstrated the ability to come and go from space at will using antigravity engines. This is really a remarkable achievement, Jonathan."

"An achievement that I fear we can no longer keep secret," said Jonathan. Then adding, "When do you expect to go after the other Syndicate stations?"

The other man replied, "The signals from our surveillance satellite in orbit around the moon indicate that they are beginning to abandon the base. We don't need to be in such a hurry. The Syndicate will need those space stations to get their people back to earth. If we take all the stations out at once, we will be stranding a whole lot of people in space with no way to get home."

"How long have you known about the Syndicate base on the moon?" asked Jonathan.

"Long enough. We had a nuclear missile standing by to take it out, if necessary," said the man darkly.

After that, the Syndicate began collapsing rapidly around the world. Emperor Napoleon X had extended his empire all the way to the Urals. He had gotten into a squabble with the United Nations, who tried to abandon the international gold standard, so he closed them down and expelled them from Switzerland. He enacted sweeping changes in provincial government throughout Europe. These reforms had diminished much of the cronyism and government corruption that had resulted in economic paralysis and prolonged depression. He reformed the taxation and banking institutions that had favored the wealthy and powerful. The anti-monarchist movements were largely silenced and forced underground.

Queen Camilla returned to Norway as the rightful monarch with much fanfare. She stood on the balcony of the Royal Palace for twelve hours on National Day, waving to the thousands of children parading up Karl Johans Gate and past the palace to receive her annual blessing. Among them were Cristiana and Joshua Voll with their two little girls dressed in festive Norwegian costumes that had been in the family for three generations. Brigid Andersen stood next to her father, Tor, in the background, always vigilant.

Once the neutron filament winder had been taken from the factory in Bucharest, the Syndicate had lost the ability to produce any more timecharging rotors. Alexandre Spinu and Sylvanus had led a group of marines to the base on the Black Sea, where they were able to capture hundreds of Syndicate combatants as they returned from the space station.

Magdalena had hired a private investigator in Paris to figure out how the investment firm handling Cédric's estate could have been so careless with his money. It turned out that it wasn't the result of carelessness at all. The money had been embezzled. The perpetrators, who turned out to be principals in the firm, were arrested and most of the sixty-five million euros were recovered. Magdalena had the money transferred to the foundation for the relief of Eastern European refugees that was being managed by Pastor Joel in Bucharest. Some of the money was used to pay off delinquent loans that threatened farm foreclosures and a cooperative was established to provide low-interest seed money for starting new businesses that provided desperately needed employment for the former Syndicate 'freedom fighters' who were starting to return home.

The group, consisting of Sandi, Vincent, Héloïse, Louisa, the Shaws and Jonathan, watched as the Admiral's plane landed and taxied along the runway of Ford Island Naval Air Station. A tug hooked up to the plane and backed it into the hangar out of sight from above. The same colonel from the previous flight appeared smiling in the doorway as the stairs were deploying. She waved at Vincent and said, "The antigravity engine works great. Thanks." Rear Admiral Paul Brundt emerged and stood at the top of the stairs, beaming. He took a deep breath of the tropical air. Jonathan met him at the bottom of the stairs and placed a ceremonial flower lei around his neck. Sandi ran forward to give him a hug. Several large suitcases were offloaded.

"Why so much luggage, Granddad?" asked Sandi.

"Didn't anyone tell you?" replied Admiral Brundt, "I'm moving to Hawaii, doctor's orders. Where is my great-granddaughter?" the admiral asked. Louisa ran to him, and he picked her up into his arms.

"Vincent," he bellowed. "I left Andrews after dinner an hour and a half ago and lost six hours in the process of coming to Hawaii, where it's just time for lunch. You keep telling me you have a solution to this problem. Now that you are done with antigravity, when are you going to start seriously working on the problem of jet lag?"

Vincent replied, "You're never going to fix the problem by just going faster, Sir. Going faster only makes matters worse, unless you fly around the globe and land in the same time zor you started at." Everyone chuckled.

He looked at Jonathan and said, "Is everything ready?"

"Yes, sir," said Jonathan. "They are waiting to take us t the memorial."

Everyone piled into the van and took the short trip to th nearby USS Oklahoma Battleship memorial. The Admiral got ou first when they arrived and walked slowly along the line of the names of the 429 sailors who had perished on the ship during the attack of December 7, 1941. "I haven't been here in years," he remarked. He stopped at the placard he was searching for and pointed to a name. "That's my great-grandfather, Ensign Paul Alexander 'Sandy' Brundt," he said quietly, touched by the sight. "He didn't die with the others, but he was badly burned rescuing some of his shipmates from the flaming waters." He stood back so Sandi could see. "I just wanted you to see this, Sandi." He somberly headed back to the van and quietly sat inside, waiting for the others.

They went to the launch site for the trip to the Arizona Memorial, where they were met by a contingent of official-looking people in dress uniforms who helped everyone off the boat. A table had been prepared for them to have lunch. They strolled along the exhibits for a while before the admiral called everyone together. Facing the group, he asked Tanya Shaw to step forward.

"I am told you are a drone pilot without peer and now you are a test pilot flying antigravity quads." He reached into his pocket and pulled out a golden insignia. "You can buy these in almost any second-hand store these days, but this one is special. It is brand new. I got it from my dear friend, Vice Admiral Forbes, who used to run the Naval Air Command for the United States Navy. These wings are what you used to receive when you completed flight training at Pensacola, Florida." He pinned the golden wings on Tanya's lapel and saluted her. "You have earned these. Whenever you decide to fly something more substantial than a quad, just let me know."

"Sandi, will you please step forward?" he said, reaching into his pocket again. "You have also earned your navy pilot's wings." He pinned the insignia on her lapel and saluted her. "I am quite confident that, given the chance, you would have graduated at the top of your class at Annapolis. Perhaps you would have decided to become a naval aviator or maybe you would have become a submarine skipper like your father. Paul Junior sank three submarines before perishing in the Battle of the South China Sea. Sandi, you sank four Syndicate submarines, and the last one you managed to sink without any loss of life. You are a true hero in the finest Brundt tradition. I am very proud of you."

Tears began to fill the admiral's eyes as he reached into his coat pocket to retrieve a wooden box. "Héloïse, will you step forward, please?" He squeezed the tears from his eyes as he handed her the box. "This is Paul Junior's Navy Cross for uncommon valor. I have been holding on to it for thirty-three years. But it really belongs to you." He turned away, unable to control his emotions any longer.

Epilogue

Vincent entered his apartment in Saint-Marc after a six-month absence. It was hot and musty in the middle of July, so he popped open some windows before phoning Sandi.

"Hello, Vincent," she said cheerfully. "Saint-Tropez is very muggy and crowded and I don't think it is anything like Mama imagined."

"Do you think she may want to return to Hawaii?" Vincent asked.

"No," she replied. "Mama is really all French, and I can't see her living anywhere else. I think we will come home tomorrow."

"Well, Hawaii is only two hours away by hypersonic transport," said Vincent.

"Get real," she said, "We will never get to ride on that plane again."

"I don't know," he replied. "When they dropped us off with Stephan in Paris, the colonel told us that with the antigravity engine, the plane only consumed one hundred kilograms of hydrogen on the trip from Pearl."

"You are just dreaming," Sandi said.

"Maybe not," said Vincent. "I stopped by La Défense this morning to meet with Jean-Luc. He wants me to come back to work for Ashleigh."

There was a cool silence at the other end of the line.

"He wants me to head up a new division to develop personal mobility aircraft with antigravity engines," he added.

"We should talk about it when I get home tomorrow," she said.

After saying goodbye, Vincent went into his office. He slid the latch at the bottom of his bookcase and swung it outwards to reveal his secret storage place, retrieving the Rothschild folio before pushing the bookshelf back into place. He removed the envelope with the microfiche films from the flyleaf of the journal and overlayed them under a microfiche reader that he had purchased in Paris. He hooked up his camera, making high-resolution photographs of the five missing pages. Then he made photos of the rest of the pages from the Cédric Rothschild Gravitron manuscript. He then loaded all the files into his computer and transferred them into an optical character recognition program that generated a computer version of the document, merging in the five missing pages. He studied the computer document carefully, comparing it with the typed version left behind by Cédric, but now including the five missing pages to make it complete.

He typed a postscript, reading as follows: 'This document was written in 2062, shortly before the principal author, J. Cédric Rothschild, died suddenly. It has been in my possession ever since. I have kept it hidden for the past twenty-four years. The revelation of antigravity and the demonstration of its efficacy is so profound that I nearly destroyed the manuscript because I feared the consequences of this discovery if it were to fall into the wrong hands. We all learned a hard lesson about what can happen with such disruptive technology from Cédric's earlier invention, timecharging. The world thought, by suppressing and banning it, they could keep it from proliferating to bad effect. They meant well, but they merely opened the door for a group with evil intent to monopolize the technology to serve its own purposes rather than bringing the benefits to mankind it should have brought. I have the same concerns for antigravity, but much more so. The technology of antigravity will change the course of history in untold ways, some good and some bad. In the wrong hands, antigravity could mean the end of free society as we know it. It is with grave misgivings that I am releasing this document to the public at this time. There is a mystery revealed in the Gospel of Matthew, when Jesus spoke regarding His Father, 'For He makes his sun rise on the evil and on the good and sends rain on the just and on the unjust.' I do not fully comprehend this passage, except that to withhold good things from humankind for fear that they will be commandeered for evil purposes removes free will in the end. May you receive the knowledge of this discovery with wisdom and discretion and use it only for good purposes. Signed, Sonja Dumitescu, July 16, 2085."

Vincent stared at the document for a very long time and then pushed the send button on his computer.

— THE END —

www.ingramcontent.com/pod-product-compliance
Lightning Source LLC
LaVergne TN
LVHW020523100826
845148LV00010B/1328